JUDGMENT CALL

JUDGMENT CALL

Suzy Wetlaufer

WILLIAM MORROW AND COMPANY, INC.
NEW YORK

It is the policy of William Morrow and Company, Inc., and its imprints and affiliates, recognizing the importance of perserving what has been written, to print the books we publish on acid-free paper, and we exert our best efforts to that end.

Library of Congress Cataloging-in-Publication Data

Wetlaufer, Suzy.
    Judgment call / by Suzy Wetlaufer.
       p.   cm.
    ISBN 0-688-10930-6
    I. Title.
PS3573.E9249J8   1992
  813'.54—dc20   91-32148
                                        CIP

Printed in the United States of America

First Edition

1 2 3 4 5 6 7 8 9 10

BOOK DESIGN BY M&M DESIGNS

For
Roscoe
and Sissy Grace

ACKNOWLEDGMENTS

This book is a testament to the family and friends who selflessly gave me the time, love, and moral support I asked for, plus much more: my husband, Eric; my parents, Phyllis and Bernard Spring; my aunt Lucille Lobene; my sisters, Elin and Debbie; my brother, Jonathan; my friends Nancy, Lori, Laurie, Jeremy, and Tricia, who read the book in its early drafts; and my baby-sitter, Willow. I also want to thank my agent, Alice Martell, and my editor, Liza Dawson, for their wonderful guidance, humor, and patience. Finally, I owe a debt of gratitude to Sandra Dibble and my other friends at *The Miami Herald*, who taught me what a good story is all about.

JUDGMENT CALL

1

The first cop on the scene was a short, balding guy in a plaid sports coat named Teddy Wasynczuk, a detective from Homicide who'd seen so many murders in his tour of duty that he actually found he was whistling as he parked his car near the corpse. At least this one didn't get him out of bed. It was high noon, and although high noon in Miami meant heat rippling off the tar like upside-down lava, he'd still be home for supper. That is, if some other poor dolt didn't get caught in the cocaine crossfire before the day was through.

The second person on the scene was Sherry Estabrook, a fact that made Wasynczuk whistle even more brightly. He loved reporters, especially if they managed to spell his name right, which Estabrook always did. She was one of the best in town. And a real treat to talk to. A flirt. A beautiful, funny, sassy-mouthed flirt.

Wasynczuk stepped out of his dented police-issue sedan and called her name. But Sherry was already too far away to hear him, crouching above the dead body and examining its wounds dispassionately. In one hand, she held a reporter's notebook, in the other a fountain pen. A moment later, she stood up, straightened her short red skirt, checked the bottom of her high heels for muck, and jotted down a few words.

"Sherry, Sherry—you mistress of Miami murders—how ya doin'?" Wasynczuk was by her side now, chatting familiarly. "When they gonna graduate you off the streets and into the air-conditioned comfort of the editor's desk?"

"*Never!*" Sherry cracked back. "I'm never going to let them." She smirked, and Wasynczuk couldn't help but notice that even her smirk was charming. As usual, she was made up with the perfection of a high-fashion model—no lipstick on her teeth, turquoise eyes carefully outlined in black, her long hair sprayed into a sexy mane. The word around the station was that Estabrook was the daughter of some muckety-muck Boston judge and that she owned a fancy college education to boot; in other words, she was way too classy to be a reporter covering the blood-and-guts beat. But her gaze was usually too cool for anyone to mention that to her face.

"Well, we'd miss you if you left us," Wasynczuk replied. "That's on the record."

Sherry flashed a smile and dutifully pretended to write it down in her notebook, then glanced back at the corpse sprawled between them. He was on his back, arms and legs splayed in an X, his neck and chest blown open by a .32 suicide special at close range. "Looks like your typical white Hispanic male," she sighed, "whose life and death will be relegated to a two-inch short on the back page of the Metro section." She rolled her eyes at the routineness of it all. "And maybe I'm crazy, but something tells me that in about three hours"—she checked her watch to be sure—"I'm going to call your office and someone is going to tell me that you Vice guys think that his death just might possibly be drug-related. Just *possibly*."

"Ah, Sherry, Sherry," Wasynczuk teased her, "you're even more cynical than me. That ain't good."

Sherry laughed. Wasynczuk had a point. Three years ago, when she'd seen her first cocaine corpse, she'd driven back to the newspaper weeping at the tragedy of a life cut short by the meaningless violence of a city gone berserk with greed. The victim had been not too different from this one—a young Latin guy in his twenties, wearing a double-breasted silk suit and an expensive gold neck chain, his body punctured by a couple of strategically placed bullet holes. Countless corpses later, she'd come to believe the victims deserved it. Or rather, that they weren't victims at all, just businessmen with very poor judgment.

"Okay, so maybe I'm cynical," she told Wasynczuk, "but I'm here, right? You'll notice nobody else in the newsroom exactly *volunteered* to venture out in the broiler pan to check out a hit. Me, I'm still waiting for my big break. The corpse that ends up to be the daddy of them all."

"You got a long wait, lady," the cop told her flippantly. He briefly turned around to scan the ruckus behind them. The medical examiner had arrived in his brown hearse-shaped van, along with three more cop cars. A small crowd was gathering, most of them from the fast-food joint a few yards away. The place was called the Seven Stars, and it was a popular dive for the Little

Havana lunch crowd of businessmen in *guayaberas* and tourists brave enough to eat at a place with a sign in the window that read, SE HABLA INGLÉS AQUÍ. The dead body lay in the shadow of the restaurant's dumpster, which explained the unusually putrid odor draping the crime scene and the proliferation of nasty black flies buzzing around the pools of sticky crimson blood.

Moments later, two of the cops who had just arrived started blocking off the area with yellow police tape imprinted with the words CRIME SCENE—DO NOT CROSS. Wasynczuk raised his eyebrows and shrugged. "Guess that means you, Miss *Miami Citizen* Staff Reporter. You better step back a few feet."

"Oh, come on, give me a break," Sherry grumbled, but she was only half-serious. "Let me stay and get all the grisly details. Oops—I mean, please let me get a closer look on behalf of the truth."

Wasynczuk shook his head. "Back up, Sherry, back—"

"Hey, wait a minute!" Sherry cut him off. She was taking one last look at the corpse, and suddenly she noticed something she hadn't seen during her initial once-over. There were four slender lines—cuts, actually, as if they'd been made with a paring knife or an ice pick—carved into the dead man's forehead. "Hey, wait a minute," she repeated. "Hey, Teddy, you see those marks in the victim's forehead? You see what I'm talking about?" She stooped down and gestured with her pen.

Wasynczuk took a quick look around to make sure none of his superiors had made it to the scene to catch him fraternizing with the enemy. None had—this hit was small time—and then he knelt down to check out Sherry Estabrook's odd observation. And in fact, she was right. The guy's forehead was sliced up, not too badly, but enough that it was obvious the killer was trying to leave his mark.

"Looks like we got a regular Zorro at work," he moaned. "I'm telling you, Sherry, they get more ballsy every day."

"So why is it you never catch any of them?" she shot back, but in a voice friendly enough not to raise his ire. "What—are you sleuths over in Homicide waiting for one big mass confession from all the bad guys?"

Wasynczuk shrugged. "One confession would suffice," he said. "But I kinda doubt it'll come in my lifetime."

"Mine either," Sherry answered offhandedly. "Mine either." And with that, she thanked Wasynczuk and headed back to her car, sticking the Press placard in the front window so she could speed across the city with impunity.

2

Sherry had been working the eleven-to-nine shift lately. No one else liked it, but she did, since good stories had a habit of breaking just when the nine-to-fivers were getting ready to split. News of the Seven Stars hit that morning had come to her via the police scanner she kept next to her bed. She'd just stepped out of the shower and was almost done applying her makeup, stark naked, in front of the full-length mirror on her closet door when the police dispatcher announced there was a homicide in the heart of Little Havana. Instinctively, Sherry had placed a quick call to the city desk to lay claim to it, dressed in three minutes flat, and then hurtled to her car, coffee cup in hand.

Now that it was obvious the corpse near the dumpster wasn't going to take ten minutes of her time during the day, she'd be free for other assignments. And for that, she needed her tape recorder, which she'd forgotten on the antique black oak credenza in her rush out of the house earlier. Sherry squealed into a fast, illegal U-turn and headed south on Dixie Highway, homeward.

Her house was on Lemonlime Road, number 43, in Coconut Grove. Sherry loved everything about the place: the umbrella-leaf avocado tree out back, the curlicued veranda, the make-believe fireplace in the living room with flamingos carved in the mantel. And she loved the fact that she'd found it herself, through a tiny classified in the newspaper. *Paradise for one. Pure Florida. Nice lawn. Lime tree deluxe. Absolute memory maker.* The paper didn't lie. The place was so perfect, Sherry told the landlord she would take it before he even told her the rent. Money didn't matter. What mattered was that the bedroom overlooked Christmas Day Park, where children played Mother-May-I under the palm trees on Sunday mornings. The landlord warned her that their shouting would wake her early, but she didn't care, and as time passed, she came to love it, too. It was a wonderful sound to break open the morning, jangling with faith and joy.

The neighborhood was home to working families mostly, a few old retired couples from up North, one single guy near the intersection with Kiwi Road. Sherry's house, like the others, was boxy and squat, of pale pink stucco, built in the aftermath of the last big war. A jalousie picture window peered onto the street— hers was the only house on the block without elaborate black wrought-iron burglar grates—and off the front door was a small concrete porch, screened in against palmetto bugs. Still, there was enough room for a wicker rocking chair from home, which was occupied most days and nights by her cat, Pansy, a creature too decrepit to even muster a *meow* against the heat. But even so, Sherry was sure, the animal was happy just to be with her in this foreign place, instead of back in Marblehead, turning to dust slowly on an overstuffed chintz love seat.

She'd moved into the place when she arrived in Miami three years back, and as time went by, Sherry found so many things to love about the house on Lemonlime Road, she wondered if she'd ever leave it. She'd even made peace with the fact that the beach was miles away; she had grown up with the water always in sight, and with the ceaseless music of waves grating the rocky shore. But soon she realized that it was better not to be reminded of home all the time. Much better. And the truth was, when there was a breeze off the Atlantic, she could smell the city's perfume of salt air and suntan lotion from her front yard. And that was enough. It was plenty.

There was only one problem with Lemonlime Road, to Sherry's mind, and it lived in the house next door, to the left: Alvin and Laura Beauregard, formerly of New Jersey—Noble Point, to be exact, a little lost town just south of Atlantic City.

Alvin was just over five feet tall, potbellied but with skinny white legs and fragile, hunched shoulders. His fleshy, damp face, deeply notched by apologetic brown eyes and a tiny O-shaped mouth, seemed unfinished, like a newborn's. At first, Sherry liked Alvin because he looked so sweet and vulnerable. But in time, she concluded his permanent look of bewilderment was a mask, hiding decades of stockpiled anger and regret.

There was, of course, so much Sherry couldn't know about Alvin, about the reasons he looked and acted the way he did. He had always wanted sons, but his marriage had been barren. He had always wanted to own a new car, and to go back to Normandy to see the beach without blood on the sand, but life didn't provide him with much in the way of money. And so, by day he worked the big pressing machines in the back of his dry-cleaning shop. And at night he fell asleep thinking of the young girls who paraded their breasts and thighs and lips for other men in one–light bulb clubs along the Boardwalk not too far from the cramped apartment where he and Laura lived.

Laura was his physical opposite: an enormous, lurching woman with strong, angry features that stood out like scars. Her eyes were blue, her hair was blue from cheap dye, and her skin— it looked a shade of blue, too, from veins surging beneath. She had married at seventeen, not to Alvin but to her boyfriend from the old neighborhood in Noble Point. He was tall and too skinny, not handsome at all but such a tender lover that she still remembered every time. He didn't come home from the war. Afterward, Laura thought she would never love again, so she said yes when Alvin asked her to marry him one night after the movies. There would be children, she was sure, to scoot away the pain and silence. But nothing came from those terrible nights of trying. And so she stood behind the cash register day after day and let the madness roam inside her mind while Alvin pressed the shirts and wrapped them in brown paper.

One winter twelve years ago, the cold in Noble Point began to hurt Laura's joints, and her fingers went more crooked with every snowfall. That was the year the store got robbed by two men with purple stockings pulled over their faces. Alvin and Laura decided to leave but had no place to go, so they went to Miami. They couldn't afford a place by the water, so they settled on Lemonlime Road; it was close enough.

For the first few years, Alvin and Laura used to trek to the beach in the old maroon Buick most afternoons, just to watch the tourists and pass the time. But after a while, that got boring, so they decided to stay home. They set up plastic folding chairs on the front lawn and spent most of the day there, frowning in their polyester jumpsuits, hiding under floppy sun hats, listening to inflammatory radio talk shows, waiting for burglars, and watching the neighbors come and go. The man across the street came home for lunch on Tuesdays and Thursdays, the same day the maid was there and his wife had her bridge club in Coral Gables. The couple in the house to their left was having problems getting rid of a relative who came to visit only God knows when.

But for the past three years, Alvin and Laura devoted most of their attention to their newest neighbor, Sherry Estabrook, whose crazy hours and crazy visitors gave them unlimited fodder for speculation. There was a see-through-skinny redheaded girl who always drove down Lemonlime Road the wrong way and then, without fail, parked her car half on the curb, half off, before scurrying toward Sherry's front door in a sideways lope. A few hours later, she'd leave looking like a different person, moving slow and steady, calling out some question or other to Sherry on the porch with the dulcet voice of a little girl: "You really think so?" or "You promise me that?" She stopped by a lot, Alvin and Laura noticed, almost as often as one particular man, an enormous man dressed like a Day-Glo surfer cowboy in flip-flops, who strode from his car to the front door as if he owned the galaxy, announcing his arrival with a giddy *whoop-whoop-whoop* noise and then an even giddier shout of *"Incoming!"*—whatever that meant. He never knocked, and the door was always unlocked for him. Some of his visits didn't end until morning, very early morning, before sunrise.

And so there was plenty to talk about, just watching the house next door, but somehow Alvin and Laura Beauregard found that they mainly talked about *her*, about Sherry, and how she had to be headed for trouble, what with the way she lived and (maybe worse) the way she looked. The way she looked, Laura once muttered to her husband, made a person want to look at her more, and not in a good way.

From where they sat, in fact, it was almost as if Sherry were too pretty—it was disconcerting to see her, actually; she moved and laughed with the head-thrown-back confidence and la-di-da glamour of a dark-eyed movie star from the days before TV. And that was part of the problem right there. She didn't fit in with the scenery on Lemonlime Road, with its pint-sized suburban palms and grainy inland sunlight. She was out-of-place, but somehow didn't seem to realize it herself. She was out-of-place putting on a city suit every day and frantically rushing out of the house as if she were late for an important meeting. She was out-of-place when she came home at dusk and stooped, knees in the dirt, to kiss her cat the way a mother kisses a baby, cooing with dizzy affection and delight. She didn't belong alone. She didn't belong in Miami, period. It just, somehow, seemed wrong.

Laura always said that if Sherry wanted to make half an effort to put things right, she could at least start with her hair, which was simply too long and too loose for a decent working girl. It was an invitation, for God's sake! But that wasn't all. Sherry's skirts were always too short (this observation was Alvin's), her heels too high, her lipstick too red.

But what bothered Alvin and Laura the most about Sherry Estabrook—and it bothered them to no end—was the way she kept her lawn. She just didn't care about the neighborhood! The hedges were never trimmed, and the grass went weeks between mowings. One day a few months ago, she stuck a dozen pink plastic flamingos all over her front yard. They were still there. Was she making fun of them? Alvin and Laura couldn't tell for sure, but it seemed that way. So after months of polite silence, they decided to hate Sherry.

"Hey, you, fancy pants, your lawn needs to be mowed *today*," Alvin would often shout, prompted by Laura, as Sherry got out of her car and walked toward her front door after work. Other days, he would accuse her of turning the neighborhood into a ghetto, and once or twice he threatened, in dead seriousness, to report her to city officials.

The insults grew even more heated after Alvin spotted Sherry's byline in the *Miami Citizen* one day. The Beauregards were great enemies of the press—"Bad news! Only bad news! They're ruining this country with their bad news!" Laura liked to complain—and Sherry was a reporter, a front-page reporter at that. It made perfect sense. No wonder she didn't care about the grass. She was too busy putting honest Americans out of work and freeing savage Death Row criminals. From that point on, the Beauregards' mission took on new zeal, although Sherry never knew the reason why.

In fact, at first Sherry thought the Beauregards really cared about her overlush lawn, so she got her boyfriend, Brazil, to mow it once or twice. But that just gave them a chance to insult him instead of her. ("Your friend should cut his hair and put on a pair of shoes. He looks like a hippie," Laura announced after Brazil's first visit. The second time, Alvin greeted Brazil by shouting, "Nice wedding ring, buddy!")

And so, Sherry, buffed and polished for four years at Miss

Eliot's Preparatory Academy for Young Ladies, had no choice but to fight back the perfectly correct way: She glowered in silence.

Four or five months passed, and the insults continued without letup. Finally, Sherry could take it no longer. After all, Miss Eliot's was a thousand miles away and she'd never been very good there anyway; wasn't she finally free of the place? And, Sherry wondered, who were these strange and horrible people to diminish her newfound paradise? They were the intruders—she wasn't. So, one Sunday morning after Laura Beauregard sarcastically asked her if she planned to pull weeds before church, Sherry launched the counterattack she'd been daydreaming of for weeks. First she darted inside to grab a special bag of trash from her kitchen, and then she came striding out of her house, headed directly toward the lawn chairs where Alvin and Laura were huddled as always, bitching away. She was moving so fast they didn't even see her coming.

But then, suddenly, they heard her.

"Oh, fuck off," she announced in a sharp-edged, matter-of-fact tone. "Fuck, fuck, *fuck* off, you fucking pitted prunes! Get a life!" She was virtually on top of them now, staring down and smiling as sweetly as possible. "I hope you heard me," she went on, "but just in case you didn't, I happened to say, '*FUCK OFF, YOU FUCKING PITTED PRUNES!*' "

Complete silence. Then: "Well, I could just die!" Laura Beauregard erupted in response, veins throbbing under crepe-paper skin. She twisted in her seat toward Alvin for a nod of approval. "What she said!" her husband swiftly agreed. "We could just die!"

"Gosh darn," Sherry cooed back, leaning so close to the couple she could count the six hairs left on Alvin's scalp, "wouldn't that be awful?" She smiled again and waited a minute for the venom to sink in before going on. "I mean, if you two left, who'd make sure everyone's lawn conformed to regulations? Who would pay the shrubbery police? I mean, Mr. and Mrs. Beauregard, who would be left to shout vindictive, petty, *fucked-up* indignities at me?"

And with that, Sherry dumped her bag of rotting fish heads, cat-food cans, and wet cigarette butts at their feet, and sashayed back to number 43 Lemonlime Road.

But that was four months ago. Since then, Sherry had seen little of the Beauregards. She'd almost forgotten that two old demons lived next door, and she never suspected that they would haunt her for the rest of her life.

3 Much later, when she'd had hours and days and weeks to search for all the clues she'd missed the first time, Sherry realized it was October 20 when the collision course with her own demons began.

She had arrived at work at one, after covering the Seven Stars hit and then rushing home to retrieve her tape recorder. First deadline was only a few hours away, and the newsroom was shifting into high gear, as clattery and petulant as a gravel truck about to head up a steep hill. As usual, the vast fifth-floor office was a mess—newspapers everywhere, trash cans overturned, empty pens and crumpled paper littering the floor and desktops alike. It was as if a hurricane had blown through the place. In fact, only reporters had, running for their daily bread and away from the editors who tried to keep them hungry. Hundreds of desks, long ago arranged in neat rows, now zigzagged across a coffee-stained, cigarette-burned carpet. Phones rang incessantly, each with a different and more irritating bell. The bulletin boards and walls were haphazardly plastered with mementos and trophies of bygone stories—a Most Wanted poster hung behind one copy machine, face doctored with a birthmark, mustache, and sideburns to look like the mayor, nearby someone had tacked up a letter from a reader who warned that the Devil was occupying one particular city desk reporter, whom she coyly declined to identify. In the margin, someone had scribbled, *Hey—if true, great story!* Two feet away, in an unclaimed shipping crate, sat twelve pairs of smelly gym socks.

But few people, Sherry included, ever noticed the unrelenting scrunginess of the newsroom. The reason was simple: From one far corner to the other, the office's huge picture windows opened out onto the dazzling waters of Biscayne Bay and its half-dozen verdant islands. The colors—shimmery turquoise against deep

azure skies, lush green speckled with bougainvillea hot pink—
were enough to make an atheist shout *hosanna*! When the sun was
shining, which was often, a magnificent white light filled the
newsroom, and if there was a breeze, which also happened most
days, the whole messy, dirty place was doused with the intoxicating perfume of sea air and tropical fauna. And so it happened
that only veteran reporters—and they were few in number; the
Citizen was teeming with young blood, all imported from up
North—ever complained about the dump where news was dug
up, twisted around, and ironed out day after day after day.

Sherry was glad she was working the late shift for a change,
in at eleven, out at nine. She was a night person; getting up in
the morning required two cups of black coffee, two sugar-coated
cherry Pop-Tarts, an icy shower, and a very loud shot of Stones
through headphones, the power turned up high. But by the time
she walked in the swinging double doors of the newsroom and
headed toward the four desks shoved together called Nerve Central, she was all jazzed up and ready to go. A quick glance left
and right let her know the day was status quo—in one corner a
group of reporters huddled in a circle, laughing, fueling up on
gossip and little cups of dark double-punch Cuban coffee. In his
glass cubicle near the back of the room, Jack Dougherty was well
into his second pack, grumbling as he read *The Miami Herald*, the
Citizen's formidable competition, making a mental note of every
reporter who got beat on a story or a quote. Her partner, Belinda
McEvoy, was gazing out one of the big windows that lined the
newsroom. That's how she got her inspiration.

Sherry dumped her briefcase on her desk and then quickly
walked over to Belinda's side. "I'm here," she said, squeezing her
arm warmly.

Belinda nodded vaguely. "Take a look at that," she said,
pointing to a sleek white sailboat slicing the water below on its
way out to sea. Her voice was sad and transparent, but somehow
still filled with wonder. When they'd first met three years ago, the
sound of it irritated Sherry utterly, it was so distant and disjointed.
Now she loved to hear Belinda talk. Her voice was a secret code,
and maybe only a handful of people could decipher it. Sherry was
one of them.

"The joys of drug money," Sherry said after watching the
sailboat for a minute.

"Doesn't necessarily *have* to be drug money."

"No."

"But it probably is, right?"

"Probably is."

Belinda sighed and absentmindedly pushed a strand of wavy red hair off her cheek. She was twenty-four then, but age seemed to elude her. One minute her eyes held the simple peace of a child; the next, they were filled with the bitterness of a war widow.

"So, my mother called last night," she told Sherry.

"Where is she?"

"Oh . . . um, Paris, I guess." She had forgotten to ask.

"How's she doing? Did you tell her about your car accident?"

"No . . ."

"You're still paying for the last one?"

"Yes . . ."

Around them, the newsroom was rumbling with signs of life. The wire machines clamored relentlessly, the clique of reporters broke apart, each heading toward Nerve Central to bargain for good play. Belinda didn't seem to notice.

"You know," she said, turning to look at Sherry, "I've been thinking about it, and she's dealing with the thing, you know, the thing with my dad, better now. Better than me, I think."

"I'm so happy to hear that," Sherry murmured, and then stopped. There were a lot of comforting words she might have added, polite phrases of sympathy she knew by heart, but she could not. For now, there was nothing to say. Belinda's grief was still too exquisite.

Less than a year had passed since Belinda's father killed himself, blowing open his brains and blowing apart what little was left of her belief in mortal grace. How she had loved him! There was no one, anywhere, like him, she had told Sherry a dozen times—a straight-backed, simply-too-elegant spook who seemed to never do a dirty day's work, a charming-when-soused alcoholic who quoted Whitman's "Song of Myself" at cocktail parties, who played polo like a prince, who painted delicate watercolors of the fishing boats at Menemsha. Aloysius McEvoy drank his way through assignments in Lebanon, Argentina, and Niger, leaving behind no fingerprints, just dumbstruck weekend lovers and awestruck lifelong enemies. For many years, he was a very good man for the Company. He got the job done quickly and invisibly. But as time passed, he began to love his own myth too much— there were indiscretions. He was spotted stumbling down a Buenos Aires street in a heavy drunk, a martini glass in one hand and a cocked Beretta in the other. A few weeks later, at an embassy party, he told the cultural attaché that he had killed fourteen men in his career, "and when I'm sober, which is frightfully rare, thank the Lord," he said, "I feel pretty shitty about some of them." Finally, when he couldn't pull off a job without botching it in some small way, the government sent him home and put him behind a desk, where he kept a Thermos of cold Finnish vodka in his bottom drawer. The paper pushing bored him. He spent his days fantasizing about the too-sweet smells of the street market in Niamey and the glittery night skies above the Argentine prairie land. He felt his liver wasting away inside him; his urine was pink and stank of blood. His eyes were turning from blue to yellow-gray; in the shower, his silver hair fell out in clumps, passing through his fingers and down the drain. His life was over, he knew it, and the rage was too much to bear silently. He had waited until the whole family was gathered at Thanksgiving dinner in Chevy Chase, all the brothers and sisters, aunts and uncles and cousins, seated around a table set in Wedgwood. He looked, eyes expressionless, from face to face around him, pausing finally and only slightly longer at Belinda to smile softly and nod. And then, without a word, he rose, walked into the garage, and shot off his head with a CIA-issued Walther.

When it had happened, Belinda was sitting next to her mother at the Thanksgiving table, head bowed, lips just parted to ask the ritual "Shall we pray?" Then the blast came, rattling the teacups in their saucers and jostling each piece of hand-polished silverware just one millimeter off kilter. Belinda rose slowly and walked into the garage—she knew no one else would do it—pried the gun from her father's right hand, kissed each of his fingers, and with one fingertip, gently shut his eyes. She had hoped to find some kind of peace in them, but saw only a glint of horror. Her own horror came later, and still she could not shake it loose.

"I think it's good your mom is with her friends," Sherry said. They were still side by side, staring out the window at the graceful sailboat below on the bay.

"I'm with friends."

"Yes, you are," said Sherry.

The sailboat vanished into Miami's glistening pale blue horizon.

"You know," Belinda said, turning from the window

abruptly, "you shouldn't be so hard on your parents. It kills me. You're just lucky they're alive, Sherry. I mean it." She had said this many times before.

"Yeah, yeah, you're right," Sherry answered automatically. But the truth was, she had no real answer. That part of her heart was vacant. She quickly pointed to another immense, gleaming sailboat on the bay below, this one heading into port. "Now here's someone who's done very well in the plumbing-supply business," she said.

"Oh, come on!" Belinda protested. "These people look completely innocent—look at them: a mom, a dad, two kids. My goodness, Sherry, you've been a reporter too long."

"Maybe you've got a point there, darlin'," Sherry agreed, relieved to be off the unbearable, unresolvable topic of family. "Hey, so what've you got going today?" she asked Belinda, trying to sound enthusiastic but not really succeeding. For the past month, they'd both been between projects, stuck on general assignment, covering quick-hit, one-time-only stories with all the gusto they could muster, which lately wasn't much. The day before, Sherry had to come up with fifteen inches of fluff about a street festival for two hundred near-corpses in Surfside, while Belinda ended up writing a short about a flu-vaccine campaign being sponsored by a legion of minicar-driving Shriners wearing round red hats with gold tassels.

"What I've got going today happens to be exactly the same thing you've got going," Belinda answered. "Jack wants to see both of us at two. Something about a project he's got an idea for." She shrugged and lowered her voice to a whisper. "This is your Pulitzer Prize, honey," she said, imitating the editor's rasp. "You're gonna win the Pulitzer this year, and maybe I'll live to see it."

"Another project with Jack?" Sherry didn't know whether to cheer or run for cover. The man was a great editor, true, but she was just getting used to eating dinner at home again.

"Suddenly makes me want to cover a fire," Belinda said with a laugh. "Makes me want to cover a beauty contest at an old-age home."

"Laura Beauregard would win."

"That's right. Christ!" She laughed—Sherry's battle with the Beauregards reminded her of some kind of demented comic strip.

Just then, Sherry spotted Brazil across the newsroom. She

hadn't seen him for a week. He had been on a vacation in Orlando with his wife and the kid. He waved at her and smiled broadly. He looked tan and wonderful.

"He wants everyone to know about you two," Belinda said, frowning.

"Do I care?" answered Sherry. "What difference does it make who knows about us? What difference in the world?"

It was just before two when Sherry's phone rang. "You're late as usual," Jack said. "Get the hell into my office. And bring that broad Belinda. I got something that'll blow your little *summa cum laude* ass to Bogotá and back. This time, you're definitely gonna win the Pulitzer."

He wished.

Hell, *she* wished, and she'd been wishing since the moment she'd landed in Miami.

For the past three years, she and Belinda had worked on too many of Jack's investigative projects to keep track of them all, and they'd come close to capturing the big one, but never close enough. There was the story about cops hiding felony records. The story about teenage strippers on Miami Beach. There was the story about corruption at the dog track.

They were all Jack's ideas. He had run the show at a dead-serious paper up North for seventeen years and then was sent to Miami to turn the beachboys in the newsroom into real men. That was *his* version of the truth. Some people in the newsroom said Miami was Jack's big good-bye; corporate was putting him out to pasture.

Who knew for sure? Jack was so unpredictable that it was common for the same reporter to love him intensely and hate him desperately within the same hour. His mood swings were notorious: Some days, he would stand on top of Nerve Central decked out in a party hat and rally the troops gathered below, telling them that the *Citizen* was a great newspaper, that they were the unsung heroes of their generation, that Miami was "the greatest fuckin' news town in the hemisphere." He would praise reporters by name, mention some small detail in an obscure story to illustrate just how "fan-*fuckin'*-tastic" someone was. But other days, Jack sulked around the newsroom, talking to no one except to dole out blame, rubbing his temples in aggravation if someone tried to disagree. That he was rarely wrong made him even easier to hate.

But Jack didn't mind being hated; he seemed to accept it as fate. With a few shots of Wild Turkey in him after work at the Bomb Shelter Bar, he would tell anyone close enough to hear his hoarse smoker's growl that he was a loner by nature. He simply didn't like most people, because most people, he'd found in life, were inherently evil. If you had any doubt about that, he'd tell you, just read the newspaper on one single day, front to back. Killers, rapists, con men, politicians—the world was full of them. It was left to the reporters to keep them from taking over.

He was a small man—he stood just a few inches over five feet—a fact most everyone in the newsroom stopped noticing once they heard him bark orders. And he was skinny, too, with the kind of lean, muscular body that would have made him a good runner if he weren't addicted to unfiltered Pall Mall cigarettes and work. His face was haggard and pinched with tension; even his smiles looked like frowns, but he wasn't a completely unattractive man. He had, for one thing, strikingly honest pale blue eyes— Sherry could picture him as an Amish farmer—and for another, he had a movie star's cleft chin. Both features, however, captured much less attention around the newsroom than Jack's most notable physical characteristic—his bald head, as smooth and shiny as a newborn's bottom. It was, in fact, such a beautiful and *touchable* head that new reporters, delivery boys, and temporary secretaries had been seen spontaneously to pat it. For a long time, Jack would simply jerk away and snarl, but one day a few months after he arrived in Miami, he showed up at work wearing a flyfisherman's cap—he was a fly-fishing fanatic; his father had been an Orvis salesman—and he'd worn it ever since, each week adorning it with ever more complicated and colorful nymphs, streamers, and bass bugs he'd tied himself.

Jack Dougherty rarely talked about his family. Occasionally, he mentioned his wife, Irene—she fixed his lunch for him every day—and once he told Belinda she reminded him of his daughter,

Emily, then sighed hard and walked away. The rumor in the newsroom was that the girl had died in a Detroit alley from a drug overdose. His son lived in Fort Lauderdale with his two kids and a blimp-sized blond wife. They showed up once a year to watch the presses roll.

"Sit down and don't give me any back talk," Jack said as Belinda and Sherry walked into his office that day. Sherry knew right away he had something major in mind, because all the big-gun editors were already there, looking uneasy. They were probably scared shitless that Jack had decided to investigate the city's country clubs.

"We got a drug problem in Dade County," Jack began, leaning forward in his chair and lighting a cigarette. Mounted behind him on the wall was a nine-foot-long steel fly rod and the 118-pound tarpon he had landed on one of his many solitary weekend excursions to the Keys. "No kidding, right? That's what you're thinking, that I've gone crazy or something. Tell me I'm right, Sherry."

"You're right, boss."

"Anyway, I got an idea. I got an idea that we're not just talking about Colombians wasting each other all over town. I think we've got the world-famous trickle-down theory at work here. Look, what I'm saying is this: I think we're talking about *seventh graders* using cocaine. I want you to talk to the seventh graders packing snow up their noses."

Jack went on for a half hour, a lot of talk for him. He wanted a series on drugs in the schoolhouse, that's how he put it. Dealers who were fifteen years old, teachers who looked the other way, straight-arrow kids who went crooked. "Why, why, why?" he said every few minutes when he paused to cough, covering his mouth with fingers turned yellow from nicotine.

"You got free rein from me. Go to the schools. Talk to the kids. Talk to them until you know what's going on. Where they're getting the stuff. Make sure they're not lying to you. If you can get names, get names. If they won't talk without confidentiality, give 'em that. And if you find out that my grandkids are using dope, you can kill 'em."

The big guns laughed nervously. Sherry was watching Garrett Newman's ageless Princeton face. He was the *Citizen's* executive editor, one step above Jack and one step out of the newsroom on his way up to the publisher's cushy suite of offices on the eighth floor. His direct contact with the grit of workaday reporting consisted of writing laudatory memos to copy editors for particularly catchy headlines and delivering puffed-chest speeches about the First Amendment at chamber of commerce functions. But Newman's crowning achievement was giving Brazil his name at the company Christmas party two years ago. "Fine work on those deeply moving photos out of Brazil, John. Very powerful stuff," he had announced in a loud and jolly ho-ho-ho sort of voice. "You take the kind of photos that make the *Citizen* a fine newspaper. Excellent work! We are proud of you."

"El Salvador, sir," John answered simply. "I was in El Salvador."

"Of course." Newman was even louder and jollier on the second go-round. "I knew you were in El Salvador." But the name stuck. Since then everyone called him Brazil, everyone except Newman.

Now here Newman was again, the titular head of nothingness, sitting in on a story conference that meant real work for only two of the people present: Sherry and Belinda. Nevertheless, he found it politically astute to say a few words, and so he authoritatively turned to Jack and lobbed a question. "When do we start?" he said, eyes squinting in concern.

"Yesterday," snarled Jack. And with that, the meeting ended.

So Sherry and Belinda went out to eat, ordered Cuban picadillo and sweet fried plantains, but ate almost nothing.

"I'm scared to death," said Belinda. They were sitting in a booth at El Roda, a former gas station turned greasy neon-lit diner run by Marielito refugees. They were the only two women in the place besides a buxom teenage waitress in red spike heels, a shiny spandex halter top, and denim shorts. All the other booths were taken up by middle-aged Cuban men playing dominoes with the shouting and intensity of a bullfight. Belinda had to lean across the table for Sherry to hear her above the racket.

"Wow, I think Jack really wants this one. I mean, he's wanted them all. But this one is like his grand farewell, like he's saying *'In your face, Newman,'* or something like that," she said, words tumbling out in her frail, childlike voice. "It must be true, Sherry, all that gossip in the newsroom—corporate must be nudging Jack out the door. Maybe they want to bring in someone more . . . I don't know, someone more *modern* or something. Someone less fanatic about ethics. Well, maybe not *ethics*, but—" Belinda shrugged in frustration. She wasn't sure how to explain it, but she sure knew how pissed-off Newman had looked when they lost the Rosa Riley baby-killer story in June because Jack wouldn't pay some mole a hundred bucks for an interview. Jack never paid for information; he said that was the way TV operated. And he never, ever, allowed reporters to trade secrets with the cops or the district attorney. That, he said, was *his* newsroom's first and most deadly sin.

But Sherry wasn't thinking about Jack. She was thinking about all the stupid questions they would have to ask, feigning curiosity, and worse, surprise.

"I don't know," she told Belinda. "The whole pretense of this thing really bothers me. Don't kids everywhere do drugs? I did drugs at Miss Eliot's. It was cool. Didn't you smoke dope in high school?"

"I was in Libya then. It was different."

Sherry tried to imagine Belinda in a chador, her wavy red hair hidden beneath black, only her speckled yellow-green eyes showing to the world. She knew she would recognize her anyway.

"Well, take it from me, everyone here in the U.S. of A. smokes a little pot and snorts a little coke in high school," Sherry said. "I mean, this could be one of those stories where people are going to read the headline and take a nap." She let out a cynical laugh. "I can see the headline now. CITIZEN FINDS MOST TEENAGERS TRY DRUGS. It might be very embarrassing."

"Oh, come on, Sherry," Belinda chided her, "you know we always pull through with something."

Sherry nodded—she had to agree. With enough digging, and sometimes a reporter had to dig very deep, every single story had at least one sexy front-page hook. This story would, too. "Okay,

okay, I got it," she told Belinda, breaking into a grin. "EIGHT-YEAR-OLD SOLD COCAINE; TELLS COPS HE THOUGHT IT WAS MOMMY'S SUGAR."

Belinda giggled. "No way, Sherry, you're getting soft," she said, "that's only good for one day on the wires. How about this: WOODSTOCK GENERATION TELLS THEIR KIDS: 'FEED YOUR HEADS.' And then we could write a whole big story about how the parents of kids today grew up in the sixties, and how that's affecting the morality of teenagers now. I actually sort of see it as a three-part series."

"It's got to have a map," Sherry said, deadpan.

"And a time line."

"And a *lot* of five-color charts."

The friends sat for a while longer, silent beneath the din of El Roda's domino wars, thinking about the story that Jack wanted and all the work that had to be done before it would appear in black-and-white, beneath a double byline, on the front page one Sunday morning.

"It's goddamn hot out," Sherry said after a while, exasperated. She was thinking about the oily heat that rises off black tar, the kind that covers high school parking lots, where she was going to be spending the next few weeks scoping out little Wallys and Wendys smoking reefer.

"Uh-huh," said Belinda. Her mind was so far away she didn't know exactly what she had been thinking about, except that it made her heart ache a little.

"It's always goddamn hot out."

She heard Sherry out of one ear. "You never lived in Niger," she said.

"Thank you, Belinda, I feel better now."

They were finished eating. El Roda was emptying out, only a few Cuban men were left, and a new waitress had come on duty, the sister of the last by the looks of her.

A few minutes passed. Sherry wished she hadn't quit smoking for the hundredth time.

"I'm not really sure Jack's right about all the kids using drugs," she said, trying to pull Belinda back to earth.

"But we don't know."

"We don't know anything yet."

After lunch, Belinda took off for a press conference in Little Haiti, something about a new job-training program for refugees.

"My last day as a regular old Lois Lane," she said to Sherry as she got into her car. "Tomorrow—undercover drug crusader." She swung one arm in the air like a swashbuckler.

Sherry laughed, more from surprise than anything else—it was so rare to hear Belinda crack a joke. She waved good-bye and headed back to the *Citizen*, where the newsroom was as quiet as a bank lobby; everyone was on the street. She wandered by Nerve Central and sat down by the day editor, Dick Radewski, who was scanning the competition.

"Got anything for me?" she asked.

Radewski looked up and fixed on Sherry with his close-set brown eyes. "I understand from the boss that you're on *super extra-special* assignment," he said laconically. "You are not to be disturbed with the day-to-day aggravation of putting out a news-paper, like the rest of us lemmings." He took a drag on his cigarette and rolled his eyes. Sherry couldn't tell if he was expressing sympathy or contempt, and she knew the effect was intentional. Radewski had spent ten years at city hall developing the best poker face in the business.

"Sorry," she said, and Radewski shrugged.

Sherry wandered away, around the newsroom for a few minutes, first checking her mailbox and then swinging by the photo desk to look at Brazil's schedule. He was gone for the next couple of hours shooting a Dolphins practice, an assignment no doubt engineered by Jack. He wanted Sherry to be alone, to get her head clear, to get ready. For the next six weeks, she wouldn't have the time or energy to care about anything but the project—his project.

She got the message. Sherry settled in behind her desk, pulled out a fresh reporter's notebook from her top drawer, and filled her favorite Mont Blanc fountain pen with emerald-green ink, just as she did before every big story. Then she unlocked her bottom drawer and pulled out her Rolodex—it was the biggest version sold, and so chock-full of high-level cop sources, gossipy street snitches, and the home phone numbers of city officials that Sherry never left it unattended—and began the arduous first step of assembling a list of potential sources. She'd have to talk to Tom Whitton, the superintendent of schools—he was always good for a defensive-sounding quote or two—and she'd need to get an interview with that new Vice detective heading up the campus-surveillance unit. She might also try to land a session with—

"Hey, darlin', I'm back!" It was Brazil, announcing his arrival with typical eighty-decibel gusto. "Darlin', I'm back and ready to roll—into bed with you. *Hah!*"

He plopped down on the top of Sherry's desk and laughed cheerfully at his own joke. "Bet you missed me." Then he leaned forward and turned his lips close to Sherry's neck. "I missed *you* just terrible, darlin'," he whispered.

Sherry shook her head. She loved him like crazy; it just didn't make sense. He had put a spell on her, she was certain, but it didn't feel too bad. In fact, it was like the feeling you get when you step off a plane in a foreign country—breathless, dizzy, and exhilarated all at once.

Sometimes she imagined returning home to Marblehead and marrying Charles, which once had seemed so inevitable, and even in the imagining, she longed for the smell of Brazil, for the sharp scent of darkroom chemicals that hovered around him always. And she longed for the sound of his arrogant Florida Cracker voice, a twangy echo of Chiefland, where he was raised on a horse farm with six older sisters. "I know more about women than you do," he told her on one of their first dates. "Sorry if that sounds obnoxious, but it happens to be true." He was the first man who left her speechless.

Charles had short blond hair and dark green eyes, the color of the sea in autumn. His hands were small and delicate, almost like a woman's. His face was round and refined; every feature was perfect. He was lovely to look at.

Brazil had long hair; it was blond, too—in fact, almost the same shade as Charles's—but his hands were enormous and callused. His face was wide to match his size, and his features were large and sturdy. Occasionally, he shaved. The first time she saw him, Sherry thought he looked like a bear.

Now when she looked at him, the bear was gone. Still, she felt that there had to be some kind of animal mixed into his blood; he was so damn fundamental. No lies, no guilt, no restraint.

Once Sherry had pointed this out to him—they were eating pizza in bed one night, listening to one of his old B. B. King tapes—and he had looked at her with amazement. "Why would anybody ever try to be something they're not?" he had asked in a slow, incredulous drawl.

"Christ, Brazil, either you are totally naive or just the stupidest person I have ever met," Sherry had answered. "Don't you know there are zillions of people who do that for a fucking living?

They don't like who they are, so they invent themselves as some-one else. They're ugly, so they make themselves beautiful, or they're poor, so they make themselves rich—"

"Or if they're like you, they're rich and they try to make themselves poor, right?" He smiled sweetly.

She started to protest.

"Don't bother," he cut her off. "I'm onto you. It breaks my heart, but I am."

The conversation had taken place more than a year ago. Sherry had thought they would never last; he had assured her they would. Now he was back from the vacation she was sure would be their death knell, and, as he had promised before he left, nothing seemed different. As he sat on her desk, happily recounting the details of the trip to Disney World, Sherry stared at him, searching in the way he moved or spoke for evidence that he had decided to become a family man for good. But none was there; he ended the description of every amusement-park ride by saying, "Baby, I wish you'da been there."

"I don't think Jeanie would have gone for it," Sherry answered once.

"Hell, I know she'd like you."

"Not *that* much."

"No, she'd like you a lot."

He was being ridiculous. Sherry changed the subject and told him about the drugs-in-the-schoolhouse project.

"Who's making pictures for it?" he asked.

"They didn't say."

"Bet it's me," he said, grinning. "Admit it. They always call on Brazil Brackett when the going gets tough. When the going gets tough, Brazil gets going."

"Yeah, I'm really sure that's what they were thinking."

"I'm sure they were."

"Brazil, try to demonstrate some modesty for once."

"Whatever for?" he asked, and he meant it.

6

The Beauregards weren't expecting Sherry when she drove down Lemonlime Road at four, and in fact, neither of them noticed at all when she turned her car into the driveway. For a change, Sherry observed, her neighbors weren't sitting, comalike, in their matching lawn chairs. Instead, Laura was standing inside the front door, looking out at Alvin, who was waddling toward something small and gray near the far corner of their yard. He must be putting a stray rock in its proper place at Laura's command, Sherry thought. Wouldn't want to spoil the neighborhood with a little nature.

But then Sherry saw Alvin swing his leg and kick the rock. And she saw him kick again, with so much energy that she could hear him grunt from twenty yards away. His face was red and puffy—he was holding his breath. Sherry stared in wonder—Alvin was absolutely obsessed. His leg kept slamming against the rock faster and faster until he stopped and hunched over, hands on knees, to rest and wipe the sweat from his forehead.

It was then that Sherry saw the object at Alvin's feet twitch—Christ!—that fucker had been kicking Pansy! The old cat was curled in a lifeless ball by his feet.

Sherry jumped from her car and ran toward him, propelled by rage.

"*You fucking asshole!* What the fuck are you doing?" she screamed. "You're dead. You and your ugly wife." She scooped up the cat in her arms. She was still alive, but barely. Blood covered her lips and ran down the fur under her chin.

"Your cat is eating our grass," Alvin said, clenched fists on hips, trying to sound indignant but sounding more scared than anything else. He looked toward his house, but Laura was nowhere to be seen.

"This is it," Sherry said, standing close enough to hear her neighbor inhale and exhale nervously. "You will pay for this, Alvin. You and Laura will pay a fucking huge price. Do you understand?" She inched closer to him. "You poor, sick fuck-head," she whispered.

Sherry carried Pansy inside and peered out her window. Now both the Beauregards were outside again, standing beside their lawn chairs, staring at her house, chattering and gesturing like windup toys.

She wanted to call the cops, but that wasn't revenge.

Revenge was punching Alvin in the gut until his ears bled, which could take years.

She called the veterinarian and told him she was bringing Pansy in—it was an emergency. Then she wrapped the cat in a towel and drove to the clinic in Coconut Grove at eighty miles an hour.

She was sobbing by the time she arrived. Pansy had stopped moving. Her eyes were closed, and her breathing came in short, shallow tugs.

The vet was a young, smooth-faced guy. She had met him once before, when Pansy got her shots a year ago. At that visit, he had suggested Sherry put the cat on an elaborate diet of pills if her arthritis got any worse.

Sherry quickly explained what had happened.

"How many times did he kick her?" the vet asked as he ran his hands over the cat's body, checking for cracked bones.

"I don't know—ten times, maybe."

He shook his head in disgust.

"Well, this definitely should be reported."

"I'm going to kill them."

"I know how you must feel." He was speaking to Sherry in the flat, sympathetic voice of an undertaker. "This is just terrible."

A minute passed. The vet kept massaging different parts of the cat's body as she lay on his table motionless. His eyes squinted with concentration.

Finally, he looked up from the animal.

"Look," he said, "I have very bad news."

"No—"

"Your neighbor broke most of your cat's ribs, and it feels to me as if her spleen and liver may have ruptured. There feels to be a lot of internal bleeding."

Tears ran down Sherry's face and dripped onto the examining table. "I know what you're going to say," she said.

"The cat is very old. Her chances of full recovery are slim," the vet went on. "She is in terrible agony. I think you ought to do what is best for her."

"I want her to live."

"I know you do."

"No, I mean it," Sherry cried. "I really want her to live. I can pay whatever it takes. I have lots of money. I can pay anything. Please, just try to save her."

"You don't understand," the vet said, shaking his head. "There is no saving her."

Sherry leaned over and kissed Pansy between the ears. "I got her when I was nine years old," she told the vet. She was stroking the cat's head with one finger and crying still. "She's always been with me. I even brought her to college. Everyone loved her." The vet nodded and gave a sideways glance at the clock above the examining table, but Sherry ignored the message. "One Valentine's Day, she ate the chocolates that Charles gave me. She was cross-eyed for two weeks."

The vet nodded again. "Sherry," he said, "the cat is suffering."

"I just want to say good-bye."

"Okay," he said. "I'm just going to get some things." He left the room.

Sherry was crying harder now. "Pansy," she said, bending so close to the cat that its fur brushed her lips, "I'm sorry to let this happen so far away from home."

In a minute, the vet was back. He was carrying a large syringe, a vial of liquid, and a plastic bag. "Would you like to be with her, or do you want to wait outside?"

"I can't watch this." She kissed the cat one last time and started to leave the room. At the last minute, she turned around and looked at the animal curled on the examining table. "So long, *amiga*," she said.

A few minutes later, the vet found Sherry in the waiting room, where she was sitting on the couch, numbly studying the patterns in the asphalt floor tiles. He patted her shoulder. "It's over now," he said.

She nodded and stood up to leave. "If I was at home, I'd bury her in the backyard."

"Yes, I understand."

"But I only rent my house here."

"Yes, well . . ." The vet looked at Sherry. "Perhaps this isn't the best time to discuss it, but I really urge you to report this to the police."

"Right." She pulled her car keys from her purse. "Thank you, Doctor. I'll take care of it."

Ten minutes later, when she arrived home, Sherry was in a daze, but she wasn't out of it enough to feel anything faintly resembling forgiveness. She needed to punish Alvin and Laura Beauregard, and she was dying to do it right away. But how? Hands shaking, she fixed herself a tumbler of gin in the kitchen and then frantically paced into the living room, to the window facing the Beauregards' house. And there they were, of course, sitting in their lawn chairs like two corpses. Sherry felt a surge of hatred rise up in her chest like a wintertime storm wave, and just as it crested, the idea came to her. It was brilliant—yes! Perfect revenge. She took her stereo speakers—they were massive, a gift from her father when she turned twenty—and loaded them into the window. Then she stuck the Stones on the record player, turned the volume up to ten, and let it go.

The noise almost blew her neighbors out of their lawn chairs. Laura looked stunned, then covered her ears and ran inside. Alvin shook his fist and followed. She let the music play for an hour, gave them a five-minute break, just long enough to think maybe the concert was over. But it wasn't.

That night, after she finally turned off the music, Sherry wrote her parents. She owed them a letter, and Pansy's death made her think of home.

Dear Mother and Father, she began. *Thanks for the note and your generous gift. I appreciate your concern, even though I am making a perfectly fine living in Miami. It was good to hear that Charles is doing well at Bullfinch and Lodge. I never doubted he would be a successful attorney.*

Sherry put down her pen. It was hard to find the right words, or any words really. She looked at the small framed photograph next to her bed. It was from someone else's life. She and Charles were freshmen then, newly in love, surging with hope, mugging it up for the camera and their friends with an extravagant kiss. Now she wondered why she kept the picture out at all. Had she really loved Charles once? Her memories were so contradictory. When she wanted, she could recall how funny and smart and caring he could be. His love was stalwart, the kind an older brother offers, even in the face of the most reckless abuses. But other times, times she could remember more vividly, he could be as small-hearted as a clenched fist.

He always told Sherry that he knew her better than anyone, that she couldn't hide from him and what he knew. For some reason, she had believed him.

He broke up with her twice, both times after she had admitted sleeping with his friends. She felt embarrassed for him when he came back.

"I'm hoping that you grow out of this," he once said as they sat in the living room of the Marblehead house. Then: "Did you like sleeping with him?"

Yes, she thought. "No," she said.

When she graduated, Charles gave her a red BMW. She still drove it.

Personally, I haven't heard from Charles for about two months, she wrote to her parents that night in Miami, lying on her bed. The TV was on with the volume turned way down. *We're both so busy that I suppose we've fallen a bit out of touch.*

Today Belinda McEvoy and I were assigned to a project about drugs and young people. There seems to be a great deal of corporate interest in the project, so I'm sure it will receive prominent front-page play. Work, in general, is going very well. There's a lot of deadline pressure, but I haven't missed one yet. In addition, I am still making lots of friends, but I'm staying in close touch with Alice. I'm sure you've heard by now that she is marrying Jamie Merrill, Katie's younger brother who went to Wharton. She wants me to be a bridesmaid, and I tentatively said yes. I don't know what will be happening at work then. But I'll try to get away to be there.

I have terrible news about Pansy. She died today—I guess she was getting very old. Thank you, Mother, for giving her to me all those years ago.

Hope all is well in Marblehead.

Yours,—S.

Sherry rolled onto her stomach to reread what she had written, and when she was done, she let out a short, sardonic laugh. Perhaps her words were a little stilted, but overall, she thought, the letter practically sounded normal—as if the Estabrooks were a normal family, "completely innocent" like the windblown mom, dad, and two kids Belinda had spotted sailing on the bay earlier that day.

But the Estabrooks were not normal, and they certainly were not innocent, despite all splendid appearances to the contrary. Sherry had known that for three years now, but still the anger hadn't faded. And sometimes she thought it was growing more virulent with every day she spent in Miami, so far away from home and its constant, insidious deception.

Sherry folded the letter in half, shoved it in the envelope, and then quickly scribbled the address: *One Hundred Endless Horizon Lane, Marblehead, MA 01945*. How pretty it looked on paper, she thought, how scenic it sounded. She closed her eyes and, just for a moment, allowed herself to remember, instead, the reality of the place, an imposing brick Georgian mansion by the sea, three stories high, with black shutters, a long, crushed-marble driveway, and a solid-brass door knocker shaped like a gavel. After the severe ostentation of the exterior, the interior was no surprise: Philadelphia Chippendale card tables of satinwood and yellow poplar, brocade-covered George I settees, bombastic Elisha Taylor Baker marinescapes on the walls, Aubussons on the floors. The rooms were so large and cluttered with precious possessions, the maids could only clean two in a single day. And so, it seemed, they were always cleaning—crouched over porcelain Chinese ginger jars and Krider & Biddle tea sets to dust them with silk rags, polishing the parquet floor on hands and knees—too busy or tired or intimidated to even look up when Sherry wandered by. The only time she ever saw their faces was when they scrubbed the French doors that opened from nearly every room onto the rough ocher beach and choppy gray waters that surrounded Marblehead Neck, and even then, the maids would not look her in the eye. They only nodded and offered a tiny "Hello, Miss Estabrook." It pained Sherry now to think she rarely answered.

But the fact was, all through her years in Marblehead, Sherry rarely answered anyone. She was mouthy and precocious and very bitchy, but no one ever called her on it. She was simply too pretty, too funny, and too smart to dismiss. That, and her last

name was Estabrook. As in Mrs. Eleanor DuFraine and the Honor-
able Laurence P. Estabrook, past president of the Bluemoor Yacht
Club, life member of the Algonquin, chairman of the Crayden
Hills Hospital fund drive, senior deacon at the First, a man with
a 10 handicap and about the same number of enemies, most of
them incarcerated at the state prison. The rest of the world, it
seemed, loved Judge Estabrook—his nickname around the courthouse was Lock 'Em Up Larry—or at the very least they respected
him. His mere presence commanded respect—he was six foot
four, built like a white oak, with a barrel chest, strong, sloping
shoulders, and legs as solid as rock-splitting roots. He dressed
the old-fashioned way, in dark, no-nonsense three-piece wool
suits from Brooks Brothers, his ties were properly indistinguishable from one another. For as long as Sherry could remember, his
hair was silver and cut close to his scalp, his wide-jawed Yankee
face set in a critical expression, his opaque blue eyes unblinking
in concentration. Even his smile had a certain dignity, but it was
a rare sight at home, reserved instead for the golf course or the
banquets, balls, and cocktail parties he and Eleanor Estabrook
attended every single weekend, month after month, year after
year. More often than not, Judge Estabrook was the guest of honor
at these events, called upon to make a toast, start the dancing,
or deliver a short speech between courses. He always complied
graciously and with dry patrician humor. He might raise his wine-
glass and pronounce, "To fairness, freedom, justice, and Lafite
Rothschild 1961! *Salut!*" or he might grandiloquently quote a few
lines from the Eighth Amendment and then ask, "Now, do you
think *marriage* is included in this part guaranteeing all of us against
cruel and unusual punishment?" And everyone would laugh and
clap delightedly, knowing, as everyone did, how devoted Laurence and Eleanor Estabrook were to one another.

And they were devoted to each other, Sherry could attest to
that. She could hear them sometimes, very late at night, talking
in their bedroom—soft murmurs interrupted by bolts of genuine
laughter. They held hands spontaneously, called each other
"lovie," sent each other flowers on the anniversary of their first
kiss, November 11, 1953, under the Soldier's Field bleachers, right
after Harvard beat Yale 13–0. Eleanor Estabrook loved the story
so much—the kiss had been a complete surprise; she had been
dating Laurence's roommate, for goodness sake!—that she told it
to Sherry every time they were alone together, which was about

twice a month, squeezed between her volunteering at a local homeless shelter two towns over, her shopping at Lord & Taylor, and her life sculpture classes at the museum. Evenings, of course, were taken up with "the Judge," as she called Sherry's father, as in, "Sherry, dear, now run along and play while I get ready for the Judge to get home from work." And for the next hour, she would preen herself like a debutante getting ready for a cotillion, even though she hardly needed to. Eleanor Estabrook, called Ellie by her many, many friends, was born glamorous, a perfect size six with naturally ash-blond hair and flawless skin, a woman who looked as if she'd been raised rich and then married *up*, because she had. But she never talked about money, of course, that would be unseemly. Instead, she preferred to talk about herself most of the time—her charities, her clothes, her crazy schedule, and most of all, her wonderful husband.

In fact, Eleanor and Laurence's affection for each other was so overwhelming a presence at One Hundred Endless Horizon Lane, it almost made Sherry feel loved—almost. But reality was, by the age of ten, she could no longer ignore or conveniently misinterpret its exclusivity. One spring night after dinner—she was fed, bathed and put to bed every evening by whatever British-accented nanny was with her that year—she crept into the formal dining room to spy on her parents, who ate by themselves when not dining out. The room was lit by candles, the table was set in Limoges and Gorham. Laurence and Eleanor sat catercorner to each other at the gleaming mahogany table, sipping wine and chatting happily. For five long minutes, Sherry crouched under a massive Hepplewhite sideboard in the corner listening, waiting to hear her name, and finally she did. "I think Sherry's ready for camp this summer," she heard her mother say offhandedly, gingerly dissecting her salad with a fork. "Vickie Marks knows a place we can send her for *twelve* weeks." Her father nodded vaguely. "What? Okay, then, all right," he replied, "but what about the place we sent her last summer?" Eleanor Estabrook shrugged. "She was *here* last summer, darling," she said. "Oh, really?" was the answer. "Fancy that."

That was all Sherry had to hear. She silently crept out of the room and up to her bedroom on the third floor, where she lay awake for hours trying to figure out why her parents hated her and what she could do to change their minds. By midnight she had hatched a plan, and for months afterward she stuck to it:

dressing in properly matched outfits, staying clean all day long, getting straight A's in English, science, and French and at least a B in math, practicing piano between lessons, memorizing a half-dozen poems by Emily Dickinson to recite center stage in the school talent show. But by Christmas it was clear her campaign was a failure—under the tree, she found a tennis racket, a canoe paddle, and three bathing suits, all earmarked for Camp Wa-Na-Ticki in the far reaches of northern Maine. She accepted them politely, but from that point onward, she stopped trying to impress Laurence and Eleanor with her suitability as a daughter. She said whatever she wanted, especially to her merry-go-round of nannies, played wherever and with whomever she pleased, which usually meant smoking dope and forming secret societies on the town beach with other rich girls just like her, she quit piano, tossed Emily in the trash, and blew off homework. And not surprisingly, she found that the change in her behavior didn't make a bit of difference. Everyone still liked her, deferred to her, and invited her to the best parties. Even her teachers at one private school and then another gave her the benefit of the doubt—her grades never dropped below a respectable B. Part of it, Sherry was sure, had to do with her looks. She had inherited her mother's lithe figure and her peacock-blue eyes and, from her father's side, a head of luxuriant pitch-black hair, which she let grow wild to spectacular effect. But her face was all her own—with its exotic high cheekbones and its sexy *get-lost* pout, she had a look of mystery and entitlement to her. And part of it, she thought, also had to do with her sharp and cynical sense of humor; her jokes were bitchy and smart, observations no one else dared to make out loud. But most of all, Sherry knew, she got away with everything because her last name was Estabrook.

The precociousness finally caught up with her when she was fifteen years old, a sophomore at Miss Eliot's, a small girl's school in an old Victorian mansion not far from the center of town. One weekend when her parents were in Chicago—her father was the keynote speaker at a convention of public defenders there—Sherry decided to throw a party at One Hundred Endless Horizon Lane. The guest list started off short: her five best friends from school and their boyfriends, most of whom attended St. Mark's Prep in Swampscott. But one of the girls, Amelia Lark, had a boyfriend who went to Salem State, and he had a few college buddies he wanted to bring along, and they had girlfriends who'd probably want to come, too. Sherry said fine, she didn't care. And, in fact, she didn't. She even thought it was sort of thrilling when midnight rolled around and sixty strangers were dancing all over the furniture in her living room, using porcelain urns for ashtrays, snorting coke off the marble mantelpiece. And when Amelia frantically pulled her aside at one point to report that two people were fucking like mad in her parents' bed, tearing the whole room apart, Sherry simply shrugged. She'd get someone to clean up the mess the next day.

But the mess didn't get cleaned up, not until much later. Because the girl getting fucked in her parents' bed left the party at Sherry Estabrook's house and went directly to the police, where she reported she had been raped. At 2:00 A.M. Sherry looked out the front window to see four wailing squad cars zooming into the driveway. The next thing she knew, everyone in the place was being lined up for questioning, and a very young, pointy-chinned patrolman was stripping the sheets off her parents' bed and shoving them in a large plastic bag marked EVIDENCE—TAMPERING WITH THIS CONTAINER IS A FEDERAL OFFENSE. The cops, however, were not unmindful of whose house they had invaded. One of them, a lieutenant named Joe O'Donnell, pulled Sherry aside and spoke to her in an unbelievably respectful manner—almost as if he were talking to the Judge himself. He asked her if she had seen anything suspicious—heard any screaming, noticed a particular young lady fighting off a particular young gentleman. Sherry said no—she didn't mention she was too wasted on vodka and cocaine to notice the nose of her face—and the cop easily accepted her version of the events. He sympathized with her. "Terrible accident we got here," he told her, "very unfortunate accident."

The cops were gone a few hours later, just before Sherry's parents arrived home, tipped off to the incident by the publisher of the local newspaper, whose wife happened to volunteer at the homeless shelter with Eleanor Estabrook. After solemnly surveying every room for damage and ordering the maids to sanitize every corner of the house, her parents shuttered themselves into her father's study for the rest of the day. It was as if Sherry weren't even there—as if they had no interest whatsoever in hearing her side of the story. And in those hours of waiting for them to come out again, for the first time in her life, Sherry was terrified of her parents, terrified they might hit her, or worse, judge her before she had a chance to explain.

She needn't have worried. When Eleanor and Laurence finally emerged, they very calmly requested a few minutes of her time, and then casually sat down with her at the kitchen table. Her mother spoke first.

"I guess you might say things got a little out of hand this weekend, Sherry dear," she began, her voice cool and controlled but not without a slightly peeved inflection. "We had no idea you were planning a party in our absence, Sherry, and—"

"Believe me, I didn't think all those kids were coming," Sherry cut her off in a weepy voice. "It was just going to be me and a few of my friends. I should have turned everyone away at the door, I don't know why I didn't, I was really stupid not to, Mother, and I'm really sorry—I really, really am."

"I'm sure," Eleanor Estabrook responded, sounding sincere enough to give Sherry a shard of hope, but then she went on as if she hadn't heard a word her daughter had said. "Let's not dwell on fault. Let's just say things got a little out of hand, correct?"

Sherry nodded in benumbed silence. All at once she knew that all the things she had been planning to tell them for the past few hours—about her loneliness in their big house, about her horror at imperiling the Judge's reputation—all those confessions would never get made on this day. There was no one to hear them.

Sherry pressed her eyes tight to stop the tears and then opened them to see her mother smiling, a tight little smile that was clearly not happy but seemed, at least, to be satisfied. "Now, Sherry," she was saying, "the Judge has a few words he'd like to share with you."

On cue, her father cleared his throat, stood, and solemnly walked to the window. As he spoke, his back was to Sherry, but she could hear his sonorous tenor as if it were being broadcast through loudspeakers.

"You have a precious gift, Sherry," he began, chin tilted skyward as if he were purposefully considering the storm clouds rolling off the Atlantic. "By dint of nature and good fortune, and with thanks to God, you have a birthright to be proud of, to uphold and to protect. That birthright is your name. My father, and his father, and many more Estabrooks before and since, have worked very, very hard to make sure our name means something. And it does, Sherry. The Estabrook name means honesty and integrity. It means respect for human dignity, fairness, moral strength. It means public service, and it means truth. Your mother and I have spent our lives carrying on these traditions. You understand that, don't you?"

"Yes, sir," Sherry responded meekly. The urge to cry was so overpowering—it felt as if the heel of someone's hand were pressed against her heart—she thought she might faint, but she knew her father would not tolerate weakness at a time like this.

"You made a mistake Saturday night," he went on, voice still loud, crisp, and measured, as if he were delivering directions to a jury. "But I'm not going to punish you for that, Sherry. We all make mistakes in our lives. The trick is not to make too many or to make the same one twice. Correct?"

"Yes, sir, correct."

A few moments of silence passed. Then: "Luckily, there has been a happy turn of events," her father continued, his back still to Sherry but his chin lower now, eyes staring straight out to sea. "The young lady who claimed to have been assaulted here, in our bedroom, has recanted her story—"

"*Recanted!* What!" Sherry interrupted excitedly. "You mean she said she made the whole thing up! That's fantastic!" She jumped from her chair and spontaneously rushed toward her father for a hug, but he didn't turn around to meet her outstretched arms, leaving her standing awkwardly in the middle of the kitchen, feeling overjoyed with relief but somehow unable to smile.

"Yes, it is *fantastic*," her father finally went on, saying the last word with slight distaste. "We can now proceed with our lives as normal. Please don't speak to anyone about this, including Alice Wheelwright."

"But Alice was here," Sherry protested, "and she's my best friend, and she knows all about it—"

"Do as your father says," Eleanor Estabrook interjected tonelessly.

"Yes," Sherry agreed, but even in the acquiescence, she knew she and Alice would be talking about the incident before nightfall. The girl had recanted! Sherry was giddy with the thought of it. She was home free! Nothing had changed! And her parents weren't even angry at her. She could keep on being Sherry—perhaps a more discreet Sherry, but still Sherry.

And that's exactly what happened. The incident was never mentioned explicitly again at One Hundred Endless Horizon

Lane, and only alluded to once, a year later, when Laurence
Estabrook called Sherry into his study one evening for "an important chat." Sherry was delighted to comply; she thought the
subject was a car—her mother had been hinting it was time she
had one of her own.

But, instead, the subject was college. The Judge wanted to
know Sherry's plans.

"Well, you know, I hadn't really given it much thought.
Maybe Bertha's Beauty Academy in Revere or something," Sherry
cracked sarcastically when he asked her. "But forget school—
didn't you actually want to discuss something else?"

"No," said the Judge. "I want to discuss college. You're a
junior now. You seem to have straightened your behavior out
since—let's say you've performed well in the past year. You have
good grades, and your mother tells me you've been elected captain of the lacrosse team. Congratulations."

"Thank you," said Sherry.

"I think you should apply to Harvard."

Sherry groaned and rolled her eyes in disbelief. "Father, just
because you went there! Please! And really, I'll never get in. You
know that."

The Judge shrugged noncommittally. "You might," he said,
looking her straight in the eyes, "if you apply yourself to your
studies, Sherry, and perhaps do some volunteering with your
mother at the shelter. Perhaps you might join the choir at the First
for a year."

"But I can't sing."

"None of them can sing," her father answered, expressionless. "Don't give me any excuses. If you don't want to try, just
tell me now."

"I don't want to try," Sherry shot back, but the truth was,
the idea was suddenly very appealing. The very fact that her
father thought she could do it was almost enough to make her
run out the door, rush upstairs, and hit the books.

"Okay, wait," she said, "I'll think about it."

"Don't think too long," her father responded dryly. "Don't
waste time thinking." And with that, he turned away from her in
his massive leather swivel chair and began to study a stack of
documents on top of a nearby filing cabinet. "That will be all."

The door wasn't closed behind her before Sherry knew, in

truth, she had no thinking to do at all. For the next two years, she sang her heart out at the First, spent eight hours a week at the homeless shelter—although she never did get used to the smell of piss and the sound of babies crying the way the other volunteers seemed to—and did her homework every single night, quickly turning her B's into A's. By the time April 15 rolled around and the acceptance letter arrived from Harvard, Sherry was more smug than surprised. She had risen to the challenge—she had proved herself to the Judge. He as much as admitted it himself. That night when her parents took her out for a congratulatory dinner at the Bluemoor, Laurence Estabrook made a point of introducing Sherry to everyone who stopped by their table. "This is my daughter, a very *special* young lady," he told them all. "She'll be attending Harvard next September."

September came; Sherry moved into Thayer Hall in Harvard Yard. Her roommate was a chemistry genius named Madeline Woo who spent fourteen hours a day at the Science Center. Her absence didn't bother Sherry in the slightest, however; it took her about one week to find the clique of freshmen with last names and home addresses like hers, and about one week after that to learn that it's true when the upperclassmen tell you the hardest part about Harvard is getting in. She spent her first year at college attending invitation-only parties, going to football games, and learning about sex with Charles.

But the fun ended sophomore year, and for one simple reason. Sherry spent the summer before it working as a receptionist in her father's office, and finally and completely she understood what the Judge had meant that day in the kitchen when he said that she had a precious birthright to uphold and protect. She understood because she had spent the whole summer awestruck, watching him in action. Too many times to count, she had seen him stay in his chambers until midnight, poring through dense legal texts, searching for moral guidance and obscure precedents. She listened to him reprimand dozens of attorneys for turning the courtroom into a circus, for demeaning the legal process with their showboating or innuendo. She knew that he always returned phone calls to the pro bono clients referred to him by the state bar association. And he did all this without a word of self-congratulation or explanation to Sherry. He did it as if it were expected of him.

And so, on her first day back at school, Sherry changed her major from fine arts (it had been Charles's suggestion; Sherry decided it was too dilettantish and irrelevant) to history, and signed up to write for the newspaper, with the barely suppressed ambition to run the place in two years, if not before. She had no plans, however, to get off the social circuit. The fact was, despite her newfound direction, Sherry remained mouthy, precocious, and very bitchy, a rich girl who loved an all-night party and fixed an excellent dry martini—all characteristics that didn't hurt her at all in her fast climb to *summa cum laude* and managing editor of the *Crimson*. The plan was to graduate, marry Charles in June, and then get her law degree at Harvard starting in the fall. And by the spring of her senior year, it looked like that was exactly what was going to happen.

But then, in one accidental moment, everything changed.

It was April 14, the day before Sherry was scheduled to fly down to Miami with Alice for spring break—Grammie Wheelwright had a condo on the beach and promised them free run of the place. Sherry was home in Marblehead packing when suddenly it occurred to her that she should bring along her father's hornbook on Constitutional law just to get familiar with some of the trivia she'd be tackling in the fall. She knew he had a copy in his study, somewhere behind his desk, if she could just find it among the hundreds of other leatherbound volumes.

Sherry meandered downstairs, stopping along the way to read a *Town & Country* magazine in her parents' bedroom—she rarely went in there, but no one was home—and to pet Pansy, who was sprawled on a window ledge on the grand circular staircase. It didn't even occur to her to knock before entering her father's study, and it was only later, when she replayed the whole incident in her mind, that it occurred to her that, yes, oddly, the door had been closed. She should have known he was inside.

But she didn't, not until she was halfway into the room and almost on top of her father, who was standing in the center of the study, face-to-face with a burly man in a slick double-breasted black suit who looked vaguely familiar. At first, Sherry thought she saw the man and her father reaching out to shake hands, but it took her only another split second to realize that was not what was happening at all. What was happening was this: The man in the black suit was handing her father a carefully folded wad of bills, about an inch thick, bound by a rubber band. And her father was accepting the money with a wide, obsequious smile, a smile she absolutely did not recognize.

"Sherry—this is unexpected." Laurence Estabrook looked up from the deal with a mildly startled expression. His voice, however, betrayed not the slightest hint of alarm. "I didn't realize you were home."

Sherry opened her mouth to speak, but it took what felt like a full minute before words came out. "I didn't realize *you* were home," she managed at last.

"Fancy that," her father replied flatly. He deftly pocketed the wad of bills. "Sherry, let me introduce you to a colleague of mine, Anthony Pertucci. Mr. Pertucci is with Pilato, Pertucci and Crown at One Boston Place."

"Oh, yes," Sherry mumbled. She suddenly knew exactly why Mr. Pertucci looked familiar. He was one of the lawyers her father had bawled out with particular ire in his courtroom three summers ago. Not respectful enough of a witness, some poor, shaking teenage girl who had been raped by a group of high school hockey players from Eastie. "Oh yes," she repeated, "I think we've met before."

The lawyer smiled brightly and then made a small jerk with his upper body in what occurred to Sherry must be a bow. "I'm sure the pleasure was all mine," he said in a smarmy voice. "And it continues to be."

"Uh-huh," Sherry answered. She hadn't heard a word out of his mouth. She was too fixated on her father, who was still wearing the obsequious grin and was staring right back at her without a trace of embarrassment in his opaque blue eyes. Could it be that she was reading this all wrong? All at once, Sherry felt overwhelmed with relief, but then one more look into her father's face—he wasn't looking at her, but through her, she realized—and she knew she had read it exactly right.

"Are you leaving now?" she suddenly blurted out to Anthony Pertucci in a voice so strident she wasn't sure if it was coming from her throat or her gut. "I think you should go, I really do. Please."

"Sherry!" Laurence Estabrook stepped toward her and grabbed her arm just above the elbow. "I beg your pardon!"

"I beg *your* pardon!" Sherry snapped back, pulling out of her father's uncomfortable pinch, but Pertucci was already backing out the door, palms up in an I-surrender gesture. *"I'm outta here,"* he said in a jocular voice, and then he winked at the Judge, exited, and pulled the door closed behind him.

For the next minute, Sherry and her father stood in silence, six feet apart, both of them looking away, out to the ocean, which was peculiarly blue and strangely calm for that time of year. In the near distance, sea gulls dive-bombed to shore to peck away at shells, and then soared skyward again, cawing plaintively. Farther out to sea, the Marblehead fleet was slowly on its way into port, the day's catch ready to be skinned and gutted, innards tossed overboard for the sharks to devour.

Finally, Sherry spoke, her voice quavering with such profound sadness and anger that she could barely hear the words herself. It took her two tries to get started.

"I saw—"

"I know—"

Then: "You were taking a payoff," she said, "weren't you, Father?"

Laurence Estabrook snorted. "A payoff?" he said, clearly amused by the phrase and Sherry's revulsion toward it. "I suppose, if that's what you want to call it." He let out an abrupt laugh.

Sherry was still looking out to sea; she couldn't trust herself to face her father and go on talking. "What do *you* call it?" she said.

Another snort. "Oh, I don't really call it anything, my dear," Laurence Estabrook said, and Sherry recognized his tone from the blithe, mock-rakish voice he used at cocktail parties. He strolled back to his desk and sat down in the giant leather chair, tipping the seat back in a relaxed manner and resting his fingertips together like a church steeple. "But if I had to give it a name, I suppose I would call it a *gift*. Or a gesture of gratitude. A reimbursement. A facilitating gratuity, perhaps."

"A facilitating gratuity? For—for what?" Sherry asked, growing more incredulous as her father's expression grew increasingly bemused, "for throwing a case his way?"

Laurence Estabrook shook his head matter-of-factly. "No, actually," he said. "In this instance, it was a gift for *not* taking his case, for manipulating the schedule so another judge would hear it. Peter Wenshaw, in fact—you know him. He's much easier going than I am on these types of crimes. Not such a big fan of incarceration."

"In *this* instance?" Sherry muttered, but it was not really a question.

"In this instance," her father answered. "As in, there have been other instances, yes."

"You've taken *other* payoffs?"

"I wish you wouldn't call them that! Really!" Laurence Estabrook clapped his hands together once and then quickly stood up, smiling condescendingly. "Let's draw this conversation to a close, shall we, Sherry? Perhaps when you have some experience as an attorney, you'll understand that not all law is practiced by the books. And for very good reason, my dear. Very good reason. Oftentimes, the system works far better when its participants have the latitude to move efficiently and quickly, to settle cases without the cumbersome apparatus of the courtroom. For the best of everyone, a person in my position must make a quick, precise judgment call to make sure justice prevails. And prevails while we're around to see it. Matters get taken care of in three weeks instead of three years, saving everyone time, energy, and money. My God, Sherry, if every case went the slow route prescribed by the rules, no one would ever go to jail! The courts would be backed up with cases from 1965, and everyone would suffer—"

"What a stinking pile of bullshit!" Sherry cut her father off. She was looking at him square-on now, body pressed against his desk so their faces were just feet apart. "I can't believe you're standing there with a fucking shit-eating grin on your face telling me why it's all right to take a bribe!"

"Now, now, Sherry—"

"Don't 'now, now' me, Father! You're the biggest fucking *hypocrite* I've ever seen in my life! All this bullshit you've been feeding me about the family honor—about how Estabrook means honest and integrity and truth—what a pile of *shit*—you're just a two-bit corrupt liar like the rest of them—"

Suddenly, Laurence Estabrook wasn't smiling anymore. His face turned rigid with anger, jaw clenched like steel on flesh, lips pulled taut, eyes narrowed into a venomous glare. He took a large step back from his desk, placed his hands on his hips, and lowered his voice into a whisper seething with indignation.

"You amaze me, Sherry, you really do," he said. He shook his head and affected a high-pitched whine clearly meant to be an imitation of Sherry's voice. *"Hypocrite! Liar!* My God, Sherry! How spoiled and naive you are, really!" He snickered, then went on. "You disapprove of the way I do business, do you?" he asked snidely. "But you certainly approve of everything it's bought you—"

"It's bought me nothing but this stupid house," Sherry protested, "which I've always hated anyway—"

"Oh, just the house?" Laurence Estabrook let out a harsh bark of laughter that seemed to last forever. *"Just* the house! Very funny!"

The immense force of his bitterness pushed Sherry back a few feet, and she almost stumbled to the ground, catching herself on the arm of a red leather wing chair. She wasn't sure she wanted to hear any more, and for a moment she considered bolting from the room, but it was too late. Her father was already breaking the news, and with it, her heart.

"It just so happens, Sherry, that my way of doing business got you out of that disgusting little mess you got us all into—that rape mess." He made an unpleasant face at the ugliness of the memory. "I spent close to *one hundred thousand dollars* cleaning up after you on that one, my dear, one hundred thousand that I had much rather have spent on a nice set of clubs for me and a new lynx coat for your mother."

Sherry shook her head as if she didn't understand, but she did. "You mean the girl didn't recant," she said numbly.

"The girl had six broken ribs and scratches on her face that looked like she'd walked into a moving helicopter," Laurence Estabrook shot back. "Not to mention rather severe bite marks on her thighs and buttocks, if I remember the police report correctly. Luckily, her father had just lost his job as a fireman, so we could be of some assistance."

"Oh, God," Sherry said. She dropped her head to her chest and instantly started to cry, heavy tears dripping from her eyes so fast that her shirt was quickly drenched through. "I'm sorry."

"Yes, you should be," her father answered flatly, "and you should be grateful that we had my way of doing business to make sure we could all go on living as if nothing had happened. Imagine, would you, what it would have done to my reputation— and yours—if the girl had pressed charges and won her case in court, as I'm sure she would have, given the physical evidence.

Tell me, Sherry, how would have I explained it all to my old friend Walter Littleton when I called to get you into Harvard?"

Sherry suddenly stopped crying. "When *what*?" she asked.

"You heard me."

"When you called to get me into Harvard?" Her voice was so small, it was almost invisible.

"That's right," her father answered in a sanctimonious sing-song. "Did you honestly think, Sherry, that a few A's from a mediocre finishing school and a couple years in the church choir were going to get you in the *front* door?"

"I worked at the shelter—"

"Oh, yes, that's true." Another burst of laughter. "Now, come on, my dear, let's be realistic."

"Okay, let's. Let's face facts, let's really, truly know the truth," Sherry answered. Suddenly, she was so drained of emotion that all she felt was a crazy, pulsing urge to move her body— to dance unhinged, to spin in circles, to run very fast and very far away. "Thank you," she said to her father, although she wasn't sure why, and then she quickly turned and rushed upstairs before he had a chance to say another word.

She hadn't had a conversation—a real conversation—with him since. She spoke to her parents only once a month, and then only in a very polite and cursory way, as if they were strangers on a luxury liner. They had yet to comment on her decision to abandon law school and move to Miami, although from time to time her father sent her a check wrapped in a blank piece of paper. Charles said it looked as though they missed her—he sometimes saw them eating at the Bluemoor—but Sherry doubted it.

And so she kept her communications with them brief and superficial, just like the twenty-line letter home she had just stuffed into an envelope marked *One Hundred Endless Horizon Lane, Marblehead, MA 01945*.

8 The alarm clock rang at six-thirty, and Sherry pulled up the shade. Clouds, but no rain.

A minute later, she was in the living room, loading her stereo with an album called *Deadly Weapon* that she'd picked up in college. The speakers were still in place, squarely facing the Beauregards' house.

"Good morning," she shouted out the window, and then turned on the stereo full blast.

She let it play until eight, when she left for work. Perhaps her house would be burned to the ground when she returned that night, she thought. But she knew the Beauregards were cowards.

When Sherry arrived at the *Citizen* newsroom, Belinda was already at her desk.

"We have to talk about our plan of attack," she greeted Sherry anxiously.

"Just let me check my mail."

"I already put it on your desk."

Sherry saw a small pile. Her paycheck on top, a memo from Jack Dougherty saying nice work covering the Rubin LeDurtin shooting, and on the bottom a sealed yellow envelope. It was from Brazil.

We have to stop meeting like this, it said. *How about meeting tonight after work instead? I'll be at your house at nine. I have good news for ya. FYI, I'm going to Hialeah today. Unreachable. P.S. Twinkie for you in top left drawer. P.P.S. Your lawn looks terrible.*

Sherry stuck the note in her purse and sat down at Belinda's desk. A paper cup of Cuban coffee was waiting for her. She had decided not to tell Belinda about Pansy right away. She was so fragile, it might really set her off.

"I did a lot of thinking last night. I have some ideas," Sherry began. It was the truth—after she wrote home, she'd spent the rest of the evening brainstorming about Jack's latest project. "I think we have to go at this story two ways. Undercover and overcover. That's a new word—overcover—but you get what I mean."

She waited for a reaction from Belinda, but she just peered across the newsroom with a vague frown.

"Okay," Sherry continued; she had found it was always best to forge ahead when Belinda got bleary-eyed for some reason or other. "This is how I see it. One, we have to pretend we're actually students in high school and hang out in parking lots before and after school and see what's going on. We've got to see who's buying what, when they're buying it—you get it, right? We need to find out if they're going to classes wasted or if they're going home wasted. It makes a difference." Sherry stopped to catch her breath, but then hurried on, excited by the ideas flowing out. "And two, we have to go inside other schools, with permission, and interview kids, get their honest opinions on all the different drugs, like what's the choice for Saturday night? What's the choice for Monday morning? Why do they use drugs, or why *don't* they, that kind of thing. This could be terrific!" She stopped again, pushing her hair over her shoulders and looking expectantly at Belinda. No response.

"I bet high schools still have *rap rooms*, you know," Sherry went on after a moment had passed, "a designated place where kids can let it all hang out. They were big in the seventies here in the United States of America. We got to check that out, Belinda. They could be a fucking gold mine of quotes."

"I'm too old to be in high school," Belinda answered tonelessly. She was fidgeting with a paper clip, twisting it open and then closed again.

"We could look like we're in high school if we put on jeans and don't wear makeup and if we start smoking Salem Lights."

"I don't wear makeup already."

"Okay. What do you suggest?" Sherry started rapping her nails on the desktop.

"No, you're right. I agree with you. I guess we can try it."

"You don't have to agree with me."

"No, I agree with you." The paper clip finally snapped in two, and Belinda nervously shoved the pieces into her desk drawer.

Sherry shook her head in wonder. "What is the matter, Belinda?" she asked. "You're acting very bizarre."

Deep sigh: "You won't believe me."

"I'll believe anything," Sherry said.

"I got in another car wreck." She covered her face with her hands in embarrassment for a second. "Please, don't say anything mean."

But she didn't need to ask. Sherry was speechless. In the past year, Belinda had been in three accidents. The first time, she rear-ended a pregnant woman, who had sued her for emotional trauma. The crash had happened when Belinda was on the way to an assignment, so the *Citizen* took on the case and settled out of court for ten grand.

The next two accidents had happened in the weeks around Easter. Both times Belinda rear-ended Cuban women in Cadillacs stopped at red lights. Insurance had covered some of the costs, but Belinda's bank account was wiped out. Sherry had given her fifteen hundred dollars so she could pay the rent and eat for a few months. "Don't think about paying me back," she had said.

"I couldn't if I wanted to," Belinda had answered.

Now, accident number four. Sherry could picture it: Belinda in a daze, messing with the buttons on her car radio, looking at her watch, humming to herself, occasionally saying, "But, Daddy . . ." in a sad and pleading voice.

"Are you okay?" Sherry asked. "Did you get hurt?"

"No. I'm fine. I think I'm fine. My neck sort of feels like I slept on it wrong. But I'm okay. My car's bashed up in the front. You know, if I wasn't about to get hysterical, this would be sort of funny. Because you're not going to believe what happened. I rear-ended another Cuban lady—"

"Not in a Cadillac."

"A Jaguar."

Sherry closed her eyes and shook her head. If the reason behind Belinda's accidents wasn't so sad, this *would* be funny.

"Is she going to sue you?"

"No, I don't think so. I didn't get her too bad." Belinda sighed. "What do you think a psychiatrist would say?"

Sherry shrugged. There were some things she just could not tell Belinda. "Where's your car?" she asked.

"Downstairs in the parking lot. It looks like a real clunker, but it drives. I can't get it fixed for a while."

"I can give you a loan—"

"Don't," Belinda said quietly. "Please don't even offer. It just makes me feel terrible. You're not my mother. You try, and you come close, but you're not." She refilled both their cups with coffee from a Thermos on her desk. "Let's forget about it for a while."

Sherry didn't want to talk about it anymore either. Belinda had her disaster yesterday. She had one, too, and much worse. "Alvin Beauregard killed Pansy," she suddenly blurted out.

"What?"

She told Belinda the story, including her plans to harass the Beauregards for the next several weeks.

"You're going to get arrested," Belinda said when Sherry paused for breath, sounding much less critical than Sherry had expected.

"The Beauregards will never call the police," Sherry came back quickly. "They're afraid I'll report Alvin for kicking Pansy."

"Do what you want, but you're acting crazy. You should just report them to the ASPCA or something."

"And then what will happen?" Sherry asked. "They'll pay a fine. That's not enough."

"It's your life."

"It's my life."

"Right," said Belinda. "Fine. Let's talk about work, okay?"

She pulled a list of the Dade County senior high schools from her briefcase. Twenty-six goddamn schools. Instantly, Sherry felt overwhelmed. Every project scared her at first. Some of them scared her for a month. It took that long for anyone to talk to her on the record about Ian Lappers, the Miami Beach cop who once spent three years in an Indiana jail for robbing a convenience store. Everyone knew about his record—the police chief, the captain, the mayor. But when Sherry asked about it, they would look right at her and say she had to be mistaken. Then, when she finally had Lappers's records in hand, his prison time noted and initialed by the mayor himself, they all asked Sherry to show some compassion. He was a man with a family, they said. His past was behind him.

Two days after the story ran on the front page of the *Citizen*, Lappers quit the force. Someone told her he had moved away, but his wife had stayed.

Sherry and Belinda talked for two hours about Jack's drugs-in-the-schoolhouse story, and when they were done, the piece of paper between them was covered with notes and coffee stains. Some of the schools on the list were marked with a red *B* for Belinda, others with a red *S* for Sherry. Those were the places they would go to alone, as themselves, *Citizen* reporters. Eight schools were circled, and *TU* was scribbled in the margin, for "Together, Undercover." Scrawled in the margins and on the back were the key questions they had to cover—all the who, when, where, and why questions they could manufacture, and then some, for Jack's sake.

"So, this is it," Sherry said. "We can go someplace undercover tomorrow morning if we want. What time does school start again?"

"Early. Like eight. I don't really even know. I can find out."

They spent the rest of the day on the phone, calling the schools beside their initials. Sherry was surprised how easy it was to get permission to go inside and talk to kids. She was right. "Rap rooms" still existed, but they had more eighties-like names now, like "the Interpersonal Center" or, at one school, the "the Us Place." The next afternoon, she was set to talk to a group of seniors at Lincoln High, a big concrete building about four miles south of the city in a standard-issue Latin suburb, where every house was a three-bedroom, one-and-a-half-bath ranch with a two-car garage. Belinda was going north first, to a vocational school near the Broward County line, a place famous for its unannounced locker searches and hallway knife fights. There probably wasn't a kid in the place who didn't have a terrifying story to tell about drugs. Belinda had won the prize of going there with a coin toss.

When they left the *Citizen* that night, it was already dark.

"You have to take a look at my car," Belinda said as they walked through the parking lot underneath the building. It was parked in a corner, dented front end facing out.

"We can take my car in the morning," Sherry said.

"A red BMW with vanity plates. That will be inconspicuous."

"Okay, never mind," Sherry conceded. "Pick me up at seven, Belinda. Don't be late."

9

Lemonlime Road was quiet when Sherry pulled into her driveway. Instinctively, she looked for Pansy waiting on the porch, and a bolt of anger and sorrow snapped through her. It would be a long time before coming home felt right again.

She checked her watch. Brazil would be knocking on her door soon.

Sherry walked straight to her bedroom and turned the picture of Charles facedown. The house was a mess. She checked the refrigerator. It was empty except for an old carton of milk, an open can of root beer, two oranges, and a box of baking soda. She fixed herself a peanut-butter sandwich. She was out of jelly again.

She sat down on the couch to eat and read the mail: a postcard from her cousin Hilary in London, a bill from the gas company, a letter from Miss Eliot's asking for more money.

A few minutes later, she heard Brazil's car pull up and the front door open. He was carrying a pizza.

"I knew you'd be fixing something extra special, but I had an urge for pizza," he said, leaning over to kiss her on the forehead. "Really, though, darlin', didn't they teach you to cook at Harvard? What good are you?"

"I was too busy learning about the meaning of life," Sherry said. It felt good to have him nearby.

They had met three years before, on her first day at work. She was covering what Jack Dougherty called "the Holybejeezus Tree of Little Havana." Some ninety-one-year-old woman, a neighborhood prophet of sorts, had seen the eyes of Jesus in the bark, setting off a frenzy of prayer that lasted for weeks. Every day, hundreds of people surrounded the tree trying to hack away a tiny piece of its holy powers.

Sherry was interviewing a sixteen-year-old Cuban refugee in a wheelchair when someone tapped her on the shoulder. A huge, sweaty photographer stood behind her. He was wearing a garish surfer's shirt, baggy turquoise sweatpants cut into shorts, and bright yellow flip-flops decorated with little plastic golf clubs and flamingos. He smelled terrible.

"Are you the new reporter?" he asked. "You look new." He smirked at her and then winked.

Sherry shook her head in disgust. Was this asshole trying to flirt with her—on assignment? Who the hell did he think he was? She turned around to finish the interview. The boy in the wheelchair said that when he touched the tree, the feeling returned to his legs.

"You going to quote this guy?" the photographer interrupted again a few seconds later, talking in an incredibly loud, conspicuous voice. He had the most hokey southern accent Sherry had ever heard. "Mind if I make some art?" He didn't wait for a response to start shooting pictures, dozens of them in rapid motor-drive succession, spinning his camera through every which angle and dancing around the two of them like a burly ballerina.

"No photos!" the boy in the wheelchair cried, covering his face.

Sherry put her hand over Brazil's lens. He grabbed her wrist.

"Don't do that," he ordered, "or I'm going to have to break your itty-bitty little arm."

"He doesn't want his picture taken."

Brazil lowered his camera for a second and bent down close to the refugee. "Hey, *amigo,* you don't mind having your picture taken, do you?" he asked with an ingratiating smile. "It won't hurt. I promise. Don't tell me y'all got a police record or something?" He laughed and squeezed the crippled refugee's shoulder like an old friend.

The boy in the wheelchair broke into laughter, revealing two rows of jagged green teeth, then reached into his pocket and ran a comb through his hair.

The photo played on page one; the story played inside.

Two days later, Brazil stopped by Sherry's desk in the newsroom.

"I'm sure you've had time now to think about what you did the other day at the Holybejeezus Tree and you're ready to apologize."

"To *you?*" Sherry asked.

Brazil laughed and asked her out to lunch. At lunch, he asked her out to dinner.

He wasn't married then; everyone knew he was going out with a girl named Jeanie who was pregnant. He didn't talk about her. He only wanted to talk about himself, and by the end of their first date Sherry had to wonder why she felt as if she was falling in love with a completely uneducated, totally obnoxious expert on everything, an enormous slob who informed her, before their drinks even arrived, that she was sitting across from one of the world's greatest living photographers. When she rolled her eyes, he pulled a memo from his pocket and delivered a playground-variety *told-you-so* smirk. It was from the publisher, and the first line read, *John—I do believe you are one of the five best photographers in the world.* A half hour later, he informed Sherry that she reminded him of someone, and when she asked who, he said, "Me!"

"But you don't get it," she had replied. "I can read Sartre in French. I know the difference between Correggio and Caravaggio. I mean, I went to Harvard."

"Oooh-we! Ain't that a hoot!" he shut her down. "I've always want to meet one of *youse*." And then it was his turn to roll his eyes. "Listen, darlin'," he went on, "it's not where you're from, it's what you *do*. Got it?"

"Got it," said Sherry, and that's when she knew she had to see this man again.

It took Sherry about a month to start sleeping with him. She had never planned to, really, but one night they were sitting in her living room talking, and he just picked her up and carried her to the bedroom. Right before they started making love, he looked at the picture of Charles on her night table and said, "Who's that faggot?"

"That's my boyfriend."

He turned the picture facedown.

And so, that's how it started. The beginning happened so fast, the words and laughter whirled by so quickly, Sherry was sure she had been hugged by vertigo. They would meet every night for dinner, and he would stay at her house until daybreak, when sometimes he took off for Jeanie's place out in far-west Dade. On weekends, they buzzed down to Key West and went deep-sea fishing or lay by the pool at their hotel. Brazil wanted to know everything about her. What did she look like when she was seventeen? When did she lose her virginity? Why didn't she cut her hair? Would she stay in Miami? He had to know if she hated Jeanie. Did she feel bad about the baby?

But Sherry never felt jealous. She had nothing to lose.

Then one Friday, about six months into their affair, Brazil didn't show up for dinner. He called the next morning. "Jeanie's going a little crazy," he whispered into the phone. "She wants to get married."

After that, he stopped calling, and Sherry didn't see him for weeks, except across the newsroom. He never even waved.

She missed him, but she never sought him out. She was too goddamn angry—angry that this man who had seemed so wonderful now made her long for Charles's sturdy and predictable companionship. The only consolation came when Dougherty pulled her aside and said Brazil had requested to be kept off assignments with her—he was feeling too damn guilty to look her in the face.

Sherry was feeling healed by October, four months after their last night together. Work had cured her. In the months alone (alone, that is, except for Belinda's moody friendship), she had never reported with such a vengeance. Jack Dougherty had rewarded her with more work, stories that took all night, stories that left her too exhausted to think.

Late in the month, Sherry heard one of the reporters was throwing a Halloween party, and she decided to buy a wig, fake eyelashes and fake fingernails, and gaudy fake jewels and go as Evita Perón, a true Miami heroine.

Belinda picked her up at nine. "You look so glamorous with blond hair," she said. "I feel ridiculous." She was dressed as a ghost, with two large eyeholes cut in a tattered polka-dot sheet. It was the first time Sherry had really laughed in months.

The party was packed with reporters and photographers, but she knew Brazil wouldn't be there. Not that he hated costumes, he just liked being himself too much to pretend he was someone else, even for a few hours. As soon as Sherry walked in the door, she felt free as if she had just crossed the border into a country where no one knew her name or even cared. She drank for hours without a flash of regret, smoked one cigarette after another, and flirted with men she never wanted to see again.

It was after two when she found Belinda sitting in the

backyard with a group of city desk friends. Sherry pulled up a
chair.

"Oh, I can top that," a reporter named Marina was saying.
"You know who used to sleep together? Egerhart and DeeDee
Roberts from personnel."

"Old news," someone moaned.

"You know about Garrett Newman and his secretary, right?"

"Old news."

"How about Brazil Brackett? Did you hear he got married?"

"No shit," someone muttered.

"Yep," Marina answered, sipping her drink. "He went down
to Key West last weekend and married old Jeanie. I guess if you
wait long enough . . ."

Sherry didn't hear anything else. She sat completely still,
suddenly sober and freezing cold, in her mind watching Brazil at
the altar of the little fishermen's church near their hotel, pulling
back Jeanie's wedding veil and kissing her lips as a baby cried.
The image mortified her so utterly that she stood up abruptly,
knocking over her drink and sending the chair toppling behind
her. But Sherry hardly noticed. She was already sprinting toward
the driveway, and Belinda was close behind her.

They were in front of the house on Lemonlime Road when
Sherry finally stopped shivering long enough to speak. She wasn't
crying, the shock was too much.

"Can you believe it?" she asked Belinda. "I just thought . . .
I mean, we were just in a fight, nothing permanent. Christ,
I . . ." She thought for a second that she could see Brazil's massive
shadow on her porch, but it disappeared. The back of her neck
ached.

A few minutes passed in silence, except for the sound of the
engine and static-laced music from a Spanish radio station. It was
near three, but the sky was silver from the streetlights of Miami.

Belinda shifted in her seat. Her ghost costume was rolled in
a ball on the floor. "I'm so sorry, Sherry," she said softly, but
Sherry was already out of the car, headed toward her house in a
daze.

Inside, the whole place reminded her of Brazil. The bedroom
smelled like darkroom chemicals, the refrigerator was filled with
his film, the walls in the living room were covered with his framed
photos. One by one, she took them down, removed the frames,
ripped the pictures to pieces, and threw them in the trash. The

process took an hour, and by the end of it, her shock and humiliation had turned into relief. She was free again. And that's what
Miami was all about.

By early December, Sherry was going out with someone new,
a thirty-five-year old, twice-divorced Colombian surgeon she met
on assignment at Mercy Hospital. He hardly spoke English, but
she liked it that way. They went out to dinner. They went to the
movies. At night, he dropped her off at the door and kissed her
on the cheek. Perfect.

Two days before she went home for Christmas, Sherry threw
her own party. She invited everyone, and everyone came, even
Dr. Colombia, wearing a double-breasted suit and a silk Paisley
tie. He brought her cocaine as a gift, which she snorted in the
bedroom with Belinda.

"Wow, I think it's snowing outside," Belinda said about an
hour later, smirking like a frizzy-haired Mona Lisa.

When the last guest left, Sherry looked at her watch. It was
four in the morning, and her silent house was littered with hundreds of empty plastic cups and messy ashtrays. Loneliness swept
through her like the winds before a hurricane. She walked into
the kitchen, picked up the phone, and dialed the photo desk at
the *Citizen*.

"Is Brazil around?"

"Sherry?" It was him. She knew he would be there. "Is something wrong?"

"I just had a huge party."

"I heard about it."

She didn't know what to say. She didn't even know why she
was calling.

A half hour later, Brazil's car was pulling into her driveway
on Lemonlime Road.

And so they became lovers again after that.

Now here was Brazil at her house as usual, bearing a pizza.
They didn't go out to eat anymore.

"I got your note this morning," Sherry said, finishing her
peanut-butter sandwich. "What's the good news?"

"This is it, me, standing before you," he said. "I'm making
the art for your famous project on drugs in the little red schoolhouse. Like I always say, 'When the going gets tough, Brazil gets
going.' Dougherty assigned me yesterday."

"Yes!" Sherry said, jumping to her feet and kissing Brazil on the cheek. "Yes, yes!"

"Just think, darlin', of all those hours we're going to get paid just to be together." He laughed. "Now don't you go acting like you're my boss on this one. If it's gonna get good play, it's gotta have good art."

"Brazil, this story is going to be on the front page no matter what. It's Jack's baby."

"You gotta deliver the goods first."

"What does that mean?"

"Look, you shoulda heard Jack today, ranting and raving about this thing. He's counting on you to turn up some pretty intense shit," Brazil said. "You can't just give him some loosey-goosey anecdotes about kids smoking reefer in the bathroom at school. He was all over the place today yelling that he wants *the fucking truth,*' like no one's ever managed to report *that* before. He's on a dang rampage to impress Newman and all those suit-wearing, college-educated faggots on the eighth floor. No offense intended."

He was making Sherry nervous. "I'm sure something will turn up," she said. "We're sure to discover some twelve-year-old who gets high with his grandmother."

"Oh, that's real good," Brazil answered. "I just love the news."

10

Sherry was already awake and rummaging through her closet when her alarm rang at six-fifteen. Belinda would be arriving in forty-five minutes for their first undercover mission.

She pulled on a pair of old jeans and an inside-out sweatshirt, and then glanced in the mirror. Christ, she thought, I look like a twenty-five-year-old reporter with a shitty wardrobe. She tied her hair in two thick braids that fell almost to her waist. Better, but what she really needed was for ten years to vanish from around her eyes. And she needed a pair of high-tops.

Time to waste. She put a pot of water on for tea and leaned against the kitchen counter, arms folded, waiting. There were two spoons and a plate in the sink that needed to be washed. A pile of dirty clothes sat on top of the washing machine. The house was too quiet, and suddenly she could feel her heart and stomach and blood stinging with anxiety.

The music was already on the turntable, Sherry thought, so why not? The image of Alvin kicking Pansy flashed through her mind. Why not? She hadn't forgotten.

"Good morning," Sherry shouted out the window at the house next door, turning on the stereo with the volume at nine. Then she walked back to her bedroom, a cup of lukewarm tea in hand, humming to herself what she imagined the melody to be, and shut the door.

Twenty minutes later, in a break between songs, Sherry could hear someone banging at the front door. This is it, she thought; it's too soon for Belinda to be here. That's got to be Alvin with a machine gun to kill me. She let another song play and sipped her tea happily, imagining her neighbor like a pissed-off cartoon character with puffed-up cheeks and steam shooting from his pudgy ears and his little O-shaped mouth.

When the album ended, the banging was still there. It was five to seven. She was surprised. Alvin was acting pretty damn persistent for a wimp.

She strode cheerfully to the front of the house and opened the door. "Hello!" she said.

But the man in front of her was definitely not Alvin.

"Police," was what he said in a light Cuban accent, rubbing a hand sore from banging. "We have a noise complaint about this address. I have to ask you to refrain from playing your music at such an extreme volume."

"Noise complaint?"

"Are your parents home?"

"Parents?"

The cop stared at Sherry, and she stared back at him. Cops didn't scare her; she spent her days with cops, and they liked her. Cops always liked pretty girls. If she really wanted good information from them, all she had to do was wear a lacy bra and a low-cut blouse. And this cop wasn't even angry, she thought, just kind of perplexed by this bizarre gringa wearing old jeans and carrying a teacup.

"My parents aren't home. I'm twenty-five years old," she said after a minute. "And I have a hearing problem."

"Hearing problem?"

"Yes. That's why I play my music so loud. I have a hearing problem. I can barely hear what you're saying."

"Okay, just keep the music down," he shouted.

Sherry burst out laughing. This was a brand-new cop. She felt sorry for him.

"Oh, hell," she said. She tried to stop laughing but couldn't. "Look. I'm having this problem with my neighbors next door."

"You are?" he shouted.

"Please . . . please. Don't shout. I don't have a hearing problem."

The cop rubbed his eyes and started to smile. He was sweet-looking, sort of short, about her age, maybe younger, with flat black hair, black almond-shaped eyes. He wore a name tag that said E. Alvarez 09251. The gun in his holster looked like a big toy.

"You want to tell me what's going on?" he asked.

"You want to come inside?"

He nodded and followed her to the dining-room table. After she turned off the stereo, they sat down, and E. Alvarez took out a notepad.

"The guy next door, the one who called with the noise complaint, he killed my cat," Sherry began, knowing that her words would end up filed in the police-department dungeon along with all the other domestic-dispute reports made that day. "He kicked her to death the other day, and let me assure you, the cat did nothing to deserve it. She was sixteen years old, very docile, and she was wonderful, really." She dabbed the inside corners of her eyes. "*He'll* tell you she was eating his grass. She didn't even know what grass was. She just slept on the porch all day long, waiting for me to get home. Alvin kicked her to death because he's a psychopathic jerk. That's the story. Okay? So I was playing my music to annoy him and his wife. I won't do it again, I promise. I'm a reporter, and I'm telling you the truth."

"A reporter?" the cop said. He stopped scribbling in his notebook. "Where do you work?"

"The *Citizen*."

"Do you mind me asking your name?" He said it politely, as

if they had just been introduced at a party. He didn't have to be so nice. Didn't he realize that he might have to run a check of her Social Security number later in the day?

"Sherry Estabrook."

"Oh, Sherry Estabrook. I know your name. I see it in the paper all the time."

A car in the driveway honked twice. It was Belinda.

The cop stood to leave, but Sherry motioned him to stay and rushed to the door to wave Belinda inside. She was wearing jeans, too, a brand-new red T-shirt with a picture of Michael Jackson on the front, and a red-and-white bandanna in her hair. As she walked toward the house, she pointed at the police car, grinned, and shook her head.

"They got you, didn't they, Sherry?" she whispered as she stepped inside. Then, to the cop: "She'll never do it again, I promise you, Officer."

"That's what she tells me," he said. Belinda spotted his name tag and started to rattle off in Spanish. *"Sí, sí,"* he answered her and laughed. *"¿Porque son amigas?"* Belinda nodded.

"We've got to go," Sherry said. They ignored her.

"¿Es Usted Cubana?" the cop asked Belinda.

"No, no! *Soy de ninguna parte,"* she said. "I'm from nowhere. But don't worry, I don't have a record." They chatted in Spanish for a few minutes. Sherry understood almost nothing, except that they kept giggling shyly. She wondered if Belinda knew this cop from some assignment, and decided that if she did not, she was acting very strange.

"We've got to go," Sherry repeated.

"I'm Belinda McEvoy."

"Eladio Alvarez." He bowed slightly. "Very charmed." They shook hands, and Sherry saw Belinda blush. "Very charmed, too," she said back. Again, she said something in Spanish. The cop laughed. Belinda laughed. Sherry looked at her watch, and the three of them walked to the driveway, where Belinda and Eladio shook hands again. Then they said good-bye as if they were ending a long evening of red wine and slow dancing.

11

All the way to Perrine High, Belinda cheerfully sang in Spanish along with the radio. Her voice was terrible.

"Stop scowling," she told Sherry. "Get psyched. You're sixteen again."

"You're acting like *you're* sixteen."

Belinda kept singing. All Cuban music sounded the same to Sherry.

They pulled into the parking lot. It was filled with cars and pickup trucks. They were in farm country, the tomato capital of the world. This whole end of the county was filled with rich farmers and migrant workers.

Belinda pulled into a space near a group of kids and turned off the engine. They both lit the Salem Lights that Belinda had bought on the way home from work the night before. Sherry shifted in her seat and stuck her feet out the window.

The kids milled around an old white Chevy, laughing, kissing, and listening to music blasting from someone's big radio box. One older boy sat on the front hood of the car, peering into a book and scribbling in the margins. His girlfriend rested her head on his shoulder.

"You and Señor Alvarez certainly seemed to hit it off this morning," Sherry said.

"He was cute," Belinda answered with a girlish smile. It was the first time Sherry could remember that Belinda had even noticed a man.

Sherry checked her watch. It was before eight, but the sun was already cruel. Her eyes followed one of the boys milling around the white Chevy. He was wearing jeans and a heavy black jacket, collar turned up. Sweat trickled from one sideburn. Every few seconds, he took a drag of a cigarette, exhaling slowly in the direction of a short blond girl wearing a red miniskirt and a tiny white T-shirt. She pretended to ignore him.

"Pretty exciting stuff," Belinda sighed.

"Really. I broke more rules when I was at Miss Eliot's," said Sherry.

They watched in silence for a few more minutes.

Sherry checked her watch again. When was the bell going to ring, for Christ's sake? She surveyed the parking lot. Kids were drifting toward the school building.

Then: "Whoa, check this out," Belinda said under her breath.

Sherry looked up to see a silver Mustang convertible pulling up next to the Chevy. It was driven by an older guy wearing Ray•Bans and a black linen jacket.

A second later, he got out of the car and quickly moved toward the kids. They had been waiting for him.

Sherry could see right away that he was a handsome man, very preppie by Florida standards, with a sharp, clean-cut jaw and Nantucket-colored hair, sandy blond. He was about her age, a little older maybe, an Anglo, tall and slender as a long-distance runner. He was wearing khakis, a buttoned-up oxford-cloth shirt, and tasseled loafers. No socks. No gold jewelry. No expression. He did not smile and barely moved his lips as he spoke. He simply patted the pocket of his jacket, and four of the kids nodded while the rest watched silently.

The bell rang.

"Now we're screwed," said Sherry. "They're going to wonder what we're doing here."

"Let's just hang in for a second."

The parking lot was nearly empty of students, and the man reached inside his coat. But something stopped him. He was gazing past his customers suddenly, squinting against the sun at Sherry and Belinda sitting in their car, Spanish music buzzing, cigarettes lit. He tilted his head toward them, asked something, and the kids shook their heads.

A second bell rang.

"What do we do now?" Belinda whispered.

"Let's pretend we're going to class."

Sherry snapped the radio off, and they got out of the car, trying to look bored. Then they began to walk, very slowly, toward the school.

"Hey." It was said softly, but unmistakably as an order.

They kept walking, although Sherry felt her knees go soft.

Again: "Hey. Come here."

"He's talking to us," said Belinda, without looking at Sherry. She turned around, holding Sherry by the elbow, and faced the man in the linen coat.

He waved at them to come closer. Sherry studied his face quickly. He looked like one of Charles's clubby friends at Harvard—he was that angular, that clean. She wished she could see his eyes behind his sunglasses, but all she could see was her own reflection, and she looked ridiculous, like an overgrown teenager in a time warp. And Belinda looked like an aging flower child.

The man stared at them, clearly perplexed. "Are you cops?" he asked.

Belinda burst out laughing. "No way! Totally negative response!" she said, sounding suddenly and completely as if she been raised in a house with a lava lamp in the living room and a pink Princess telephone next to the bed. Sherry couldn't believe her ears; the accent was perfect: pure, unrepentant teenager. "What a wild concept!" Belinda went on, jaw dangling and eyes open wide in utter shock. "Cops! Ugh—I mean, *really!*"

The man smiled, evidently convinced. "No?" He looked at Sherry.

"No way," she said, trying to imitate Belinda and coming close enough.

"Who are you then?" he asked.

"We want to buy dope," Sherry said. She didn't know what had come over her—maybe Belinda's unexpected bravado—but she liked the sound of it. "We go to Saint Aidan's. Something happened to our connection. He doesn't come around anymore. Somebody told us to try here."

The man relaxed his shoulders. "Just give me a minute," he said. "Let me take care of these kids before they're really late for class."

He walked back to the waiting group, then deftly reached into his jacket and passed out small bags of grass, collecting bills with his other hand. The transaction was over in less than a minute, and he was back.

"Okay, what do you want?" he asked them. "Hurry up."

"Do you have any coke?" said Belinda.

"Not on me, no. But if you come tomorrow, I can have some fine Bolivian product. Eighty dollars. Yes or no?"

Sherry looked at Belinda. Was this supposed to be happening?

"Okay," she said. "Tomorrow. We'll be here."

The man looked at them and frowned. "Why aren't you in school?" he asked abruptly.

"We're, like, totally skipping," said Belinda, accent still going strong. "It's been a while since we had any coke. It was bumming us out a lot. I mean, like it was really getting hairy."

Sherry nodded, speechless. Did Belinda learn to talk that way in Niger or Libya?

Then, Belinda again: "I mean, like, Gary could get us almost anything we wanted. We don't know what happened to him. Do you know? You don't have to answer, but I was worried, I mean, *we* were worried, because we thought he was wicked cute."

"He was a cop," the man answered matter-of-factly. "And his name wasn't Gary. It was Joe. He cut out because they were onto him. No one has seen him for a while."

Belinda gasped and started to sniffle. She leaned on Sherry's shoulder. "Did you hear that? He was a *cop*. Totally, like, a cop! He could've busted us," she said.

"Don't be stupid," the man answered sharply, obviously irritated. "He wasn't going to arrest anyone. The police want to arrest *him*."

This was too much, Sherry thought. This was too much for one morning. She tried to stay calm, but all she could think about were the wonderful headlines writing themselves in front of her eyes—COP SOLD DRUGS IN HIGH SCHOOL PARKING LOT—TO KIDS HE WAS JUST "JOE." She looked at Belinda, who started to ask another question. Sherry stuck a finger into her back to shut her up. If this guy was as smart as he looked, he would figure them out in one more minute. "Okay, well, we're going to split now," she said, pushing Belinda toward the car. "See you tomorrow."

It was nine-thirty when they reached the *Citizen*. Jack spotted them as they walked through the swinging doors to the newsroom. He could tell right away they were giddy.

In a minute, the whole newsroom was staring at them. "Give me a high-five," Sherry whispered to Belinda, and she did. Out of the corner of her eye, she could see Brazil. He was smiling broadly at her, and he raised his fist in a victory salute.

"In my office. Now," Jack barked.

Sherry and Belinda followed his order and shut the door. Jack sat behind his desk. "Spit it out," he said, pointing his cigarette at them and leaning over his desk, as if to hear better.

When they were done telling the story, Jack finally leaned

back in his chair. His eyes were closed. "Holy shit," he said softly. "I was right."

"You were right," they echoed him.

"You have a lot of work to do."

"It doesn't look like it's going to be too hard," Sherry said.

"Don't be an idiot, Estabrook. God, I hate dumb women," Jack snapped back. The fuzzy introspection in his voice was gone. "You gotta get moving. All you've got is one good anecdote. So what? We need to find this Joe guy and get an interview through his fucking lawyer, and we gotta track down the kids who bought from him, find out if they feel betrayed or lucky or just like fucking idiots, which they are, by the way. And we gotta spend a few minutes with the moron of a principal over at the school, see how he feels about this little episode on his grounds. Not to mention all the parents we gotta get on the horn. You got tons of work to do. Shit, I can't believe how much work we have to do. What do you have for this afternoon? Belinda's going to that voke up north, right? What about you? You're going to where? Hialeah High?"

"No, Lincoln. I'm sitting in on a rap room."

"Sounds like a waste of time."

"Yeah, I could cancel, but let me give it a try," Sherry said. "I've got an appointment there in around an hour."

"Okay," Jack said. "Get out of here and keep me posted. And, girls, don't screw up."

Before taking off for Lincoln High, Sherry rushed home and put on a suit, heels, and makeup. She wanted to look like an adult, someone the kids could respect. Someone they could trust. When she looked in the mirror, she had to laugh at the twenty-minute transformation she'd made from goofy teenybopper to glitzy newslady. Neither was real, but the chic reporter was definitely easier to behold. "It's showtime," she said to her reflection.

A few minutes later, she was pulling up in front of Lincoln

High, a sprawling, flat-roofed, small-windowed structure built in the sixties of pale yellow cinder block. It sat, low-slung over concrete, in the heart of a solidly middle-class neighborhood, each bare concrete-block ranch house built square in the center of one-eighth acre of flat lawn so neatly trimmed it looked like Astroturf. The whole area was built at one time for the influx of Cuban refugees who managed to escape with the contents of their bank accounts, and many of them had never moved again. Instead, they'd made their lives over in Miami as shopkeepers, construction workers, and government bureaucrats, and they tended their modest homes and their property and their families with exquisite, traditional care. The high school reflected that. It was known for its devout booster club, its polite students, its unusual cleanliness. A large hand-painted sign out front announced, BEWARE OF THE LIONS!!! 10-2-1!!! WAY TO GO!!! Sherry recalled that a recent article in the *Herald* had claimed the community's fabric had begun to fray with the "Americanization" of its youth, but she decided you'd never know it by looking at Lincoln High. Even the parking lot exuded order and good old-fashioned values. It was filled with beautifully polished American sedans, Cutlasses, Bonaires, and LTDs, most of them circa 1975, hand-me-downs that looked brand-new.

The rap room was stuck in the far back corner of the first floor, not far from the locker rooms by the smell of it. Sherry checked her watch—she was early—and so she sat down in the center of one of the blue couches that encircled the room. A poster on the wall said, I AM SOMEBODY, and on the blackboard someone had written, LEAVE ST. MARY'S FOOD BANK DONATIONS HERE, with an arrow pointing toward a box overflowing with Goya cans. The room was littered with used tissues and a few cigarette butts.

The bell rang, and suddenly the hall outside was filled with voices and laughter. A middle-aged man smoking a pipe walked into the room and looked blankly at Sherry. He put down his briefcase, took out a small calendar, checked the date, and then looked up with a tight smile. "Ah, yes. We don't get many visitors, Miss Estabrook," he said. "I'm Mr. Warren. I run the counseling service here." He turned his back to her and tapped his pipe on an ashtray. "I hope you're not on some kind of witch-hunt."

"No, absolutely not," Sherry said firmly.

"Really. That's nice," Mr. Warren answered sarcastically. He had no choice but to suffer through the visit: principal's orders. "All right then." He sat down across the room and gazed past Sherry, out a window, as if he wished she weren't there. "Before the kids get here, I want to set up some ground rules." His voice sounded both snide and weary. "No questions. No names. Just an observer. The kids know you're coming. They're really excited. You'll hear some wild stories. But these are just kids. Remember that. Most of them are liars."

"They're *liars*?"

"Let's say they exaggerate a lot."

"Kids usually tell the truth."

"Not to pretty reporters, they don't," he said. The room started to fill with students. Mr. Warren nodded at her and stood up to erase the blackboard.

Sherry smiled at the teenagers as they walked in the door. Most of them giggled and smiled back. One of the girls walked over to her and asked, "Will you put me on TV?"

"I'm a newspaper reporter," Sherry said. "I'm just here to observe."

A second bell rang, and Mr. Warren shut the door firmly. He looked at the two dozen kids sitting on the couches and on the floor. "We have a visitor. This is Miss Estabrook, a reporter for the *Miami Citizen*. She's going to tell you what she's doing here, and then she's just going to observe. You can say whatever you want today. Just be yourselves, please."

He turned to Sherry.

"Hi, everyone," she began, trying to sound as friendly and sympathetic as possible. "As Mr. Warren said, my name is Miss Estabrook, but you can call me Sherry if you like. I'm here because I'm writing an article about how kids today feel, like what's on their minds, about school and parents and even about drugs."

The room erupted in excited laughter. "We love 'em!" somebody said loudly, and the kids roared in approval.

"Please, just be yourselves," Sherry said, trying to appear unimpressed by the bravado ready to be unleashed. This was obviously what the competition meant by "Americanization," she thought; no typical Cuban mom and dad would knowingly tolerate the use of marijuana, let alone cocaine. From her experience, they still believed in hard work, virgin brides, and hell as a destination. Their kids obviously had their doubts; definitely an interesting angle for Jack's piece, it occurred to her—drugs creeping into even the most traditional communities in Miami. "Thanks for letting me visit." Sherry smiled.

"Are you on TV?" a short boy across the room asked.

"No, I work for a newspaper," Sherry said.

"How old are you?" another girl asked.

"I'm twenty-five," said Sherry. "I graduated from high school about nine years ago."

"Are you married?"

The question came from a thin, angular boy who was standing in the corner, legs spread and hands behind his back like a soldier. His black hair was slicked straight off the forehead, revealing a narrow face carved with acne scars. His eyes were small, piercing, and so dark Sherry couldn't see the pupils. He was wearing a sharp-pressed white shirt, unbuttoned almost all the way, with three or four thick gold chains around his neck.

"Manuel, this class is not about Miss Estabrook," Mr. Warren said. "Take a seat, please." The boy waited a few moments and then slowly sat down on the arm of a couch. He didn't take his eyes off Sherry.

"All right. Let's begin," Mr. Warren said. "Last time, Lucy was explaining why she ran away from home last summer, and we were helping her find positive solutions—"

"I want to know if Miss Estabrook has a boyfriend first," Lucy interrupted.

"Not really," said Sherry, smiling. Lucy smiled back forlornly. "Oh, that's too bad," she said, seeming anxious to say more but then catching Mr. Warren's scowl. "Okay, well, I was talking about my parents," she went on. "It's not really my mother who is the problem. It's my father. He just doesn't trust me or nothing, like my sister *always* has to chaperon me, even when I'm just going to the movies or something."

Lucy talked for another quarter of an hour, and then, when she was done, there was silence. Mr. Warren asked if any students had advice for her. Still silence. "Boring!" Sherry scribbled in her notebook. She looked up and noticed the class was watching her.

"I want to answer Miss Estabrook's questions," the boy sitting on the edge of the couch said after a minute had passed. "Mr. Warren, that's what we should do now." It was a command. The rest of the students sat silently, some of them nodding.

The teacher turned to Sherry with a sigh of disapproval and

resignation. "Do you have any questions?" he said gruffly, checking his watch. There were eighteen minutes left to class.

"Well, yes, I do," she said. This was her one chance to get some good anecdotes and maybe pinpoint a few kids to interview later, alone. "I'd like to know if kids here, kids your age, are using drugs. May I ask that question?"

"Yeah, you can ask that question," said Manuel. "Hah!" He smiled at her with thin rose-colored lips. His face was so scary, Sherry thought, it looked like a Halloween mask.

The class broke loose as the kids excitedly shouted out one story after another. One girl said she smoked dope every day, it made her happy and relaxed. Other kids talked about getting high at parties, in the parking lot, at lunch. One boy said he got his grass from his stepfather, "and sometimes we get wasted together." A few kids laughed and clapped approvingly.

Then, harshly, an interruption: "You all think you're so cool."

It was Manuel. He was standing again, staring at Sherry, hands behind his waist like a marine, head tilted back slightly. "They all think they're cool." He looked around the room. No one said a word.

"You're all babies."

"We don't judge each other in here," said Lucy, but it wasn't really a challenge.

Sherry started to speak; she wanted to pierce the sudden tension, and maybe, before the bell rang, hear a few more stories from the rest of the class. But it was too late. The halls were filled again with hundreds of kids, and Mr. Warren was shaking his head. He walked over to Sherry. "A total disruption," he said disparagingly. "Don't plan on coming back."

She nodded and stuck her notebook in her purse. The whole thing puzzled her. What had just happened anyway? Could she use any of it in the story? She made her way through the crowds in the hall, and felt a rush of relief as she walked out the door into the squinting sunlight of the parking lot.

She was just about to step into her car when she heard someone calling her name loudly. "Miss Estabrook—don't leave." Then, suddenly, there was a hand on her shoulder.

It was that kid Manuel.

The next thing Sherry knew, he was two inches from her face. He had backed her against her BMW with the silent, effortless dexterity of a tango dancer, and he now was staring straight into her eyes without blinking.

Sherry raised one hand to shove him away, but it was useless. His presence was so overheated, she could practically feel it melting her joints. All at once she realized she couldn't move, except to drop, and she wasn't going to let that happen.

She met his gaze.

The sight was repulsive. Manuel's red-pitted crescent-shaped face was so close to hers that she could feel the warm moisture off his lips, and he was smiling with serpentlike satisfaction at the effect. He was unbelievably ugly, and he knew it. Sherry had never seen anyone like this kid in her life, but now that she wanted to look away, she couldn't. She couldn't even lower her eyes. Somehow, he wouldn't let her. Was he touching her? No—both hands were on his hips—but he wanted to. She could sense it. And why was he smiling? Nothing was funny. He was frightening her, and that pissed her off.

"I want to tell you *my* story," Manuel said.

"Your story?" Sherry asked, trying not to sound incredulous. A story about what? About being a pushy asshole? About wearing enough gold chains to sink a flotilla? Maybe some other day in a few years.

"Yeah," he said. "My story. It's unbelievable."

"Can you tell me what it's about?"

"No, you need a tape recorder."

"I have one in my car."

"We can't talk here." Manuel took a couple steps back from Sherry and grinned with the look of someone who owned a very juicy secret. He glanced left and right to make sure no one was within earshot. "I have some incredible information for your article," he said, "information no one else can give you."

Sherry wanted to blow him off—something about him was too damn creepy for words—but the lure of exclusivity had already snagged her. She couldn't resist. What reporter could?

"Do you want to talk in my car?" she asked.

"No, I can't talk now. I've got football practice. I'm the quarterback. Did you hear about us? The Lincoln Lions?" Manuel smoothed the side of his hair back with one quick, confident move. "Ten, two, and one. My name was in the newspaper two weeks ago. Did you see it?"

"No," said Sherry. "I don't read the sports pages."

"That's okay," he answered mock sincere, patting her on the shoulder and then letting his hand linger there familiarly. "You don't have to."

Sherry smiled tightly. "Gee, thanks," she said sarcastically, shrugging off his hold.

Manuel didn't miss a beat. He quickly resumed the Marine stance he'd affected in the rap room, stomach in, chin out, buttocks tight. She noticed he was taller than she was by an inch or two, and so wiry that the veins in his arms and neck stuck out worse than a junkie's. But this kid was no addict. His eyes were too alive, his language too controlled. And his clothes—gaudy, yes, but very expensive: linen shirt definitely the real-thing product of some Italian designer, hand-tailored black leather pants and unscuffed red-stitched cowboy boots made of some exotic creature like ostrich or rattlesnake. Thanks to a recently rich daddy somewhere, he looked as if he were in costume. Suddenly, Sherry wasn't frightened anymore. Here was a kid who would someday be a cop, she thought. A bully and a tattletale—the perfect combination.

"I'm sixteen," he said.

"Yeah," Sherry said offhandedly. "I've got to get going. My boss expects me back by now. Why don't you call me or something?"

"No," Manuel said. It was an order, the same kind he had given his teacher not an hour before. "Meet me at five o'clock, in the park around the corner from here. There's a picnic table. I'll see you there."

Sherry wanted to put it off. She was seeing Brazil later. But the kid was so insistent—and there was that promise of information for her alone, another Sherry Estabrook coup and something Jack would just gobble up—she just couldn't say no.

13

The picnic table was in a corner of the park not far from Lincoln, under a giant, shady banyan tree and overlooking a playground where about a dozen kids were running around. Sherry popped a fresh cassette in her tape recorder and waited. She was early for a change; it was ten to. She watched as two young mothers—they looked like old friends—gossiped and laughed as their kids played in the sandbox. It took Sherry a minute to realize that one of them was nursing—a tiny baby was tucked inside her blouse, head nestled to breast, only visible when she stood up and, without missing a beat, casually reached into the sandbox to wipe her other kid's nose. A few feet away, another mother was changing her young son's diaper on a bench, and Sherry suddenly remembered the stench of shit that pervaded the homeless shelter near Marblehead and the terrible way the newborns would constantly wail to be held. How did these women stand it? Sherry wondered. Didn't they ever get bored with planning birthday parties for their kids, with making chicken Marsala for their husbands, with watching the soaps in the afternoon while they sorted the wash? Didn't they realize life had more to offer than making the world turn for a little family?

At exactly five, Manuel pulled up to the park in his black Camaro. Sherry could see him checking his hair in the rearview mirror before eagerly jumping out and strutting toward her with the self-confident gait of a sleazy car salesman. "Hey, Miss Estabrook," he said, smiling brightly, "I knew you would come."

"Uh-huh." Sherry nodded noncommittally. She hoped this would take about a half hour. She was meeting Brazil at home at six.

But fifteen minutes later, she had forgotten she even had a date that night; she was totally and completely focused on the boy sitting by her side who was smiling blithely, speaking in a relaxed monotone, and telling her the most shocking, terrifying, *newsworthy* story she had ever heard. It took all of her energy just to listen, ask questions, and hold her pencil without trembling so uncontrollably he might laugh and walk away.

"Go on, please," she told him.

"No problem," he agreed simply, "that was my third job. It was clean. No problem. I got the guy right in the neck. Boom. Smooth. Not even a whimper. Just, like, a gurgling sound from the blood. It always sort of gurgles when you shoot them in the neck. But they don't get a chance to say anything. It's better that way, because sometimes they can beg for you not to do it, you know, they can say something about their kids or something, and it gets messy."

"Yeah, of course," Sherry heard herself saying.

"One time, this guy gave a fight, and I didn't get to waste him right off, and he said, you know, something about his mother, and I felt bad. I mean, I didn't feel totally bad, but I thought maybe I should just forget it and split. But he had seen my face and all, so I had to finish the job. So. Boom." He chuckled softly, as if he had just made a joke.

"How many times have you done this?" Sherry said, voice flat. She didn't want to sound judgmental. He had to keep talking.

"Okay, I thought you were going to ask that," he answered. "I've lost track exactly. I used to know for sure. If you'd asked me a few months ago, I could have told you the perfect number. But now, I'm not positive anymore. I think it's up to eighteen."

Sherry turned off the tape recorder. "Give me a second," she said, flipping the page of her notebook, trying to act calm, as if occasionally stopping an interview were routine. "I've got to write some things down."

"No problem," said Manuel. He stood up and stretched lazily.

Sherry pushed her pencil to the paper, trying to force a steady hand. *An assassin,* she wrote, *a hit man. Works for Lopez ring out of Coral Gables. Kills people.* She wrote those words again. *Kills people.*

Sixteen years old. Remembers eighteen murders. Thinks there may be more.

Shoots victims in neck. Makes $2,500 a hit. Started when he was fourteen.

Father is bricklayer/construction job chief with El Duque, been with him long time, makes decent money, he sez

One sister, Sonia. younger

Captain varsity football team, All-American quarterback
Loves Madonna, MC Hammer, big Nintendo fan
Sez favorite designer is Armani (!)
Girlfriend named Blanca, "real nice," he sez
Drives new Camaro, black, with custom detailing
Sherry glanced at Manuel, and he gave her a friendly smile.
I believe that he is telling the truth, she wrote. *I don't know why, but I know he is.*

Sherry closed her notebook and snapped on the tape recorder again. "Could you please tell me how you got started?" she asked.

"No problem." Manuel took a deep breath. "There's this guy on the football team. His older sister goes out with a guy in the family. I didn't know that then. But, okay, this was two years ago. And my friend on the team asked me if I wanted to go to the coolest party. It was a Saturday night, down on Brickell, in a fancy building, a skyscraper on the beach, and I said, yeah, absolutely. I told Blanca, that's my girlfriend, that I had to baby-sit Sonia, and I went with Alfred to the party.

"This party, man, it was the most unbelievable thing to me! I had never seen anything like it, except on TV. All these gorgeous ladies, wearing these tight dresses, and guys all wearing leather and Rolex watches, and I was blown away! I said, this is it! This is the life I wanted. I knew right then, this was the life I wanted very, very much. I would kill for this life.

"So, we go to the party, and before you know it, I'm sitting on the couch with some beautiful woman, and her boyfriend walks over, and he's about thirty. I thought I was going to get killed. I mean, I have my hand on her knee, and I think this guy is going to waste me. But instead, he starts to laugh, and he's says, 'Go ahead, Sondra, baby, I want you to kiss him.' So she leans over and gives me the longest kiss. And when she's done, she leans back and says, 'Hey, Baby Lips, I love you.' "

Sherry held her hand up for Manuel to stop. This was coming at her too fast. "So *what* happened at the party?" she asked. "Did someone ask you to work for the family?"

"No, not that party," Manuel said. "A few parties after that. A guy named Eddie came up to me and said, 'Hey, Baby Lips, how'd you like to make some money? Nothing in life is free.' So I said sure. He said he wanted me to drop off a package in Lauderdale. He said he would drive. And so I did it a few days later. And I did it real good, so I got called to do drops a few more times for Eddie. It was easy. But then, one day out of nowhere, Eddie meets me after school, and he says he has a bigger job for me. It was a hit that night.

"So, three guys from the family went with me. It wasn't as bad as I expected, you know? I thought I might flip out or something, but hey, nothing. And I was so good, everyone was talking about it. After a little while, they started letting me do it alone. It's safer that way."

"You were good?" Sherry asked. "What made you good?"

Manuel rubbed his chin. "That's a good question," he said, as if suddenly he were addressing an eager pupil. "You're very smart."

"Thank you," Sherry said. She smiled at him numbly. She could barely believe she was managing to speak, let alone ask good questions. She had dreamed of landing huge stories in her career, but never one this big. And now, here was an exceedingly polite killer in designer blue jeans landing it for her before she even had to cast the bait. She shook her head in grateful disbelief. "What made you good?" she repeated.

"Well, everyone respected me, you know?" Manuel came back swiftly, as if he had practiced the answer before. "I was fast. It was always over quick. I always got the job done. I didn't get scared. And I didn't get all girly about it."

"Girly?" She didn't want to press him too much—he might close down.

"You know, like a girl. I didn't cry. I didn't laugh. I didn't talk about it afterward. No offense to you, being a girl, as you are."

"Thank you," Sherry said automatically.

It was dark. The playground was empty. For the first time since she had moved to Miami, Sherry felt freezing cold, and she was dizzy. Here, happening to her now, was the greatest story of her life, the one she had been waiting for since she'd left home, the one that would get her the prizes she needed, the interviews on the morning talk shows, the guest lectures at journalism schools. She would never have to spell her last name for a source again, because from now on, Estabrook was going to mean raw, honest journalism, it was going to be a name that meant something real. Sherry was so overpowered by the thrill of the idea, she didn't care that she had to chat it up with a very sick little murderer for the next few weeks. In fact, she didn't hate Manuel anymore. He was so agreeable. He answered all of her questions in detail. He was patient when she stopped to write notes. It was all going to be very easy. She wasn't going to have to search the streets for a teenager who smoked dope with his grandmother. She was never going to have to go begging for news again.

"I have to go now," she told Manuel with regret. "But I want to talk to you a lot more. Will you meet with me again soon?"

"Name the time and day," he said cheerfully. She wanted to hug him.

Sherry turned off the tape recorder and stuck her notebook into her purse, but something stopped her from saying good-bye. There was a question she wanted to ask. She could do it now or wait until later. Either way it was a risk. She might never see him again. He could change his mind about the story, or he could get killed. So she had to ask now, but she had to ask so that he would want to answer, so that he would still like her.

"Manuel," she said softly, shifting closer to him on the park bench. "Why are you telling me this?" She nodded, trying to let him know that it was okay to answer. Any answer would be just fine.

For a moment, he said nothing, but licked his lips as if he was thoughtfully preparing an answer.

"Manuel?"

"I have my reasons," he answered at last. It was so dark Sherry couldn't see his face. "There are reasons . . ." His voice drifted off and then came back again suddenly, gathering conviction. "It's like—I want to start over, okay, Miss Estabrook? I want to start fresh, you know, make a new life for myself. I'm not saying what I did was wrong—it was *business*. Everybody does business that way down here. But I want to be my own man now."

"So why not just quit the family?" Sherry asked. "Why not just leave town?"

Manuel shrugged, as if he had never considered the options before. "I'm not killing for them anymore," he said offhandedly. A pause, then: "And I will leave town, you know, as soon as my story appears in your newspaper. I'm going to stay with some friends in Mexico. It's all set up. You gotta realize, Miss Estabrook, a man like me is always in total control. No problem."

Sherry nodded to show her understanding, but the truth was,

she still felt slightly uneasy, as if he were answering only half her question. She decided to try one more time, as gently as she could. "But I'm still not sure I understand, Manuel," she said. Her voice was sympathetic, soothing. "Why are you telling *me* this?"

Another shrug, this time with a shy smile. "I thought you would want to know, Miss Estabrook," he said. "When I saw you, I thought—"

"Thought what?"

"May I call you Sherry now?" Manuel asked.

"Yes," she said.

"Sherry, when I saw you, I knew you would understand."

"Understand?"

"Yes. I knew you would understand me. You'll understand my story, right? You were sent to me, like an angel or something. I've been waiting for you."

"Thank you," said Sherry. She had been waiting for him, too.

Sherry drove home in a daze, clutching the steering wheel with one hand, the other clutching the tape recorder that sat in her lap. At a red light, she rewound it briefly and played it back. "And he said he had a bigger job for me. It was a hit," Manuel said. "Uh-huh," she heard her voice in the background. "It wasn't as bad as I expected, you know? I thought I might flip out or something, but hey, nothing."

"Uh-huh." Her voice again, monotone with shock. The light turned green, and Sherry clicked off the machine.

A few minutes later, she pulled into the driveway and saw her living-room light on. For a second, she was struck with fear—were Alvin and Laura inside?—and then she remembered her date with Brazil. She had to be an hour late, but in a few minutes he would understand everything.

She found him sprawled on the couch. "Glad you decided to

show up, darlin'," he said. He was almost mad, holding off only to find out whether she had been in a car wreck or trapped in the flash flood that hit west Dade that evening at sunset.

"Brazil," she sat down beside him. "I don't know how to tell you this. The most amazing thing has happened." She struggled for words—was there any way to tell the story that would convey its hugeness to the man beside her? Just her telling of it would make it smaller. It had to come out of the mouth of Manuel, out of the mouth of a teenager who shot his victims in the neck because it was easier that way; otherwise it would sound like a ridiculous lie.

"Start at the beginning," Brazil said with a long sigh. He sounded bored—nothing fazed him, and it aggravated Sherry to no end. Suddenly, she wanted to tell Belinda first, to hear her reaction: "Are you kidding? Tell me, he told you *all* that? Tell me again. . . ." She wanted to call Jack at home, hear him slowly exhale smoke over the line, and whisper, "Oh Jeezus, Sherry. Jeezus Christ on a crutch." But here she was with Brazil, she was late and jittery, and he was watching her. She had to tell him now.

"Look, something really big has happened," she began. "A huge story has happened to me. A huge story. There's never been such a big story."

"You saw the governor fuck a sheep on the statehouse steps?"

He laughed loudly. Sherry glared at him, and frustrated tears began to drip down her cheeks. "Listen," she said as she rewound the tape to the beginning and angrily wiped her face with the back of her wrist, "this is what a sixteen-year-old kid told me today, okay? Just listen to this, okay? Don't say anything until the end."

She let the tape roll. They listened in silence until it was over, Brazil still sprawled on the couch, staring at the ceiling. Sherry sat on the coffee table.

"Holy shit," Brazil said after she clicked off the machine. "The kid is dead. As soon as this hits the paper, the friendly Lopez family is going to plug *him* in the neck."

"What about me?" Sherry asked.

"Oh, you're safe. I mean, maybe you should get out of town, go to Tallahassee or something, for a few weeks after the story runs so you avoid getting subpoenaed, but the *Citizen* will keep you out of jail."

Sherry stared at Brazil, astonished. "You asshole!" she shouted. "What about me—my career? Is this incredible or what?"

Brazil started to say something—he was older, he had been at this hack trade longer, he was sorry, but he had to bring her down—something like that. It was just one story, one award, maybe two. But the paper keeps coming out, and you've got to keep spewing it out every day, month after month, year after year. One good story was great. But it was just *one* story. After a while, people forget, even people in the newsroom. He was going to tell her, but he loved her too much right then. She was so brave, trying hard to break free from that distant place called Marblehead, where this would all be so improper.

"Sherry, this is amazing. Dougherty is going to love it," Brazil told her. "You're a star."

She leaned over and kissed him on the forehead.

"Now let's eat," he said, sitting up.

"No, I've got to call Belinda." Sherry ran to the kitchen and dialed. It rang ten times, but there was no answer. She tried again. "Shit, where could Belinda be? It's nine o'clock." Brazil shook his head and shrugged. "Let's eat. You can try her again later," he said.

"Let's eat? Are you kidding? I can't eat," Sherry snapped in response. She dialed Jack's number. His wife answered. He wasn't home either—he'd be back late. She asked if it was an emergency. "No, I guess not," Sherry said. She hung up and stared at the phone. She had to tell someone. She thought of calling Charles, but what would he say? He wouldn't understand at all.

Sherry walked back into the living room where Brazil was leafing through the *Vogue* on her coffee table. "I could shoot fashion pictures and be rich and famous," he said, without looking up. "We would have to live in New York City, though, and it's too dang cold there."

"*Please*, Brazil."

"*Please*, Sherry," he said back. He stood up and tried to hug her, but her body was stiff. "Okay, I get it. You're a bit uptight about this. Calm down. Everything is going to be okay."

"No, nothing is going to be okay," Sherry shot back. "Everything is going to be changed."

"Okay, everything is going to be changed. We still have to eat."

"You have to eat. You always have to eat."

"Yes, I like to eat."

"Well, it shows."

"It shows?"

"It shows, yeah. You and eating. God! Eat, eat, eat. And pizza. Always pizza! You drive me crazy. Why don't you just inject the grease and cholesterol into your veins?"

"You got some in the refrigerator?"

"Please, Brazil. This is important," Sherry pleaded. "Let's listen to it again."

"I'm leaving," he said, gathering the cameras in a sack next to the couch.

"Don't leave!" she cried. "I can't be alone. I'm sorry. Let's eat. You eat. I'll watch."

"Fine," he said. "There's a pizza in there. We have to heat it up."

"Fine," said Sherry. She walked into the kitchen and stuck the pizza in the oven. Then she tried Belinda again. Still no answer. It was crazy, Belinda being out so late. She never went out after work. She curled up in bed and watched soap operas on Spanish TV or she wrote long letters to friends in Khorammābād and Djakarta and Puerto Madryn, children of other spooks who found her life in America full of foreign intrigue.

Sherry stood in the kitchen and watched the oven for a few minutes. She could hear Brazil flipping magazine pages in the next room. "I need a shot of Stoli," she said after a while. "Let's go get some."

"Okay," Brazil said. "Excellent idea."

They were about to get in the car when Sherry ran back into the house. "Hold on," she said. She was back a minute later with the tape recorder. "You never know when Alvin and Laura are going to seek revenge," she told Brazil.

"Yeah, good thinking," he said. "Really, really good thinking. I'm so glad one of us is thinking rationally."

15

Sherry was in the newsroom at seven; she couldn't sleep. Not even for an hour.

She had to be in the office, to be close to the sting of the news, to make sure Manuel wasn't among the night's body count. She couldn't lose the story now, before her reporting of it made it real.

"Anything exciting going on?" she asked the overnight rewrite man as soon as she arrived in the newsroom. She tried to sound nonchalant, and apparently it worked, because the guy didn't even look up to answer. "Got a dead wife up in Hallandale," he said flatly. "Domestic."

Sherry sighed with relief, and then wandered back to her desk, stuck the headphones over her ears, and switched on the tape recorder.

"Okay, is it on?" she heard Manuel ask.

"It's on."

"Okay, so I'm going to tell you my story now."

"Uh-huh." She sounded irritated. That was yesterday.

"I want you to promise you won't give my name to the police before this article runs in the newspaper, only afterward, you know what I'm saying?"

"Look, I'm a *reporter*," Sherry had answered testily. "I'm never going to give them your name, if that's what you want."

"I want you to protect me."

"Okay, the *Citizen* will protect you." Sherry heard her voice get bitchy, and she cringed at her obvious impatience. She was lucky he hadn't walked right then.

"I mean, protection just until everything is under control again."

"Fine," Sherry agreed, stifling a yawn. This dumb kid didn't realize his "story" would probably amount to one four-line quote in an eight-hundred-line story. "Why don't we get going now, okay?"

There was a brief silence on the tape, and Sherry remembered that was when Manuel had extended his hand to her, to seal the terms of their agreement with a shake. She recalled how firm his grip had been for such a young kid. He covered her hand with both of his and squeezed tightly.

"This is a true story." His voice was louder now. She could see him leaning purposefully toward the machine's tiny microphone.

"Uh-huh."

"Do you want to ask me to state my name?"

"If you want. We're not in court." Not yet, Sherry thought now.

"My name is Manuel. I'm sixteen years old, and this is the story of my life." Not even a pause. "I kill people—I've killed a lot of people for a very, very famous cocaine family in Miami, the one run by Mimi Lopez. I'm not doing it anymore. But I did it for two years. I don't have any regrets. I made a lot of money. You could say I'm rich now. I drive a very, very nice car. I bought it myself—cash. I bought my girlfriend a necklace with diamonds in it. See these pants I'm wearing? They're real leather, from France. They cost two hundred-fifty dollars, and I didn't even think twice about buying them. My shirt cost a hundred twenty-nine dollars. I got it at Mayfair in the Grove. I shop there all the time, with the rich people. You could say I'm a classy guy. Everyone respects me. You can tell by looking at me."

Here he had looked at Sherry for a reaction.

"Can we start at the beginning?" she had said.

"Yes, sure. Of course."

A few heartbeats of silence.

"Don't you want to ask me questions?" Manuel had said. "I'm getting the feeling you don't believe me. But I can prove every word I'm saying."

Sherry clicked off the tape recorder and glanced around the newsroom nervously. She was suddenly overcome by a fusillade of fear. What if Jack didn't believe the story? She would have to bring Manuel into the *Citizen*, parade him around, make him repeat all the gory details, let a bunch of editors dissect his heart and brain with skepticism. Would he agree to that? He seemed to trust her; she couldn't betray him. If Jack asked him too much, he might balk. He was just a kid. They couldn't push him too far.

The phone rang, and Sherry swung around to pick it up, banging her knee hard on the side of her steel desk. "Just me," Brazil said at the other end. He was in early, too. "If I was you, instead of sitting there looking like you've got fire ants in your brassiere, I'd transcribe the fucking tape. Jack is gonna want to see it in black-and-white. He likes you, Sherry, but you can't sell the story alone. Let Manuel sell it to him."

"Transcribe it. Right," she said, and hung up. Across the newsroom, Brazil gave her a thumbs-up sign, but she didn't see him. She was too busy banging down the keys on her computer.

Two hours later, as the newsroom awoke, Sherry was deep into the transcript. "You know, like a girl. I didn't cry. I didn't laugh. I didn't talk about it afterward," she typed, the words swiftly appearing, neon green on the black screen in front of her. "No offense to you, being a girl, as you are." She rewound the tape to make sure she got it down right.

"No offense to you, being a girl, as you are."

Then a light, happy voice sang out behind her: "No offense to you, being a girl, as you are? *What*? What is this, Sherry?"

Sherry swiveled around in her chair and stared in wonder. It was Belinda. Belinda—in pearly orange lipstick, heavy black eyeliner, and turquoise eye shadow. She smiled coyly and twirled around once as if she were Miss Georgia in a swimsuit competition. She was wearing a low-cut, frilly lavender dress, tied at the waist with a deep purple scarf. It must have been one of her mother's castoffs, a relic, circa 1974, that probably saw Katherine McEvoy through a half-dozen boozy embassy cocktail parties in Buenos Aires. Belinda flopped down into her chair and scuttled in close to Sherry. She pursed her lips, giggled, and then put her head down on her lap and squirmed like a baby in bathwater.

"Belinda?" Sherry was alarmed.

"What?" Her head was still down on her lap, and she was tapping both her feet on the floor in a jittery tempo. Suddenly, she looked up. "I had a date!" she said in an astonished whisper. "I had a date last night with *Eladio*!"

"Eladio?" Sherry searched her mind. Not Eladio Gomez, the West Miami selectman, too fat and ugly and too old. Not to mention the arm he'd lost in the Bay of Pigs. Eladio Lan-Castro, the fire commissioner in Miami Springs? Impossible, he wasn't even on her beat.

"Eladio—the policeman, for God's sake, Sherry," Belinda said, grabbing Sherry's hand. "The policeman I met at your house. He called me last night after work."

"How the hell did he get your home phone number?"

"He got it. He's a cop. He called the phone company. He has a friend there." She giggled again.

"You're acting like you got laid," Sherry said, shaking her head. In three years, she had never known Belinda to go out on a date. When Sherry asked, she claimed she was still getting over a dreamy, black-eyed poet named Abdullah, to whom she'd lost her heart (and her virginity) in Damascus or Dargol or somewhere like that. She'd met him while she was in journalism school; he waited tables at a café near the university. After three passionate weeks, in which they swore everlasting love to one another, Abdullah unceremoniously dumped her for a fourteen-year-old local girl with big boobs and an even bigger dowry. Belinda learned her fate when she caught them screwing in the back of her car, which she had lent to Abdullah on the premise that he was taking his mother to the ear doctor. After that, she told Sherry, she had decided never to trust a man again, any man except her father. And after he died, she realized she'd gone too far even with that allowance.

"Good God, Sherry," Belinda said, laughing at the suggestion that she and Eladio had slept together, "don't be so American. It was our first date. We got to know each other. We went to dinner at Versailles, and we took a long walk on the beach and we talked. He's very interesting."

"A Cuban cop in Miami is interesting?"

"Yes—he's *so* interesting. He thinks about stuff."

"*Stuff?*"

"Yes—*stuff*. Important stuff. You know, about life, and sadness, and love." Belinda laughed sweetly at the thought. "He thought *I* was interesting. He said I was pretty."

"Oh, my God," Sherry said. "You can't fall in love now."

"Too late." Belinda giggled again. It was terrible to see her acting this way, Sherry thought, like a goddamn cheerleader who'd just landed a date with the captain of the football team.

"I have something important to tell you," Sherry said. But she could see she was bringing Belinda down, and she stopped. She banged two keys on her computer and stored the copy on the screen. "Start from the beginning," she told Belinda.

"Okay, okay." Belinda stood up and then sat down again, tucking her legs beneath her and pulling down the lavender dress to cover her knees. "I got home at seven-thirty or so, and, um, I had stopped at Kentucky Fried Chicken to get dinner, and I was about to sit down and eat it when the phone rang, and it was him. He asked for 'Miss McEvoy.' I thought it had to be the insurance company again, about my last accident—which he says he can help with, by the way—and I said it was me, and he said it was Eladio Alvarez, and he said who he was, but I knew right away anyway. I thought I was going to faint. I was going to *faint*, Sherry. I could feel my heart beating. Has that ever happened to you? You feel it beating in your chest?"

"Yeah," said Sherry. The tape recorder sat in her lap.

"So he starts off by apologizing for disturbing me at home, and then he asks if I would like to have dinner with him. And I was so stupid, Sherry. I said, 'Tonight?' Can you believe I said that: *'Tonight?'* He probably meant this weekend or something, but I went and said, 'Tonight?' And he said, 'Yes, if you like, that would be an honor.' And I gave him directions to my apartment. He lives three blocks away! So he came over about a half hour later and I met him downstairs and we took a walk down Calle Ocho and we stopped at Versailles. He likes it, too, can you believe it? I told him we had eaten there about a thousand times. So we sat down at a table, and we got our menus. . . ."

Sherry looked at her watch. Jack should have been in the office already. "Are you going to see him again?" she asked Belinda.

"Tonight!"

"You can't see him tonight."

"What?"

Sherry rubbed her eyes and pointed to the tape recorder in her lap. "We're working on a huge fucking story."

"We still have to eat, Sherry. And we're not writing it tonight. We have all those schools to go to—"

It's not the same story anymore, Sherry thought. It's a story about one kid, and maybe, well, maybe it wasn't Belinda's story anymore, either. But she *wanted* Belinda with her. They were a team. They'd written a half-dozen of Jack's big stories together. And she needed Belinda to help her prove to the cops and Garrett Newman and everyone else that the story was real. Maybe Belinda didn't have to meet Manuel—that part could be all hers—but

Belinda had to help her verify all the murders, run down all the details, pinpoint the exact day and hour of every kill, to tell her she was writing it with the right touch. She wanted Belinda with her to the end of it. She didn't mind the double byline. It would be better with a double byline. It was such a huge story, it had to have a double byline.

But here was Belinda acting like an idiot, about some man, a dumb cop no less, and this could really screw up the story, Sherry thought. She needed Belinda, but Belinda had to be completely with her in this.

"Sherry?" Belinda was watching her, and a look of hurt had replaced the misty-eyed delight of a few minutes earlier.

"Belinda, I don't want to bring you down. I'm unbelievably happy about you and Eladio. I think it's great. I'm jealous." Sherry squeezed Belinda's small hand warmly. "But while you were out with Eladio last night, I was interviewing a kid from Lincoln High who is an enforcer for the Lopez cocaine ring. He's killed eighteen people, and he wants to tell us all about it."

Belinda leaned forward in her seat, her knees rested against Sherry's. She gasped softly, and then whispered, "You talked to him?"

"I talked to him for almost two hours. He told me everything. He's sixteen years old. He plays on the football team, and he kills people for twenty-five hundred a pop. And now he wants to come clean."

"He's telling the truth?"

"Yes. Absolutely. I really think so."

"Why on earth did he tell you?"

Sherry smiled—this was the kicker, the real human hook into the story. "He said he wants to make a new life for himself," she explained, her voice bubbling with excitement, "and he thought I looked like I would understand."

"Oh," Belinda said, nodding knowingly. "He feels guilty."

"Yeah, I guess," she said vaguely, remembering Manuel's casual disclaimer about business-as-usual, Miami style. "I suppose he must, deep down."

"And he's killed how many people?"

"Eighteen, he thinks. He can't remember exactly."

"Have you told Jack?"

"Only Brazil knows."

Sherry held up the tape recorder. "It's all in here." She

handed Belinda the headphones, rewound the tape, and let it play.

 At eleven, Sherry and Belinda went together to Jack's office and closed the door behind them. He was banging out a memo on his typewriter—he never got used to the new computers—a cigarette stuck in the corner of his mouth, ashes lightly falling onto his lap with each deep drag.

After a minute, he stubbed out the butt and looked up. Sherry noticed that he raised one eyebrow skeptically as he glanced at Belinda's lavender getup. "Yeah?" he said.

Sherry and Belinda sat down in two metal chairs facing Jack's cluttered desk. A cloud of gray cigarette smoke hung over them, despite the small fan whirling in the corner. A police radio rumbled in the background, a dispatcher flatly announcing an attempted murder in progress somewhere in Liberty City.

"Jack, the story has taken an *unexpected* turn," Sherry said. Belinda was right: They had to be as understated as possible. Too much hype would kill the story in the first minute. Let it slowly blow Jack away.

"An unexpected turn?" Jack was not enthused.

Sherry nodded.

And then she started at the beginning—Lincoln High, the rap room, the intense kid in the corner named Manuel, the incident in the parking lot.

"So I met him at five, in the designated spot," she continued. "I have to admit I was doubtful that he would have anything for us, Jack. He seemed so clean-cut. But he surprised me.

"He says he works for the Lopez family. He says he committed murders for them for about two years. He thinks he assassinated eighteen people in all. He wants to talk about it."

She stopped. Next to her, she could feel Belinda sigh against the tension.

"Holy shit," Jack said. "You got it on tape?"

"Yes, and I have the whole conversation transcribed." She handed him the computer printout.

"Don't move," Jack said. He lit a cigarette, pushed the fly-fishing cap off his forehead, and started to read Manuel's story. Sherry and Belinda watched his face closely, but his expression was blank. In the background, they heard the police dispatcher ask all units to respond to shots fired at a Liberty City address. A few minutes later, a cop's voice crackled over the radio. He asked the dispatcher to contact the medical examiner. Two dead.

Jack looked up ten minutes later and dropped the sheaf of paper on his desktop.

"If this is true, this is the greatest story I ever heard," he said quietly. "I mean, Jesus fucking Christ." He stood up and walked over to a tray of hand-tied fishhooks mounted on the wall and appeared to consider them solemnly, shaking his head back and forth in slowly expanding disbelief. "I never heard a story like this," he said at last. "Here I'm thinking it's sort of like Larry Pilato's story about that killer baby-sitter up in Chicago, or maybe like that story out of Austin a few years back about Barry Loomis's little killing spree just before he fried, but this is better than that— it just fucking is *better*." He was picking up steam now, and a reluctant but gleeful smile broke across his harried face. "What we got here is the story about our whole sick society in a micro- cosm, it's a story about pure, unmitigated evil—it's fucking every- where, girls! I love it!" He turned to face Sherry again, and looked her straight in the eyes. "You're my star," he whispered as if the admission were too weighty to announce full voice. "You're going to put us in the books, kid."

"Gee, thanks for all your confidence, Jack—" Sherry began; she was glowing, too. Suddenly, she felt an enormous burst of affection for the man, for everything he had given her since she begged her way in the door of the *Miami Citizen*, all the hard assignments, all the freedom to run with them, and all the trust that she could hack it with the best of them. She wanted to thank him for having faith in her when she needed it most, really, truly thank him, but Jack cut her off unceremoniously. He was pacing the office now, practically running from one end to the other as he shouted out commands. In his excitement, his cap had flown off, exposing his baby-bottom head to the newsroom, but he didn't seem to notice. The ideas were exploding too fast and furious. "You got to find out everything about this kid, and I mean *everything*, Estabrook. And you, too, McEvoy. I'm talking details, details, fucking details." He stopped momentarily to stub out a Pall Mall and light another in an agitated flurry of motions. "The two of you," he said, when he picked up again, "you got to find out how many pores this kid's got at the end of his nose, you got to find out the fucking bra size of his second-grade teacher. I want to know what he eats for breakfast, how many shits he takes a day. We have to get so deep into this kid that we end up knowing him better than he knows himself. Fuck, we got to know him better than we know ourselves." He jerked his body into a halt and faced Sherry and Belinda foursquare. "Got it?"

"Got it," they answered in cheerful unison.

"And, of course," Jack snarled out of the side of his mouth as he exhaled a long column of smoke, "of course, the kid's gotta take a lie-detector test."

A lie-detector test! Sherry rolled her eyes and turned to Belinda for a supportive nod, and Belinda complied. "We could scare him off," she protested quickly. "We could lose him."

"We could look like idiots, Sherry, if this is bullshit."

"We could verify everything he says." Sherry hadn't expected to hear Belinda's voice, but now it filled the room with unusual assertiveness. "He says he killed some guy behind El Pub on January fifth, and we check to see if the police found a body behind El Pub on January fifth. He says he shot the guy in the neck. We call the medical examiner and make sure the guy was shot in the neck. He says he was paid twenty-five hundred bucks. We don't know, but we do know he has no other job, his dad is a bricklayer, and somehow he still manages to own a brand-new Camaro."

"It's not enough," Jack said. "Really, Belinda, I'm surprised at you. Look, I want the story to be true. I *love* it. Baby Lips! Shit! But we got to get the kid a lie-detector first. It's just a formality. It'll take two hours. But it's got to be done."

Belinda started to say something again, but Sherry stopped her. She wanted to stick to the strategy, to act calm and detached. "I'll ask him. He might say yes," she said. "It might be okay. He wants to cooperate—"

"Which makes me think something," Jack interrupted her. He was pacing the office again after swooping down to pick up his cap and shoving it firmly onto his head. A moment of silence passed, and then he stopped by the window and looked at the crystalline bay, letting go a long, uncomfortable sigh. "Why is this kid really talking? I don't buy the phony-baloney answer he gave you. Does he want money from us?"

Sherry shook her head. "No, I believe him, Jack, I really do. It's like he said, he wants to start over again, make a new life for himself—that's a very *human* urge. I think something deeply psychological is going on in his head."

Jack snorted and let out a harsh laugh. He looked at her and smirked. "I can't wait to see that stripped across the top of the front page: *'deeply psychological.'* Don't give me that crap. Find out what the real reason is. And set up a lie-detector with Sherman Otis."

Otis kept the lights dim in his small, dingy office, and from where she sat in the corner, Sherry could barely see the expression on Manuel's face as Otis's assistant taped wires to the boy's right arm, hand, and neck. She could only guess what he was feeling, and she prayed it wasn't regret.

He had been relaxed and talkative on the way over, not even mentioning the test that lay ahead. It was just after three when she picked him up outside Lincoln High, and she was glad to see he was in a good mood despite the relentless downpour that had been drenching the city since morning. In fact, Manuel didn't even mention the weather, except to ask if she had a cloth to wipe off his new Gucci loafers. When she didn't, he shrugged and quickly changed the subject, cheerfully telling Sherry about the football game the day before and how his team had won on a last-minute touchdown pass. Afterward, he didn't tease her or complain when it took her three tries to parallel-park the Beemer in the alley behind Otis's office. All in all, he had been so typically—so predictably—*unthreatening* that Sherry had to wonder why Jack was all bent out of shape about her safety. Manuel should never be in control, he insisted. They could never again be alone together. If they went out to eat, the *Citizen* would plant someone in the restaurant. If they talked in the park, he'd plant someone there, someone with a kid, so Manuel wouldn't suspect. If they had to visit the scene of one of his hits, someone would tail them. Those were the new ground rules. Doesn't matter if he's lying or telling the truth, Jack had said, the kid is a psychopath. Drugs make people sick. Sherry could act nice to him, but she couldn't be his friend. She could not trust him.

But Sherry wasn't so sure. She would put up with Jack's rules, but she thought she could trust Manuel. Or at least she thought she could understand him. He was a very screwed-up kid who had lost his moral compass in a city with crime beckoning from every direction, but now he wanted to get back on the right path, to put his past behind him. What was wrong with that? And the fact was, Sherry thought, Manuel might be very dangerous with a gun and orders to shoot, but he simply was not a danger to her. He genuinely liked her—when they met at the park at lunchtime to confirm the trip to Sherman Otis's office, he had brought her a single red rose and a delicate gold bracelet with a tiny heart dangling from the middle. When she told him she couldn't accept the jewelry—company policy—he smiled sweetly and said he understood. No problem.

And now here he was, gladly taking a lie-detector test. In fact, he had been so eager to comply with her request that he had led the way up the staircase to Otis's office, taking two steps at a time. The door was locked, so he knocked politely, and they were let in by a young blond woman who wore thick square glasses. She introduced herself as Amy, Otis's assistant, and ushered them into the dank inner office. It was a small room, paneled with fake mahogany. The floor was covered with chipping brown-and-white linoleum.

Otis sat in the corner at an old metal desk. He rose when they walked into the room. He didn't introduce himself or extend his hand to Sherry; he simply jerked his head in a nod and then gestured for her to take a seat in the corner, next to a window with the shade pulled down. He pointed to a utilitarian wooden chair in the middle of the room for Manuel, and asked him to place his right arm on the table next to it.

Jack had warned her that Otis would act unfriendly, and she disliked him already. He was a tall, fleshy man, wearing brown polyester pants, a white shirt, and a stained brown tie. His eyes were small and shifty beneath faint eyebrows. He looked like a prison warden, and in fact, he was a former army man and a cop, eighteen years on the homicide squad in Allentown. He'd come to Miami to retire, but his move coincided with the sudden white-hot popularity of cocaine and Miami as its port of call in America. Now he worked seven days a week for a dozen of the city's best lawyers and, occasionally, for the *Citizen* and its competition. In seven years, he had built an impeccable reputation for being virtually foolproof, and one of his biggest fans was Jack Dougherty. He had told Sherry that Sherman Otis was the best lie man in the business. Never wrong.

Five minutes passed as Amy wired Manuel to a large metal box covered with red knobs, switches, and dials.

"How you doing?" Sherry asked him, to break the silence.

"No talking please," Otis said sternly, adjusting the paper roll emerging from one end of the machine.

Five more minutes passed, and finally the assistant nodded at Otis. He stood up and walked over to Manuel. "I want you to stare straight ahead at that"—he pointed to a rectangular white screen on the wall—"and to answer every question fully, please."

Manuel nodded, and Otis returned to his desk. He clicked on the lie-detector machine, and a low buzz filled the room, like static from a broken radio.

"State your name, please."

"Manuel. No last name to anybody but Sherry, that was the deal."

"State your address."

"No address neither."

"State your age."

"Sixteen."

"State your profession."

"I'm . . ." Manuel glanced quickly at Sherry, but he could only see her in outline, her legs crossed and head tilted. "I'm not employed currently."

"Do you go to school?"

"Yes. I go to Lincoln High."

"What is two plus two?"

"Four."

"Five minus three."

"Two."

Otis watched the needle on the machine before him bob up and down, etching a thin red line across white paper. Sherry thought she saw him frown slightly.

"What is the capital of the United States?"

"Washington, D.C."

"Where were you born?"

"Miami, Florida."

Now Sherry was sure she saw Otis frown.

"Where were you born?" he asked again.

"Miami." Manuel seemed fine. He continued to stare straight ahead at the white screen, motionless. She couldn't even see him breathing.

"Do you know Sherry Estabrook?"

"Yes."

"How did you meet Sherry Estabrook?"

"She came to my school to talk to the kids about drugs. I followed her into the parking lot."

"Have you told her a story about your involvement with a cocaine family in Miami and your part in several murders over the past two years?"

"Yes." Jack had briefed Otis on the phone so that he could develop questions for the lie-detector test. Sherry knew that Otis was skeptical going in. There was an edge in his voice; he sounded nasty, even angry.

"Do you have a police record?"

"No." This was something Belinda had already tried to check, but her moles wouldn't let her get into the juvenile files without some information in return. And she didn't want to ask Eladio for help.

"Have you ever been caught shoplifting?"

"No way."

"Yes or no, please," Otis said sternly.

"No."

"Where did you purchase your car?"

"My car?"

"Yes," Otis snapped, sounding impatient.

"At Bob Carullo's, out in Kendall."

Otis watched the needle bob back and forth. Amy stood up from her chair near the door and looked at the red line emerging from the machine. She sat down again and scribbled a few words in a small notebook.

"Is your father employed?"

"Yes. He works for a construction company. He's been doing it a long time."

"Are you a member of the Lincoln High football team?"

"No."

Sherry jerked forward in her seat—what was this? *Not* a member of the Lincoln Lions? Hadn't Manuel told her he was an All-American quarterback? It was such a great and ironic piece of color, in fact, she had been planning to stick it in the lead of the story.

"You informed Miss Estabrook that you were a varsity football player, true or false?" Otis asked, and for the first time, Sherry was grateful for his persistence. Manuel had better have a damn good explanation for this little macho fib, she thought, or else she had some serious backpedaling to do.

Manuel shifted uncomfortably in his seat, and Sherry thought she saw a trace of awkward embarrassment cross his face. "True," he said after a short pause. "Because I used to be. I'm not on the team anymore. I quit. But I made the team in September. You can ask anyone."

Sherry let go a long sigh of relief; she knew there had to be a logical reason for his version of the events. She wanted to hear more, and so, obviously, did Sherman Otis. He moved closer to the machine and scrutinized its readout closely as he asked the next question.

"Why did you quit the team?"

Manuel didn't miss a beat. "The coach was an idiot," he said. "Too many stupid rules."

"Too many rules?" Otis repeated tonelessly.

"I don't like rules," Manuel responded matter-of-factly, and Sherry felt a surge of delight. She could just picture the headline, perhaps not good enough for the front page but certainly sexy enough for the jump: TEENAGE KILLER DIDN'T LIKE RULES; PLAYED HIS OWN GAME FOR LOPEZ FAMILY. Wonderful, she thought, just wonderful. She looked at Otis for his reaction.

But there was nothing to see. Otis had stepped back from the machine and was now standing with his hands on his hips, his face lowered, as if he were critically considering a speck of dirt on the floor.

"You told Sherry Estabrook that you have been employed by

the Lopez family of Coral Gables for two years. Is that true?'' he asked.

"Yes."

"Please describe your affiliation with the Lopez family."

Manuel was silent, and for the first time he took his eyes off the white screen. He looked desperately at Sherry.

"I don't know."

He's balking, Sherry thought, he's freaking out. This asshole Otis is pushing him too hard; he's just a kid. And then it occurred to her—Manuel didn't know what "affiliation" meant. Why should he? He was just in high school. She wanted to blurt something out, to rephrase the question, to defend Manuel from Otis's doubt. I'm losing the story, she thought. He's killing my story.

"Please describe your affiliation with the Lopez family."

Still no answer.

Sherry couldn't stand it a moment longer; she leaned forward in her seat and addressed Manuel in a commiserative whisper.

"Manuel, he means, tell him about your *relationship* with the Lopez family," she said.

"No talking," Otis cut her off.

"He didn't understand you." Sherry glared at Otis, but he didn't meet her challenge. He'd lifted his gaze from the floor and fixed it on the machine.

"Okay, I get it now," Manuel said. Sherry could see him take a deep breath and make a fist out of his left hand. One foot began to tap the floor nervously.

"Okay, it started two years ago. I was at a party. I got invited by a guy I know from school. I didn't know the people throwing the party. But this friend brought me. I got into that crowd, okay? I went to a lot of their parties, and after one of the parties, a guy came up to me and asked me if I wanted to make money. He said I couldn't expect to keep coming to the parties forever unless I did some work."

"Please state the man's name," Otis interrupted.

"He's dead now."

"He's dead?" Otis asked.

"I had to kill him," Manuel answered. His foot wasn't tapping anymore. He stared straight ahead, expressionless, awaiting the next question.

"*I had to kill him.*" The statement, delivered in a prideful, almost cavalier tone of voice, knocked Sherry for a loop just when she thought everything was under control. Manuel had told her the story of his recruitment and induction into the Lopez family two times now without having mentioned this particular detail. For a moment, she wondered if she should be angry with him, or even doubt other parts of his story, especially after the little football-team glitch, but the concern quickly faded when she caught the look on Otis's face as he monitored the lie-detector readout—he was wearing a full-blown scowl now, conveying the kind of recrimination that could only mean Manuel was telling nothing but the truth.

Otis cleared his throat, took a deep breath, and continued with the questioning. "Please complete your account," he said. "When did this party occur?"

"I can't remember the date," Manuel replied, shrugging. "It was when I was in tenth grade, sometime in the fall, probably in October. Eddie was waiting for me after school in the parking lot.

"He asked me if I wanted to make some money, and I said sure. He said I had to kill somebody that night. He would give me a gun. It would be an easy hit. He would go with me, with some other guys.

"I thought he was joking," Manuel chuckled at the memory. "I said, 'No way, man!' So Eddie went like this"—Manuel held up his palms—"and he started to walk away, and then he turned around to me, and he told me it was five hundred bucks. So I said yes, okay. I could do it.

"That night I ate dinner at home with my mother and my sister. I don't remember where my father was. He was working late or something. I told my mother I was going to Blanca's. At eight o'clock, I walked to the corner, and Eddie picked me up. That's how we arranged it. So we drove to Sweetwater, I don't remember the exact address, but it was an apartment building. Two stories. The guy lived in back on the second floor.

"Eddie gave me a gun, a .32 suicide special, I think. It had a silencer on it, the real cheap kind made out of a plastic Coke bottle, you know? Anyway, he told me to go to the apartment, knock on the door, and give the code. The guy inside was expecting me. When he opened the door, I was supposed to shoot him quick and then get back to the car. He told me not to look at the guy. That puts a curse on the job.

"Okay, so I was shaking and everything." Manuel licked his

lips and paused to catch his breath. "I wanted Eddie to come with me, but he said he had to stay with the car so we could get away fast in case someone called the cops. I really wanted him with me, but he said no. He called me a *muchacha* for being scared.

"So I went to the apartment, and I knocked on the door. Believe it or not, the guy didn't ask for a code or nothing. He just opened the door, and I shot him in the chest. It didn't make any noise, really. Those cheap silencers work good. It sounded like a plug popping or something. But there was blood everywhere! I guess I hit a vein or something. My shirt got all splattered with the shit.

"For a second, I just stood there and I looked at the guy. He fell right in the doorway, and he was sort of still twitching, you know, like this." Manuel jerked his body slightly, as if he had just touched a spark of static electricity. "Then all of a sudden, he stopped moving and his eyes rolled back, and I thought, Okay, good, he's dead. And then I tried to push him into the apartment with my foot so I could close the door, but he wouldn't budge. He weighed a ton or something. I kept pushing him with my foot, but he's just lying there." Manuel stopped for a moment and frowned briefly. "The worst part was, his blood got all over my sneakers, and I'm thinking, Shit, my mother paid *sixty* bucks for these. How am I gonna hide this from her?

"So after a minute, I just said forget it, and I stuck the gun in a paper bag, like I seen guys on TV, and I run back to the car. I'm not even in the door when Eddie takes off.

"He asks me if I did it, and I say yeah. Afterward we went to McDonald's. Before we go in, Eddie tells me there's a clean shirt for me in the backseat, so I put it on. When we get inside, he asks me if I'm sure the guy is dead. And I said, yeah, I'm sure. And then, I guess, I started to laugh, and then he started to laugh, and the two of us were sitting there laughing our heads off for a while. It was funny, you know, it was so easy. I never knew it would be so easy."

Manuel shrugged, then went on.

"Okay, so after the hit, Eddie drove me home and he gave me the money and he told me not to tell anyone, not even Blanca, or I would be dead. He told me like he was a friend, not like he was trying to scare me or nothing. He just wanted me to know the way things worked. He was a good guy."

Another small shrug.

"And so that was it. I went inside, threw out my sneakers in a plastic bag, and went to bed."

Manuel turned to face Otis and nodded in a firm, businesslike way. The story was over.

"Is the story you've just recounted the truth? Yes or no?" Otis asked.

"Yes."

"That will be all," Otis said, snapping off the machine.

 That night Belinda went out to dinner with Eladio again. This time he picked her up in his car, a clunky, clean American sedan with a mother-of-pearl cross dangling from the rearview mirror and Jesus on the dash. He'd made reservations at a steak place on Hallandale Beach, and he carried a roll of bills in his pocket so Belinda could order whatever she liked.

Eladio was dressed up for the occasion: pleated white pants and an embroidered *guayabera*. He didn't go on many dates. His aunt Nerida was always trying to fix him up. He was twenty-three, she said, it was time to get married and start a family. But the truth was that the last time he really liked a girl was in high school, when he had a desperate crush on Alicia Barreda. When he passed her in the hall at St. Ignacius, he practically went blind from longing. Even in her drab gray-and-green uniform, she was too beautiful; he thought she looked like an angel, unsoiled and forgiving. He dreamed about her every night for two years. They would have lots of children together—five boys and a girl, for her. Someday he would be the chief of police, and they could move out of Little Havana to Coral Gables, to a sprawling ranch house with a trimmed lawn and an expensive turquoise swimming pool.

In reality, Eladio never spoke to Alicia, not one word, until the night his older brother, Tommy, Jr., brought her home for dinner, and even then he barely was able to ask her to pass the beans. She smiled at him so sweetly he was sure she could read his mind.

She finally did kiss him six months later, softly on the cheek like a whisper from heaven, to thank him for his wedding gift. That June, she married his brother, and from that day on Eladio forced himself at night, tangled in sweaty sheets, not to think of her again.

The years passed, the pain eased. Alicia and Tommy had two children. She looked different to Eladio now; he thought that maybe he had stopped loving her. But he hadn't felt intoxicated by a woman until he saw Belinda that morning at the reporter's house in Coconut Grove. The moment she walked in the door, he fell into her eyes. They were golden.

That night before he called her, his body tingled with anxiety. She was a *gringa*—would she laugh at him, reject him outright for his lilting English and shiny black hair? She said she was from nowhere. Would she stay in Miami long enough for him to show her love? He dialed the number despite the fear in his veins, thinking of the sad tenderness in her voice, of her delicate fingers, of her eyes.

So she had said yes, dinner that night would be wonderful, and there was something in the way she answered that made him believe she was expecting his call. Had she felt it, too, or was he dreaming again before he should be?

He loved every second of that first night, the long stroll down Calle Ocho, the dinner of secrets, the walk on the moonlit beach afterward. Her life was almost too amazing for him to comprehend all at once, too rich with places and feelings, and too filled with tragedy. He felt small next to her, dwarfed by her suffering and by her survival. But she had sensed that. She told him not to make too much of her life. Everything that happened to her, she said, happened by accident.

He told her of his life. It had started in Miami, and would probably end there, too. He was born one year after his parents arrived in the city from magical Cuba, running scared and bitter from that madman Castro. The grief—his mother cried for years! She and her husband left behind everything: their new Ford, her satin wedding dress, their sunny apartment in Havana with eight, yes, eight, rooms, and all the friends and relatives who could not bear to say farewell themselves.

Belinda leaned close to him to hear his words. Her eyes were glistening with sympathy. She had seen refugees, many of them, in Addis Ababa and Niamey, and made up their stories in her head. The men walked the streets like zombies; the women peered from the windows of their clay-and-tin shacks, faces glazed with remembrance.

Tell me more, she said to Eladio.

He was born at home, in his parents' bedroom, with Aunt Lily and Aunt Maria there to help his mother through the pain and the sweat. It was a long labor—twenty-six hours. Dr. Lantal arrived just before he did. He was a fine man, a surgeon in Havana who gave up good money to tend the exiles in Miami, and though many could not pay him, still he came in the middle of the night.

He was killed last year when two gangs of drug runners chose to settle their debts on his block. So many shots punctured the air, everyone said, it sounded like a war zone. One lady who saw it all from her window told the police that the doctor, wearing an apron and carrying a big wooden stirring spoon, had dashed from the kitchen of his tiny house to the street, shouting, "Enough! Enough! Stop the killing!" He was struck in the temple, and he died that night, in a hospital. Eladio had been a pallbearer at the funeral.

Belinda said she remembered the story. The *Citizen* had given it big play—family doctor making chicken soup for a patient with pneumonia murdered while trying single-handedly to stop a cocaine shoot-out. She was almost certain that Sherry had written the story, but she didn't want to ask Eladio about that now. She wanted only to hear his voice, telling her about his life with an intimacy she had not shared since Abdullah left her.

And so, he went on, he was raised in Little Havana, in a one-story house with six cramped rooms. His father managed a picture-framing shop near Brickell Avenue, it was nothing fancy, but it had a good reputation and he made a decent living. His mother bore one more child after him, a daughter named Lucille. She's eighteen now, Eladio told Belinda. She got married last year and had a baby six months later. His mother and Aunt Lily closed themselves in Lucy's old bedroom and cried a week. When they emerged, they went straight to the kitchen and cooked huge pots of picadillo and beans, and brought them to Lucille's apartment. His mother stayed for two months.

They both laughed at this story. Mothers! Belinda quoted a favorite writer: "Children begin by loving their parents; as they

grow older, they judge them; sometimes they forgive them."
Eladio nodded solemnly. He understood, but knew that the words
must have meant more to her.

He paid the bill, and they drove to the beach on Key Biscayne
for a walk in the neon glow of a purplish autumn moon.

He had been a quiet kid, Eladio told her there, and he suspected that most people assumed he wasn't thinking much. But
just the opposite was true. He thought too much—all the time—
it drove him crazy sometimes! He would be sitting in class, and
his mind would be churning with crazy ideas. He would imagine
sneaking back to Cuba aboard an old boat, disguised as a fisher-
man, and making his way to Havana through the jungle and
across many villages, and finally finding Castro and killing him—
slitting his throat with a sugarcane knife! He would fantasize
about a great celebration exploding in the streets of Miami: huge
floats covered with roses and loud Cuban music and wild dancing.
He could see the tears of joy running down his mother's face.

Belinda had stopped walking then; hearing him say these
words filled her with sorrow. She told him how she, too, often
dreamed of making her mother happy again, but they were impossible, frustrating dreams. A hundred times a day, she would relive
that cloudy Thanksgiving afternoon when a lone blast pulverized
the fragile silence of her home, and she ran to the garage to find
her father lying in a pool of sticky crimson blood. "Sometimes I
dream that I open the door, and he is standing there smiling
innocently, and he asks me what the matter is, as if there was no
shot at all, as if I were hearing things, like some kind of loon,"
Belinda told Eladio. "And sometimes I dream that the bullet
missed his brain, and he is alive, and he tells me that he loves me
as I hold his head in my lap, and we get him to the hospital before
it's too late." She was looking frantically into Eladio's black eyes
glowing in the moon's hazy shadow.

"But then, even when I'm dreaming, I know it's just a dream.
I can smell the gunpowder so strongly it stings my eyes."

Eladio wanted to embrace Belinda then, to show her that he
would share the memory and the anguish—he would take it from
her, set her free. He pulled her to his chest and hugged her tight.
It only lasted a minute, and when he let go, they started walking
again, holding hands, toward the car for the ride home.

They were on the highway headed south when Eladio decided to break the silence—it hadn't been uncomfortable, only

too somber for such a wonderful night—with a lighthearted account of his day. He had rescued two Kansas City tourists from the clutches of a confidence man peddling promises on Flagler Street and then helped an old lady coax her cat out of a sewer pipe. Belinda twisted sideways in the car seat while he happily prattled away. She was watching him closely, not really listening, trying to decide if she should tell him about Manuel and the lie-detector test. Sherry had told her not to—"I forbid it! God, Belinda!" she had practically screamed in the newsroom an hour earlier. "He's a cop, he'll have to tell Homicide. If he doesn't, he'll get screwed. You're putting him in a terrible position." Belinda thought about Sherry's words and decided she was probably right. It would be terrible. Eladio would have to keep a terrible secret. But it would only be for a few days, until the story ran. No one would have to know that he didn't report the murders right away. She would deny ever telling him. She would claim they'd never met.

He would *want* to know, she thought, watching Eladio as he carefully steered the car down the highway, keeping it just under the speed limit. That was the most important thing—Eladio would want to know about something that mattered so much to her. How could she not tell him?

"I had a very interesting day myself," she began softly. And then Belinda started at the beginning.

19 The newsroom was quiet. It was eight o'clock; most reporters had wrapped it up and headed for the Bomb Shelter. Sherry sat alone at her desk, reading an old copy of *The Economist* she found in the mail-room garbage pail. Belinda had left for her date with Eladio at seven.

Jack was pacing back and forth in his small office, occasionally looking out the window at the bay, hands on his hips except when he plucked the cigarette from his mouth to tap the cinders in an ashtray shaped like a flamingo.

They were waiting for Sherman Otis to call.

Sherry skimmed through an article on gun control. Gun control—shit! She laughed wryly, thinking of Manuel and his first ten-buck .32 with the Coke-bottle silencer. She had dropped him off at the park a few hours ago. He was in a buoyant mood, confident about the outcome of Otis's analysis of the thin red line that had measured his words in the dingy office above the blood-testing lab. "Don't worry," he had said to Sherry lightheartedly. He squeezed her hand, got out of the car, and waved good-bye. "See you tomorrow."

The memory irked her—his parting words had been so strange. "Wear red," he had told her almost as an afterthought, leaning jauntily through the passenger-side window. "You look pretty in red."

She wasn't accustomed to men telling her what to wear; in fact, she realized now, no man had ever tried. Once before church, when she was about thirteen, her father suggested she wear a pair of white gloves he had given her as a birthday gift. She had refused, knowing that his secretary had selected them, which she told him. And Charles had never commented on her clothing, except for an occasional complaint that she wore too much black.

Did Brazil ever tell her to wear red? Did he ever tell her she was pretty, for that matter? Did he ever give her a single red rose? Or a bracelet with a tiny gold heart? Sherry looked up from the magazine and searched for Brazil at the photo desk across the newsroom, but he had already gone home to Jeanie and the kid. Why were American men so allergic to romantic gestures? she wondered. Here was Manuel, just a teenager, for Christ's sake, behaving like Don Juan—unembarrassed! No wonder Cuban women always looked so smug.

Suddenly, Sherry saw Jack waving excitedly for her to come to his office. He held the phone to his ear. Otis had finally called. She jumped out of her chair, slamming her knee on the corner of an open drawer. For a split second, she keeled over in pain—shit, the same damn knee as that morning! She pressed her fingers against the bruise, and then limped across the newsroom as fast as she could without screaming.

When she made it to Jack's office, he was behind his desk, furiously scribbling notes on a piece of yellow paper. She tried to read the words upside down, but she had never learned short-hand. That was something only the veterans still used.

Jack motioned for her to sit down. He wasn't saying much; Otis was doing all the talking. After a minute, Jack looked up at Sherry and nodded, a huge conspiratorial smile breaking across his face. "Let me tell Sherry," he said.

Jack covered the mouthpiece with one hand. "You got a live one," he said.

"What? What—is he telling the truth?" She wanted to hear it straight.

"Here, talk to Otis," Jack answered, tugging a cigarette out of one of the packs on his desk. He handed her the phone.

"Mr. Otis, this is Sherry."

"Yes, hello," he said curtly.

"Can you tell me about the results?"

"Well, as I just told Jack, the boy you brought to the office today is, by and large, telling the truth."

Sherry felt a rocket take off in her chest. I knew it, she thought, I knew it from the first words out of his mouth. The story is alive—it's alive!—and it's mine to run with. She stood up and carried the phone to the window. She didn't want Jack watching her too closely. There was nothing he hated more than emotional reporters, and she was afraid he might catch the way her fingertips had started to tremble.

Sherry took a deep breath. "So, he's telling the truth?" she asked Otis to be sure, trying desperately to sound nonplussed.

"By and large."

She lowered her voice, afraid Jack might detect the irritation in her tone. "What exactly does 'by and large' mean?" she demanded.

"My professional judgment is that the majority of what the boy says is true. I also believe there may be some critical parts of his testimony—of his account, rather—that may be inaccurate or that he may be omitting for some reason. For instance, I suspect he is not being honest about his motives for speaking with you, but this is just a suspicion. I'm a professional lie-detector analyst, not a psychiatrist," Otis said, speaking slowly and unemotionally, as if reading from a prepared text. "In addition, Miss Estabrook, the manner in which your subject described his acts of violence also gives me cause for concern, but I can't exactly state why. Perhaps he is exaggerating them, or then again, perhaps he is understating them. I'm not sure. I suppose it is up to you to determine what the truth is."

"Yes, I suppose it is," Sherry said. She was ready to end the conversation. Sherman Otis had said what was necessary; now it was time to forget the whole unpleasant encounter in his office and get on with the story. "Well, thank you, Mr. Otis," she said loudly enough for Jack to hear.

"One more thing—" Otis cut off her hasty farewell.

"Yes?"

"I feel it is my professional responsibility to tell you to be extremely careful around this individual. He has a pathological mind," he said, sounding to Sherry like a cranky junior high school teacher lecturing a group of tardy students. "He is a dangerous human being. He is not to be trusted."

"Thank you," Sherry said. It was her turn to be curt. Otis was talking to her as if she were some kind of cub reporter, two days out of journalism school. "I can assure you I have the situation under control." She handed the phone back to Jack.

"Thanks, Sherman," she heard him say familiarly, as if he sensed a kindred spirit in the no-nonsense man on the other end of the line. "I want you to know, we'll probably stick your opinion in the story someplace. Okay? Great. Thanks, old man. All right. My love to Greta and the kids. Yeah. Okay. So long."

He hung up and turned to Sherry. The huge smile was gone now, replaced with a look of frigid seriousness, the kind of expression Sherry recognized from his black moods. "Where's Belinda?" he asked. He sounded edgy, ready to erupt with energy.

"She had a prior engagement, something she couldn't get out of," Sherry answered quickly. She had prepared this response earlier, while waiting for Otis's phone call.

Jack frowned. This was screwing up his plans. He wanted to talk about the story tonight, to start plotting the reporting that needed to be done, the details that had to be uncovered, the questions that had to be asked, and asked again. The story was going to be huge work—they had to start right away. He was going to throw every resource the *Citizen* could spare on this one—eight reporters, four photographers, three editors, plus him. They all might not get much sleep for the next few weeks. Besides Estabrook's profile, there had to be sidebars, four or five of them at least, about serial murderers, about the Lopez family, about the Miami cops and how they couldn't catch a goldfish in a tank if you handed them a net. He'd get someone to do a workup on how cocaine gets from the fields of Bolivia to the streets of

Miami, and how a hit man like Manuel fits into the scheme. He needed someone to do a big, scary, research-heavy piece on kids who kill. Maybe they'd run the whole thing as a pullout section, he thought for a second, and then instantly canned the idea. No, he decided, this was a package for the front page if there ever was one.

"We gotta get Belinda in here, now," Jack barked, but Sherry shook her head. "It can't be done," she said. Her voice pleaded: Please don't ask for details. It worked. Jack thought of Belinda's father, the whole mess that Thanksgiving, and he backed off. Forget it, he thought. Shit, they'd start in the morning.

"Both of you, in here, eight A.M.," he said. "And don't talk to anyone about this. Don't go blabbing it around the newsroom, or next thing you know, we're going to have the fucking D.A. all over our butts. And if you gotta tell that boyfriend of yours, please tell him to be discreet, though I'm not sure he knows the meaning of the word." Jack stopped to stick another cigarette in his mouth. He was expecting Sherry to say something, but she sat in front of him, silent, her mouth slightly open and her eyes unblinking, stuck in a look of quiet shock. She was thinking of how much her life had changed in the past two days, and how long she'd been waiting for exactly this, an event that would make sure it was never the same again. After a moment, she shook her head, as if to wake herself from a trance.

"Yes, Jack," she said. She thought maybe she was answering a question he had asked a few minutes ago.

"Go home," he replied. He wanted to be pissed-off at her for losing her cool and going numb, but he knew what she was thinking. This kid she had found—he was a cold-blooded assassin, for crying out loud—and now she was going to have to spend countless hours alone with him, ask him hundreds of questions with ugly answers, and then get it all down on paper like a fucking poet. It was enough to scare a girl to death. He didn't want to, but he understood what she was going through.

"Go home, Sherry," he said again. "Get some sleep for both of us."

20

But Sherry couldn't sleep; she'd never felt more awake in her life. Suddenly, she was dying to get outside, to run around, to shout out loud, to share her pumped-up glee with someone who would share it back. She dashed into the newsroom and flew over to her desk. Before she had time to stop herself, she picked up the phone and dialed a number she knew by heart but had never called before. Brazil at home.

It only rang once, then:

"Hey, there. Brackett residence." The voice at the other end was high-pitched and twangy, almost southern in its inflection but more delicate than that—damn it all, Sherry thought, this had to be Jeanie. In the background, she could hear the unmistakable tenor of Brazil's belly laugh and a baby delightedly squealing in response.

"Hello? Brackett residence," Jeanie tried again when Sherry was too stunned to answer. "Hey, you two, stop that screaming, I can't hear nothing. Hush it up!"

For an instant, Sherry considered slamming down the phone, but the overwhelming need to talk to Brazil stopped her. She cleared her throat and affected an officious voice, almost British in its clip. "Yes, hello," she said, "I'd like to speak with John Brackett, please. It's the newsroom calling."

"Who?" Jeanie asked. The happy squealing in the background was louder now, with Brazil mooing like a cow, and then, for some reason, shouting out the alphabet in a booming voice. "Sorry, we got a little game going here, I can barely hear myself chew gum," Jeanie apologized with a light laugh. "You want Brazil, right?"

"Right," Sherry snapped. "Yes, I need to talk to Brazil right away."

A moment later, he was on.

"Better be damn good!" he exclaimed as hello. "I told you assholes I'm not working tonight. It's my son's birthday."

Sherry grimaced. He hadn't told her. "Brazil," she whispered. "It's me."

No response, save a short, frustrated sigh. "What is it?" he asked tonelessly.

"I have to see you," Sherry said. "We got the lie-detector test back from Otis, and—"

"No go, *amigo*," he cut her off, and Sherry noticed the laughing in the background had stopped. In her mind's eye, she pictured Jeanie holding the baby on her hip, glaring at Brazil accusingly. "Can't be done," he said. "I'm not working tonight. I got a commitment here at home."

"Oh, come on, Brazil—" Sherry cried.

But the phone was already dead, and inside the cozy house on Tall Palm Lane, the laughing began again and Brazil leapt toward his son, pulled him into a hug, and started nibbling his neck with all the love he could muster. He only looked up for a second when Jeanie left the room. He knew he didn't have to worry. She didn't get mad about Sherry. At least that's what she always told him.

And it was the truth. There wasn't much Jeanie cared about these days. Life was good, she told herself, a person could fuck it up with too much worrying.

This was a new philosophy for her. It was her first philosophy, really, she decided. Until recently, she'd just spent her life getting by and getting pissed-off. Now that everything was in place—her being married to Brazil and all—there was nothing to worry about. She had what she wanted. It wasn't a regular marriage, but she had known for a long time that she would never have a regular marriage. How could she? She was lucky to be married at all, to have a father for the kid and a place to live for both of them. There was food in the fridge, and the baby had a doctor. She wouldn't have to go to the emergency room with all the other poor people if he ever looked sick, the way she'd had to with the first baby, before he died.

It killed Jeanie, it really did, that her first baby was buried so far away, in Boise. She kept a picture of his snow-covered little granite gravestone in her top dresser drawer. She saw it every morning when she pulled out her underwear. That was the only time of the day she allowed herself to feel sad. The rest of the day, if she ever felt pissed-off or bored, she would stop dead, take a deep breath, and try to remember how much luck she finally had. And it had all come care of Brazil.

They had met three years ago. She was twenty then, a waitress at the last diner before the road pierces the swampy darkness of the Everglades. Brazil had stopped in for a coffee, on his way to a photo assignment in Tampa, some murder trial. They got to talking, and he took her number. She thought she would never hear from him again, but he called a few weeks later and then drove out and took her for a drink at the Mosquito Bite Bar in Sweetwater.

It was easy to talk to him; he was so talkative back. She had never met a man like that, one who just said whatever he was thinking. So after she had a few shots of Jack in her, Jeanie started telling Brazil the story of her life. It was pretty pathetic, she warned him before she started, but he didn't seem to care.

It began in Lost Corners, Wyoming, a tiny little nothing of a town, one zillion miles from anywhere, not even close to Casper. Her mother died when she was two from some kind of cancer all through her body—Jeanie didn't even remember what her face looked like, so she grew up imagining that her mother looked like Doris Day.

Her father was the town drunk; she had to live with that. The kids in school kept pretty much away from her, except the horny boys, of course. She got straight D's—that was something she couldn't do anything about, she figured, she was born stupid. She didn't talk much to anyone. She'd go to school, come home, clean up the trailer, best she could. It always smelled like puke because of her father. Then she'd watch TV, and at five or so the old man would wander in, and she would put together some kind of dinner for him before he went out again.

When she was sixteen, she got pregnant. It was bound to happen. Her father drove her to Cheyenne for an abortion. She didn't know who the father was; it could have been her own. He knocked her around a few times when he was on a bad drunk, but he never touched her again after the operation. Guess he got scared, and it was expensive. Cost him a hundred-fifty bucks. There was no point finishing high school after that, Jeanie told Brazil. What was it going to do for her? So she packed her bags and headed for Boise—one of her boyfriends told her there were a lot of jobs there for people like them. And he was right. It took her an hour to find a job at a sub shop and a cheap motel to live in one block away. The shop was called Herman's, for the owner, and there was a nice man who worked there behind the counter as a short-order cook. His name was Ralph, a black guy. He was always very polite to her, never made lewd comments or tried to put his hands all over her when she had to squeeze by him to get the silverware. After work, he would walk her back to the motel, and they would make small talk about the weather. One day, he told her he was from Atlanta. He left the city when his wife died. She never did find out why he came to Boise. But there he was, like her, and she really felt like they had something in common, something sort of deep. So she didn't mind one night when he kissed her. She was so damn lonely she invited him upstairs, and he made love to her in her creaky, narrow bed. She thought it was nice because he kissed her afterward. She liked that.

A few weeks later, she was waiting on two guys, they were construction workers from the looks of them, and suddenly she had to run behind the store and vomit. She knew what that meant from Lost Corners. Another baby was in her stomach.

She was going to tell Ralph, but something inside told her not to. She didn't want him to hate her, he was too nice a man, and she wanted to make love to him again, at least a few more times. But it didn't work out that way. A few mornings later at work, she had to vomit again. She ran out behind the shop and threw up all over the garbage pails. Then she walked inside, hung up her apron, and told Herman that she quit. She ran back to the motel, packed her one bag, and headed for the highway. She was going to hitch to Fort Lauderdale. She'd heard from another waitress that you could make big tips there during spring break. All the rich college kids just threw money away. And it never rained.

She was only sticking out her thumb for ten minutes when a trucker stopped for her. He was headed for Shreveport, and he made it sound like a nice place, so she decided to give it a try. It was a few weeks before spring break anyway.

Jeanie asked the driver to let her out at the first truck stop she spotted after the ENTERING SHREVEPORT sign. She figured there might be a job for her there, and she was right. The owner was real happy to have her; he even let her stay with him and his wife until she found a place to live. She thought maybe things were finally going to work out for her.

So Jeanie worked at the Stop-on-By, and everything was just
fine for a while. She threw up almost every morning, but she was
getting used to it. The truckers gave her pretty good tips, and
she was saving up to rent a real apartment—no more motels, she
decided. After a few weeks, she set out to find a place, and she
ended up with a room in a rickety Victorian house on a bus route
that ran right by the Stop-on-By. She thought the other people in
the house seemed nice enough. There were three guys, two of
them were named Joey, and the other was named Joe-Bob; she
liked that because it sounded so southern. And there was a girl
who lived in the house, too, Valerie. She said she was a cleaning
lady in the city.

Because Jeanie worked nights, it took a while before she realized that they were all junkies; that is, they shot heroin into their
veins all the time, in the morning before work and at lunchtime
and at the dinner table after work and in front of the TV at night.
Jeanie liked to smoke dope every now and then, but she had
never stuck a needle into her own arm. The thought scared her.
She was afraid it would hurt.

One day Jeanie called in sick because she was feeling so
shitty—she figured she was about six months along by that time—
and Valerie came into her room. She was really pretty, Jeanie
thought, so skinny and so foreign-looking with high cheekbones
and slanted green eyes. She sat on the bed next to Jeanie, and
then, without even asking, she started to run her fingers through
Jeanie's hair and rub her shoulders slowly, all the while humming
to herself and sometimes calling Jeanie her "poor baby." After a
while, she got up and glided out of the room, and came back a
minute later with a piece of yellow rubber tubing and a syringe.
She softly told Jeanie that she was going to make her feel all better,
and then she shot her up.

It didn't take long for Jeanie to fall in love with Valerie and
her China White. All night at work, she'd fantasize about being
at home with Val and the boys and the secret they called their
"medicine." But pretty soon she was running out of money—the
Stop-on-By just didn't pay enough, even when she was especially
nice to the truckers to get big tips. So she started letting them fuck
her, usually in the cabs of their trucks, out in the parking lot. It
only took a minute, and she never even had to ask for money
afterward. Usually, they'd just slip her a ten, and she'd stick it in
her apron pocket without a word.

She went into labor Halloween night. She had just served some trucker lemon-meringue pie when she keeled over behind the counter. One of the other waitresses drove her to the hospital. Before they wheeled her into the delivery room, she phoned Valerie and told her she was about to have the baby. "Don't tell them about us," Valerie had cried out in response. She sounded totally fucked-up and paranoid. "Don't tell them about us, or they're going to send the cops to arrest us." Jeanie told her not to worry. She wondered when she and the boys were going to come to the hospital.

The baby was born addicted. Jeanie hadn't counted on that. So the hospital started them both on methadone and kept them in a dingy ward for junkies for a few weeks. Every once in a while, a social worker would stop by her bed and ask how she was doing. Jeanie told him she was fine; she just had to get back with her family. But when she was finally strong enough to leave the hospital and take the bus to the Victorian house, Valerie and the Joeys and Joe-Bob were gone. The place was empty, except for a couple of spent syringes in the kitchen. Jeanie put the baby down on the floor near the refrigerator and cried for three hours. Then she went upstairs and packed her bag and headed for the highway.

She was hoping to make it all the way to Fort Lauderdale this time, but she only got as far as Daytona Beach. No one wanted to pick up a hitchhiker with a baby. Sure as hell wasn't going to be a blow-job in the deal.

It was hot as a furnace in Daytona, and Jeanie didn't have enough money to get a motel room, so she walked the streets until she found an abandoned house in the black part of town. She laid newspapers and rags down on the floor of one room on the second floor, and that's where she and the baby, Ralph Junior, slept.

God, how she loved that baby! He was so tiny and mocha-colored, and he had her eyes. When she looked into them, it was like staring at herself, but so, so much more beautiful it made her chest hurt. He was a real quiet baby, too. He almost never cried. He just loved to watch her, and he loved to stick his fingers in his mouth, all five of them at a time sometimes. The only thing that worried her was his appetite—he didn't like to eat very much, which was lucky because her boobs didn't seem to make very much milk. And she wondered when he was going to learn to smile.

Of course, Daytona didn't turn out as she'd dreamed. It was hard to find work when she was carrying a baby around, and pretty soon she was getting desperate. So she decided to look for work and food alone. During the day, she would stick the baby in a cardboard box, wrapped in a flannel shirt she found in a garbage pail, and hit the streets. Still no one seemed to want her, so she had to turn tricks on the beach just to make enough money for a little bit of food and Huggies.

One day when she got home from the beach, she found Ralph Junior all covered with his own puke and flies. His soft brown skin had turned swampy yellow, and his eyes wouldn't open, even when Jeanie screamed out his name and desperately jiggled him up and down. She tried to force her breast into his tiny mouth, but the baby just lay there, looking like a tiny mummy. Finally, she wrapped him up in the shirt and ran into the street. She tried flagging down cars to take her to the hospital, but no one would stop. She was weeping, crying out, begging people to help her, but no one would even look her in the eye. So she started to run, holding Ralph Junior tight to her chest. She knew the hospital was near the highway, so she ran in that direction, but no hospital appeared. Then she ran in the opposite direction for a few blocks. She was covered with sweat, and her face was red with tears and hatred and grief. Finally, a cop drove by, and she screamed out at him. When he stopped, she climbed in the front seat and dropped the baby between them. "Save him," she cried.

There was a long wait at the hospital, or at least it seemed like a long time before a doctor finally made his way into the tiny curtained room where Jeanie sat on the examining table, Ralph Junior lying motionless in her lap. The doctor—he was so young that Jeanie hoped he knew what to do—barely said a word to her. He placed a stethoscope on the baby's chest and then stuck a thermometer up his tiny butt. When he pulled it out and read its verdict, he shook his head and rolled his eyes. "How long has it been this way?" he asked Jeanie, pointing at the infant. "Just today," she answered, swamped with guilt. He left the room, and a few minutes later a nurse came in and gave Ralph Junior a huge shot in his inner thigh. He didn't even twitch. "Your baby has an infection," she told Jeanie in a slow, obnoxious voice, as if she were talking to a foreigner. "You have to give him medicine every day. Can you remember to do that?" Jeanie nodded. "Can you pay for some pills?" the nurse asked matter-of-factly. Jeanie shook her head no; she was crying again; the hot tears rolled down her cheeks and fell onto her jeans. The nurse left, and a few minutes later another nurse came back with a small bottle. "This is penicillin," she said. "Take this dropper and fill it halfway and squeeze it under the baby's tongue twice a day. Do you understand? One dropper, twice a day, morning and night. You have to come back in a few days so we can look at him again." She pulled the curtain back and looked accusingly at Jeanie. "Don't forget," she said, and then she walked away.

As soon as Jeanie got outside, into the suffocating heat of Daytona Beach, she knew what she had to do. She had to get back to Boise, back to Ralph at the sub shop. He would take her in his arms and kiss her on the lips, and he would hug his little son, and surround them both with hope and love. She had been wrong to run off. Now she had to get back.

Suddenly, Jeanie felt overwhelmed by exhaustion. She slumped down on the seawall. Why was she so tired, especially now when she needed all her strength? She was hungry and hot and incredibly tired. She had to get back to Boise before she died. She needed money fast. But there was no way. She could barely move; just holding up her head wore her out. She thought of Ralph Junior, of how much he needed her, and she thought of his daddy and the lovely way he used to caress her back. God protect me, she prayed to no one in particular. I'm gonna have to hitch.

It was dusk when she finally reached the highway. She was walking slowly, rocking Ralph Junior in her arms, cooing to him, watching him closely for signs of life. He lay heavy next to her breast, his eyes still shut fast, his tiny face covered with a patina of dewy sweat. Jeanie stuck out her thumb.

Her first ride came an hour later. It was an old lady in a Buick, heading for Atlanta. Jeanie took this as a good sign. She told the woman that the baby's daddy was from Atlanta, but they didn't talk much after that. She could tell the woman didn't approve of her: a dirty white girl traipsing across the country with a sickly half-black baby. What was this world coming to?

Outside Atlanta she got a ride all the way to St. Louis. Two hippies picked her up, a guy and a girl, and the two of them sang Grateful Dead songs almost the whole time, sang them just like that, without a radio or anything.

She was more exhausted than ever when they reached the city, and she was getting really scared about Ralph Junior. His skin was still yellow, and he wouldn't take her milk, no matter how much she begged him. She'd given his medicine twice, but both times his little pink tongue expelled it. His fuzzy hair was soaked with sweat, but his palms and the soles of his feet were dry as paper. He smelled terrible; she hadn't changed his diaper since the trip began, and she began to think that maybe his own shit was making him sicker.

She slept by the side of the road for a few hours after the hippies let her off, and at daybreak she stumbled into a truck-stop rest room and puked. This time she knew she wasn't pregnant, just sick enough to drop dead. Barely anything came out—all she'd eaten for days was a hamburger roll covered with ketchup that she'd found by the side of the highway near Atlanta and some potato chips and Tab that the hippies had offered her. Ralph Junior was looking terrible, too. She wasn't even sure he was still breathing. Jeanie put her ear to his lips and listened for a hint of life. She heard nothing. Time was running out.

She dragged herself to the highway and stuck out her thumb. Pretty soon, she felt rain come splattering down and she wrapped the flannel shirt tighter around Ralph Junior. Hours passed; night came. She stared desperately into the passing headlights. Finally, when Jeanie thought she could stand up no longer, a truck slowed and then pulled over. She climbed into the cab and asked the driver where he was going. "Boise," he said. She placed the baby on the seat next to her, stuck the medicine dropper under his tongue, and then leaned over and fell into a dark, comatose sleep. She woke only three times during the rest of the journey, and then only briefly, to eat the driver's leftovers and force medicine into Ralph Junior's mouth. But the baby never seemed to swallow it, no matter how desperately she pleaded.

It was dawn when they hit the city, and Jeanie was so fast asleep that the driver had to shake hard to rouse her. Finally, Jeanie came to, unfolding her body slowly; she was full of pain. The sunlight stung her eyes, but she definitely recognized the intersection where the truck had stopped. The sub shop was only a few blocks away! Thank you, she thought, thank you, God!

When did she notice the smell? Was it right then, as she was thanking God for getting her home? She'd never really know. Suddenly, she felt the trucker staring at her, and at the same exact moment she inhaled the overripe stench hanging in the air of the cab.

"That baby don't cry," the trucker said to her. It was more a timid question than a statement of fact. He sounded worried.

Jeanie met the trucker's gaze, and then, moving as if she were in a trance, she looked down at Ralph Junior, beside her in the seat. The flannel shirt was covering him from head to toe; only one little hand peeked out. She pulled back the cloth slowly, murmuring his name over and over. Tears were already dripping from her tired eyes. But she didn't even need to see the baby's tiny scrunched face, looking blue and bruised in the morning light, to know he had left her for heaven. He was dead.

She couldn't really remember what happened next—everything happened so fast, and there were so many people everywhere. The trucker called the police, and an ambulance came and took her and the baby to a hospital somewhere in the city. Someone took the baby from her, took him right out of her arms even though she was trying to scream for them to stop; she wasn't sure the words came out. She was too weak to speak, too tired to even tell them her name and to explain to them what had happened, how she was trying to get back home, to the baby's daddy, a man who was going to make everything all right. When she woke up, she was in a strange bed, wearing a white-and-blue nightgown, in a room overlooking the same highway that had taken her from this town a year before.

She fell back asleep even though she didn't want to—she wanted to know where they'd taken Ralph Junior. She was afraid they were going to bury him like a dog, in a mass grave someplace. She called out for help, but when a nurse appeared in her room, Jeanie was too weak to speak a full sentence, and finally she stopped trying.

Maybe a few days passed, she wasn't sure, maybe it was just a few hours. When she finally woke up, there were two young men in her room. They said they were from Social Services. Would she talk to them, please?

So Jeanie told them everything that had happened, about how badly she had wanted to get back to Boise, how Ralph Junior wouldn't take his medicine—for crying out loud, she tried to make him! They nodded calmly at her and took notes, and occasionally one of them, the man wearing glasses, asked her a question. She was sobbing most of the time; just thinking about her life made her wish it was her dead instead of Ralph Junior, and she told the men that, and again they nodded. After they left, a nurse was stationed in her room around-the-clock, but it didn't occur to her until much later that they thought she was going to commit suicide. The truth was, she hated herself too much to even make the effort.

When the men came back a second time, Jeanie pushed herself up in bed and glared at them. "Where did you put my baby?" she asked. "I ain't answering a single question until I know where he is."

The man with the glasses cleared his throat and jotted down an address. "He was buried at the Mount Clarion Cemetery. We can take you there after you are released," he said, handing her the slip of paper. "He has a nice gravestone. The city took care of everything, Miss White."

A few days later Jeanie dressed in some clothes the men brought to her. They told her the District Attorney's Office had decided not to press charges against her—she was shocked by the news. She had no idea anyone was thinking of putting her in jail for what happened. It was an accident! The men said they understood. It was a terrible accident.

They waited in the car while Jeanie visited Ralph Junior's grave. She had expected to cry, but no tears came. She figured she was all cried out. She'd probably never cry again. She walked back to the car and asked the man with glasses if she could use the camera on the backseat to take a picture of the grave, and he said sure. He would even take it for her, and he did. Then they drove back to the city, and they dropped her at a halfway house for battered women. She could stay there until she found a job. A few days later, she wandered back to the sub shop. She already knew in her bones that Ralph wouldn't be there, and she was right. The manager told her he had left a few days after she quit. No one knew where he'd gone. And he was sorry, there were no jobs right now. She could try again in a few weeks. One of the waitresses was pregnant; she might not last too much longer.

Jeanie hung out a while longer at the halfway house. She liked the women there; no one passed judgment on her, and no one forced her to talk about it. She spent most days in the arts-and-crafts room, making ashtrays from clay and learning how to knit. With help from a middle-aged lady named Maria, she even made a royal-blue wool scarf. It didn't look pretty, but hell, she figured, it was the first thing she had ever finished in her life.

It was at the halfway house that Jeanie met a nice woman named Linda, who was in there with two little kids. Her husband used to beat the shit out of her, she told Jeanie, and after taking it for six years, she'd finally left him for good. It would be hard, but she was going to strike out on her own; she was going to Miami. And Jeanie decided to go with her.

That's how she ended up at the truck stop near the Everglades. She'd been there for a year before Brazil wandered in the door on his way to Tampa. Life had been pretty good for her—simple and quiet. She lived in a little shack in an unincorporated town near the edge of Dade County. Her rent was $130 a month, and she could eat the leftovers from the restaurant. She didn't socialize much; every once in a while, she would go out for drinks with another one of the waitresses, but men were out of her life. She'd had enough. It was time to heal.

She didn't want anything from Brazil after their first night out together, but he kept calling and wanting to give her things. He'd bring her clothes and a bag of groceries, or little trinkets to decorate her house, and he even bought her window shades once and hung them up, too. For the longest time, she wondered when he was going to make a move on her, but he never did. She finally had to kiss him, and after that they became sometime lovers.

He didn't get mad at her when she told him she was pregnant about a year after they met. She thought he looked sad. He took her hands in his and said he would support her forever and ever, but he couldn't marry her, he was in love with another girl, a girl named Sherry who worked at the newspaper. He promised Jeanie he would never abandon her, and she believed him.

She was happy enough with the arrangement. Brazil visited her once a week or so, and he always brought food and money, enough money that she could afford decent pregnancy clothes this time. She even had enough cash to buy a color TV and a used car. She finally had her own car. She felt free.

One night Brazil stormed into the restaurant, his neck red and bulging with anger. He sat in a booth, just sat there twitching and mumbling loudly until Jeanie got off work a few hours later. When they got back to her place, he told her it was over with the girl at the newspaper, and he wanted her to move into his place in Miami. She didn't have to work anymore. They would get married.

And that's the way it happened. A few days later, she packed up her things—she had a lot more to her name these days—and she drove into the city and settled into Brazil's funky three-bedroom bungalow not far from the waterfront. Three months later, John Junior was born. She never did find out what Brazil and Sherry had argued about, and once at a party, one of the other photographers told her that they hadn't argued at all—that Brazil had told everyone that the wedding was Jeanie's idea. This news confused her, but it wasn't in her nature anymore to worry about confusing things. Whatever Brazil wanted to say was okay. She had what she wanted. The baby was strong and happy, and she was teaching herself to cook. Life was good.

The truth about his marriage to Jeanie would always be Brazil's secret, as long as he lived. How could he ever admit it out loud? One day, on the way back from an assignment taking head shots of the mayor of Perrine, he had to stop by Sherry's house to get some film out of the refrigerator. He let himself in, got the film, and headed out the door again, but before he knew it, he was in her bedroom. At first, he thought he would just turn the picture of Charles facedown, as a joke to amuse Sherry when she got home from work, but then he saw her diary sitting there on the bed, and he couldn't help himself. He had to know what she really felt about him. And so he opened it up, and he began to read.

Most of it was pretty boring stuff—she wrote a lot of bullshit about her parents and how she felt betrayed by her father for some reason; it wasn't really clear. He flipped forward a few pages, and he finally spotted his name. It was a recent entry, from two weeks earlier. *Brazil was over for dinner tonight. Pizza again. No wonder he has a stomach like a truck driver. I don't know. We've had so many good times together, and sometimes I really think I love him, but times like tonight, I look in the mirror after he leaves, and I ask myself: What are you doing with this strange man? I mean, he's got another girlfriend, and she's going to have his kid. Our relationship has got to be the biggest dead end I've ever maneuvered myself into, and didn't I just get myself out of another dead end with another man? Oh, Charles, so terrible in his own way, so pretty and self-absorbed, like a ballerina, and so fragile just beneath that Yankee exterior. I wish I didn't know how much I could get away with, hurting him. He waits for me like our old dog Scooter used to wait for Mother at the back door. And his tail would thump thump thump when she got home and she would give him a little scratch behind the ears. That was enough for him.*

Brazil didn't get mad very often; that was something he boasted about to Sherry all the time. He was a man who had total control over himself. That's why he never flipped out on assignment, with bullets flying and blood spurting and cops screaming for everyone to duck. That's why he was such a great photographer. Nothing rattled him.

But this shit Sherry had written got to him. She thought he was *fat*, did she? And she called their relationship a dead end—that especially pissed him off because she had never come right out and said it to his face. Sure, he had Jeanie. It was no secret, but he told Sherry a thousand times that the thing with Jeanie was under control. Obviously she didn't believe him.

Well, screw her.

Brazil skimmed the next few pages, scanning for his name, and he found it at the top of a page dimpled with water stains. Had Sherry been crying?

Brazil laughed at me when I told him how upset I was about Pansy's arthritis. He said I should just "gas" her, that a cat with bad joints is as good as a hunting dog with polio. He just can't take me, or anything, seriously. Why do I love him so much?

She had written a disjointed paragraph about work, and then her handwriting suddenly turned furious and choppy: *I can't concentrate anymore. What's with me tonight?* she had written. *I guess the truth is, I'm sick of sharing Brazil with Jeanie. Her existence makes me feel like I'm constantly on trial. Is he going to love me tomorrow? Will I make the grade? It's wearing me out. I find myself crying at the oddest times—in the shower, during sappy TV commercials. Ridiculous! I mean, didn't Father (of all people) say the trick in life was not to make the same mistake twice—and here I am caring too damn much about what one man thinks of me. I swore to myself that would never happen again. Maybe I should just go back to Charles. He'd have me. Maybe that's what I should do. Maybe next time I'm home, I'll sleep with him and see if the old feelings are still there. They could be, maybe.*

Brazil's face burned with fury. She was planning to go home and fuck Charles! That lying bitch! He wanted to rip the pages from her diary, shred them, and scatter them across her bed, where *they* had made love so many times, and she said she loved him, hated Charles, and that she didn't care about Jeanie or the fact that he was a 100 percent red-blooded Florida Cracker. She had said that didn't matter at all. She said she loved him. She lied, not once, but a hundred times. Screw her.

Control—that's what he needed. Brazil breathed deeply, stopped, squared his shoulders, and then exhaled slowly. He did it again and again, until he stopped shaking. After a few minutes, he closed the diary and carefully placed it back on the spot where he had first discovered it. Then he smoothed out the covers on Sherry's bed so that she would never suspect his visit. She must never know.

Brazil locked the front door behind him and got back into his car. For a second, he wasn't sure what he should do. He could go home and take the phone off the hook, or he could go into the office and make some pictures for the Travel section that he had been putting off, or he could go out for drinks with the gang at the Bomb Shelter. He put the car in gear, and before he knew it, he was speeding down Alligator Alley, headed for Jeanie, and as the miles slipped by and the night got darker and darker, he couldn't help getting more and more pissed-off. It was as if he had memorized the words from Sherry's diary—he just couldn't get them out of his head. By the time he pulled into the parking lot, he had decided he was going to dump Sherry first. Why should he wait around—was he just another Charles, who acted like a fucking dog named Scooter? No, he would end it. He would marry Jeanie. It was the right thing to do anyway.

He had never expected to get back together with Sherry. He didn't even expect to see her again, if he could help it. He had pulled some strings at the photo desk to make sure they were never assigned to the same story, and he completely swore off *Citizen* parties and the Bomb Shelter. But then one night he was working late at the paper, and when the phone rang at 4:00 A.M., he half expected it to be Sherry on the other end. And as soon as he heard her voice, so full of grief and longing, he knew he had to be with her that night, right away.

Life was funny, Brazil often thought after the affair began again. Here he was married to Jeanie, and things couldn't be sweeter with Sherry. Life was good. As long as Sherry didn't start talking about going home, life was good. And these days, it seemed as if she had put Marblehead far behind her. All she cared about was this kid, Manuel, and how his story was going to change her life forever.

21

The next day, Sherry wore red.

It was Saturday. Manuel told her he had to wash and polish his car in the morning and then drop his sister off at the mall, but after that, he would be "totally psyched" to meet her at the park at one o'clock. Jack arranged for Laura Cohn, one of the rewrite editors, to hang out with her kid in the park that afternoon at overtime-and-a-half. She was supposed to act inconspicuous and watch Sherry's every move at the same time. If Sherry raised her right hand above her head and waved, that was the signal for Laura to call the city desk from her car radio, fast. Jack would contact the police.

The plan was this: Sherry and Manuel would meet and talk at the park for a while. Sherry had come up with a list of questions, which Jack had doubled in length. She would ask as many as she felt Manuel could handle in one sitting. Then they would get in her car and visit a few of the places where he had committed murders, and Sherry would tape his accounts of each hit, to be verified later with police records. That was to be Belinda's job, and Sherry had to make it as easy as possible for her, Jack said—get every detail: What was the victim wearing, how old was he, did he have a mustache or a scar or a tattoo, what time did Manuel pull the trigger, what kind of gun did he use, where did he shoot the guy, how many times, which way did the body fall? Everything mattered. Get it all, Jack told Sherry, and she promised she would.

She arrived at the park early, and she was surprised to find Manuel already there, sitting at the picnic table. He stood up as Sherry approached, and held his hands up in the air as if to indicate he wasn't armed with a weapon.

"No gifts this time," he said, smiling warmly, "company policy." Sherry laughed. "What commendable behavior," she answered, relieved to see he was still in good spirits. On the car ride over, she had a panicky premonition that he was going to call the whole thing off. Instead, he was in the same buoyant mood as the night before, maybe even more so. He seemed anxious to talk.

They sat down next to each other at the picnic table, and Sherry placed the tape recorder on the seat between them. "Let's make this as inconspicuous as possible, okay?" she said. She wanted him to understand that she was going to look out for him from now on. She was an ally, a coconspirator, a friend.

She smiled familiarly. "Hey, Manuel," she said to set the tone for the day, "I *really* like your shirt." And in fact, she did. It was a khaki-colored knit polo with a small, flat collar—definitely off the rack from some upscale European boutique in the Grove, the kind of place she was always urging Brazil to shop, much to his disgust.

"How about these pants, too?" Manuel answered, obviously pleased by Sherry's attention to his attire. "Armani. Just like I told you, I love Armani. They cost me three hundred bucks."

Sherry nodded slowly, as if she was duly impressed. "Three hundred bucks, wow," she said. "They look really slick."

"I picked them myself."

"Well," Sherry said, "you obviously have an eye for fashion, Manuel. Maybe that's a career for you after this whole thing blows over—"

But Manuel cut her off with a cackle. "I'm no fucked-up *homo!*" he snarled.

"Of course not," Sherry quickly agreed. She didn't want Manuel defensive before the day even began. "Say, Manuel," she said immediately, her cheerful voice steering the conversation in a new and more pleasant direction, "what do you say we get started, okay?"

"Good," Manuel said. "I got a lot to tell you."

"And I can't wait to hear it." Sherry sounded delighted, but inside she was beginning to quake with anxiety. Now, she thought, comes the hard part.

Sherry took one long, deep breath and then faced Manuel foursquare, staring straight into his black eyes with as much earnest warmth as she could muster. She had a short speech to deliver before they started, a speech practically dictated to her word-for-word by Jack that morning after he got back from a meeting with all the big bananas on the eighth floor—Garrett Newman, Loren Rosenberg, Casey McDowell, two clones in blue suits sent by the publisher, and a pack of lawyers. Nobody was crazy about a Saturday morning meeting, but they all came. Jack Dougherty didn't cry wolf.

Newman was ecstatic about the story—Jack could practically see the words "Pulitzer Prize" flashing in his eyes like a red neon sign. He commended Jack for running the kid through a lie test, and for assigning some of the best reporters on staff to come up with *major* sidebars. He especially liked the pieces on kids who kill and the Lopez family's savage history. He loved the fact that Belinda McEvoy was involved in the backup research; she was good, he said, very good. And he also *loved* the idea of a map of Manuel's hits and of staking out Lopez family hideouts for new color photos of Señora Lopez and her henchmen. But as soon as Newman was done with the praise, he starting harping on how important it was to get the story out fast, before the kid disappeared or changed his tune or decided he could make some money by talking to TV. Rosenberg chimed in—the kid was obviously nuts, the story had to run before he realized what he was getting himself into. Estabrook should wrap up the reporting in the next week, start writing it fast so that someone good—he used the words "more experienced"—could start rewriting it, and then get the hell out of town so that the District Attorney's Office couldn't find her when the story hit the street.

That's when the lawyers started talking all at once, and they sounded absolutely frenetic. They didn't like this at all, not at all, this was obstruction of justice. The *Citizen* couldn't know about eighteen murders and just sit on the information! The D.A. would slam them to legal hell and back again. Even the First Amendment wouldn't protect the newspaper this time.

But Jack held firm, and finally the lawyers bickered long enough among themselves to come up with a plan to keep the *Citizen* out of court for the next hundred years: Sherry had to tell Manuel to go to the authorities with his story.

"What we need, simply," one lawyer explained, as the rest of them nodded in relief, "is a tape recording of the reporter telling the subject that he could or should take his information to the police, and of course, what we would need on the tape would be the subject saying that he *only* wanted to divulge the information to the reporter.

"There is no doubt the reporter will be subpoenaed as soon as the story appears, but if we're lucky, Manuel will turn himself into the police as soon as the story runs."

Jack let out a short laugh. "When the story runs, the kid is going to vanish into thin air if he knows what's good for him," he said.

"I think it would be prudent for us not to think that out loud," another lawyer responded quickly. "In the best scenario, the boy will turn state's evidence and get a reduced sentence for helping the D.A. locate and prosecute his employers. We could go far toward exonerating the *Citizen* if we urge him to cooperate with the authorities after the story runs."

"We'll see what we can do on that front," Newman said, trying to prevent a profanity from Jack. "We appreciate your counsel. The reporter is meeting with the boy today, and Jack will tell her what she has to say."

Jack stood up. The meeting was over; he had to talk to Sherry before she took off for the park. He left without saying good-bye to the lawyers; niceties were Newman's job.

He found Sherry at her desk, loading a fresh cassette into the tape recorder. Belinda sat nearby, going over the list of questions. Jack couldn't help noticing that her hair, ordinarily tangled and swept back in a ponytail, was combed out and hanging over her shoulders like an elegant gold-threaded scarf. She was wearing makeup again, and long dangling earrings. She really did look like Emily; the likeness startled him.

Belinda looked up and caught Jack's haunted eyes. He quickly looked away—the last thing he needed today was Belinda pulling him aside and asking, in that little-girl voice of hers, if anything was wrong. She did that from time to time, and it irritated the hell out of him. Still, he was careful not to let it show. That whole thing with her father had been so brutal, and how she kept it inside . . . he felt for her, he really did.

"In my office, ladies," he grumbled, and walked away.

"Okay, we just met with the lawyers. God, I hate lawyers," he said as soon as they were sitting down. He was pacing back and forth, looking even more agitated than usual. He pulled a cigarette from the pack in one swift, automatic motion. A stall. How was he going to put this?

The truth was that he wanted Sherry to follow the letter of the attorneys' plan but sort of ignore the spirit of the thing—she should go ahead and tell Manuel about going to the police, but she should somehow imply that turning himself in was only one option, take it or leave it. Since the whole conversation had to be taped, Sherry couldn't sound like she was discouraging the kid from spilling his guts to the authorities, but something—maybe the way she looked at him or smiled—had to tell him that it was perfectly okay to keep the story between just the two of them. Jack didn't want to lose this kid, give him away to the cops and then, goddamn it, to every other two-bit reporter in the city and the country. Shit, if the kid went to the cops, his whole story would be spelled out in some ridiculous press release. *Police are questioning a juvenile who claims to have information about eighteen drug-related shootings in the Miami area over the past two years.* That would be the first leak. Within two days, the kid would be on all the fucking morning talk shows, a beefy Miami cop by his side. The *Citizen* would only be another microphone sticking in the chief's face at the daily press conferences on the case. That couldn't happen, Jack was thinking, not to this story, not to these girls, not to him.

"The lawyers are real uptight," he finally said. "They're afraid that we're obstructing justice." He said it sarcastically. It was ludicrous—as he'd told them at the meeting, reporters aren't cops. That's the oldest rule in the book.

"But, even though I know it's crazy, and you know it's crazy, and everyone and their fucking mother knows that we aren't here to do the cops' work for them," Jack said, "the lawyers think we have to do a little cover-your-ass action." He paused for a reaction.

Sherry was already panic-stricken but trying hard not to show it. Another obstacle! Didn't anyone want to see this piece run? She was sitting on the greatest story in Miami, and everyone had some bone to pick. Give the kid a lie-detector test. Never go anywhere alone with him. Verify every verb, noun, and preposition out of his mouth. And now the lawyers were antsy. What hoop did Manuel have to jump through this time?

She was hoping Belinda would say something; a protest from her might sound less biased and frantic to Jack. But she was silent, and when Sherry gave her a quick sideways glance, she noticed Belinda was frowning slightly, looking distracted, as usual.

In fact, Belinda's mind was clicking away with a rush of confusing ideas. Maybe the lawyers were right—maybe they should go to the police with Manuel's story. After all, the kid was a killer, not of one or two men but *eighteen*, and not in self-defense or a fit of insanity. And he has all this information, like where Mimi Lopez lives, and where her cocaine comes from and where it goes afterward. Maybe, Belinda thought, all this stuff was so big and so important that the story—the big banner headline, the beautiful double byline, and all the gloating afterward—just didn't matter. As soon as it hit the streets, Manuel was going to disappear, by his own free will or by someone else's, and probably she and Sherry would win a zillion awards and get to have lunch with the publisher, but—but justice would never be done. Isn't that what Eladio had been trying to say last night when she told him about this, the greatest story on earth? God, just a few hours earlier, hadn't she convinced him that she was right, that the story *had* to run? It had been easy to persuade him—he was so sweet and so awed by her, it was positively scary—and he had promised not to utter a word about Manuel to any living soul. But now, sitting in Jack's office with the words "obstruction of justice" hanging in the air, Belinda wondered, had she done the right thing?

"The lawyers want us to tell the kid that he can go to the cops with his story if he wants to." Jack was speaking again, and Belinda focused tensely on his words. "Now this doesn't mean that you should go telling the kid it's a good idea to blab his story to the authorities, but you should let him know that it's an option. And we got to have the whole thing on tape."

Sherry's answer came quickly. "Great," she said, frustration seething in her voice. "What if he goes and takes the suggestion? Then we lose the story—good-bye and good luck! Don't you realize that he'll do whatever I say? If I say he can go to the cops, he'll go the cops! It's like giving away the story!" She stood up and walked to the window. Her back was to Belinda and Jack because she was afraid she might cry. "I just don't get it—I don't get it at all. Doesn't anybody want this story as badly as I do?"

Belinda joined Sherry next to the window and gently draped an arm around her shoulders. "I don't know, Sherry. Maybe this is for the best—"

"Are you crazy?" Sherry cut Belinda off. Sometimes Belinda was such a pushover it drove her crazy. "Why don't I just send him to Channel Ten or to the *Herald* or tell him to stand in the middle of South Dixie Highway at rush hour and shout it at passing commuters? We're just giving it away. Once he goes to the cops, it's not our story anymore."

"That's just not true, Sherry. Calm yourself." Jack was leaning against his desk, arms folded across his chest and head slightly bowed, as if in prayer. "You don't tell the kid he *has* to go to the cops, you tell him that—if he wants to and only if he wants to— he can go over to headquarters. That's all. And that way, the *Citizen* is squeaky-clean. We did our civic duty. We told the kid he could tell the authorities, and he decided he wanted to tell only us. Boom. That's it, and we're home free."

Jack lifted his head and sighed sadly. "Sherry, don't you see it's all in the way you say it?" His voice was softer than she'd ever heard it. He almost sounded like a regular dad, sweetly pleading for his little girl to come out of the bedroom after her first broken heart.

Did she really have a choice? If she was going to play at all, she had to play by their rules. Understood. Sherry walked back to her chair and slumped down into it. "All right, okay," she said. "Let me handle this."

One hour later, she was sitting next to Manuel under the spreading banyan tree, and her heart was thumping like bird wings in her chest. She couldn't screw up.

She pushed a small button to activate the tape recorder between them.

"Manuel, there's something important I want to tell you before we start talking today." Had she screwed up already? Maybe she shouldn't have used the word "important."

Manuel looked at her quizzically. The smile was fading from his pockmarked face. "Is something wrong?" he asked.

"No, no, not at all. I just want to tell you something that's on my mind," Sherry said. She wondered what her voice would sound like on the tape. Too stilted? Too neurotic?

"Look, Manuel, we've spent some time together, and we've had some very interesting conversations about your past, and I was just thinking that I should let you know that you have the option of telling your information to the police or to the District Attorney's Office." There, she had said it, almost word-for-word as Jack had instructed. She was supposed to stop at this point and gauge Manuel's response before going on with the second part of the speech. Sherry was still staring into his eyes, but even in the sulfur light of the afternoon sun, they remained impenetrably dark. What was he thinking? It was impossible to know. For a few seconds, he was motionless, and then suddenly he jerked forward and snapped off the tape recorder.

He leaned within an inch of Sherry's face. "Why are you

telling me this?" he snarled in a low whisper. His anger was so sudden and explosive it petrified Sherry, and she had to fight the desperate instinct to raise her right hand in the air and wave frantically in the direction of Laura Cohn and her kid on the swing set.

"Manuel, please," Sherry said. She was practically begging him for patience with her voice; still he would not break his gaze. "Why?" he snapped. His face was frozen in a gruesome grimace, and in her mind Sherry could see him pulling the trigger of a gun held snug against someone's neck.

A few seconds of silence passed, crackling with the static of fear. "I had to," she finally whispered. "Please . . ."

Manuel leaned back, and she saw his shoulders relax. He nodded knowingly, and a tight conspiratorial smile slowly broke across his sliver of a face. "I see," he said. "Your boss?"

"My boss, yes," Sherry said, glancing down to make sure the tape recorder was off. "My boss and the newspaper's lawyers."

"They said you should tell me to go to the cops?"

"No, no," Sherry said; her heart was still pounding hard, and she struggled to keep her voice controlled. "They told me that I had to tell you that you had the *option* of going to the cops. Not that you *have* to, but you can, if you want to. The newspaper has to protect itself from a lawsuit." She paused. She knew she shouldn't say the words poised on her lips, but she spoke anyway. "I know the cops would absolutely die for your information, but you can just tell your story to me alone, if that's what you want."

Manuel was warming to this turn of events. He clicked on the tape recorder and smiled at her with the intimacy of a lover.

"You were saying I have the option of going to the police with my story." His voice was firm, authoritative. He was going to help her play the game.

"Yes," Sherry answered. Suddenly, she, too, felt bold. "You should know that the *Citizen* urges you to take your story to the authorities, who might reduce your sentence in return for information. Of course, we can't promise lenient treatment from prosecution, but you should know that the police and the D.A. would be very interested in your story. We can arrange a meeting, if you'd like." She looked at Manuel next to her. He was smirking, clearly delighted by their scheme.

"Thank you for informing me of this option," he responded, carefully enunciating the last word as if he had never said it before.

"But I prefer to tell only you, Señorita Estabrook. That is my decision."

"Are you absolutely sure?" she asked. Jack had told her to say this loud and clear.

"No, thank you," Manuel answered politely. "My mind is made up." He leaned forward again and clicked off the tape machine. He raised his eyebrows, smiling broadly. "That ought to do it, right?" he asked.

"Yeah, I guess so," Sherry said. She hoped Jack didn't ask about all the on-and-off clicking on the tape. She would tell him she was fiddling with the machine, trying to make sure it was working.

"So now we can really get down to business?" Manuel asked, looking at the gold watch on his wrist like a businessman late for a meeting. It was a trait Manuel shared with her father; she'd seen that very gesture a thousand times. Sherry checked her own watch. Unbelievably, only five minutes had passed since she arrived at the park. How could so much happen in so little time?

Sherry activated the tape recorder and watched the wheels spin for a second. "Today," she told Manuel, "today I want to talk about you. I want to get to know you a little better. And after we're done talking here, I'd like to get in my car and take a drive, visit some of the places that you"—she paused, not exactly sure how to put it without offending him—"places where you had jobs."

"Sounds good," Manuel said blithely. The idea of talking about his life seemed to please him. "One condition, though."

Sherry tilted her head. Her expression said, Anything you want.

"After I tell you all about me," Manuel said, "you tell me all about you."

The request caught Sherry off guard. She didn't want to talk about herself; it would be a waste of time. But she could give him a quick rundown: born in Boston, the daughter of nice parents, a few years of college, then Miami—not too many details, no mention of Charles or Brazil, no talk about her future. "Okay, we can talk about me," she said, "but it will be pretty boring."

"I doubt it," Manuel said. He was using his Don Juan voice again, and Sherry had to smile. God, he was only sixteen! If he wanted to practice his lady-killing techniques on her, he could.

"All right," Sherry said, trying to set the conversation back on track. "Let's get going. Why don't you tell me where you were born, where your parents are from, what they're like, stuff like that. You know, tell me about your family and what you like to do with your free time, and what you want to do after high school. All that good stuff."

"You want to know why I am the way I am, right?"

"That's right," Sherry said. He'd seen right through her elaborate setup. This kid was sharper than she was giving him credit for. "I want to know what makes you special."

And so, Manuel started at the beginning. His father, Juan, was twenty-two years old when he left Cuba in '69 with dreams of striking it rich in America. He scraped together a few hundred dollars loading fruit at the waterfront, and finally arrived one evening in New York just as the lights in the skyscrapers came twinkling on. He had never seen anything so glittering and magnificent in his life. He wept from loneliness and hope.

He had planned to stay with his mother's cousins, whose address he carried on a tattered piece of paper in his shirt pocket. But when he finally made it to their tenement around midnight, they wanted nothing to do with him.

Juan slept that night in an alley and woke to find that the city was not so beautiful by day. He walked the grimy streets until he finally found work, just about closing time, at a Puerto Rican food stand on East 110th Street. That night and for many nights afterward, he slept on a bench in the park, and he was awakened every morning by the jab of a nightstick in the ribs and a cop's bland warning to move along.

A few months later, he met a Colombian girl who bought fruit at the stand every night on her way home from work. She was a cleaning lady at the mayor's mansion. To Juan, her job was impossibly glamorous; each day this little Maria with pitch-black eyes was so close to wealth and power, so close he could taste it on her lips when he kissed her. A few weeks after their first night together, she told Juan she was pregnant, and they married without much fanfare at a church near her apartment. Manuel was born three months later, on a frigid January morning just before sunrise.

Five years passed. Maria rose at four every morning, deposited Manuel with her mother in the apartment across the hall, and left for the mayor's mansion. Juan was out of the house an hour later, standing behind the cash register at the food stand. At noon,

Maria would leave her first job for her second: cleaning a widow's penthouse on East End Avenue. At nightfall, she would head back to her apartment in the ghetto, gather Manuel into her arms, and walk across the hall to start dinner. Juan would get home at eight, and a few hours later they would all fall asleep to the buzz of the black-and-white TV.

One night, lying in bed with Maria, Juan began to weep. He looked around the tiny, airless apartment with its peeling wallpaper and leaky sink, and he saw one thing: Havana. He was back home in the slum. He had never left.

"We have to get out of here," he told his wife. He didn't know what they should do or where they should go, but he knew that he would never be rich if he stayed trapped in New York, where money was even scarcer than happiness. In five years, he had learned only a dozen words of English; still, his eyes told him everything he needed to know. The rich men in this city looked just like the rich men of his homeland. He would never find his fortune in this city of concrete and cold winters. Why should he live out his life here? He missed his mother, and he longed for the sweet fragrance of flowering Allamanda trees, and he wanted to feel the seductive breeze of a turquoise ocean on his face again.

They would go to Miami.

And so, a few weeks later, Juan, Maria, and Manuel left New York forever. Maria was pregnant again, and the trip was hard on her. But when they arrived, Juan quickly found work unloading bananas at the waterfront, and a city social worker who met the bus at the station helped them find a cramped but clean basement apartment not far from Calle Ocho. It even had a double bed for Juan and Maria, and it was in that bed that Maria gave birth one rainy August morning to a daughter named Sonia. A Cuban doctor named Lantal had come to the apartment to help, even though Maria had told him, through her tears and panting, that she could not pay.

The first time Manuel saw his father strike his mother was a few weeks after Sonia was born. He came home from work drunk; that wasn't uncommon, but usually he just collapsed on the bed. This time, his anger was still alive, and it was as harsh as an acid bath. Maria was washing the dishes when Juan walked in the door. The baby was sleeping in her cradle near the sink, and Manuel sat at the small kitchen table, watching his mother and chatting with her happily in Spanish. Suddenly, the front door slammed, and Juan stormed into the kitchen. Before Maria could even turn around, Juan grabbed her hair and swung her around so he could slap her across the face with the back of his hand. When she hit the floor, Juan kicked her in the stomach with his heavy black work boot. "Whore!" he screamed. "You give me a daughter, but you fuck another man to give me a son. In my house, I want respect. Respect me, Maria." And then he spit on her and left the room.

Manuel jumped off his chair and ran to his mother's side. She was weeping silently, and blood ran down her face, from her eye to her chin. "Don't worry, angel," she told her son. "He doesn't mean it. He loves you." Manuel didn't understand the meaning of his father's words, but he grew to over the years, as he saw Juan beat Maria with frightening regularity, each time accusing her of being a whore who only produced sons for other men.

When Manuel was eleven, he came home from school to find his father sitting at the kitchen table with a half-empty bottle of peach brandy in front of him. Maria was standing over the sink, her chin tucked to her chest as she did the dishes. "Come celebrate with me," Juan said grandly when the boy peeked into the room from behind the door. Manuel reluctantly walked closer to his father. "Come here, don't be scared," the man urged, laughing warmly. "Have a drink of this and celebrate with me. We're going to be rich! Your papa got a job with El Duque today. El Duque was Tomas Zorro, the obese, flagrantly corrupt lord of Miami's burgeoning construction industry. Juan pulled Manuel close to him and forced the bottle to his lips. Manuel tipped it back and drank in a gulp, just as he had seen his father do so many times. The liquor hit him like a sledgehammer, but he fought the urge to spit it out on the floor. His father laughed raucously. "Have another," he said, pushing the bottle on Manuel again. "Be a man. You gotta be strong if people are going to respect you." Manuel looked pleadingly at his mother, but she continued to wash the dishes in silence, her eyes riveted on the sink before her. He tried to run from the room, but his father caught him by the shoulder and forced the bottle to his lips again and tilted it back. Manuel felt the heavy liquor drip down his throat and chin. He began to cry and knew what was coming next. The hard slap caught him on the side of his face, and broke the skin near his left eye. He bolted for his bedroom as the sound of his father's laughter filled the small apartment.

After a few months with El Duque, Juan had enough money to buy the family a three-bedroom house in a new suburb south of Miami. It wasn't much bigger than the basement apartment in Little Havana, but it had a backyard and a driveway for the old blue Chevy that Juan bought from another bricklayer for two hundred dollars. Otherwise, life didn't change much. Juan still came home drunk, and he still slammed Maria around the house until he fell into a deep sleep on the broken couch in front of the TV.

"I used to stand in front of the mirror and stare at myself," Manuel told Sherry in the park that day. "And I would wonder, am I big enough yet to hit my father?" He smiled sardonically. "But I never got big enough.

"Look at me," he continued in the same voice, laced with irony. "I'm a small guy. I take after my mother." Sherry shook her head sympathetically. She tried to look as if she understood Manuel's dilemma, but she was really wondering why Manuel hadn't just put a gun to his father's neck. He had killed so many strangers—then why not this man who had tormented his mother for twenty years? The question hung in front of her like ripe fruit, but she was afraid to ask, to maybe put the idea into his head.

"Does he still hit your mother?" she asked.

There was a long pause. Manuel's face closed down, his eyes were blank, and his mouth fell into a thin, almost lipless grimace. "She died two years ago," he said.

"Oh my God, I'm terribly sorry," Sherry said.

"He killed her." Manuel's delivery was flat, and he watched the tape whirl around and around in the small machine on the bench between them.

"He killed her?" Sherry asked, incredulous. It was all beginning to fit together. Revenge—all the murders were revenge for his mother's death. He was killing his father, over and over again. She felt ecstatic—the copy grew into a bigger blockbuster with every answer. She couldn't have fabricated a better story line. Where would she put this critical element—should she stick it in the lead? Or maybe better to lay it out it in a sidebar. She needed all the details.

"He hit her and that killed her?" she asked.

"No." The answer was uncharacteristically terse.

"Was there another way he killed her?"

Another long pause. Manuel wiped the corner of one eye, but Sherry wasn't sure she saw a tear.

"She killed herself. But she did it to get away from him."

"Did she leave a note?"

"No."

"But you know it was because of your father?"

Manuel smiled bitterly, as if to say the answer was obvious.

"The sick part," he said angrily, "is that my father blamed me because she used my gun. He said she would have never done it if she hadn't found the gun in my room."

"That *is* sick," Sherry agreed. She imagined the scene in her mind: Maria, hunched over from years of beatings, is putting away her son's laundry when she finds a revolver in a drawer. At first she is frightened, and then she is overcome with happiness and relief. She lifts the gun up, kisses the chamber, and then points the barrel—

"I found her," Manuel interrupted Sherry's thoughts.

"In your bedroom?"

"Yes," he answered. It was almost a question. How did she know?

"That must have been terrible for you," she said. In her mind, she saw a flash of Belinda, finding her father in the garage and gently shutting his eyelids.

"I was pissed-off," Manuel said flatly.

"And sad, too?"

"Yeah," he said, although he didn't sound too sure of the answer. "I was sad, but I was really pissed-off. I mean, I saw her lying there, and I just started yelling at her. I was crazy, like I wanted to kill her for doing something so stupid. If she had just lived a little longer, I could have gotten her out of there, away from him. I was going to buy her a little house of her own, you know, set her up. She was going to be happy."

"You were already working for the Lopez family when this happened?" Sherry asked. This could screw up the revenge angle.

"It happened right after my first job," he answered, "a few days after, I think."

Sherry nodded. It still might work. "Did you ever think that your mother's death might have something to do with the jobs you pulled afterward?" she asked. She wanted him to say yes, to tell her that he thought of his mother's face every time he pulled the trigger, or to say that he imagined he was killing his father with each carefully placed gun blast. She needed him to say yes. It would make the story perfect.

Sherry stared at Manuel expectantly, but he kept his head down, his eyes fixed on the tape recorder.

She started to ask the question again: "Manuel, do you think your mother's death—"

"Is that what you think?" he asked abruptly.

Sherry leaned closer to him and shook her head. She didn't want to spoil his answer. "I don't know, Manuel. That's why I'm asking you," she said gently.

"It never occurred to me that I did it because of my mother," he said slowly. "But maybe that's why I kept on doing it."

Sherry was silent, waiting and hoping for more words to come from Manuel's tightly pursed lips. But for a full minute he said nothing, and his eyes remained on the tape deck.

"You're smart to figure out an answer," he said finally. "I knew you would."

A few minutes later, they were on their way to the site of one of Manuel's hits. What with Manuel's obviously pained description of his mother's death, Sherry figured they had covered enough tender territory for one day.

Shifting the car into reverse, she turned and smiled brightly at the boy beside her. And as always, Manuel smiled back, with a thin, ironic grin she was just beginning to get used to. "Okay, lead the way," she said. They were headed for the apartment building where he had committed his ninth or tenth murder. He couldn't remember which.

Manuel directed her through the shady streets of Coral Gables until they reached a shiny new high rise on Tomar Boulevard just inside the Miami city line. Sherry was surprised. It was a pretty ritzy place, with curved balconies and a uniformed doorman—an apartment there had to cost at least two grand a month. She pulled the car into a "Guests Only" spot in front of the building.

"Okay, follow me," Manuel said, jumping out of the car and striding briskly toward the back of the apartment building.

She caught up with him near the pool, where he stood, head thrown back, squinting hard against the sun as he carefully studied the high rise. A minute passed, and then another. Sherry watched him closely, watched his eyes jerk back and forth between two balconies. Finally, he settled on one, cleared his throat, and lifted a finger toward the sky. "See that apartment there, on the floor right below the penthouse, the one with the flower boxes," he said calmly, "on the corner?"

Sherry nodded.

"That was the apartment."

"Yeah, I see it," Sherry said, counting up to the fourteenth floor. The tape recorder was nestled on top of her purse so that it would pick up Manuel's voice but no one could see what they were up to. "How'd you get into the building?" she asked.

A smug half-smile. "No problem," Manuel answered. "I just told the doorman that the guy was expecting me. I was wearing a real nice outfit so I wouldn't look like I was there to rip off the place or nothing."

"Good idea."

"Yeah," he said, "I thought of it myself."

They sat down at a table next to the pool. A large red umbrella shielded them from the sun. The place was empty save for a flabby guy splayed out on a distant chaise longue. He was snoring.

"So tell me about the job," Sherry said. She checked to make sure the cassette was spinning. "Who was the victim? Why did you have to kill him? What did he do?"

Manuel shrugged. "His name was Pablo something, like Nevilla, I think, but I don't know what he did," he said. "I never asked."

"But he did something to piss off the family, right?"

"I guess so."

Sherry raised her shoulders in a small accidental shudder— did Manuel notice?—and then repeated his words back to him, to rattle the memory. But nothing, and she was left for a moment imagining the victim, whoever he was, sitting in his expensive apartment fourteen stories up, maybe watching *Jeopardy!* on TV or balancing his checkbook, maybe not even knowing that he had done something so bad that Mimi Lopez wanted him dead.

"So you went up in the elevator," Sherry jump-started the story for Manuel.

"Yeah, it was right around dinnertime because I remember I could smell someone cooking something good, and I went up in the elevator, and I found the apartment," Manuel said, "and I knocked on the door, and the guy looked through the peephole."

"What did you do?"

"I smiled and I waved at him, like I knew him or something."

"And?"

"And he opened the door and smiled back at me. Then he said something, like, 'Are you Carlos?' and I said, 'Are you Pablo?,' and when he nodded, I said, 'I have something for you.' " He stopped to laugh. "Most people I killed were pretty stupid," he told Sherry.

She nodded, picturing the words in 24-point type, the ideal blow-up quote. "And then?" she urged him on. "What happened after that?"

"And then I stepped inside the apartment a few feet, and the guy shut the door, and then I pulled out my piece and I shot him in the neck. It was an accident. I was aiming for his face, but he sort of jumped back, and I got him in the neck. That's how I figured out that it was a good way to kill a guy fast. Quick kill, not too much blood."

This time Sherry's shudder was full blown, and she stole a quick sideways glance to see if Manuel had noticed her horror at his grisly account. He hadn't; he was still considering the fourteenth-floor apartment with a self-satisfied smile, the kind of smug expression that might be worn by an artist reviewing his masterpiece in a museum.

"You're proud, aren't you?" Sherry asked timidly; her stomach felt a bit queasy. She already knew the answer.

Manuel dropped his chin and focused his eyes on something in the distance, something Sherry could not see. "I'm a professional," he stated simply.

Sherry nodded vaguely; suddenly her mind was too busy churning with ideas to answer otherwise. He claims he's a *professional*, she thought, but of course! Manuel must have completely turned himself off to the vileness of his crimes by compartmentalizing them as "work," the same way a butcher inures himself to sawing a bloody cow carcass in half or a dentist inures himself to drilling down to soft, oozing gum tissue day after day. *Bingo*, Sherry nearly uttered out loud. It was just as Jack always said: Reporters have to be one part Mother, one part Spanish inquisitor, and one part Freud. As usual, he was right.

"Okay," she blurted out with new energy, "a few more questions before we go." She asked Manuel to describe the victim, his clothes, his face, his hair, and he cheerfully complied. The man had been about twenty-five, he said, very cool, with black hair pulled into a ponytail and a thin mustache. He was wearing a pale pink sports coat and white shirt, buttoned up to the top, both by Fendi, he thought.

"Did he say anything?" Sherry asked.

Manuel burst out laughing, as if he had just heard an uproarious joke. "You can't say much after you get it in the neck," he said.

"Oh, yes, of course." Sherry felt like an idiot. Her ivory-tower upbringing was showing again, but Manuel didn't seem critical, just amused. She struggled to think of another serious question, came up blank, and, in frustration, started flipping through her notebook to find the long list provided by Jack. She had covered everything, it seemed, everything except the angle of the bullet.

So, quickly: "Can you tell me exactly how you shot him?" she asked, sounding a little more officious than intended. "Exactly where you held the gun?"

Manuel screwed up his face in concentration. "I guess I came in the door this way," he said, suddenly standing up and turning his back to Sherry. "And then the guy turned to the left a little, and I stepped toward him like this." He gestured for Sherry to get up and play the part of the victim. "Here," he said. "Stand like this." Sherry followed his directions. They were facing each other, two feet apart.

"So I guess I pulled the gun out of my inside holster like this." He made a quick gesture. "Now you jump back." Sherry stepped back a few feet. "No, not so far," Manuel said, pulling her a little closer to him by the arm. "Okay, so I guess then I just did this." He lifted his right arm and turned his hand into the shape of a gun. He took a step forward and pressed his index finger to Sherry's neck, right against a soft spot next to her esophagus. She could feel her pulse pounding beneath the imaginary barrel of his fingertip.

"And then, click, I pulled the trigger."

He stared into Sherry's eyes, a sly but clearly delighted smile playing on his narrow lips. She met his gaze, but she was afraid to speak until he dropped his finger from her neck, afraid that her voice would betray her. Finally, he let his hand fall back to his side. "The end," he said.

Sherry shook her head to correct him. "Not quite," she said, trying hard to sound unrattled. "Which way did the body fall?"

Manuel squinted up at the apartment again and frowned. "I'm not sure I remember exactly. Is that okay?"

"You don't remember?" Sherry asked, but almost instantly she regretted the question. How many butchers would remember the unpleasant details of their job?

"I don't remember. I didn't exactly hang around afterward," Manuel answered, and Sherry felt relieved that he didn't sound put-off with her at all. "I just stuck my gun back in the holster and I left. I remember feeling good because I didn't get any blood on me."

Sherry swallowed and took a deep breath. Again, a surge of queasiness. She forced herself to think of Dr. Feldman, her pudgy-faced dentist back in Marblehead, of his smarmy smile after he drilled open her molars to fill a cavity. She quickly ducked her head. "I'm a professional," she murmured to herself three times, so quietly Manuel did not notice. After a moment, the queasiness subsided, but she wondered how many of Manuel's stories she would have to hear before she became as inured to the gory details as he was. She looked up to see him sitting down again at the poolside table, leaning forward with anticipation. He wanted more questions, and she didn't want to disappoint him.

Sherry sat down, too. "How did you get out without the doorman seeing you?" she asked.

"He saw me. I didn't care. They weren't going to find the guy's body for a while because I shot him with a silencer, and Eddie was picking me up in a car with stolen plates." He paused. "And, oh, yeah, I forgot to tell you, I closed the door with a handkerchief. No fingerprints. I told you I was good."

Sherry nodded again and flipped through the pages of Jack's questions. She was feeling weary, as if she had enough for one day. The story was great—Christ, things couldn't be going any better—but she needed a break, if only to digest everything she had learned about Manuel and his complicated psyche. She wished Belinda were with her. Or even Brazil. How long had they been at it anyway? She checked her watch. It was almost four o'clock, but Manuel showed no signs of tiring. She could probably make it through one more hit.

"Okay, I think we've covered everything here," Sherry said. "And we'd better get going. I think we only have time for a little more today." She sighed hard to herself. Was Jack really going to make her go through *every single* job with Manuel? She already had enough quotes and background to write a thousand inches.

But Manuel had so much more to show and tell her. As soon as they were back in Sherry's car, he eagerly directed her to the spot where he killed Eddie, the man who got him started with the family. It was the parking lot of a fast-food dive called the Seven Stars, a few blocks off Calle Ocho on a narrow, unpaved side street littered with empty Coke cans and newspapers. The only other building nearby was an auto-body shop surrounded by a six-foot chain-link fence. The smell of motor oil and spray paint wafted through the car window. Sherry thought the restaurant looked familiar—she vaguely remembered covering a hit there a week or two ago—but before she could place the memory, Manuel was talking again.

"Something smells good!" he said as Sherry shifted the car into park. "I'm going to get dinner. May I buy you something?"

"No, thank you." She'd lost her appetite back by the pool.

Manuel sprinted inside. A few minutes later, he was back with a hamburger, fries, and a cherry shake. He carefully laid a napkin out in his lap and unwrapped the food. "Are you sure you don't want a bite?" he asked Sherry.

"No, thank you," she said again. She rolled up the car windows, turned on the air-conditioning, and hit the circulation button to cut out the smell and the high-pitched whine of cutting metal from the car garage. "You don't mind," she said to Manuel. It was not a question.

She watched him eat for a minute. He looked as if he were starving, champing away at the hamburger greedily, stopping only to lick his lips between bites.

She turned away and looked out her window.

"Okay, let's get started," she said to Manuel. He was halfway through his hamburger, and a rivulet of grease trickled down his chin.

"Right." He swallowed the last bite and politely wiped his mouth with a napkin. "I remember this one real good."

He told Sherry it started when he got a call at home from Fernando, Mimi Lopez's chauffeur. They had met at a party a few weeks earlier. Manuel said he couldn't believe that Fernando remembered his name, and he was more than happy to meet him at an Argentine grill joint in Little Havana that night for dinner. Something big was up.

Fernando was waiting for him when he arrived at the restaurant, and he waved him over to the table. "He was real friendly, like we were old friends," Manuel told Sherry. "I couldn't believe I was sitting down to eat with Mrs. Lopez's chauffeur. This is somebody very important."

She nodded, and Manuel continued with his story.

Fernando ordered for both of them, and it was a dinner that must have cost a hundred bucks or more: nonstop beer, three or four appetizers, huge steaks, beans, plantains, and two big bowls of sticky-sweet flan. All the way until dessert, the two of them just shot the breeze. They talked about the Dolphins, about cars, about the girls who went to their parties. Then, just after the flan arrived at the table, Fernando laid down his spoon and looked at Manuel with the seriousness of an undertaker.

"Do you know what discipline is, Manuel?" he asked. "Discipline is what keeps the family together. Discipline is what keeps the family strong. Discipline is what protects people like you and me. Now listen, Manuel, *amigo*, somebody has been disloyal to the family, and he has to be disciplined." Here Fernando stopped for a long swallow of beer, Manuel remembered. Then, he said: "Mrs. Lopez doesn't believe in second chances, you know that. This person who betrayed us has to go." He ran his finger across his throat sideways.

"And that was when it occurred to me," Manuel told Sherry. "I was the iceman. *Me!* For Mrs. Lopez's special job. *Jesucristo,* was I psyched! It was like"—Manuel stopped for a few seconds to think and then suddenly burst into a gleeful smile—"it would be like if you got promoted to TV or something!"

Sherry barely suppressed a groan—TV was for talking heads, not real reporters—but what was the point of explaining that to a sixteen-year-old? She nodded as if she understood exactly how excited he must have been. "Wow, that must have been awesome," she said, trying hard to not dampen his enthusiasm. "But then, Manuel, but then Fernando told you that you had to kill your friend Eddie, right? That couldn't have been too great."

Manuel looked irritated by the question. "Yeah, that sorta sucked," he said. "I was surprised and shit, but man, Eddie *really* fucked up."

"Oh, I'm sure," Sherry heard herself agreeing congenially. "What did he do?"

"If you can believe it, he sold to a cop," Manuel told her, rolling his eyes at the sheer stupidity. "Some stupid cop named Joe who sold coke to the kids at Saint Aidan's High."

"Maybe Eddie didn't know—"

"He knew, he knew," Manuel cut her off. "Of course he knew. I mean, he had to, he was in business with the guy for a year or something."

"Oh, I see," Sherry said. It made sense. "And so?"

"And so I said good-bye to Fernando and walked to the nearest phone booth to call Eddie. They wanted the job done fast, and he was home, so I was golden."

"Did he suspect anything?"

"Nah," Manuel said, "he trusted me. But I gotta tell you, the guy was a total loser by that point. I mean, he kept on *thanking* me for calling him." Manuel let out a harsh laugh. "I told him, 'Hey, what are friends for?' "

Sherry pretended to laugh back.

"So then I asked him if I could stop by his place, and he said no, I couldn't—there were cops everywhere, staking out his place. But lucky for me, he was hungry as hell, and he was dying to eat, so he said he could sneak out the back and meet me at the Seven Stars near his house. I told him to meet me near the dumpster." He smiled at Sherry conspiratorially. "Like, see, the dumpster is set behind these bushes in the back of the parking lot. It's real dark there. It was the perfect setup.

"Anyway, that night about nine, I said good night to my father and went into my room. He didn't even hear me or nothing. He was too shit-faced. So then I crawled out my window, and I caught the bus to Calle Ocho. Believe it or not, I even got there early. I had to count the pebbles to pass the time. I was bored."

"I'll bet," said Sherry. Again she furtively checked the tape cassette to make sure it was working. For God's sake, she thought, every word Manuel said was a knock-out quote, the kind of ironic understatement that would look great in boldface type. She could imagine it now: "Passing the time before assassinating an old friend, 'I was bored,' the teenager told the *Citizen*." The stuff of killer journalism—honest, powerful, *important*. "Tell me what happened when Eddie got there," she urged him to go on.

Manuel nodded eagerly. "Okay," he said, "like I said, I remember this part real good because I couldn't believe my eyes when Eddie showed. I mean, he was a total slob—like I said, a *loser*. His hair was all greasy, like he hadn't taken a shower or nothing, and his eyes were crazy—wide open and flipping out, you know. He was scared. Not of me, of course, but of being in deep shit with Mrs. Lopez."

"Right," said Sherry. She felt her shoulders tightening up at what was coming. "So you got it over with quickly, right?" she suggested hopefully.

Manuel sighed wistfully. "I tried," he said.

"You *tried*?"

"Yeah, but the first shot didn't kill him. It shoulda, because it was a direct hit to the neck, but I don't know, it just didn't. I mean, he was just lying there on the ground, moaning and groaning, calling out for Mary and Jesus and this saint and that saint. And then he started saying, 'Manny—why'd you do it to me?' and shit like that, so I just *boom*, nailed him in the chest. That quieted him down. Hah!"

"I'll bet it did!" Sherry heard herself saying again to cover up another brief bout of queasiness, again forced from her mind with the image of Dr. Feldman's goofy smile. Suddenly, she remembered why the Seven Stars looked so familiar—a week before, she'd stopped off on the way to work to check out a corpse near the dumpster. All at once she realized that the victim had been Eddie. If Manuel hadn't happened into her life, she would have written it off, just like the cops, as just another meaningless cocaine casualty. But she knew better now, much better, lucky for her. "I guess Mimi Lopez was pleased," she prompted Manuel for more details.

"Completely and totally." Manuel beamed. "And you're impressed, too, no?" he asked.

"Oh, sure," she answered automatically. "Although I don't really think—"

"What are you doing tonight?" Manuel cut her off.

"Working," Sherry answered quickly. Hadn't she already told him she couldn't see him socially? But perhaps he didn't grasp the concept—all their meetings probably seemed social to him.

"Can you get away for dinner?" he asked.

"No," Sherry answered firmly. "Manuel, I explained this to you before. The *Citizen* has certain rules, and one of them is that reporters are not allowed to see their sources off the job, okay?"

"Your company has dumb policies," he grumbled.

"Maybe after the story runs," Sherry said, trying to sound reassuring. She couldn't lose his allegiance.

"Okay." Manuel smiled again.

"And anyway, I thought you had a girlfriend," Sherry said.

"Blanca, yeah."

"Well, I'm sure she wouldn't be thrilled by us going to dinner."

"She wouldn't have to know about it," Manuel answered. He had obviously given it some thought already. Sherry didn't respond. She wanted him to keep talking about Blanca. Great background for the story. Her silence worked.

"Look," Manuel said, "Blanca's just not that important to me, okay?" He rolled his eyes as if what he was saying were elementary. "She'd just a prop, you know what I mean? She looks good, she talks nice. But she's pretty stupid. All she wants to talk about is love."

"A *prop*?" Sherry asked. She'd never heard that before. "Is that what boys are calling girls these days?"

Manuel shrugged. "I got it from the guys in the family."

"Oh," Sherry said, trying to suppress an incredulous giggle. "And it means?"

"Like I told you." Manuel was completely exasperated now. "It means a girl you just keep around for . . . show."

"Oh, for *show*," Sherry said. Obviously, Manuel was too polite to utter the word "sex" in mixed company. "And tell me, how does Blanca feel about being a prop?"

"She doesn't care!" Manuel groaned. "You just don't get it, do you? She's just a dumb girl!"

Sherry couldn't help herself. "Am I just a dumb girl?" she asked, head aslant in an attempt not to appear too offensive. "Manuel, you sound a little sexist to me—"

Manuel held up his hand to cut her off. "You and Blanca are totally different," he said.

"Yeah, I'm *much* older." She laughed, recalling how she and Belinda had struggled to look like teenagers the week before.

"It's not an age thing," Manuel insisted, his tone conciliatory. "Blanca is a sweet kid." He sounded as if he were talking about a ten-year-old. "You're a woman."

"Oh, really?" Sherry said. Suddenly, her irritation at Manuel's sanctimonious attitude toward women had vanished, replaced by amusement. Without a gun, Manuel was just another big-talking, chest-thumping horny teenage boy with zits and a perpetual hard-on who would get his comeuppance soon enough, as they all did.

"You've *lived*," he told her authoritatively.

"Oh, really?" Sherry asked. "How can you tell?"

"The way you look, the way you talk, the way you move."

"The way I *move*?" Sherry couldn't wait to tell Brazil about this conversation.

Manuel leaned closer to her. "You're very sexy," he said. Sherry wanted to groan.

"I like your lips."

"I'm sure Blanca has nice lips, too," she said.

"They're okay."

"Does she know—"

Manuel stopped her cold. "She doesn't know anything," he snapped.

"Anything at all?" Sherry pressed him gently. "It must be hard not to tell her."

"Not especially."

"Are you afraid she wouldn't understand?"

Manuel shifted uncomfortably in his seat. "No," he said carefully. "It's not that. I have to protect her."

"From?"

Manuel stared at Sherry blankly. He didn't seem to have an answer. "What time is it anyway?" he asked finally.

Sherry checked her watch. It was past six. "Time to get going," she said, pulling back her sleeve to show Manuel the time. "Nice watch," he said approvingly. It was a gold Cartier, a gift from her father one Christmas in college.

Sherry turned over the engine and pulled out of the parking lot. She was relieved the working day was almost over.

A few minutes later, she dropped off Manuel at his house, a bare concrete-block ranch identical, at first glance, to its neighbors except for a mangier lawn and the peeling paint on the triangle of pine clapboards over the front door. But the longer Sherry looked, the more she noticed something was awry. One of the curtains in the front window hung sloppily off its hooks, and there was a hole in the screen door precisely where a boot might kick it in. To the left of the steps, she spotted two empty cans of beer, crushed by someone's heel. The old Cutlass in the driveway was dented front and back, and the front window was cracked. Inside the house, the blue neon light of a TV glowed, but not a single light was on. Suddenly, Sherry felt an unexpected bolt of sympathy for Manuel. What a dismal place to grow up in.

"Okay, so what time tomorrow?" Manuel interrupted her musing.

"Oh, Manuel, not tomorrow, okay?" Sherry said. Belinda needed time to corroborate today's hits with police records. "I'm real busy with meetings tomorrow. How about the day after?"

Manuel was clearly displeased—Sherry watched him closely for any signs of suspicion but saw only childlike disappointment on his sliver of a face. He nodded. "Pick me up after school, right here, three o'clock."

"Okay," Sherry said warmly, taking a final look at his house. "And, Manuel, take care of yourself until then."

Sherry drove straight to Hildegarde's, a honky-tonk of a bar on the waterfront in Coconut Grove as yet undiscovered by tourists. Instead, it was jammed every night with mysterious characters of every color and persuasion—jazz musicians in town from New Orleans, failed writers from New York, bohemian sailors from everywhere and nowhere. Over the din of their laughter, Hildegarde herself, a part-Sioux, part–Puerto Rican artist from Greenwich Village who followed a long-lost husband to Miami, would often take the cheap microphone near the bar and sing rock and roll classics in her aging alto. But most of the time the sound track was the blues, heavy on Elmore James and John Lee Hooker. It was Brazil's favorite place for dinner. Fantastic clam cakes. Sherry had seen him down a dozen in one meal.

Hildegarde recognized her as she walked through the door and escorted her to a table on the patio with a view of the bay.

"Brazil just phoned, he'll be a few minutes late," Hildegarde said, pulling out Sherry's chair. "I'll get you a bourbon."

"Double it."

"Your wish, my command," she said, and sashayed toward the bar.

Sherry massaged her shoulders and let out a long sigh; it felt as if she hadn't taken a full breath for hours. She was happy Brazil was late—it would give her a few minutes to unwind. She arched her back, rolled her head from side to side, and then looked up to gaze across the shimmering bay.

Miami is simply, *utterly* beautiful, she thought, resting her eyes for a moment on a graceful catamaran lazily cruising into shore and then tilting her head back to take in the cerulean blue of the city's skies at dusk. She inhaled deeply, filling her lungs with the gentle fragrance of paradise—the scent of exotic perfume, ripe mangoes, and salt air, and then exhaled just as slowly. Up the coast, she could see the skyscrapers of downtown lighting up for the night, looking like so many glistening upside-down icicles—it was a spectacular sight, and Sherry shook her head in amazement. It was almost impossible to believe that a city so breathtaking in its beauty could create a business so ugly that it could spawn a boy like Manuel, she thought. But then again, wasn't Miami also a city of hope and new beginnings? A place where anyone could shed his past and start fresh? That was also so much a part of its splendor.

She remembered the day she decided to make Miami her home. It was during her spring-break vacation with her best friend, Alice—exactly one week after she'd discovered her father accepted—hell, he *solicited*—bribes. That, and so many other horrible truths.

The night before the trip, as she packed and unpacked her bags in a frantic explosion of loathing and grief, she'd made up her mind that she wasn't going to tell Alice about what happened in her father's study. She wasn't going to tell anybody in the whole world about it, ever. Just thinking of what she had seen and what he had said made her want to vomit—the whole flight she was so queasy, she told Alice she had a hangover—and talking about it would only make things worse. And so she vowed to spend the whole week forgetting what she had just learned, hopefully forever, by whatever means necessary.

And the means were easy to come by in Miami: booze, coke, and sex. Grammie Wheelwright required their presence once a day, at lunch, but the rest of the time they were free to sit by the pool sipping pastel-colored cocktails, or flit from chic art-deco bar to bar along South Beach, linking up with the Latin high-fashion models, Eurotrash, and idle young rich from New York, Detroit, D.C., and Boston who spent their nights snorting high-grade cocaine and their days sleeping off the effects. Within twenty-four hours of landing at Miami International Airport, Sherry and Alice were deep into the city's expansive, expensive party scene, taking a late dinner at the Strand, waiting until eleven to meet the crowd at the Edison, then dancing and drugging until dawn at one sweaty nightclub after another, finally collapsing into the arms of that night's anonymous dance partner for a quick, cocaine-rush fuck in the back of a car or on the beach. Alice was a veteran party doyenne—she often boasted that she only attended three classes a week at St. Anne's Junior College—but even she was outdone by Sherry that week. She carried a juice jar of vodka with her everywhere, started snorting coke midafternoon, danced more wildly than anyone else, and screwed more men. But when Alice questioned her abandon—"You don't want to bring a little gift home to Charles," she warned—Sherry told her she couldn't help herself. There was something about Miami that had set her free; after all these years of slaving over the books and breaking her ass at the *Crimson*, she could finally let go. "It's in the air," she told Alice, and it wasn't a lie, because Sherry was already in love with the air in Miami. It was warm and soothing, thick with liquid heat and the sweet perfume of trees pregnant with vibrant fuchsia and cadmium-yellow flowers. It was intoxicating. Why in the world, she wondered, does anyone ever leave here?

The day before the vacation was to end, while Alice was making a mandatory visit to Grandpa Wheelwright at a Surfside nursing home, Sherry rented a car and took herself on a long tour of the whole county. She drove from far south Dade, through the scrubby tomato fields of Perrine, to the northeastern edge of the city, where a wide low-slung bridge spanned the foamy green water to Miami Beach. On the way, she passed by the mossy villas of Coral Gables, and made her way—very quickly—up and down the boulevards of Liberty City, where poverty seemed to hover over the tenements like a polluted cloud. She drove through Little Havana, where shop windows were crammed full with gaudy life-size statues of Jesus and Mary, and then onto El Portal, where she saw women doing grocery shopping in their bikinis. The tour finished in Coconut Grove, where Sherry stopped at a bar to get a piña colada. "This is the Greenwich Village of Florida," a waitress with a juicy southern accent told her when she asked about the neighborhood. "Now, I've never been North, so I wouldn't know, but it is a really . . . *unusual* part of town."

Unusual, maybe, Sherry thought. Unreal, definitely. She looked at the too-blue sky above, like a Technicolor musical from the fifties, and half expected Carmen Miranda to burst out of the bushes, head covered with a hat of bananas and cherries and golden-red mangoes, belting out a sassy song about the easy life awaiting her in Miami.

The waitress was still babbling away. "It used to be it was just us Crackers down in Miami," she said, pronouncing it "My-am-uh." Sherry had never heard *that* before. "But now we got all types from down south, you know, south of the border." She clucked her tongue and twisted her mouth in a frown. "Miami is changing. Why, it's like a foreign country now! You don't know a thing about anybody anymore! It's a city of strangers." Sherry nodded happily. This was the place she was looking for.

The next day, just a few hours before she was scheduled to fly out of town, Sherry zipped over to the closest Neiman-Marcus and bought herself a white silk blouse, black Ferragamo pumps, and a crisp, professional business suit—they cost sixteen hundred dollars on her mother's charge card, but she couldn't have cared less—then she drove straight to a blocky white limestone building by the bay that she had been eyeing all week: headquarters of the *Miami Citizen*. Thanks to the paper's masthead, she knew exactly whom she was going to find there, the managing editor.

"Sherry Estabrook for Jack Dougherty," she announced herself officiously to the guard at the front desk, and the tone (and the outfit) worked just as planned. "Fifth floor," he replied politely. "Go through the double doors, straight back, third office on the right."

Three minutes later, Sherry was sitting in Dougherty's office, calmly explaining why he should offer her a job—excellent grades at Harvard, three years of daily newspaper experience, and an iron-clad guarantee that no one—*no one*—could match her aggressiveness, tenacity, and energy. "If I don't work harder for you than anyone else, if I don't break more stories, uncover more sleaze, get more quotable quotes, find more Deep Throats, than anyone else, I'll pay *you* for the money lost on my hire," Sherry said, and by her matter-of-fact tone Dougherty knew she was not kidding around. He'd seen plenty of ambitious cub reporters in his time, but none this ambitious. And her credentials weren't bad. Skimpy on the experience, but she made up for that in gall. He liked her. He liked her very much.

"Did you have an appointment?" he asked when she was done laying out her argument.

"No."

"You just decided to stop on by, huh?" Jack pressed her, deadpan.

"Yes." Sherry smiled briefly. "I always think it's best to see someone in person, to cut through all the bullshit of introductory letters and piles of clips and six or seven meaningless interviews with underlings who don't have any hiring power. Screw all that. I wanted to make my case directly to you. So I came in."

"You speak Spanish?"

"I'll learn."

Dougherty burst into laughter. He believed her.

"You ever seen a dead body?"

"Blood doesn't scare me," Sherry answered.

"That mean no?" Dougherty asked.

"That means no," Sherry said, "I'm not afraid of anything. You'll see. I'll get my hands as dirty as any reporter in this place. I'll talk to everyone—cops, construction workers, poor people, rich people, everyone. I'm ready to do whatever it takes."

Dougherty sighed and lit a cigarette. He'd been in the business long enough to read a person in five minutes or less, and what he was reading here was an extremely rich, quite talented, overconfident, and very good-looking young woman on one very complicated psychological mission.

"What you running from?" he asked her.

"What?" Sherry shook her head as if she hadn't heard the question. "Pardon me?"

"What you running from?" Dougherty asked again. "You have a fight with your boyfriend? Your parents kick you out?"

"No to both questions," Sherry answered assertively. "Absolutely *no*."

Dougherty shrugged. He'd find out the real answer soon enough. "Okay, you're hired," he said simply. "You start at three-fifty a week." He paused to gauge her reaction, but there was none. "First day is—"

"Right after graduation, June sixth," Sherry interrupted him. She jumped out of her chair and rushed toward him to shake hands. "You just made the best decision of your life," she told him. "You won't be sorry."

And he wasn't. From the day Sherry started on the *Citizen's* city desk, she had kept her promises. She was willing to take on the grungiest assignments, go to the farthest-flung locales, put in the most hours softening up difficult sources. She worked late nights, weekends, holidays. If there was a shooting or a fire near her house, or where she was eating dinner out—police radio always buzzing nearby—she'd call in and volunteer to cover the story. Before her first year at the *Citizen* was up, she didn't have to ask Dougherty to promote her, he offered to, moving her onto his special investigative team, giving her the choicest, toughest assignments. She never failed to deliver with the same revved-up, pushy ambition that had so impressed him at their first meeting. He half expected it to fade one day, just as he half expected her to someday spill her guts to him about her troubles back home, but neither happened. In fact, the only time he ever heard her mention home was to explain, in an expressionless voice, why she was volunteering to work Christmas Day. Her parents, she told him, were spending the holidays on the Continent. She didn't know if it was true or not, and she didn't care with a single cell in her body. She still didn't.

"Yoo-hoo, Miss Estabrook?" Suddenly, Sherry heard Brazil calling her name in a high-pitched singsong. "Where the hell are you, darlin'? I've been sitting here for five minutes."

"Oh, just thinking," she said.

"About me, of course."

"Of course," she said sarcastically, but not without affection. She noticed the drink in front of her and took a long sip. "You're late."

"Big powwow about your fucking story," he told her. "Everybody and their mother has an opinion about what kind of art it's gonna need. Hell, good ol' Newman even made it to this meeting, ranting and raving about 'going for the gold,' and 'giving one hundred and one percent.' What a dingdong! Finally, Vinnie shut him up and started handing out assignments. If you can believe it, they got Mary Lou flying to Medellín tomorrow to shoot pictures of Mimi Lopez's little ol' digs down there. Understand it's got forty-four rooms in all. And they say there's no money in teaching violin to handicapped children!"

He laughed heartily at his own joke.

"What about my story?" Sherry interrupted the guffaws. "Who's doing it?"

"You're looking at him, darlin'." He gave her a familiar told-you-so smirk.

"Well, you sure as hell aren't taking a photo of Manuel."

"Yes, so I've been informed," Brazil said. "But, frankly, I don't know why we're trying to protect this kid. He's a fucking killer. As far as I'm concerned, we should plaster his picture across the top of the front page."

"And then we can go sit along the Miami River and wait for his body to float by."

"It's going to float by whether we run his picture or not," Brazil said. "The kid is dead the minute your story runs. He seems to be the only person who doesn't realize it."

"No, no," Sherry insisted, putting down her drink. "He knows what he's doing. He has some plans to take off for Mexico as soon as the story hits the streets. He says he's got it completely under control." She paused for a moment to arrange the thoughts rushing through her mind, then went on. "And plus, Brazil," she said, "if he doesn't get out in time, the D.A. will protect him. He's their star witness in a very, very big case."

Brazil laughed incredulously. "If that's how you want to deal with your guilt," he said, "fine by me."

A waiter appeared at their table, just in time.

"Crab cakes," said Brazil. Sherry ordered a salad.

"You have *got* to learn to eat," Brazil said after the waiter left.

"I'm trying to keep my girlish figure." Suddenly, she smiled. "Oh, God, that reminds me, Manuel told me today that he thinks I'm sexy. He likes my lips." She finished off the bourbon and signaled the waiter for another.

"Whoa," said Brazil. "I don't like that at all."

"Don't worry, dearest. I'm yours forever."

"That's not what worries me," Brazil said. "Sherry, you're in this too damn deep. This kid's got a fucking crush on you."

"No, he's just a flirt, like every other Cuban man ever born."

"Maybe, yeah." Brazil stopped to think. "But it's dangerous for this guy to be liking you like that. It's gonna backfire."

Another bourbon arrived. "You're just jealous," Sherry said.

"I'm just worried about you," Brazil came back angrily. He hated it when Sherry acted sanctimonious. "I don't get jealous."

"You're jealous of Charles."

"That faggot?"

"Oh, and you're not jealous."

"I'm not." He was going to win this argument. "It's just that Charles—and I don't know why the fuck nobody calls him Charlie or Chuck like a real man—gets in the way of us having a future."

Sherry rolled her eyes. "May I remind you that you're married?" she asked.

"I got married because I realized that Charles had turned us into a dead end."

Sherry jerked her head forward. Dead end? she thought to herself—Brazil doesn't talk that way. Sometimes she was certain he could read her mind. And the fact was, she had stopped thinking about the end of their relationship after Brazil had returned to her the night of her Christmas party. What was the point? He was going to stay married to Jeanie, and she was going to have to find somebody new sooner or later. They had a few good years left in them. The inevitable only made every kiss sweeter, every moment alone more poignant. Just the week before, she had written in her diary that loving Brazil was like loving a dying man.

"Sherry?" Brazil's voice was tender; he was afraid she'd finally figured out that he had read her diary. But one look from her convinced him that he was still safe.

"Oh, Brazil, let's just drop the whole subject, okay?" she said a little wearily. "Let's just eat and get home to bed."

"Sounds just divine to me," he answered.

24

The phone was ringing when they walked through the door of Sherry's house an hour later.

"Ignore it," Brazil said, pushing Sherry toward the bedroom. He was already half-undressed.

"It could be Manuel." She grabbed the receiver in the kitchen. Brazil clumped down the hall, pants around his ankles, and sank noisily onto the bed. Sherry could hear him turn the picture of Charles on her night table facedown with an intentionally loud crack.

"This is 7113," she said into the phone—the last four digits of her phone number. She'd started doing that when an army of old people started misdialing her house, looking for some nursing home at a similar number. Now it was something of a trademark that amused her friends.

"Excuse me?" said a confused voice at the other end of the line. It was a long-distance call.

"This is Sherry," she said quickly, a little annoyed.

It was Alice, practically hysterical, calling from Marblehead.

"Sherry, I've been trying to reach you for *days*," she began breathlessly. "The wedding is almost here, and you haven't called to find out about your bridesmaid's dress or anything. Is everything all right? I know you're busy working and all, but you have to get the dress fitted before it's too late, or everything will be all screwed up."

The dress? Had Sherry actually told her she would be a bridesmaid? The wedding wasn't for months, right?

"Alice, my God, first tell me how you are," Sherry said, stalling.

"Oh, just crazy with last-minute wedding details." Alice sounded a little calmer. Sherry could hear Brazil pacing around the bedroom, but she ignored him. The words "last minute" had made the muscles in her shoulders cramp painfully.

"Now, when's the wedding exactly?" Sherry said, trying to sound as if the date had momentarily slipped her mind.

"November twentieth," Alice answered quickly. "Sherry, it's in *three* weeks!"

Three weeks? That's just when the Manuel story would be wrapping up.

"Look, Alice, I'm sorry, I've been working on a really big story. My mind is totally elsewhere," Sherry said. "I'm not even sure my boss will let me get away. I'm sure he won't."

No response.

"Alice?"

"Sherry, you can't do this to me. The wedding party is all set. What am I supposed to do—tell Jamie to uninvite one of his ushers?" Alice started to cry softly, and Sherry could picture her trying to stop the tears by pressing the corners of her lovely hazel eyes with an index finger. "And you would miss my wedding? After everything we've been through together? I would *never* miss your wedding—Sherry, what has happened to you?"

"Please don't cry, Alice."

"I'm not crying." A muffled sniffle.

"This is a hard business," Sherry offered. "I'm working on a very important story—you'll understand in a few weeks. I just can't leave Miami now. I just can't."

"I thought"—another watery sniffle—"I thought you were my best friend." The words spilled out in the delicate, injured voice of a little girl.

Sherry felt strangled by guilt, and sadness, too. She couldn't even remember meeting Alice; they had been friends that long. When other girls bickered and broke alliances in high school, they had stayed together, loyally escorting each other through ridiculous failed romances with the boys from St. Mark's, bad encounters with dope, false-alarm pregnancies, and one real one—Alice's.

But were they still *best* friends? Were they even friends at all anymore? In her gut, Sherry knew that Alice was reaching out for someone else entirely—she wanted the Sherry who existed before Miami, before she had started working seven days a week to cover race riots in Liberty City and cocaine murders in Little Havana, before she had encountered the unrelenting sadness of loving Belinda and embraced the exquisite pain of loving Brazil, before she had begun hating the Beauregards like death, before she had ever met a boy named Manuel.

But then, hadn't Alice been there always, through the party at One Hundred Endless Horizon Lane, through every boring up and down with Charles, through that wild, unhinged spring break when she decided to make Miami home? And it was crazy, Sherry thought, but she couldn't help remembering the time they pricked their fingers with a needle in her bedroom, mingled their blood, and in dead seriousness declared themselves eternal sisters. How time passes. . . .

"Oh, Alice, I'll be there," Sherry said. "Of course I'll be there."

"You will?"

"I couldn't let you down."

"I knew you couldn't."

Brazil appeared at the door to the kitchen, naked except for his orange flip-flops. Sherry held up a finger to indicate the call would take only another minute.

"Alice, I have guests," she said. "Tell me quick what I have to do."

"Is there a Neiman-Marcus near you?"

It figured. "Yeah, in Fort Garbage Pail."

"What?" Alice asked.

"In Fort Lauderdale."

"Oh," said Alice, sounding relieved but a little perplexed. She wasn't sure whether she had misheard Sherry the first time. "Just go to their bridal department and give them my name, and they'll fit you for the dress. You'll just love it, Sherry, it's a fabulous black velvet—"

"Black?"

"Black is *the* color for bridesmaids this season."

"What does Hannah think?" Sherry asked. They had always referred to their mothers by their first names.

"It was her idea."

"Well, it sounds like you two are getting along."

"Yeah," said Alice almost apologetically. "She's actually okay these days."

"Great."

"Yeah," said Alice. "So, Sherry, what's this big story you're working on? Will I see it on the news?"

"Alice, I'd love to tell you all about it, but I have to go." She could hear Brazil snoring like an old drunk in the bedroom, but she wasn't sure if he was asleep or only trying to annoy her.

"Okay, okay," Alice said sympathetically. Then, quickly: "But Sherry, one last thing before you run—look, is it okay that we have you, um, with Charles during the wedding procession? I mean, he'll be escorting you down the aisle—is that okay?"

Sherry lowered her voice to an urgent whisper. "Charles and me? Can't you give me some other usher?"

"Not really," Alice began. Sherry could tell she was winding up for a long, rehearsed explanation, but she cut her off. "We're not going out anymore," she said, still whispering.

Silence. Then: "I'm sorry, Sherry." The statement came in a voice that said, This is not negotiable.

Sherry sighed to herself. "It's okay, Alice," she said.

The snoring had stopped, and Brazil was up again. The TV was on, tuned to a Hawks game. She heard the announcer exclaiming something about Larry Bird. How perfect, she thought, they're playing the Celts.

"I've gotta go," Sherry said.

"Right, right," said Alice. "Call me, please, Sherry, when you're all set with the dress, just so I can mark it off my list."

"Promise."

They said good-bye, and Sherry rushed down the hall to the bedroom. Brazil was sitting on a chair by the TV, enraptured by the game. He didn't even look up when she scurried into the room and started pulling off her dress.

"Don't be mad at me," Sherry said. "Things are bad enough as it is."

"Uh-huh."

"I have to go home in three weeks for Alice's wedding."

"Uh-huh." Brazil's eyes were fixed on the screen; Bird sank a three-pointer.

"Just when the Manuel story is wrapping up . . ."

"Uh-huh."

"And I have to be escorted by Charles down the fucking aisle. Believe me, it wasn't my idea. Alice said I *had* to do it—"

Brazil clicked off the tube and swiveled around to face Sherry. "What in the hell—" he said, standing up abruptly. His voice was rough, but his eyes, darkening from see-through blue to gray-green as if a cloud were passing overhead, betrayed him: He was more sad than angry—and mainly he was confused, totally confused. Sherry had only seen him look this knocked off center once before—the drizzly night they slammed into a fawn driving back from Sanibel Island through the Everglades. Brazil had been driving, not looking at the road, of course, but instead staring at Sherry, excitedly telling her a detail-laden story about his great-aunt Opal of Opa-Locka and her two husbands. Then: *thuuunk.* The car had swerved from left to right, hitting the sandy embankment on both sides before swirling through a 180-degree turn to a dead stop. "What in the hell—" Brazil had said.

Sherry remembered that Brazil cried when they found the crumpled body of the fawn a hundred yards back. Its eyes were still open. It was just a baby, really.

He wasn't crying now, but he looked as if he might.

Sherry opened her mouth to tell Brazil not to worry, but he stopped her cold by raising his hand and clapping it over her mouth.

"Don't tell me not to worry," he said.

"Well, don't." It was the best she could offer. She was trying to think of something funny to say.

Suddenly, Brazil caught Sherry around the waist, pulled her into bed, and dragged the covers over their heads. Even in the dim light, she could see the wounded, vulnerable expression on his wide Cracker face. He lay tight beside her, kissed her palms, and held them to his chest. "Look here, my little darlin'," he said with a false bravado that broke Sherry's heart, "don't you go running off with that guy."

His head was nestled between Sherry's chin and shoulder, the way she always lay against him, and he draped one heavy leg over hers, using it to draw her so close there was no air between them.

How odd this felt—to have Brazil hug her the way a child hugs his mother during a thunderstorm—and to hear him so frightened of losing her. And how strange for it to happen now, especially, when she was more wedded to Miami than ever.

"Don't worry," she told Brazil, smoothing his hair and kissing his forehead lightly. "I have to go home, but I'll come back." It sounded wrong, she thought, and she tried again, softly, so the man beside her couldn't make out the words, "I have to go back," she said, "but I'll come home."

25 Belinda woke up the next morning at 6:11 A.M.—she didn't use an alarm clock. She slept with the shades open, always had. It was the best way to get adjusted to different time zones. Or so her father had always said.

It had been a tough night; in fact, she wasn't even sure she had fallen completely asleep. Her morning mind was tangled with half-dreams and scattered, unfamiliar images: There was a dry-brown mountain peak piercing thin air with the audible high-C pitch of a violin; a school of silvery fish, small as plugs and shaped like bullets, pirouetting up a waterfall; there were little girls in bejeweled black chadors playing "Mother-May-I" someplace very dusty—where in the world? She shook her head to jostle the images away.

She longed to talk to Eladio, to have him anchor her back to earth. How long had it been since their last conversation? Nearly seven hours. And it would be another twelve before they would see each other again. He had to spend the day in court for some criminal-trespassing trial, and she had to spend the day poking around the police archives, verifying Manuel's murders without raising any eyebrows. No wonder she had such trouble sleeping. She hated this whole Manuel story. It involved such deceit.

But she knew there was no getting away from it, of course. What could she do—tell Jack that she wasn't interested in working on the "greatest fan-fucking-tastic story on earth," as he called it? Just the other day, he had pulled her aside in the newsroom and congratulated her for landing on the kind of Pulitzer Prize–winning jackpot that "any reporter would die for." It was just luck, of course, and they both knew it. He was just trying to be a good guy. It was Sherry's story.

And Sherry—she couldn't tell Sherry she wanted out. A year

or two ago, maybe, she could have told her to ask for another partner on the story. But that was before the Thanksgiving dinner of her father's farewell.

Belinda had returned to Miami the day after the funeral. She hadn't asked her, but Sherry was there at the airport, waiting patiently for a flight three hours late, appropriately dressed in black. "I'm falling," Belinda had said to her in a hoarse voice as they stood at the baggage carousel, and in fact, she looked like she might collapse to the floor at any moment. But that wasn't what Belinda was afraid of; she was terrified of hitting the ground from the unrelenting free-fall she had been in since the moment she shut her father's eyes in the garage.

"Can you keep me standing?" Belinda asked Sherry.

"Whatever it takes."

Sherry put her arm around Belinda and hugged her close. She felt thinner than ever, and her frail body, cloaked in a heavy, oversized black raincoat, was trembling all over, as if an errant arctic wind had found its way to the Miami airport.

"Sherry?"

"Yeah, Belinda?"

"Does it show?"

"No."

"Are you sure?"

"I'm positive, Belinda," Sherry lied, hugging her again.

She had stayed with Sherry that night, sleeping in bed with her, just as she used to sleep with her mother years and years ago, when her father was off on some weeks-long adventure. She woke up crying twice, and both times Sherry had helped her back to sleep with soft, wordless murmurs. Then, in the morning, Sherry fixed her a huge breakfast of eggs and bacon and muffins. It meant a lot to Belinda; she knew it was the first time Sherry had ever prepared a meal in her life.

If that had been all that Sherry had done, of course, getting out of the Manuel story would still be possible. Not easy or comfortable, but possible.

But in the months that followed, Sherry had kept Belinda standing, just as she had promised.

When she froze on assignment, Sherry was always there to ask the next question or to call in the lead to the news desk or to sell the story to Radewski at Nerve Central so it wouldn't be buried in the back pages. When she couldn't sleep at night, Sherry would talk to her for hours, until the demons faded long enough for her to close her eyes. And when she rear-ended Cuban ladies in their Cadillacs, Sherry was there with her money. She didn't even have to ask.

And so Belinda knew she would spend this day, and God knows how many more, traipsing around Miami police headquarters surreptitiously making sure this Manuel boy was telling the horrible truth.

She slipped on a faded blue denim skirt and a rumpled white button-down shirt and pulled her hair back into a low ponytail. The phone rang.

"Hi, Sherry," Belinda said, picking up the receiver.

"You all set to go?"

"Yep." Belinda picked up a notebook from her bureau and flipped through the first few pages. "I've got the dates and the details. Now all I need is the proof. Simple."

"I hope so."

"Me, too."

"Look," Sherry said, "I've been thinking, can Eladio help you? He has such great access—"

"The answer is no," Belinda said. Her voice was so firm it startled both of them. "I told you, Sherry, he's not getting involved. He could lose his job. It's bad enough that he knows all about this and he has to keep it a secret."

"Okay, okay," said Sherry. "Well, good luck. Keep me posted." She didn't ask how Belinda was going to get her hands on the murder records, and she didn't want to; she had too many other details to worry about. Belinda would get it done; that was all that mattered.

26

The moment she pushed open the door to the information office at police headquarters, Belinda knew Officer Aloe was on duty. She could tell by the noise—the wildly cheering audience on *Wheel of Fortune* boomed from a TV mounted in one corner—and she could tell by the smell of the place.

It smelled like aloe.

The officer on duty—her real name was DeLisa Watson—was a high priestess of aloe.

If you heard her out, which was a painful process that all cop reporters had to suffer through at least once in their careers, DeLisa Watson would tell you that the aloe plant has been used for centuries to cure hives, warts, dry skin, oily skin, bee stings, psoriasis, pimples, sunburn, and wrinkles. And did you know (she would ask, wide-eyed with astonishment) that many great ladies, including Cleopatra and Cher, have sworn by aloe to enhance their natural, inborn sex appeal?

Yes indeed, DeLisa Watson would tell you in a slow, sugary Deep South drawl, aloe possesses a special ability to actually massage *deep hidden* layers of skin cells and make them *come alive*. Aloe relieves stress! she would exclaim with the fervor of a true believer speaking in tongues. It releases inner beauty! It reverses the aging process! It increases the human sex drive—and improves performance in the boudoir!

Then: "Might I interest you in purchasing some su-*perb* products produced by Everything Aloe, a fine Miami cosmetics emporium?"

Probably a dozen *Citizen* reporters had a tube of the stuff lying around. Belinda had escaped, until now. And now, she was ready to spend whatever it took to get what she was there for.

"Officer Watson—hi!" Belinda said cheerfully, plopping down in the office's couch and curling her legs underneath her. "What's new with you?"

DeLisa Watson quickly shut the TV and smiled at Belinda with the warmth and affection of a hungry spider.

"Don't tell me your name," she said, coming around from her desk and parking herself next to Belinda on the couch. "I'll remember it." She squinted her eyes and knocked her forehead with the back of her wrist. "Oh, dear!" she drawled. "I must be the most forgetful person on earth! I am terrible with names, I just am!"

"Belinda McEvoy."

"That's right! Of course!"

"From the *Citizen*."

"Why, I *knew* that!" She playfully pretended to slap Belinda's arm. They were old friends already.

"Well, it certainly is hot outside," Belinda began. Ever since her arrival in Miami, she had noticed that the locals constantly commented on the heat. What did they expect, anyway?

"Hotter than a chili pepper!"

"I'll say," Belinda answered, "and to think I have to keep myself looking cool and pretty for a date tonight." She pouted thoughtfully.

"A date!" exclaimed DeLisa Watson. This was too good to be true. "Why, isn't that marvelous! I am a big fan of love!"

Belinda nodded. She noted that DeLisa Watson wasn't wearing a wedding band, but she did have perfectly manicured nails painted a bright and pearly pink. In fact, everything about her was manicured, from her straightened black hair, coiffed into an improbable 1950s-era flip, to her police uniform, which she managed to frilly up with a fake cameo brooch at the collar and a crocheted white sweater.

"You know," DeLisa Watson was saying, now facing Belinda with an expression of deep concern, "you know, you have to love yourself before you can love another."

For a split second, Belinda considered saying, "Amen."

"So true," she answered instead.

"I love myself," DeLisa Watson intoned.

"That's great," said Belinda.

"I love myself, and so I take care of myself." She said "myself" the Old South way, Belinda noticed, as if it were two words. "Do you love yourself?" Again, two words.

"I think so," Belinda responded. She knew what was coming.

Then, solemnly: "Do you take care of yourself?" DeLisa Watson asked.

"Oh, no, not really. Not nearly as well as I should," said Belinda, trying to sound sincere and worried. "For instance, I really don't take good care of my *skin*."

DeLisa Watson leapt up from the couch as if a firecracker had exploded beneath her cushion. "Girl!" she practically shouted, "you have come to the right place!" She locked the door to the office and then rushed to her bottom desk drawer and pulled out a huge flower-print carpetbag filled with tubes, bottles, and jars.

Twenty minutes later, Belinda had spent close to fifty expense-account dollars on everything aloe, and she and DeLisa Watson had become spiritual kin.

"Now tell me true," DeLisa Watson asked as she tucked Belinda's money into her wallet, "don't you feel like you are about to embark onto a brand-new journey?" She didn't wait for an answer. "Life will never be the same!"

Belinda smiled sweetly. She was ready to make her move, but DeLisa Watson had more business to conduct. She leaned closer to Belinda on the couch.

"Now tell me, who is the lucky man you'll be dating tonight? Is he someone special?"

Why not tell her? Belinda thought—she'll eat it up.

"As a matter of fact, I'm going out with a Miami policeman."

An audible gasp. "You are!" DeLisa Watson looked as emotionally overcome as the mother of a bride. "I am so proud of you—and with your aloe regime, you two will be so happy I could cry!"

"It's Eladio Alvarez," Belinda offered. "Do you know him?"

DeLisa Watson squeezed Belinda's arm and shook her head in amazement. "I just *love* that man," she said. "He is so handsome! And so kind! You are a lucky girl."

"We're not married yet!" Belinda strained to smile; it was getting harder and harder to keep up the mock cheeriness.

"With aloe"—DeLisa Watson paused for emphasis—"you will be soon."

Belinda smiled again but did not answer; she couldn't prolong this conversation another minute. She had to do it *now*—before she lost her nerve and before DeLisa Watson lost the rosy glow of a cash commission. Belinda stood, slung her purse over her shoulder, and started for the door. But as she reached for the doorknob, she turned suddenly.

"Oh, DeLisa!" she said, as if thunderstruck by her own silly absentmindedness. "I almost forgot! I need a couple of police reports from you."

"Just give me the dates," she answered happily, picking up the phone and dialing the three-digit extension of Central Files.

Belinda jotted *Homicides: January 11, October 20* onto a slip of paper and handed it to DeLisa Watson.

The cop stared at the paper for a moment, turned it over a few times, and then scrunched her face into a perplexed frown. "I'm not seeing something," she said. There was a slight edge to the drawl.

"No, that's it," Belinda answered, keeping her voice upbeat. "I need all the homicide reports from those dates."

"You what?"

"I need the homicide reports filed on those dates," Belinda said, as if it were the most ordinary request in the world.

DeLisa Watson tilted her head to one side and considered Belinda closely. Was someone trying to make a fool of her?

"Are you looking for something?" she asked.

"Yes," said Belinda. "I'm looking for all the homicides on those dates."

"I got that."

"Right," said Belinda, shrugging. "So?"

"So," mimicked DeLisa Watson, "what are you looking for? I mean, what's the story about?" She used a long thumbnail to cut off the phone connection with Central Files.

"I'm not sure yet," answered Belinda. "A bunch of us are working on a story about cocaine's toll on Miami—in human terms. We're taking a look at a number of unsolved homicides."

"In human terms? I see. Haven't y'all done that story before?"

"I suppose so," Belinda said, tiring of the charade. "And I suppose we'll keep doing it until there's no more cocaine in Miami."

"Listen here, honey," DeLisa Watson shot back, "there are more than four hundred homicides a year in metropolitan Miami. You expect the police to solve them all?" She pulled her lips into an angry grimace. "You reporters sure don't like Miami, do you?" It was the voice of a cop speaking.

"No, we love Miami. But it's sick right now." She had heard

Sherry use this excuse with belligerent cops on a dozen occasions. "We want it to get well."

"Isn't that nice of you," DeLisa Watson said icily.

The two women studied each other.

Belinda checked her watch. "Look," she said finally, "I still need those reports."

DeLisa Watson pursed her lips into a small, smug smile and arched her eyebrows suspiciously. "And you need *these* dates for some particular reason?" She waved the slip of paper in the air dramatically as if it were evidence in a murder trial.

"Yes!" Belinda shot back. A miscalculation—she saw DeLisa Watson harden even more. Belinda quickly forced a tame, apologetic smile.

"Really, DeLisa," she said sweetly, leaning into the cop's name with her best southern accent, "it's just a simple request." She reached into her purse and pulled out a purple tube of aloe lotion. "This is much more important to me—but a girl's got to make a living!"

"Don't I know it," said DeLisa Watson, clearly relieved to be back on familiar ground. Her shoulders relaxed, and for a full thirty seconds, she seemed to be considering the tube of aloe in Belinda's hand. "That's a fine product you have there," she finally added. It was a peace offering. "I myself use it—and it's guaranteed. Like it says, total satisfaction guaranteed or your money back—and you know where to find me!"

The tension of a minute before had evaporated—another problem, Belinda thought, cured by aloe.

DeLisa Watson picked up the phone again and dialed the basement. "Hi, Herb? It's DeLisa up here in PIO," she said. The flirtatious drawl had returned. "Yeah, hi, honey, how you doing? Uh-huh. Oh, good. Now, how you liking that aloe after-shave?" Long pause. "Now what? Well, listen, Herb, you just keep on using it, and I'm telling you, you *will* see results. Uh-huh." She giggled.

"Uh, Herb, sweetness, I am sending down a lovely woman here from the *Citizen* newspaper, and I would like you to pull two reports for her, the homicides on January eleventh and October twentieth of this year," DeLisa Watson said. "Yep, just give 'em to her, honey, and let her Xerox them right there—okay? And, Herb, you keep using that aloe!"

DeLisa Watson hadn't even hung up when Belinda smiled

brightly and bolted out the door. A minute later, she was face-to-face with Herb, her right hand outstretched for the reports. She couldn't wait to get out of the building.

"Computer's still printing 'em out, miss," he told her, laughing at her pushiness but not in an unfriendly way. "You reporters!"

"Us reporters—yep!" Belinda shot back, sounding accidentally bitchy. She didn't want to take her frustration out on some poor desk officer, and especially not on this one, another sucker to DeLisa Watson's hard sell. "Sure is hot out there," she said to change the subject.

"Wouldn't know it down in this dungeon," Herb replied matter-of-factly, and suddenly Belinda liked him quite a lot—a Miami resident not delighted to talk about the weather. Then again, he barely looked like a local. He was more the Brooklyn schoolteacher type: His hair was mousy brown and disheveled, his eyes were dark and intelligent, but he was pudgy and pale-faced from too many hours in a thankless job. That, and his whole body sagged, as if he had long ago thrown in the towel to the world's ironies and injustices. She guessed he had three kids at home—he was around forty—and a wife who worked nights at the supermarket bagging groceries to make the mortgage. While she was gone, he spent his evenings cleaning the house and reading Tennyson.

Abruptly, the printer stopped buzzing and spit out two sheets of paper. "Here we go," said Herb. He picked up the reports to hand to Belinda, but then pulled them back just as she was about to take them.

"Oops," he said. "Can't have these. Says here at the top that these cases are still under investigation. You know what that means." He rolled his eyes sympathetically.

Belinda knew exactly what it meant—it meant she'd slammed into a brick wall. According to police-department regulations, reporters were not permitted to look at any case that the detectives in Vice happened to consider "too sensitive" to appear in the press. They claimed publicity might blow their cover or screw up a prosecution down the road. But in the newsroom, everyone knew that nine times out of ten "under investigation" meant the cops were suspectless and clueless, and they didn't want the world knowing about it.

"Give me a break!" Belinda groaned. All that aloe goop and

girl talk with DeLisa Watson for nothing? "Look, Herb," she appealed, "I don't have to copy the damn things. I just need to take a quick look at them, to verify a few measly details."

Herb shook his head. "Sorry," he said, and sounded as if he meant it. "You know I can't let you see these. I don't love my job, but I'm not quite ready to retire, if you know what I mean."

"Yeah," Belinda sighed. "I sure do." She paused for a moment for effect. "I want to keep my job, too. And that's why I have to see just a few simple facts on those reports—time, location, victim, and cause of death. That is all. I don't want any narrative or description. Believe me, I like doing this even less than you do. That is the honest-to-God truth."

Herb shook his head again, but then quickly glanced left and right. Belinda immediately sensed his indecision.

"Herb," she said, "look, I know the homicides occurred. All I need are a few very basic facts. I can absolutely guarantee they will not appear in the *Citizen* in any way, shape, or form that will indicate I got them from you."

"They won't?"

"Absolutely not," Belinda said firmly. "I just want to verify information we already have, okay?"

Once again, Herb looked left and right to make sure they were alone. "All right," he said, voice dropping to a whisper. "But this is the deal. Let me read them to you, okay? That way, I can say you never saw them if anyone asks."

"Fine," said Belinda, whispering, too. "That's great. Let's start with January eleventh, all right? Who was the victim?"

Herb checked the report in front of him. "Pablo Nevilla," he said quickly.

Belinda checked her notes and nodded. "Time?" she prompted him.

"Estimate of six to seven P.M."

"Location?"

"It's 1515 Tomar Boulevard, apartment 1407."

"Cause of death?"

"Um—hold on a second," Herb told Belinda. "I just got to read through it a bit." He scanned the report's narrative section, reading to himself: *"Victim's body found at 0800 hours by victim's brother, who was worried because victim had not answered repeated phone calls to his apartment. Victim was discovered faceup on floor near entrance to apartment. Medical examiner reports victim sustained several stab*

*wounds to the face and eyes with an ice pick–type instrument and had
what appeared to be the letter M carved into his forehead with the same
instrument. Cause of death was single gunshot wound to the right side
of the neck. No signs of forced entry. No signs of struggle. No signs of
burglary or robbery."*

Herb clucked his tongue. "Drugs," he said. "They make people sick."

"You're not kidding," Belinda agreed. "But what did you say was the cause of death?"

"Oh, yes," the cop said, "single gunshot wound to the neck."

"Right," said Belinda. Big surprise. "How about the October twentieth hit? Who was the victim?"

The cop shuffled the papers and switched to the next report. "Eddie Rodriguez," he answered.

"Time?"

"Let's see—the body was found about eleven A.M."

"Location?"

"At 1023 Southwest Fourth—the parking lot of a restaurant called Seven Stars."

"And last but not least," Belinda said, "cause of death."

"Hold on," Herb said, and again he rushed through the narrative, reading it quickly to himself: *"Victim discovered by night manager J. Bromberg at 1100 hours near garbage dumpster behind restaurant. Victim was fully clothed, lying on right side. Medical Examiner E. Sozio called to scene, reported victim sustained mutilation to face, chest, and arms with ice pick or other sharp weapon. Left ear removed and apparent ritualistic marking M or N made in victim's forehead with sharp instrument. Cause of death gunshot wounds to chest and neck. See addendum for autopsy report."*

"Well," Herb told Belinda, "looks like you got the same sicko here."

Belinda shrugged noncommittally.

"Cause of death: two gunshots, chest and neck."

Belinda smiled appreciatively. "I am much obliged," she said, jotting down the last piece of information and closing her notebook. "Herb, I owe you one. Thanks a million."

The cop smiled. "Now get lost," he told her, and she was gone.

27

The newsroom was in full throttle when Belinda arrived a few minutes later. Deadline was approaching, and she could hear Radewski shouting for copy as reporters frantically clicked out the day's news at their computers. She envied them.

Sherry was at her desk, headphones clamped over her ears, transcribing the latest interview with Manuel. Belinda peered over her shoulder at the screen. *Um, let's see, I think I got paid two grand for that one,* she saw Sherry type. *It was a good one . . . I got him right in the neck. Very quick. He didn't even see it coming.*

Belinda knew she would have to verify this one, too. But why bother? The kid was more honest than most politicians the *Citizen* quoted, but no one double-checked their claims.

She tapped Sherry on the shoulder. "Hi. I'm back."

Sherry pulled off the headphones and looked up at Belinda anxiously. "Did you get them?" she asked. "Did you get the reports?"

"I got what we needed, Sherry, and everything checks out."

"Yes!" Sherry jumped from her seat, grabbed Belinda by the wrist, and dragged her into Jack's office. "Hello, boss, hello!" she announced, slamming the door closed behind them. "Everything checked out!"

Jack jumped up from his chair. He looked at Belinda for confirmation but got none. She was staring vaguely out the window to the bay, thinking about the hundreds of shades of blue below. They were lovely, and it made her sad that she hadn't noticed them earlier.

"Belinda?" Jack said.

"Yes, yes," she answered slowly. Suddenly, she felt exhausted; it was an effort to speak. "It's true, Jack. I got a cop to read me the reports you wanted me to verify, and they both check out perfectly. It's as if Manuel wrote them himself."

"Like? Like?" Sherry prodded.

"Like, um, both victims were shot where he said they'd be, in the neck or chest or whatever, and the addresses check out, et cetera, et cetera. . . ." Her voice faded off, but Sherry and Jack didn't seem to notice. They were smiling at each other.

"Holy shit," Jack said. "This kid isn't fucking around."

"I knew it," Sherry agreed.

"How'd you get the reports?" Jack asked. "Any problems?"

"No," answered Belinda, still gazing at the shades of blue. "Officer Aloe was on duty. I'm going to expense about fifty bucks' worth of her stuff. And then, after that, I had to beg and plead with the cop down in Reports because the cases are allegedly under investigation, but he eventually read me the important stuff."

Jack nodded and lit a cigarette. "Under investigation—shit!" He laughed wryly. "Any case those poor suckers can't close!"

Sherry laughed in agreement. She was watching Jack closely, waiting for his next set of directions, and it came fast enough.

"All right, good work, girls," he said. "Now, Belinda, I believe Sherry has about six more hits for you to verify. How many more reports do you think you can get from the cop in the basement before he shuts down on you?"

"Maybe one or two." She shrugged.

"That's good enough," said Jack. "We don't want the police cracking this case before we do."

"Uh-huh," Belinda mumbled. Her thoughts had drifted from the bay to the apartment on Tomar Boulevard where Pablo Nevilla had been shot. Something about the hit made her want to cry— what was it? An image played in her mind: The guy's brother, shaking with dread, pushes open the door of the apartment and sees the "victim"—his *brother*, good God—lying in a pool of sticky crimson blood on the floor. He wants to bolt, but he fights the impulse and drops to his brother's side and then—what had she done?—he puts his brother's head in his lap, and maybe he shuts his eyes and kisses him good-bye.

Sherry and Jack were watching her.

"I was just thinking," Belinda said finally. "I really hate this kid Manuel." She stopped for a second to gather her energy. Then: "Do you hate him, Sherry?"

"Do I *hate* Manuel?"

"Yes. That's what I asked."

Sherry pulled her face into an expression of frustration and disgust; Belinda recognized it from the times that Sherry described her neighbors or confronted an I-don't-talk-to-reporters cop on assignment. She walked over to Jack's desk and took a cigarette out of the pack. "Excuse me," she said, trying to sound nonplussed, "I think I'm having a momentary relapse."

Sherry took a deep drag and slowly exhaled into the air above Belinda's shoulder. "Well, that's an interesting question," she said after a few moments had passed. "No, I don't think I hate him. I think he's a boy who's had a very sick past, who is obviously a sociopath on some levels. And I think he needs a lot of help if he's really going to start a new life like he wants to. I don't especially like him, but I don't *hate* him."

"He's killed all these people," Belinda said.

"They were drug dealers," Sherry answered, exasperated.

"They were brothers and fathers and sons and husbands."

"Yeah," said Sherry, "and they decided to make their living selling drugs to other people's brothers and fathers and sons and husbands."

"So they deserve to die, right?" Belinda was standing close to Sherry now. "Manuel was doing a public service, right?"

"No! Christ, Belinda—but it's not like he was wasting innocent bystanders. He was playing by the rules of a game they all bought into. That's the way they do business around here."

Belinda stepped back and looked at Sherry in amazement. "I think you're making excuses for him."

"Making excuses? Why in the world would I make excuses for Manuel?"

"Girls, girls!" Jack interrupted before Belinda had a chance to answer. "Now just shut up, the two of you." He was sitting on the corner of his desk, looking at the floor and rubbing his temples. "I don't like what I'm hearing—two hens squawking about something that doesn't mean diddly-shit.

"Who cares if Sherry hates Manuel or if she loves him to death?" He was staring at Belinda now. "We're not here to *judge* this kid. We're observers. We're on the outside looking in. We watch . . . and we listen . . . and then we write. It's that simple. We're *reporters*. If you don't like what we do, you don't belong in my newsroom."

Belinda turned to gaze out the window again. She longed to

be sailing out on the bay, the glimmering blue waters slipping by so fast that watching them would give her no time to think of anything else.

Sherry's voice, low and percolating with controlled anger, caught her off guard.

"Don't threaten Belinda," she said.

Silence again. Belinda kept looking out the window, but she felt as if she might weep if someone touched her.

Sherry waited a minute and then spoke again. "I said, don't threaten Belinda, Jack." She wasn't going to let it go.

"Hey, I don't want touchy-feely intellectual types in my newsroom. They muck it all up," Jack came back. "Either you're a reporter or you're not. I can't be running a fucking encounter session here."

"Belinda *is* a reporter, Jack," said Sherry. "She's asking questions. That's what it's all about." They were talking as if Belinda weren't in the room.

"You want this story or not, Estabrook?" Jack asked. "Or do you agree with your friend here that we should run him in to the cops?"

"She wasn't saying that," said Sherry, although she wasn't exactly sure what Belinda wanted. She only knew that she had to protect her. "Please, Jack, you know she'll come around."

"I sure hope so."

"Don't worry about it," Sherry said. She took a few steps over to Belinda and pulled on her sleeve. "Let's get working," she said softly. Out of the corner of her eye, she could see Jack nod approvingly at the suggestion. He wanted this story done and out there before someone else in the newsroom caught the jitters. He'd seen it happen before on ball-busting stories: All the wimps, preppies, do-gooders, and intellectuals got nervous just before press time. He wasn't going to let it happen with this one.

"Yeah, just do the story," he told Sherry and Belinda as they left his office. "We'll talk about it later."

28 Belinda didn't say anything for nearly an hour. She sat at her desk, five feet from Sherry, silently studying her computer, reading the day's top stories, written by reporters lucky enough not to know word one about a boy named Manuel. She stared straight ahead, eyes clamped onto the green letters as they popped onto the black screen in front of her, thinking of absolutely nothing.

She didn't know what to think.

Sherry watched her for a few minutes, waiting for her to look over and explain—even if it was just with her eyes—what in the world was going through her head. But Belinda wouldn't meet her gaze, and after a while Sherry turned away, back to her work and Manuel.

At six o'clock, Belinda's phone started ringing.

She didn't pick up.

"You trying to avoid someone?" Sherry asked.

"What?" Belinda answered. It was the slow, dazed voice of someone woken from a dream.

"Why didn't you answer your phone?"

"Did it ring?"

"It was just ringing right now," Sherry said. "I guess you were concentrating so hard you didn't hear it."

Belinda looked at her phone, squinting, as if she had never seen the thing before.

Suddenly, she turned and looked at Sherry. "Why do you do that?" she asked urgently.

"Do what?"

"Why do you make me hate you and then go and do something that's really nice, like something only a sister would do?" Belinda said. "Why can't you be just one person?"

"I am one person." This was really out of left field, Sherry thought.

"You are not."

"I am, too," said Sherry.

"No, you're not. One person couldn't love Manuel and also go around loving me."

"Ugh!" Sherry groaned and made a face. "Please! I don't *love* Manuel."

"Well, maybe you don't love him, but you love what he's going to do for you, for you and your big career," Belinda said.

Sherry was ready to disagree, but she knew this argument could go on forever, and she wanted it to stop—she needed it to stop. It was too damn frustrating to debate all these abstract questions about Manuel when the answers simply didn't matter.

"This is ridiculous," she told Belinda. "Can we just stop talking about it all the time and just do it? What the hell is this place, *The New Yorker*? We're reporters. We've got a story. Let's just do it."

Then she added, "Look, the story will run, and before you know it, a whole cocaine ring will be out of business, and everything will be back to normal."

Belinda looked surprised. She had only imagined Manuel getting blown away the hour after the story hit the streets. End of episode.

"Yeah," Sherry added quickly, catching a shadow of interest cross Belinda's face. "Manuel takes off for Mexico, but the story has all the dates and times and locations for the cops to get search warrants and the D.A. to get subpoenas"—she paused for dramatic effect—"and next thing you know, Mimi Lopez and her seven dwarfs go off to prison for the long haul, and everyone lives happily ever after."

Belinda liked the sound of it, but then . . .

"What if Manuel gets killed first?" she asked Sherry. She hoped there was a good answer.

"He won't. I swear to you. I'll make sure he knows a few days before the story runs."

"You promise?" Belinda asked.

Sherry held up the three middle fingers on her right hand. "Scout's honor," she said. Belinda was frowning. "No, I mean it, really," Sherry added, dropping the gesture. "You've got my word."

"Okay," Belinda said solemnly.

"Okay." Sherry felt as if she had just left the dentist's office.

Thank God that was over. "Belinda, just stick it out with me until the end, all right? I know you're not crazy about this story, and you'd rather be spending time with Eladio—which is *perfectly* understandable—but it will all be over soon. Trust me."

Belinda let go a long, resigned sigh. "I trust you, Sherry," she said. "Of course I do."

 When Eladio finally called again, a half hour later, Belinda heard the phone loud and clear. She couldn't wait to see him, to tell him all about this day and then to put it behind her.

They had planned to go out for a bite at Versailles, then catch a movie, but Eladio sounded exhausted. He asked Belinda if they could eat in, at her place. The proposal jolted her. "But I don't have anything defrosted," she objected. "But my apartment is really a mess."

"I don't care," said Eladio. "Belinda, I just want to relax and be with you."

"We can find a quiet restaurant."

"Listen, I'll pick up dinner at El Pub, and all you have to do is set the table."

"I don't even know if I have clean silverware."

"Belinda," Eladio said gently. It was an appeal. He wanted to free her from all her fears, but he didn't know where to begin. "Don't worry," he reassured her. "We're only going to eat dinner."

"Yeah, but . . ."

"Don't worry," Eladio said again. "Nothing will happen."

"Yeah," Belinda answered. "That's what I'm afraid of."

And so Belinda rushed home to clean her tiny apartment.

It was just three rooms, really, and four square feet of a foyer. It was located at the end of a long hall on the third floor of a yellow stucco apartment building on one of Little Havana's narrow, nondescript side streets. She had found it through an advertisement in *Diario Las Americas* that read, *Inexpensive shelter. Three windows. No roaches.*

She loved it the minute she saw it—even through layers of dust she could tell it was just what she was looking for, a home as cramped and dark and warm as a womb. She felt safe there, all alone, but safe.

She paid two hundred dollars a month for the place: a kitchen barely big enough to hold a rickety, humming refrigerator and a gas stove so old it had to be lit with a match every time.

The bathroom was next to the kitchen, and across the hall was the bedroom. It had three windows, but Belinda had to keep the shades pulled most of the time. Not twelve feet away, across an alley, sat an identical apartment building. Sometimes at night she could see a young girl solemnly watching TV and brushing her hair in the room directly facing hers. She was there every night, looking so lonely and tragic that Belinda sometimes wondered if she was sick. She never seemed to sleep.

Belinda's bed took up most of the room. It was a futon, actually, which she laid on the floor and covered with a handwoven blackish-green blanket from Marrakech. There was a small wobbly wooden dresser along one wall—she bought it at a furniture warehouse on the outskirts of town for forty-nine dollars a few days after she arrived in Miami. The rest of the room was filled with cardboard boxes, some of them stacked four high. She didn't know what else to do with them: They contained her whole life—her diaries, written in five languages, her letters, most of them from her father and grandmother, dozens of little trinkets and souvenirs from all the places she'd called home, photographs of friends left behind, her clips. Every once in a while, she would stick her hand into one of the boxes and see what she pulled out. Last time she extracted a postcard her father had sent from Belize. They were living in Buenos Aires at the time, in a big white house near the embassy. *My little pumpkin fritter*, he had written, *Daddy misses you! Business is going well, but I can't wait to get back and give you some kisses! I saw an iguana sunning himself on the road yesterday. Made me think of that dinner Teeta cooked us—oh no! Tell mommy I said hi. Love and kisses my angel girl. Papa Bear.*

Belinda wondered what Eladio, who had lived in the same house from the day he was born, would think when he saw all the boxes. She had been here for *three* years. Wasn't she ever going to unpack?

She checked her watch. Ten minutes until he was due to arrive with dinner.

Belinda smoothed the rumpled blanket over her futon and used a swift hip check to shove the dresser drawers closed as far as they could go with all the clothes jammed inside. Then, spinning around, she pushed her shoes into the closet and tried to stack the boxes into neat columns. Still, it was no good. This room of solace and healing, where she had lain awake many nights making peace with ghosts living and dead, suddenly looked totally wrong and inadequate. It looked unfinished.

Belinda scurried down the narrow hallway to the kitchen and searched through the cabinet under the sink for a tablecloth her mother had sent her from Lisbon, a gift when she got her first apartment during college. She found it, still crisply folded in a cellophane wrapper, underneath the white enamel tub she used to wash her stockings. But when she laid it over the butcher block, the tablecloth draped over the sides and covered the kitchen floor. She crumpled it into a ball and shoved it back under the sink. It was no use. . . .

The doorbell buzzed.

"Wait, wait!" Belinda cried frantically, not knowing what she meant or what there was left to do. She scanned the kitchen again, and suddenly remembered the candles in the napkin drawer. She had bought them last year, just before a hurricane blew through town. Should she put them out now? Or would Eladio think that she was trying to seduce him by making the place all dim and glowing? Would it look like she was trying too hard? And didn't Latin men like virgins anyway? Then again, maybe they would make the apartment seem cozier. Maybe they would warm the place up, make it seem less dingy, like a grown-up lived there or something—

The buzzer again. "Belinda?" she could hear Eladio through the door.

"Coming—"

She pulled the candles from the drawer and stuck them in the center of the table, unlit—a compromise.

"Belinda?" A little bit louder now.

She pushed a strand of hair off her forehead and pulled open the door.

"Hi!" they both said at the same time, then laughed awkwardly.

Eladio stepped inside the apartment and glanced left and right. "Very nice," he said politely, although all he could see was a miniature kitchen crammed with old appliances. "So, we're eating here?" he asked in the same tone, pointing to the butcher block. Belinda watched his eyes for any reaction to the candles. There was none.

"Nope, we're eating in the grand ballroom."

Eladio took a step out of the kitchen and peered down the hallway.

"It was a joke," Belinda said.

"Oh! Right!" He laughed and put the bag of food down on the counter. He looked at Belinda expectantly, but she bowed her head and then looked away. It wasn't the first time that she reminded Eladio of his little niece Alexandria, so docile and already afraid of the world. He'd asked his brother about it once, and he had shrugged lazily in response. "Some kid has been hitting her at school," he said matter-of-factly. "It'll pass."

But would it ever pass with Belinda?

"So, let's eat, okay?" Eladio said.

They unpacked the bag of food in silence, standing next to each other in the tiny kitchen, somehow managing not to touch.

They sat down across from each other. "Oh, candles!" Eladio said to break the silence. "Do you mind . . . can I light them?"

"You don't mind?"

"What?" Eladio looked surprised. "Do I mind? No, no. I like them. I never get to eat by candlelight. It will be nice. Here, let me shut the lights." He reached over his shoulder and hit the switch.

It was suddenly pitch-black in the room, and they both laughed nervously. Belinda jumped up to turn on the lights, but Eladio stopped her and pulled her onto his lap. "Let me kiss you," he said gently.

"It's okay," she said, trying to stand up.

"No, let me." He kissed her once.

"You don't have to feel sorry for me," Belinda said when it was over. She reached over the stovetop and found the matches in the dark. "Everyone feels so sorry for Belinda." She lit the candles.

"I don't feel sorry for you," Eladio said, but he did.

"Sherry feels sorry for me."

"Sherry is—" He didn't want to say something wrong, but he had wondered about that gringa from the moment he first saw her, serenely sipping tea while harassing her neighbors because of some dispute over a *cat*. "Sherry is very unusual."

Belinda nodded. "Yes," she said. "Thank God for that." She stood up and pulled some silverware from a drawer. Eladio noticed she was suddenly much more relaxed, humming softly to herself as she served them both sloppy portions of black beans, rice, and picadillo.

He started to tell her about his day—four boring hours sitting on an uncomfortable courthouse bench waiting for his case to be called, a half hour of rehearsed testimony, a long, meaningless break while the attorneys whispered with the judge, another thirty minutes on the stand being cross-examined by an agitated lady lawyer, and then another long and meaningless recess, this one ending with the announcement that the two parties had reached some complicated settlement even he did not understand. What was the point of being a cop, he asked Belinda, if criminals never go to jail?

"I don't know," she answered, shaking her head. She thought about Manuel, who would probably never serve a day behind bars. "It makes me wonder if the people in Iran know something we don't." She remembered a public flogging she saw when she was ten; it had given her nightmares for weeks, but it had also convinced her that crime was something to be avoided at all costs. "I mean, over there, if you rob a store, they cut off one of your hands. If you sell pornography, they put out an eye. If you rape a woman, well, um . . . you know . . . it's not very nice, but it does the trick."

Eladio laughed. "Yes, but this is America."

"Right." She sighed. In her mind, she could imagine Manuel sitting in a comfortable rocking chair outside a ranch in Montana, whittling a piece of wood and watching the buffalo graze.

"Well, I had quite a day, too," she said. They were done with dinner and she started clearing the dishes. "I had to get a couple of reports from the PIO to verify Manuel's story."

The mention of the boy's name made Eladio recoil.

"Maybe you shouldn't tell me about this," he said quickly. "The less I know, the better."

Belinda turned and faced Eladio. "But I *want* to tell you about it," she said. "That's terrible, isn't it?"

"No, no, it's not terrible at all." He stood and embraced her, and this time she didn't fight it.

"You're right," she said after a minute had passed. "We shouldn't go around discussing how I'm breaking the law. It sort of puts you in a bad place."

She could feel Eladio's body stiffen. "You're not breaking it *too* bad," he said hopefully.

"No—" Belinda laughed ironically. "And believe me, there are people at the paper who would argue I'm not breaking it at all. I'm just doing my job. I'm not a cop, and I'm not a judge, and I'm not a lawyer or a priest. I'm a reporter."

"Reporters can go to jail."

"Oh, don't worry," Belinda said, laughing more fully now. "I'm not going to jail. If anyone goes, it will be Sherry. And I'm not so sure she would mind."

"Oh, really, Belinda, come on—"

"No, really," she cut him off. "Really, Eladio—journalism is the only career where going to jail can help your career. Hooray for the First Amendment and all that stuff."

"Okay," said Eladio, still sounding slightly perplexed. "Let's just drop the subject, okay?"

"Okay," said Belinda. They were still together in an embrace, leaning against the sink. Eladio kissed her again. "Can we go into the living room or something?" he whispered into her neck.

"I don't have one."

"Oh . . ."

"We can go into the bedroom." She braced herself for Eladio's reaction—now was the time he would balk and push her away—but he only hugged her tighter.

"Okay," he said, picking up one of the candles. "Lead the way."

"Lead the way?" Belinda repeated, just to make sure.

"Yes, beloved," Eladio answered, "lead the way."

For the next three hours, they lay in each other's arms on Belinda's narrow bed, exchanging secret dreams and promises in the flickering amber light. Finally, after a few murmurs of agreement, they rose and headed silently toward the door, to Eladio's cruiser on the street. There was no need to talk anymore—everything had been said. Their love had come quickly, but that was because it was meant to be—for both of them—after so many years of bittersweet longing and hushed sadness. They sped to Cape Florida, where they had slipped into love on their first date. It felt right to be there again.

The beach was empty and still, and the moment Belinda saw the mesmerizing glow of the moon dancing on the water, she felt she had to go in, to go under. She walked, almost in a trance, toward the shoreline, pulling off her clothes piece by piece until she was standing bare, back to Eladio. She held her breath, shut her eyes, and plunged beneath the waves.

Eladio followed her to the water's edge without thinking, stripped, and threw himself forward, expecting a jolt of cold thunder. But the bay was as warm and soothing as a baby's bath.

"Over here." He heard Belinda calling him when he came up for air. He paddled to her.

They both knew what was going to happen, and they smiled tenderly at each other at the new beginning it promised. They swam together to the shoreline, and there, in a cushion of soft and yielding sand, they made love.

30

Sherry picked Manuel up at ten the next morning at a corner near his house. He was skipping school that day—his idea completely—so they could cover as many hits as possible before his father started asking him where he was going every afternoon. But Sherry didn't object; for her sake and Jack's, the sooner the story was done, the better.

"You look lovely today," Manuel told Sherry as he climbed into the BMW. "As usual."

"Thanks," Sherry answered brightly. She was finally beginning to accept the fact that Manuel's constant flirtation was nothing more than that. It was cultural affectation. After three years of being hooted, clucked, and whistled at in Miami, Sherry told herself, she should be used to it. "I'm ready to cover a lot of ground today," she said. "How about you?"

"Totally!" said Manuel. He gave her a congenial wink, and Sherry wondered why she ever thought he was ugly. "I got three good ones for you," he told her. "You're gonna love them, I swear."

"Lead the way."

Manuel excitedly started to direct her toward North Kendall Drive, but then stopped himself abruptly, slamming the dashboard and then his forehead with the heel of his hand.

"Wait, wait," he said, gesturing for Sherry to pull over to the side of the road. "I've been meaning to ask you something real important."

"What is it?" Sherry asked hurriedly, and all at once, she felt her stomach roll over and her skin start to sting like prickly heat. Had he suddenly changed his mind about talking to her? Decided to leave town early? Go directly to the cops? Sell his story to TV? No, no, it couldn't be, Sherry reassured herself. This whole thing was making her paranoid.

"Hey, I said pull over." It was Manuel, sounding plainly irritated.

"Oh, sorry," Sherry said. She immediately slowed the BMW and steered it into the parking lot of a hardware store. "This all right?

"Fine," Manuel said. He turned in his seat to face Sherry, and she couldn't help but notice his entire wiry body was suddenly flexed. Even his fists were clenched. "Now, I want you to look right in my eyes, *right in them*," he said, voice low and deadly serious, "because I gotta ask you an important question, and I need to know if you're telling me the truth."

Sherry almost protested—"I always tell you the truth," she was going to say—but what was the point of lying? Obviously, Manuel was already wary of her coy journalism techniques and vagaries; one more false move and she might lose his trust, and with it the whole incredible story.

She turned toward him, pushed her hair back over her shoulders, and fixed her eyes on his. "Ask me anything," she said.

Manuel nodded once. "All right," he said. "I need to know one thing: What did that lie-detector guy tell you about me?"

Sherry felt an immediate bolt of relief, and she burst into a huge, relaxed smile. This wasn't going to be a threat to the story at all—quite the opposite. "Oh, that's *easy*, Manuel," she practically gushed. "He said you were telling the truth!"

"Good," Manuel said. He was suddenly relaxed and smiling

broadly, too. "I knew he would." There was a short pause, then he quickly added, "So you believe me, too, right?"

"Right," said Sherry. She made sure she was still looking him in the eyes. "Don't tell me you were worried?"

Manuel shook his head with unusual vigor. "No," he said resolutely. "It's just that I was afraid you were going to do something stupid, like try to find someone in the Lopez family to back me up, or something. You could get yourself killed that way." He let go a short snicker.

"No kidding," said Sherry. For a moment, she considered telling Manuel they were finding all the backup they needed in the police reports on his hits, but she decided against it. Better just to let him believe her trust in him was complete.

"So are we all settled on this?" she asked.

"All settled," Manuel said. He turned back to face front, adjusted the seat to a more reclining position, and leaned back, hands behind head. Then, almost as an afterthought, he pulled a pair of aviator sunglasses from his shirt pocket and pushed them on. Instantly, Sherry had to repress an ironic giggle. Together with his perfectly pressed linen shirt and sharply creased blue jeans, the glasses made Manuel look like an undercover cop. She could spot them at a hundred paces, any good reporter could— they always looked so neat and Boy Scoutish as to be utterly out-of-place anywhere. And Manuel even had the right expression— a perky smugness that practically announced, "I'm carrying a big gun in my sock!" Of course, he wasn't—she'd checked many times—but his face had that certain cockiness she'd grown quite familiar with, covering the police for three years.

"Lead the way," she said again.

For the next half hour, Manuel directed Sherry down one road and then another until they came to the far reaches of Kendall, a huge chunk of scrubland at the county's western border that had recently been converted into a monotonous collection of sprawling, indistinguishable subdivisions. One billboard after another advertised their charms—FAMILY FUN BEGINS AT APIAN RETREATS, and THREE BEDROOMS STARTING AT $66,000, COME HOME TO CASTLE VILLAGE! Finally, just after they passed a sign boasting, TRANQUIL-LITY, SECURITY, AND VALUE AT FAIR LAWN GARDENS! YOUR PERSONAL PARADISE 40 MINUTES FROM MIAMI!, Manuel told Sherry to take a right. This was the place.

She pulled into the development and immediately saw what the billboard meant by security: a small wooden booth, manned by a teetering guard probably born before the turn of the century. "What do I tell Grandpa?" she asked.

"Just wave and smile like you belong."

Sherry followed Manuel's instructions, and the security guard cheerfully motioned her through the electronic gate. He even offered a buoyant "Have a nice day" as she drove past.

"That was easy." Sherry laughed.

"Always is," Manuel replied matter-of-factly.

A minute later, they were parked in front of a group of town houses a few blocks into the development, clustered among baby palms and white concrete driveways on a flat and artificially winding street named Dove Song Drive.

Manuel rolled down the window and looked around, grimacing in frustration. "All these places look the same," he said, and Sherry had to agree. The town houses were identical two-story structures, standard new-Florida fare, heavy on the maroon-stained pinewood and arched windows.

"I think it was this one." He pointed to one of the houses and broke into a gratified smile. "Yeah."

Sherry turned off the engine, pulled up the emergency brake, and jotted the address in her notebook.

"Okay," began Manuel, taking a deep breath. "This is the one where I had to kill the dog. I hated to do that."

"Uh-huh," said Sherry. She was fiddling with the volume on the tape recorder. "You had to kill the dog."

"Yeah, I thought it was going to bite my leg off."

"It was barking at you—"

"Yeah, and I was afraid someone might call the police."

"So—"

"So." He pretended to pull the trigger of a gun.

"And then?"

"And then I did the hit and went home."

"Right," said Sherry, "but who'd you shoot?"

For the next few minutes, Manuel described the hit in familiar detail. He got a call from one of Mimi Lopez's lieutenants, who told him to show up at the town house around four. The guy inside was named Miguel D'Escara. He was expecting company. Ring the doorbell, step inside, close the door, say, "Mimi sent me," do the hit, and then split.

It sounded easy enough, Manuel told Sherry, but he knew there would be complications when he rang the doorbell and heard the dog barking. Then D'Escara wouldn't open the door. He kept asking who was there.

"It's Manuel."

"Manuel who?"

"You know, *Manuel*."

This went on, Manuel recalled, until he finally figured he had to take a chance.

"Mimi sent me," he said, half expecting a shotgun blast through the door. Instead, it swung open, and Miguel D'Escara stood there, smiling uneasily. "Why didn't you say so earlier?" he asked.

Manuel stepped inside, closed the door behind him, and reached for his gun. "That's when the dog went crazy, and I had to waste him," he told Sherry. "It was one of those huge fucking Doberman pinschers, you know, the kind with all the teeth."

"Yikes," said Sherry.

"Anyway," Manuel surged on, gaining momentum with the telling, "D'Escara knew he was next, and he tried to make a run for the back of the house. There's a door back there that goes to the backyard."

"Uh-huh," Sherry said.

"He got as far as the refrigerator." Manuel released one of his I'm-a-professional smiles and looked to Sherry for acknowledgment.

She nodded. "I assume you got him in the neck," she said.

"Well, I got him in the back first," said Manuel, "and once he was down on the floor, I nailed him in the neck for good luck."

"Right," said Sherry, snapping off the tape recorder and checking her watch. Thanks to their little conversation about the lie-detector test, they were running slightly behind schedule. She didn't want to rush Manuel through the process, but all of his hits were beginning to sound the same. That, and the fact that she didn't want to get a reputation around the newsroom for holding up a big package. She'd never missed a deadline before. This time she was going to beat it. Two or three more hits with Manuel, and she was going to tell Jack she was ready to start writing. She'd already heard through the newsroom rumor mill that the companion stories on the Lopez family and serial killers were wrapped, and the one on the cops was nearly ready. All she needed was a few more quotes on Manuel's personal philosophy to add to the stuff about his mother's suicide, and she'd have everything for her profile. And, Sherry reminded herself, she needed to ask Manuel if he'd ever met Mimi Lopez. She doubted it—word was she was utterly reclusive—but it was worth a try. Sherry made a mental note to fit the question in sometime in the next few days. "Okay, Manuel," she asked. "Where next?"

Nearly an hour later, they pulled onto an unpaved street on the slummy southwestern section of Homestead, a sprawling town of farmers, new developments, trailer parks, and lime groves tucked at the bottom of the county. Sherry knew that across the railroad tracks Homestead wasn't such a bad place to visit; it still felt like a small town with its barbershop and home-made-doughnut place. But in the poverty-stricken black neighborhood where she and Manuel now sat, the sun, now straight up and bearing down like a hammer, gave deep shadows to the shotgun shacks scattered here and there amid tall stalks of wild grass and piles of melting garbage. There wasn't a soul in sight.

"Over there." Manuel waved toward one of the shacks. "That one with the green roof."

Sherry drove a few yards and parked the car in front of a dilapidated clapboard one-story house shaped like a railroad car, its front porch half on the ground, half off. There were no panes in the windows, and what was left of the paint was peeling off in long strips. The house next door was in better shape, but not by much. Still, three young children played in front, squirting each other with a hose and shrieking with delight.

"Looks abandoned," Sherry said, jotting a description of the scene of Manuel's hit in her notebook.

"Well, they do drugs there," Manuel answered.

"Oh, I see." She turned on the tape recorder. "On your mark, get set, go."

This was an easy one, Manuel told her, because he didn't have to worry about the cops. They never bothered with this part of town.

The target was a black girl called Lulu. "She'd been snitching or something like that," Manuel explained. "I'm not really sure what it was. But she was doing something wrong."

The night of the hit, Manuel said, a guy he didn't recognize picked him up near his house about midnight; he'd had to sneak out his bedroom window again, which he didn't appreciate, but that was life. They drove in silence for a long time—the guy never took his eyes off the road—until finally they passed a sign saying WELCOME TO HOMESTEAD. DON'T EVEN THINK ABOUT SPEEDING.

"That sign really cracks me up," Manuel broke off his narrative to tell Sherry.

"Yeah, me, too," she agreed, hoping he'd say more. This was just the kind of revealing personality detail she needed. "Every time I see that sign, I think, Watch out—it's the mind police!"

"*Mind police*—right! Exactly!" Manuel latched on to the expression enthusiastically, repeating it over and over, and then he suddenly burst into a rapid-fire rush of words. "You know, the whole world is always telling you what to think. How to act. Who to be. Do this—don't do that. You know? You can never be yourself," he said, practically bouncing in his seat from excitement as he spoke, and it occurred to Sherry that he had probably never had the opportunity to talk about his feelings this way before. What she was seeing was revelation and release at once—a breakthrough in their relationship and another coup for the story.

"You think people should have more freedom, right?" she suggested, careful not to close him down with any hint of judgment in her voice or the wording of her question. She remembered Manuel telling that lie-detector expert, Sherman Otis, that he hated rules.

"Yeah, *right*," Manuel answered, apparently a little surprised and very pleased that Sherry had grasped his line of thinking so quickly. "You see what I mean. People should have more freedom to do what they want. There are too many rules in this world for a guy like me. I'm the kind of guy that everyone will understand a *hundred* years from now—that's what I told 'em, and they *laughed* at me, those idiots." He shook his head incredulously, looking out the window as if he were talking to himself. "But it's like they teach you, everyone laughed at Christopher Columbus when he said the world was round. You know? And now there's a fucking school named after him in Hialeah. So, I'm like him, right? I'm different from everyone else. I'm *advanced*."

"Advanced? What do you mean?" Sherry asked, but she knew exactly what he meant. She was trying to buy time, trying to figure out what she had just heard him say. Had he said someone laughed at him? She had to know who, but she was more convinced than ever that she couldn't close him down, not at a vulnerable time like this, when he was exposing his soul to her as never before. Jack was going to flip when he heard these quotes.

"Yeah, advanced, you know," Manuel was answering her question, and she could feel him growing even more introspective beside her, as if he was winding up for a long, complicated explanation. He leaned back in his seat, took off his sunglasses, and rested his fingertips on his temples. His eyes were distant, foggy with thought. "I'm ahead of my time, okay?" he said. "I got a unique way of doing things. And I don't want to sound stuck-up or nothing, but my way of doing things is the right way, okay? I know how to make people respect me. That's why I was so good at the business. I was *too* good for them—"

"And so they laughed at you?" Sherry asked softly before he could go on. It was more a murmur than a question.

But it was enough to shock Manuel to alert. He abruptly sat forward in his seat and turned to face Sherry foursquare. "No one laughs at Manuel Velo," he snapped, his eyes squinting and his jaw set rigid with indignation.

"Oh, oh—I'm sorry," Sherry quickly backed down more out of reflex than intention. Manuel's anger was as intimidating as a slap across the face. "It's just I thought I heard you say some people laughed at you—the way they laughed at Christopher Columbus, remember?"

There was a full minute of silence between them, and Sherry wished she could look at Manuel, but his glare prevented it.

"Oh, yes, I remember now," he said finally. His voice was toneless, except for a slight edge of irritation. "I was talking about the other students in the rap room at Lincoln High School, of course. They're all a bunch of babies. They don't understand me. They have no idea how much I know about the way the world really works."

"You might even say they're idiots, right?" Sherry gently suggested, trying to shake loose the memory for him. She could picture the scene in her mind—Manuel, in his typical Marine stance, officiously informs his classmates that someday he'll be as famous as the man who discovered the New World. And, of course, the place explodes in laughter. Manuel is livid and humiliated. He almost blurts out that he used to work for the Lopez family, that he killed eighteen people, that he earned thousands of dollars while they flipped burgers at McDonald's. But instead he calls them idiots and vows to himself that someday his story will be told. A few days later, in walks the *Miami Citizen* saying, "Talk to me about drugs."

Everything, Sherry thought, is beginning to make perfect sense.

"Yeah, they're idiots," Manuel quickly agreed. "You saw them."

Sherry nodded her head agreeably. She was trying to figure out if she should try to keep the conversation going or if she'd pushed him far enough. One glance at Manuel's agitated rapping on the dashboard told her all she needed to know.

"Well," she said cheerfully, "let's get back to this Homestead hit, okay?"

Manuel was happy to oblige, and he quickly ran through the details.

The girl he was supposed to get rid of, he told Sherry, was easy to find. She was crouched in the far corner of the shack they were sitting in front of now, her back to the door, smoking crack in the light of an incense candle. "I'll never forget," Manuel said, "how nice the place smelled. Like that pine stuff my mother used to wash the floors with.

"Anyway"—he shrugged—"she didn't hear me coming because she was sort of singing to herself. Well, not really singing. Humming. And rocking back and forth on her heels. I think she was really wasted.

"So, like usual, I was going for her neck, but she turned all of a sudden, right when I was behind her, and I got her face instead, like near her nose. It was a mistake, but it worked."

Sherry took a deep breath to fight off a sudden and totally unexpected attack of nausea. Again she forced herself to think of her dentist in Marblehead and his smarmy smile after pulling the drill from her mouth. And again the image did the trick; her queasiness subsided, but not completely. "Her nose," Sherry repeated numbly. But she couldn't help imagining this girl—Lulu was such a sweet and curious name—humming wistfully to herself one second and lying in her own blood the next, dead in the corner of a room the scent of a Minnesota forest. How long was it before anyone noticed she was missing?

"Need anything else about this one?" Manuel interrupted Sherry's thoughts in a businesslike voice.

"Nope," Sherry answered, turning off the tape recorder and turning over the engine. She checked her watch again. This next spot could be their last hit together—with these new quotes about Christopher Columbus and personal freedom, she certainly had enough to write the story now. "Point the way," she told Manuel, and he effortlessly directed her to Cutler Ridge, yet another Dade suburb built all at once by a northern developer gunning to sell paradise at a nice price.

Manuel steered Sherry to a modest brown-shingled ranch house on Thanksgiving Street. Two little kids—they looked so similar, Sherry was sure they had to be twins—tossed a Wiffle ball to each other in the driveway.

"You hit someone *here*?" Sherry asked.

"Believe me, these people didn't live here then," Manuel answered. "At least, they weren't around when I nuked the guy."

Sherry turned on the tape recorder.

He had pulled this hit alone, he said, borrowing his father's car. It was right after track practice last spring. He knocked on the front door, and when no one answered, he walked around back. The guy was swimming laps in the pool.

"Easy shot," said Manuel.

"Didn't anyone notice?" Sherry asked incredulously. She looked around the neighborhood—it was so bucolic, Ozzie and Harriet would have felt right at home.

"Oh, you know, they've got one of those tall redwood fences," he reported, as if he were a friend of the family. "They did me a big favor."

Sherry nodded. "Do you know who you shot?" she asked.

"Some guy," said Manuel. "Bill Somebody."

Sherry stared at him blankly. She was trying to think of something right to say, but she was almost out of steam. He took her silence as an invitation to go on.

"Hey," he began, "I really never gave too much thought to the people I hit. The way I figured, they did something wrong. They pissed off Mimi. That's a big mistake in our business. Mimi is the queen, you get it? Everyone respects her." There was a short pause, and then, almost as an afterthought, he added, "Like they respected me, you know? If I hadn't quit the family, I could have been king someday. That's what they all said."

"Oh, really?" said Sherry. This was yet *another* new and intriguing angle—what an incredible day of interviews this had been! "They said you could really go far inside the family, huh? Tell me about it."

"They said I'd go to the top!" Manuel said.

Sherry threw a quick glance at her watch. There was still time to ask Manuel about Mimi Lopez—perhaps this really *was* their last interview. She couldn't wait to get in front of her computer and get this news onto the front page.

"Say, Manuel," Sherry asked, "I've been meaning to ask you, did you ever meet Mimi Lopez?"

"Yeah, twice," he responded automatically. "I mean once."

"Once or twice?" Sherry asked him in a teasing voice. "Make up your mind."

"Once," Manuel answered firmly.

"And?"

"And what?" Manuel said back.

"And, what's she like?" Sherry asked. She turned off the engine and rolled down the window, a signal to Manuel that she was ready to hear a long story, if necessary.

He accepted the invitation. Slowly, a self-satisfied grin broke across his narrow face, and he purposefully readjusted the car seat so that he was practically lying flat on his back, his face tilted toward the sunroof. He removed his sunglasses, tucked them in his shirt pocket, and closed his eyes, not in sleep, but in a look of fond remembrance.

"Mimi loved me," he said.

"Oh, really," Sherry urged him on. Suddenly, she was irritated at herself for not asking him about this sooner—it sounded like this was going to be a great sidebar—but she was also irritated at Manuel for not mentioning it sooner. He was such an egomaniac sometimes, Sherry thought, he couldn't stand to share the spotlight! "How come Mimi Lopez loved you?" she asked.

Manuel sighed. "She loved me for killing Eddie like I did. After the Eddie hit, she called me in to her house."

Suddenly, he sat bolt upright. "Hey," he said, "let me show you her house, okay? You gotta know where it is, right?"

"Sure," Sherry said, pleasantly surprised by Manuel's ever-increasing cooperation. In fact, she already knew Mimi Lopez's address—the reporter working on the Lopez sidebar had wheedled it out of a good source at the DEA, but there was no point in Manuel knowing that. "Lead the way," she said. "It's someplace in the Gables, right?"

"Gables by the Sea," Manuel answered proudly, as if he were the one who lived in the fancy seaside enclave of million-dollar mansions. "She's got one of the classiest houses there. Not too obvious or nothing. Just very, very rich looking."

A few minutes later, Sherry realized Manuel was absolutely right. The house was beautiful but—unlike its neighbors—hardly ostentatious. Set well back from the road with immaculately groomed grounds, it was a sleek, slightly asymmetrical split-level with pale pink stucco walls and a Mexican red clay-tile roof. A stranger driving by quickly might notice the house's size—it was enormous—but nothing else. A closer look showed the house to be laden with expensive, albeit subtle, details: stained-glass windows here and there, carved white pine verandas, a crushed marble driveway. Someone studying the house from across the street, as Sherry was, might notice something else—every curtain drawn in the middle of the day.

"This is where she lives," Manuel said. "Mimi Lopez."

"Wow," Sherry said, trying to sound impressed. "Tell me how you got in here."

Manuel eagerly complied, lying back in his seat again, closing his eyes.

One night shortly after he killed Eddie, he said, he was awakened in his bedroom by rapping on the window. He pulled open the shade to see Fernando, Mimi's chauffeur, who told him Mimi wanted to see him right away.

"I said to him, 'Man, it's the middle of the night!' and he tells me the Señora is up all night. She sleeps all day. That's just the way it goes. I wasn't gonna argue!" Manuel laughed.

After they arrived at the house, he went on, Fernando pulled into a driveway and maneuvered the limo into the garage. Then he motioned Manuel to follow him down a long hallway, up a flight of stairs, and down another hallway into a sparsely furnished living room: two black velvet couches, a matching chair, a glass table covered with papers and a pair of bifocals, and a TV set in the corner. The house was silent.

"Wait here," Fernando told him, and vanished.

He was still waiting an hour later, when finally he heard a distant door open and close and then footsteps. A moment later, he said, a petite, black-haired woman entered the room, smiling warmly. "I'd seen her face before, you know what I'm saying?" Manuel asked Sherry, turning to look at her earnestly. Sherry nodded quickly—she certainly did. Mimi Lopez looked like his mother. And even if she didn't, Manuel thought she did. That was all that mattered.

"She told me to sit down, and then she sat down right next to me," he went on. "And she says, 'I am so happy to meet you.' Then, if you can believe it, she tells me she's sorry the house is such a mess but that she just moved in because the feds were chasing her. I remember, she said, '*Jesucristo*—the feds are always on my back!' It was funny."

"What did she say after that?" Sherry asked.

Manuel leaned back and closed his eyes. "She said, 'Manuel, I wanted to meet you because you have done very good work for me.' She was looking right into my eyes. And then she said, 'I want you to know I am watching you. Closely.' "

"Is she pretty?" Sherry asked. She wasn't sure the question was relevant, but she really wanted to know.

"Beautiful," Manuel responded solemnly, "and very sexy. Very, if you know what I mean." He licked his lips. "But she's not stupid-looking like most beautiful women, you know. She looks like what she is—*La Reina*."

Sherry nodded with interest. This was a woman she'd love to meet—brainy, independent, and totally corrupt. What a slew of questions she would fire off, given the chance. Sherry probed to see if Manuel knew anything else. "You know," she said, "I've heard Mimi Lopez's husband was a real . . . *businessman*." The truth was that the reporter working on the Lopez family piece, a new Dallas transplant named Eric Rockland, had told Sherry a few days earlier that Mimi's dearly departed, Raoul Lopez, had succeeded on sheer savagery; no one in Columbia dared to cross him. If he hadn't been killed by syphilis, he would probably be the richest man in Latin America. His wife, Rockland told Sherry, was a lighter touch. The DEA knew that she gave a million bucks a year to an orphanage in Bogotá called the Holy Haven for Little Wanderers. Still, she ran the business very *efficiently* and was quickly becoming one of the top competitors in Miami's battleground. Her only weakness was her sons, all eight of them. She forgave their excesses too easily, or such was the word on the street, according to Rockland.

"I don't know about her husband," Manuel responded to Sherry's question dreamily. "All I know is about Mimi."

"And how much she loved the Eddie hit?"

"Right," Manuel sighed. "She told me she knew killing Eddie wasn't easy, but that I did the right thing. You can't fuck up that way."

"Did she say anything else?" Sherry asked.

Silence.

"Manuel," Sherry repeated. "Did she say anything else?"

Finally, Manuel nodded. "Yeah," he told Sherry, "she said I knew how to make people respect me."

"Wow," Sherry said, "that must have felt great."

"I never felt better in my life," Manuel answered. "And then she hugged me, and she kissed me, just like she really meant it."

"Wow," Sherry said again.

Just then, the recorder between them on the seat clicked to a stop, and Sherry held up her hand. "Hold on," she said cheerfully, "just got to get another tape in my purse." She rummaged for a full minute before she found one, all the while trying to keep up the mood that was making Manuel so wonderfully open and thoughtful in his answers. "What have we got?" she babbled, "another hour before you need to get home? We can just pick up where we left off—"

But Manuel cut her off. "Forget it," he said, suddenly pulling himself up and rubbing his eyes as if he were awakening from a nap. "I'm not interested in doing any more interviews today."

Sherry nodded quickly—she understood completely; the day had been draining for her, too. "No problem," she said, "I'll just drop you off early." She turned over the engine and steered the car back onto the road leading to 95 North.

For two miles, there was silence in the car. Sherry glanced right to make sure Manuel was okay, and he certainly seemed to be: leaning back in his seat again, legs spread and back arched in a pelvic tilt, hands behind his head. He never wore a seat belt.

Then, just before they passed the turnoff for Coconut Grove, Manuel spoke:

"Let's go to your house," he said quietly. "It's right near here."

Sherry hit the brake with unintentional force. The car behind them swerved left and leaned long on the horn.

"Oh, fuck you, too!" she shouted. "People are such assholes."

Manuel was watching her.

"You turn right at the light," he said calmly, "to get to your house from here."

"Right, right," said Sherry. She was suddenly and completely discombobulated, and knowing that made her even more unnerved. This was completely unexpected! She was sure Manuel had finally accepted the terms of their agreement—no socializing—but here he was pushing her on it again. It was enough to make her scream from frustration.

Or was it? Sherry stole a fast glance at her hands on the steering wheel and knew, if it weren't for her white-knuckled grip, she would be shaking. Could it be she was scared to bring Manuel home? Scared he might hurt her? Sherry almost let out an incredulous laugh—she was being absurd. Hadn't she just persuaded Jack to get rid of those ridiculous spies he had tailing them everywhere, assuring him she trusted Manuel as much as she trusted the goddamn chief of police? And hadn't she just got a glimpse into his deepest heart, only to find a confused kid who hated his father, missed his mother, and entertained ridiculous delusions of grandeur? She had nothing to be scared of but her own imagination.

Sherry slowed the car to twenty and glided up to the stoplight. Thank God it was red. She was thinking fast.

This must be a test, she decided quickly. He's saying, "I've told you everything about me. Now it's your turn." He must be trying to even out the score a bit.

She looked over and saw Manuel staring at her hopefully.

That's it, Sherry thought—he wants to find out if my friendship is for real. I'm too close to the finish line to blow the race now.

The light turned green, and she pulled a hard right.

31 In the driveway, Sherry started to hum the theme
song from *Dallas*.

"Here we are," she said, waving her hand
grandly in the direction of her compact pink house. "Southfork!"

Manuel laughed. "Yeah, I like that show," he said. "But
you've got a ways to go before you live in Southfork. Maybe after
you write my story, you'll be rich."

Sherry tried not to laugh out loud. "Maybe," she answered.
A second later, she unlocked the front door, and Manuel eagerly
walked inside. He switched on a lamp by the living-room
couch.

"So this is it," Sherry said, but Manuel, his usual edgy energy
now back full force, was already out of her sight, busily scanning
the place, studying the pictures on the walls, the letters on her
kitchen table, the magazines on the couch.

"Who are these people?" he asked. He was standing in front
of the fireplace mantel, which was lined with photos. Sherry
walked over to his side.

"Well, these are my parents," she said uneasily, nodding
toward one of the pictures. She didn't want Manuel to get the
wrong idea—she was *not* going to discuss her family with him.
"And this is my cousin Hilary. She's living in London now."

Manuel moved over a few feet and picked up another photo,
scrutinizing it with a slight frown.

"Who's this with you?" he asked.

"That's my best friend, Alice. She's getting married soon."

Manuel put the picture down and moved on.

"This is your grandmother, right?"

"Right."

"She looks like your mother. You look like your mother."

Sherry shuddered, but assumed it was a compliment.
"Thanks," she said.

Manuel picked up another photo and smiled. This was what he was looking for: Charles.

He was wearing long khaki shorts and an Andover T-shirt, holding a beer in one hand and a wriggling green lobster in the other. Behind him, lit by the cool white sunshine of Cape Cod, lay the wide curved porch of his aunt's place and a sliver of choppy dark blue ocean. The picture always made Sherry's heart hurt a little; she knew that even as the shutter snapped shut on their smiling faces, they had been in their death throes. She had moved to Miami the following week.

"And who is this?" Manuel asked. His voice bore an edge of anger, and Sherry wondered if it could actually be jealousy that she was hearing.

"That's an old friend," she answered carefully.

"Your boyfriend?" Same voice.

"No," Sherry said. "Just an old friend. I've known him since I was eight. We went to Sunday school together."

Manuel looked at her with raised eyebrows. He didn't believe it for a second.

"You can tell me," he said. It was the same line she used on him not an hour earlier.

"We dated one summer a long time ago," she said.

"Who's your boyfriend now?"

"I don't—"

Manuel gave Sherry a look of reproach. "I've seen him," he said, "at night. Leaving here. He drives that blue Dodge."

Sherry turned and started to walk stiffly toward the kitchen. Jesus Christ, she thought, he had been spying on her! Maybe Brazil was right. Maybe he did have a schoolboy crush on her. Which was not good at all. But then . . .

But then, Sherry thought, wasn't that to be expected? Her shock began to fade into amusement. After all, she was letting Manuel boast, confess, and pontificate to his heart's delight. He wouldn't be male if he didn't love talking about himself, and love the person attentively listening. Still, Sherry thought, she couldn't let Manuel's emotions get out of control. That wasn't fair, and it wasn't good journalism. She would say something about it today. She would say it now.

A moment later, Manuel wandered into the kitchen and poured himself a glass of water from the faucet. "The coach used to say we should stay real hydrated all the time," he said cheerfully. "You gotta drink six glasses a day—"

"Hey Manuel," Sherry cut him off. She was speaking softly, trying hard to modulate her voice. "Manuel, I wish you wouldn't come by my house when we're not together. Remember, our relationship is not social, okay?"

"I'm just checking on you," he said matter-of-factly. "Just making sure you're safe."

"I'm fine. You don't need to check."

He shook his head and took another sip of water. "You never know," he said. "Miami is a dangerous place. You should get a dog or something."

Sherry began to relax; he sounded sincere enough.

"I *had* a cat," she said.

"A cat's not going to stop a robber, Sherry," Manuel said seriously. Then: "What happened to it?"

The question caught Sherry off guard. For the past few weeks, it seemed that everyone, including Brazil and Belinda, had forgotten about Pansy. But she hadn't. Every day when she got home from work, she felt Pansy's absence even more strongly than she had felt her presence when she was alive. It was crazy, really, how much she missed the cat. But Pansy had been so ridiculously sweet and devoted—and so harmless—that she'd been a much-needed antidote to the rest of Sherry's life. Suddenly, Sherry felt tears coming. "She died," she told Manuel weakly.

"Hey, I'm really sorry," he answered right away, putting down his glass of water and handing a tissue to Sherry. "You must have really loved that cat."

Sherry nodded. Her head was lowered, and she covered her face with her hands, but the tears dripped through her fingers anyway.

"I had her a long time."

Manuel moved closer to Sherry, and his voice suddenly took on the earnest and sympathetic tenor of a doctor with bad news. "Well, you know, Sherry," he said, "pets get old, and it's really the best thing to do—to put them to sleep."

"It wasn't that way," Sherry said. She was still crying; it had been days since she let herself remember the image of Alvin kicking out Pansy's guts as she lay there defenseless, curled in a ball.

"My neighbors killed her," Sherry blurted out. "They *murdered* her." And then she told Manuel the story.

When she was finished—it took a while through the tears—she saw Manuel stand ramrod straight, as if he had a dagger for a spine. He marched into the living room and glared out the window at the house next door.

"These people?" he asked.

"Yeah, them," said Sherry, joining Manuel at the window. "Laura and Alvin Beauregard."

"How old are they?"

"I don't know," said Sherry. "Old."

Manuel nodded officiously. "Do they work?"

"No. They're retired, I guess. I don't know what they do all day," she answered bitterly.

Manuel nodded again. He was studying the house closely, memorizing it.

Suddenly, Sherry remembered the time. "Oh, dear—Manuel, I've got to get you home for dinner," she said. "I don't want you ending up in trouble."

He was still motionlessly watching the Beauregards' house, eyes blank with concentration.

"Manuel?" Sherry said. She nudged him gently on the elbow. "Home?"

"Oh, yes," came the answer. His voice was distant; he'd gone next door.

They were getting into Sherry's car a minute later when Brazil pulled into the driveway. Sherry nearly fainted. This was too much.

"It's your boyfriend," said Manuel. He let go of the door handle and carefully smoothed his hair. Sherry could see his eyes focus—pupils spinning like a high-powered camera lens—on the man behind the wheel of the clunky blue Dodge.

"We've really got to go," Sherry said forcefully, trying to recapture Manuel's attention. She pulled open her car door and at the same time desperately waved Brazil away with a flurry of frantic waist-high hand motions. But something told her that he wasn't about to obey the pantomime, especially after he saw Manuel. She knew there was only one way to avoid confrontation and disaster—a quick getaway. She climbed into the front seat and gestured Manuel to get in, too. "He'll just have to come back later," she said brightly, turning over the engine and revving it high.

But Brazil had already leapt out of the Dodge and was hurtling toward the BMW. He couldn't believe Sherry had brought that smug-faced little killer home. Had she lost her mind?

Sherry saw Brazil get closer and closer in her rearview mirror. She rolled up her window and shifted the car into Reverse.

"What the fuck!" Brazil was banging on the side of the BMW. "Open it up, Estabrook!"

Sherry forced a lighthearted laugh. "He's just kidding," she told Manuel.

"Doesn't look like he's kidding to me."

Brazil heaved himself onto the trunk and started thumping his fist on the rear window.

"Stay here," Sherry instructed Manuel as she put the car in Park, jumped out, slammed the door, and walked back to face Brazil.

"What the fuck are you doing?" she seethed.

"I had the exact same question for you," Brazil shot back. "You brought that nut cake to where you live—you must have gone absolutely insane."

"Shut up," Sherry ordered in an urgent whisper. "He's going to hear you."

"Frankly, my dear," Brazil answered loud and clear, "I don't give a damn."

Sherry didn't have a chance to respond. Manuel had appeared at her side.

"How do you do?" he announced, throwing back his wiry shoulders and extending a hand to Brazil.

But Brazil ignored the offer with an exaggerated roll of the eyes. He hopped off the trunk of the car and planted himself five inches from Manuel, dwarfing him in every dimension.

"What the hell are you doing here?" Brazil asked Manuel

in a tone so deliberate and condescending Sherry barely recognized it.

"I'm visiting—"

"You invited yourself over here, that's what," Brazil cut him off. He stepped closer to Manuel, forcing him to either stare at his chest or look up at his chin six inches away. "That's not polite. That's not what Sherry wanted. And that's not the way it's gonna be.

"I want you to get something straight," Brazil went on. "Sherry is *not* your buddy. She is *not* your girlfriend. She is a *reporter*, and you are a *source*. It's very, very simple, *amigo*, like a good old-fashioned business deal. You understand that, don't you, *amigo*? Sherry doesn't have any emotions for you, and you should not—and will not from now on—have any emotions for her." Brazil paused long enough to see the stricken expression on Sherry's face.

"You *comprendo*?" Brazil concluded in an insinuating drawl. "I knew you would."

Manuel stumbled backward a step and fixed his eyes on the pavement. He said nothing, but Sherry quickly filled the silence.

"Brazil, really . . ." Sherry exclaimed, sounding unnaturally bright and friendly, as if the whole encounter had been some kind of silly misunderstanding. "Really now!" Then, with one swift move, she turned her back to Manuel and dropped her voice to a whisper. "I'll call you later," she said to Brazil, pushing him toward his car. "We'll have dinner, okay?"

Just as fast, she turned back to Manuel. "Hey, what do you say we get going?" she asked. He was still studying the pavement, head down, but he obediently climbed into the front seat beside her. They weren't out of the driveway when he abruptly lifted his head and glared at Sherry.

"I've killed for less, you know," he said. His voice was low and controlled.

But Sherry's was not. She immediately broke into a frantic, peppy, pleading singsong. She wasn't going to lose Manuel over one of Brazil's typically melodramatic outbursts, not now.

"Manuel, I want to explain something to you, okay?" she began. "Are you listening? Promise me you'll listen. Please, please, listen to what I have to say."

He nodded sullenly.

"That was my boyfriend. He's got a very strong—a very

opinionated—personality. He doesn't really approve of all the time we spend together. Please don't take it personally. It's not going to affect our relationship."

They drove in silence for a mile.

"You could do better," Manuel said finally. "A *lot* better."

She smiled as if she sympathized with his concern. "Maybe," she said. "But, Manuel, I'm sure you'd like him under different circumstances."

"What makes him think he's so great?"

"Well, he's a great photographer." Sherry wasn't sure the conversation was going the way she wanted. "That's not really the point, Manuel. He doesn't really care about *you*. He cares about *me* spending too much time with one person. Like I said, don't take it personally."

"He's jealous."

"Maybe."

"Well, maybe he has reason to be."

Sherry's hands gripped the steering wheel. What kind of nebulous answer could she manufacture this time?

But Manuel didn't give her time. He was talking again, same voice, low and controlled.

"If he took better care of you, he'd have nothing to worry about," he said. "Some guys just don't have any class. They don't know what to do, you know, to make a woman happy. They just don't have what it takes."

Sherry noticed Manuel was sounding more like himself again. He was sitting up in his seat now and staring out the window straight ahead.

"I knew it the first time I ever saw you," Manuel went on, voice bolstered by new confidence. "I could tell you didn't have a man taking care of you. I'm not bragging, but I think I have a sixth sense or something when it comes to women. I know what they want."

"Uh-huh," Sherry muttered. She wasn't really listening to his words; she was listening to his tone, and it sounded just fine. A nice, speedy recovery—thank God.

They pulled up in front of his house. As usual, the TV was on but the lights were out. With her window open, Sherry could hear the dull roar of volume turned up very high. It sounded like Manuel's father was watching a wrestling match—so much unhinged screaming.

"Is everything okay now?" she asked Manuel.

He turned to face her, his narrow face set in a skewed and happy grimace.

"Everything," he said, "is going to be just beautiful."

The next morning Belinda found a note from Sherry on her desk. The handwriting was terrible, as usual.

B, dearest: Jack sent me up to Boca to interview some shrink he knows who can talk about kids who kill. Patsy Cullen was supposed to do it, but one of her kids got the chicken pox. I'll give her my notes. Won't be back till tomorrow earliest.

I've got three more hits for you to verify. The details are attached.

But forget business. I tried to call you last night about 10 times but you were out (with Eladio again?) I had an unbelievable day yesterday. Lots and lots of good quotes from Manuel, but then he came over to my house and we ended up bumping into Brazil who proceeded to throw a temper tantrum in my driveway. Then last night, Brazil spent about three hours screaming at me. He thinks Manuel has made me crazy, wants me to quit the story, quit the paper, work as a go-go dancer or something like that. . . .

I need you! Where are you? I leave at the end of the week for Alice's wedding. Jack agrees I've gone through enough of the hits with Manuel, we await your verifications. Lucky for you, you won't have to hassle the desk guy over at Miami again, all these hits were elsewhere. As soon as you're done, we have to start wrapping it up. Time is of the essence, as they say. Talk soon, okay? Yours, S.

Belinda read the note twice. She missed Sherry, too, and was dying to hear about Manuel's visit and Brazil's driveway harangue, so why did she suddenly have a stomachache? She leafed through the pages Sherry had attached with a paper clip. They laid out the details of three murders, scrawled in red ink, in the same extravagant script.

"¿*Cuando*, Sherry?" Belinda asked out loud when she was

done reading. "When will this be over?" The newsroom hummed and clicked back, oblivious, with the high-pitched *zzzt-zzzt* of wire machines, the low din of questions being asked in a hundred different voices, the nonstop *tck-tck-tck* of words hitting the screen. Downstairs, a bell clamored, and then, as if to answer Belinda's question, came the muffled roar of the presses.

She was out the door and headed for the garage when her phone started ringing.

The cop behind the counter at the Homestead police station was asleep when Belinda arrived, slumped in a ratty maroon La-Z Boy recliner, arms flung open in the abandon of a dream. He was a big man, shaped like a pear, wearing a hand-knit, bumpy brown cardigan over his uniform and a pair of fancy red cowboy boots. His face was jowly, gray with whiskers, and hung down to his chest like an old bulldog. Belinda hated to wake him; she wasn't sure if he would talk or growl.

"Hello," she said softly.

The man in the chair sucked on his cheeks like a nursing baby, shifted from one wide hip to the other and tucked his chin deeper into his chest. He was down for the count.

"Hello," Belinda tried again.

No response.

She tapped on the counter with her fingernails. Nothing.

She cleared her throat. Nothing still.

She clumped out of the station and then back in again, slamming the screen door behind her.

Then: movement. The cop raised one leaden arm, lazily swatted at an imaginary fly, and let it drop, knuckles hitting the desk beside him like so many glass marbles.

"Yowch," he muttered.

"Hello," Belinda said, this time with volume. "Hello there, SIR!"

She finally had him. He opened one watery blue eye and—without moving a cumbrous muscle—gave Belinda the slow up-and-down. "Uh-nnn," he groaned, and shut his eye again. Finally, words: "I don't know," he said.

Belinda laughed, but the cop did not. He wasn't joking.

She paused for a moment and then tried again. "This will just take a second," she said.

The cop groaned.

"I'm out of here in five minutes, in five minutes or less. I'm telling you—"

"All right, all right." The cop cut her off.

He rose from his chair with exaggerated effort—one heavy limb at a time—and hitched up his belt. The whole process took a minute or two.

"All right now, what can I do you for?" he asked finally. Belinda recognized instantly that she had a real Cracker on her hands. Was it too late to put on the drawl? It had to be worth a try anyway.

"I'm Belinda McEvoy. *Miami Citizen*," she said. "How y'all doing today?"

"A reporter?" The cop scowled. "I thought you were here to complain about getting towed off Krome Avenue, like everyone else in this town is complaining about. But you're a reporter, huh? I'm not authorized to talk to reporters."

"You don't have to *talk* to me," Belinda said sweetly. "Y'all just gotta pull one little report for me. Homicide last July of a black female, first name Lulu."

The cop rubbed his eyes and looked around the office uneasily. "I'm not supposed to talk to you," he said.

"Right," said Belinda. She batted her eyes provocatively and smiled like warmed-up molasses.

"Lulu," the cop said. It was more of a sigh than a statement.

"Right," Belinda drawled. "Remember her?"

"Yeah, surely do." The scowl was gone, Belinda noticed, and it was replaced by something resembling perplexed frown—what did this mean? He wasn't angry anymore, not at all. He was pained. Christ!—this cop was *sad.*

He looked at Belinda quizzically. "We surely miss Lulu around here," he said.

"That so?" said Belinda. She was intrigued—utterly—but she couldn't press her luck.

"She was a good kid. Mixed-up terrible, but a good kid."

Belinda nodded, head aslant, eyes crinkled at the edges with heartfelt compassion.

"What you want that report for?" the cop asked. "We ain't solved it yet."

"Well, exactly," Belinda improvised. "Me and my friend at the paper are working on a story about unsolved homicides. Maybe we can help y'all out on this one."

"I doubt it."

She couldn't help herself: "Why not?" she asked.

"Cuz whoever killed Lulu was a cold-blooded s.o.b., and he ain't never gonna get himself found," said the cop. He pulled up his pants again. "Shot her right up the nose. Right here," he shoved one meaty finger up his left nostril. "Blew her head off. She dint hurt no one. He dint have to go and do that."

"What a shame!" said Belinda.

The cop considered Belinda carefully for a moment and then shuffled over to a metal filing cabinet near the recliner. After a bit of rummaging, he pulled out a yellow homicide report, read it over, and shuffled back to the counter. Then, gingerly, he put it down between them and released a long unhappy sigh, blowing out the air through puffed-up cheeks.

Belinda started to read the report, hurriedly jotting notes into her pad. *Victim, b.f. Lulu LaTerche, was reported missing by family members 7/23, 1440 hours, after she did not return home for two weeks. Body of deceased was discovered by Buddy Mann, a homeless person known to frequent the area. Mann was questioned and released.*

The cop was watching Belinda intently—eyes squinted in an effort to decipher her shorthand upside down—and twitching so anxiously she was afraid he might grab the report away at any moment. She needed to distract him.

"This Lulu," she asked, drawl still rolling, "was she a friend of yours?"

"She was just fifteen," the cop answered. He pulled a soiled handkerchief from his pocket and blew his nose.

"Sounds like you knew her real well."

"We all knew Lulu." A long pause and then a sharp intake of breath. "She was always in here for somethin' or 'nother—druggin' or stealin' from the Seven-Eleven down the road here. We got to know her real good. We'd known her since she was just ten."

Belinda had stopped reading. "Just ten?" she asked.

The cop nodded, and his jowls bobbed up and down. "She weren't a bad kid, like I said," he went on. "Lulu—she was just . . . just *grown up* for her age. She dint have no mama takin' care of her, and her daddy was poor. He tried to keep her good, but she had some fierce will in her. We said round here that Lulu was a firecracker." He seemed cheered, suddenly, by a memory. "She baked us some cookies one time," he said. "She weren't much for bakin', but it was the heart that mattered in it."

Belinda nodded sympathetically. She wanted to listen, but she needed to keep focused. She turned back to the report and continued jotting its details into her notebook. *Victim was found in NE corner of abandoned residence in 400 block of Roberts Road. Identified by police officer at the scene by articles of clothing, pink chamois skirt and pink fishnet stockings. Cause of death: gunshot to the face.* Belinda scanned the report for any mention of a crack pipe or a marijuana butt—hadn't Manuel claimed Lulu was wasted when he killed her?—but there was none.

"She was just barely fifteen." The cop was talking again. "You shoulda seen her papa cry. That man wailed so loud they could hear him in Miami. It was a piteous sight."

"Why would someone do such a thing?" Belinda asked. She really wanted to know.

"Had to be someone with not a heart nor a soul," said the cop. "Someone who'd just kill a girl like that. She had to see it coming, the way he did it." He stuck his finger in his nose again. "Even made the medical examiner barf."

Belinda was writing faster now. She had to get out of this place, out into the fresh air.

The cop had left the counter and was rustling through the top drawer of the station's desk. After a minute he found what he was after and brought it over to Belinda.

"Here's her picture," he said, holding out Lulu's police mug shot. "She was a cute thing."

Belinda sighed heavily. The cop was right. Even in the stark white light of a lineup photo, Lulu was beguiling. Her hair was pulled tight into two short fuzzy ponytails atop her head, and her almond-shaped eyes were wide with delicate melancholy.

"Pretty," said Belinda.

"Surely was," said the cop.

Belinda was done taking notes. The hit, of course, was Manuel's handiwork.

"I thank you," said Belinda. She pushed the report along the counter toward the cop, who stared at it without moving.

"Son of a bitch," he whispered under his breath.

"Surely was," said Belinda.

 There were nine pink message slips on Belinda's desk when she returned to the office. Each one read: *Call Eladio—VERY URGENT.* He had been phoning every half hour since she left.

She pounded out his number frantically and got an answer on the first ring.

"Belinda? Is that you?" Eladio said. His voice sounded strange and muffled.

"Eladio—what in the—"

"Can you meet me in a few minutes, down where we were last night, right near where we parked the car?"

"At Cape—"

He cut her off. "Right. There. Can you?"

"Yes," she said. Her heart was slamming in her chest like bumper cars.

He hung up without saying good-bye.

Belinda grabbed her keys and scrambled toward the elevators, but Brazil stopped her cold, stepping in front of her just before she reached the swinging doors out of the newsroom.

"Whoa!" he said. "Got a hot date?"

"Please, Brazil." She had never really liked him. "I've got to get out of here."

"One second now," he drawled, scratching his neck lazily. "Would you happen to know where Miss Estabrook has misplaced herself to?"

Could he talk any slower? Belinda wondered. "Why don't

you ask your wife?" she snapped, trying to get around his over-sized frame. But Brazil calmly sashayed left to block her way.

"Now that's unfriendly!" he came back with an openmouthed Cracker smile, apparently amused by Belinda's suggestion. "You can't possibly mean that." He laid a hand on her shoulder and let it linger there a moment. "Let's start again, shall we? Now, where is Sherry?" he asked.

"Fine," Belinda said briskly. She wasn't going to waste her time fighting with him now. "She went to Boca for an interview. I don't know when she's coming back. Leave her a message, for Christ's sake!" She finally elbowed her way past him, and seeing the elevator stuck on the first floor, rushed toward the stairs and took them two at time until she reached the garage five flights down.

Something is terribly wrong—the words pulsed through her head over and over again as she maneuvered her car out of the garage and gunned onto the long white causeway tying Miami to Key Biscayne. *What could be so terribly wrong? What did I say to hurt Eladio last night? Did I say too much? Did I sound too crazy? Yes, I sounded too crazy. He wants to end it with me—that must be it. He realizes this is all a mistake. He wants to break it off before it's too late, before we go too far. He's going to tell me we're moving too fast. He wants to think it over. He's thought it over. He needs some space.*

The speedometer on her dash nudged 80, and the Tercel, its unrepaired front bumper still hanging low to the pavement, rattled and shook as if it might fly apart. Belinda turned the volume on the radio up high to blank out the noise.

A few minutes later, she took a hard right out to the beach and quickly spotted Eladio. He was leaning against the passenger door of his cruiser, hands deep in his pockets, looking out to the bay.

She screeched into the spot next to his and jumped out of her car. She knew what she was going to say. Anything—*anything*—he wanted was okay with her, but couldn't they give it one more chance? Maybe making love *had* been a mistake. They had gotten carried away. She understood his concerns. It *was* happening too fast. She wasn't going to try to force him into anything. He could leave if he wanted, really. Or maybe they could see each other less—that would be fine. Maybe just once every two weeks. Or once a month. Which did he prefer?

She opened her mouth to begin, but Eladio was talking already.

"Belinda," he said, "my angel, thank God you're here!" He pulled her into his chest with a desperate embrace. "Thank God you're here." He kissed her eyes and lips.

"I was so worried—"

Eladio nodded, trying to catch his breath—he sounded as if he had just sprinted a mile. Sweat dripped down his face and into the collar of his uniform. "I'm sorry I left so many messages," he said. "I had to get in touch with you before PIO did."

"PIO? The cops in the news office? What are you talking about?" Belinda was trying to sound concerned, but in her heart she was so relieved she wanted to weep. This wasn't about them at all! It was about *work*, and work was meaningless to her now. "Eladio, what's happening?" she asked calmly, dabbing the sweat from his brow with two fingertips. "Is it something with Officer Aloe—you know, DeLisa Watson?"

Eladio leaned on his car again. He inhaled and exhaled deliberately.

"Well, she started it all," he said. "You told her about us, right?"

"I just—"

"Did you?" It sounded almost like an accusation, but the expression in his eyes told Belinda he was too sad and confused to be angry.

"Yeah," she answered. "It seemed like a good idea at the time. I was trying to soften her up. I needed some reports for Sherry's story about the kid."

"Yeah." Long pause. "You shouldn't have done that."

"What? You're not supposed to go out with reporters?"

"No, it's not that," said Eladio. He took her hand and squeezed it reassuringly, gazing out toward the beachhead where they had lain together the night before. "Apparently, after your visit she went to the chief's office and got him all riled up about some story the *Citizen* is doing that's going to destroy Miami's image and make fools out of the police."

"She did that?" Belinda gasped. Hadn't she and DeLisa had a grand old time? Hadn't she bought enough of that ridiculous aloe goop? "That bitch!"

"So the chief calls the internal-investigation office, and they call me—"

"You?"

"Yeah," Eladio sighed. "I think DeLisa had some crazy theory that I was supplying you inside information about certain unsolved homicides. She told the chief I was working as your major source to discredit the department."

"This is crazy!" said Belinda. She wanted to laugh, but Eladio still had the ashen face and tremoring hands of an earthquake survivor.

"It isn't crazy," Eladio said. "This was bound to happen. It's that story you're working on. It's going to get us all in trouble."

"I hope not," Belinda said. It was her turn to hold his hand reassuringly, and he seemed to relax slightly. "But I guess I should warn you that there's going to be a sidebar about how the cops haven't got a clue about Manuel's little killing career."

"Haven't got a clue! Mother of Jesus, Belinda!" Eladio exclaimed, wagging his head in disbelief. "There are more than four hundred homicides in metropolitan Miami each year, you can't expect the police to solve them all—"

"I've already heard it," Belinda interrupted him gently. "DeLisa gave me the same line."

"It's not a *line*," Eladio insisted. "Come on, Belinda, you know that the cops can't even bother with Manuel's kind of homicides. They're just drug hits. They're unpreventable. We've got our hands filled keeping *innocent* people safe. You've got to understand that."

"I do," she said, and she meant it. "Let's just forget about this whole thing with DeLisa, okay? I promise I won't talk to her again. In fact, I spent the whole day talking to cops who *don't* work for the Miami PD. And, you know, that reminds me, you won't believe what I found out over at the Kendall substation—"

"Belinda, I really don't want to hear about it, especially now," said Eladio.

"No, no—this really isn't about the story. It's a minor detail," she came back. She was excited. "I've been dying to tell someone all day."

Eladio nodded, resigned.

"You know how Manuel goes around talking like he's this big, tough macho man, right?" she began. "Well, today I was checking out one of his murders out at some development in far west nowheresville, and you know what I found out?"

Eladio shrugged no.

"I found out that in one of his hits, he killed the victim's dog, and guess what?"

Eladio shrugged again. He was trying not to listen.

"It was a little tiny yapping Pekingese! You know how big those are?" She held her hands about a foot apart and laughed in amazement. "The guy is a total coward!"

"Right," said Eladio. As far as he was concerned, all killers were cowards.

Belinda wasn't done. "And then I was down in Cutler Ridge, and I found out he shot some poor eighty-eight-year-old geezer when he was swimming in his pool—*eighty-eight years old!*—just like a sitting duck—"

But before she could go on, Eladio stepped forward and clamped his hand over her mouth. "*¡Basta!*" he said. "I can't hear any more! Belinda, they called me and grilled me for two hours. They were all over me. If I know anything about this story, I'll get fired, okay?"

"They questioned you for two hours?" This *was* serious.

"Yeah." Eladio clenched his teeth at the memory. Did he know that Belinda McEvoy had pressured Officer DeLisa Watson to get her a series of reports pertaining to unsolved drug-related homicides? Was it true the *Citizen* was preparing an article about the department's inability to crack serial-killer cases? When was the story going to run? And would it, the chief demanded, really claim Miami was "sick like cancer" and that all the cocaine killings were taking an "incalculable human toll?"

"I had to lie. I don't like that," Eladio told Belinda as they watched a sailboat tack against the wind out of the bay. "I had to tell them I didn't know a thing about it."

Belinda felt ashamed, and then came a sudden bolt of anger— at DeLisa Watson, at Manuel, at Jack, and at Sherry, too. What a mess she had got them all into while she buzzed around town in her BMW, oblivious, letting Manuel thump his chest about this great hit and that great hit. And now she was up in squeaky-clean Boca, getting intellectual with some shrink. If she wanted one more killing verified, she'd have to get into the trenches and do it herself.

"I'm really sorry," Belinda told Eladio, and she meant it so much it made her heart ache. "I promise you, the story will be over really soon. Sherry has to go home for a wedding. We're wrapping it up this week."

Eladio let go a long sigh. "I hope so," he said wearily. "But I bet PIO is still going to be calling you. They may tell you that you can't use any of the information in the police reports DeLisa got you. They're going to say the cases are still under investigation."

"Well, we don't need them anymore," Belinda said. "We just had to know if Manuel was telling the truth."

Eladio raised his eyebrows.

"He is," said Belinda. "Unfortunately."

"I don't have any idea what you're talking about." He pulled his face into a silly expression to show he was joking.

"Okay, okay." It was safe to laugh now, and so Belinda did. She hugged Eladio around the waist and kissed the smooth skin just below his ear. She tasted salt and shut her eyes tight in piquant bliss, remembering why.

"You know," she said after a minute, her face pressed close to his chest, chin touching his shiny silver badge, "I was afraid you called to break up with me."

"Belinda—" Eladio started to admonish her, but stopped before she could detect the sadness and frustration caught in his throat.

Of course she had been afraid of losing him, he told himself, just as she had lost one man and then another in the space of too few years to make sense. And so fear was at her core now, pumping capricious life through her veins like a mechanical heart. If he didn't know her as he did, he'd have decided right then that Belinda was someone very tragic, damaged beyond reasonable hope and repair. But she wasn't beyond saving, Eladio thought. He could do that.

"Belinda," he said gently, "How could you think that I would leave you? I mean, we had last night—you were being crazy to worry."

She shook her head. It did seem crazy now.

"I promise you," Eladio said, knowing that life was too brief and unpredictable to wait, "I will never leave you. Never. I'll stay with you forever if you let me."

"I'll let you." She said the words into the starched shirt of his uniform, just loud enough for him to hear.

Eladio kissed her forehead and waited, praying silently to God that she would open her yellow eyes just for a second, so he could look into them when he asked her to marry him. But she kept them closed, and so, finally, he asked anyway.

And she said yes.

The psychiatrist's name was Adam Klein, and he practiced out of an office connected to his house by a pink marble path. That's all Jack told Sherry before she shot up the coast for Boca Raton.

Maybe he had wanted her to be surprised. Maybe he had wanted her off guard. She had to wonder; Klein's house wasn't the kind of detail people forgot to mention.

It was, instead, an immense and breathtaking place: a late-modern configuration of white granite and stucco, acute and obtuse angles, white ramps and railings and curved glass-block walls, sitting like a monument to new money and lots of it, one grassy acre back from a still and shimmering inland canal.

This guy Klein, Sherry thought incredulously as she steered her car around the wide circular drive and surveyed the house from one distant corner to the other—this guy is a friend of Jack's?

It made even less sense a few minutes later when she crossed the threshold of Klein's cluttered, Byzantine office, ceiling arched to the sky like a chapel and illuminated by an evocative stream of pink-golden light. A young redheaded butler in a chartreuse silk jacket had wordlessly led Sherry there—it was in a building all its own a hundred feet from the main house—unlocked the door with a giant key on a black satin cord, and fixed her a cup of peppermint tea. He was gone before she could ask when to expect Dr. Klein. She had the feeling she would have to wait.

And so she decided to check the place out—how could she help herself? It was like a jewelry box spilled on its side. There were books everywhere—splayed on the purplish Oriental carpets, piled five high on Queen Anne brocade chairs, lying open and upside down on a massive black oak desk in one corner. She twisted her head this way and that to check out the titles: *Hopscotch*, by Cortazar, *The Human Brain*, by a bunch of doctors, *The Moviegoer*, by Walker Percy, *The Once and Future King*, by White— hadn't she read that at Miss Eliot's?—*What We Talk About When We Talk About Love*—this was serious stuff, Sherry thought—a volume of Cheever short stories, so worn that yellowed pages were falling out, and here was one she recognized! *As I Lay Dying*—Belinda had recommended it a thousand times. It was sitting on a spindle-legged table, on top of a dark red leather-bound copy of the Bible and underneath a paperback copy of *Walden.*

Sherry thought she heard a door click open, but when she spun around, there was no one there. No Dr. Klein, not yet.

She headed to a wall covered with photographs—maybe she could get a look at the doctor before he showed. But in all the pictures, and there were dozens, she couldn't pick him out—the men seemed either too young or too old to inhabit this curious lair. One picture did catch her attention, though. It showed a small girl—she was probably about four—wearing a summer dress the color of watermelon standing next to a blackboard with a pensive expression. Sherry stepped closer to the photo to make out the faint childlike lettering scrawled across the slate.

I No DaDdY-O, it read.

How odd, Sherry thought. Was it some kind of inside joke?

The other photos weren't as mysterious: a terribly skinny dark-haired woman in big square sunglasses—Klein's wife, no doubt—leaning against the railing of a speedboat in a leather string bikini, cigarette poised just at her lips; two young boys—so Klein had sons, too—posing with a strung-up Marlin, shimmering yellow and silver, just dead.

A few inches away, Sherry spotted a small, framed ink drawing of two elephants in a giddy mating dance, and underneath, in fancy script, the words GET IT ON! WHAT THE REPUBLICAN PARTY MEANS TO ME. Beside it hung a grainy black-and-white poster of Che Guevara, beret aslant as always and impenetrable eyes staring fervently into the distance.

Sherry wandered over to the big desk in the corner. It was blanketed with scraps of paper, some blank, others scribbled with a few words or sentences. *Suffering is the origin of consciousness*, one said, *tell Mia.*

She kept reading:

Re:Martie B./ early incest?

"julio's awesome cookies/2 cups butter, 2 eggs, half cup almond extract, juice of one lemon, sifted whole wheat flour (2–3 cups/whatever feels right)/cinnamon maybe/sprinkles

thursday: get dead tickets!! 555-2771"

Re: janet l./sez she was "obsessed" with father, 4X in one hour. note phrasing/sez mother "obsessed" with death 3X. using third person to describe own actions/feelings. referral to memorial?

Off in one corner, Sherry spied another piece of paper, covered with carefully printed words: "I being lost, being poor, being blind/ Have only my dreams, that is all/And I, I have cast them beneath your feet/Tread softly, surrender, don't fall."

It was part of poem, Sherry thought, a poem she knew from somewhere. She flipped over the scrap—it was on a piece of brown paper torn from a grocery sack—to look for the author's name, and that's when she saw her own, printed clearly on a small piece of yellow paper.

SHERRY ESTABROOK/citizen/jack d. likes/trusts. story:kids who kill/why?/needs "total" confidentiality/wednesday 3 pm/needs one/two hours

Sherry checked her watch. It was three-fifteen already.

She headed back toward the couch. She didn't want to stop looking, but something told her it would be smart to be sitting down minding her own business when Klein finally appeared. She checked her watch again and, looking up, suddenly noticed three simply framed diplomas hanging, almost hidden, on the wall behind a richly carved high-backed chair. She took two steps closer—could it be?—she took another step . . . yes! This Klein guy went to Harvard. Harvard College '69, Harvard Med '73, Beth Israel Hospital '75. What in the world was he doing down here in Boca, living in this hippie drug-dealer's dream den, scribbling poetry on paper bags?

"Hello, Sherry Estabrook."

Suddenly, someone was by her side.

Sherry jumped back a step in surprise and caught her first glimpse of Klein—or was it? This couldn't be a doctor. He was wearing blue jeans ripped at the knees, a faded Keith Richards T-shirt, and purple suede clogs. She hadn't seen those since high school.

He stuck out his hand. "Adam Klein at your service," he said.

It *was* him.

"I was just looking—" Sherry rushed through the words, pointing awkwardly toward the diplomas as if she'd been caught spying. "Um, you know, I went there, too."

"That so?" said Klein. "Not too many of us down here. We're refugees." He whispered the last word conspiratorially and then let out a loud laugh.

"I love your office," Sherry said. She needed a few minutes to study this strange person before they got down to business. It wasn't just his clothing that threw her off. For another thing, he was blue-eyed and blond, with the fine curly hair of a picture-book angel. In fact, Sherry thought, if it weren't for his little potbelly and the shadow of fair whiskers on his chin, Klein would look about thirteen years old. He even had the face of a bar mitzvah boy: plump, hopeful, and sincere, and the beaming eyes of someone infused with untested faith. His lips were fixed in a mischievous, elflike smile. There was something so completely unaffected and appealing about him, Sherry thought, could he be for real?

"My office, well, it's certainly *unusual*," Klein answered cheerily, looking around as if he were seeing the place for the first time himself.

"All this furniture—"

"It's just wild, isn't it?" he asked, eyes open wide in wonder. "You know, I just pick up shit I groove to here and there, and I stick up whatever I want on the walls, and presto, you get this wigged-out place!"

Sherry stood silent. She was listening to his voice—his accent—all those flat *As* and the way he said *"they-yah"* when he meant to say there—Klein sounded so wonderfully familiar she just wanted to sit and listen to him forever.

"You've got to be from Boston," she said.

"North of Boston. Marblehead, to be exact."

"You're kidding!" Sherry practically jumped out of her skin. "So am I!"

Klein laughed. "Yeah, yeah," he said. "But something tells me that the planets of Adam Marcus Klein and Sherry—don't tell me, Ames? Merrill?—Estabrook didn't exactly cross orbits in our little Marblehead universe."

Sherry stared at him and shook her head in confusion.

"Now, Sherry," Klein said, sounding as if they were old pals.

"Marblehead High—did you go there? Temple Sinai? Michael's Deli? The Salem State skating rink Sunday mornings? Oy, no! You were busy worshiping the Father, Son, and the Holy Whatsoever at the First."

"I know where Michael's Deli is," she protested.

"Great pumpernickel, right?"

"Right," said Sherry. Was he teasing her?

Klein frowned, and even then, he was smiling.

"Now, I'm sure you are mucho busy, Sherry Ames Merrill Lowell Lamont Estabrook the Third, so shall we get started on the real business of things today?"

Sherry nodded, but she couldn't let the conversation go at that; this guy was too intriguing. How did he ever end up in Boca? What was he doing to afford this enormous house? Was he really married to that emaciated glamour bunny in the photographs? How did he know Jack? And who was that bizarre redheaded butler?

"So," said Sherry, obediently heading for the couch, "what brought you to Florida?"

"Long story."

"I like long stories."

"I'll shorten it," said Klein, settling into an overstuffed blue velvet chair, kicking off his clogs and crossing his legs. "I practiced in Boston. Did it for two years. Big problem: All my patients were neurotic, but I liked them that way. They were interesting. They were smart. They didn't need a doctor. Unfortunately, they wouldn't believe me when I said so." Klein shrugged. "One day, I'm reading the paper, and I see some article about Miami, and I say to myself, 'Now, here's a bunch of neurotics who need me!' Packed my bags, and moved to Boca—which was as close to Miami as my wife would allow. I opened my doors, and the crazies flooded in. They're happy. I'm happy. End of story."

"You have got to be kidding."

"No," said Klein. "Why do you say that?"

"It's just not how people usually end up someplace."

"Really?" asked Klein, uncrossing his legs and leaning forward, elbows on knees. "How do people end up one place or another? Isn't that an interesting question? Isn't the answer to that question totally central to a person's character? A person can just *happen* someplace, which might indicate some certain lack of direction or ambition, or a person might put himself someplace, which might indicate a very revealing phenomenon at work. Why did the person pick *that* place? Is it different or similar to the place he left behind?" Klein rubbed his temples thoughtfully. "You know, talking about this makes me realize how much my move to Florida says about Adam Klein. Utterly fascinating, yes, but probably only to me and my immediate family, most notably my mother, Esther. Correct me if I'm wrong."

Sherry stared at him and said nothing. She had lost him a while back.

Klein continued to look at her expectantly.

"I'm sorry," said Sherry. "Did you ask me a question?"

Klein leaned back in his chair and laughed. "Not really," he said, tilting his head in surprise. "I guess not! I must be losing it."

Harvard '69—no kidding, Sherry thought.

"Well, shall we get down to it?" Klein was talking again. "The famous Mr. D. tells me you're working on a piece about kids who kill. Sounds tantalizing."

"He talked to you about confidentiality?"

"My lips are sealed." Klein pretended to zipper his mouth.

"Okay," Sherry began, "we're actually writing about *one* kid who kills, who killed, actually. He's actually finished killing now."

She anticipated a question, but Klein sat silently, watching her. His expression had turned dead serious in concentration, and suddenly he didn't look so young, or so naive, anymore.

"The kid is sixteen, okay?" Sherry wanted to lay it all out for him short and neat. "I met him at his high school when I was working on another story. He followed me out to the parking lot, and he ended up telling me about these killings, these hits, he was involved in."

"That he was *involved* in?"

"That he committed."

"That he *committed*, right."

There was no use mincing words, Sherry realized. She told him Manuel's story from the beginning.

"Wow, heavy," Klein said solemnly when she was done. "I can't believe you've been carrying this kid's story around inside you for all these weeks. That must have been tough."

"Yeah, sort of," said Sherry.

"And you know he's telling the truth? He took a lie-detector test with Sherman Otis, right?"

"Yes," Sherry said firmly. "He's absolutely telling the truth."

Klein climbed out of his chair, stretched his back, and then sat on the floor cross-legged. For the next three minutes, he stayed in that position, head in his hands, face covered. Sherry could almost hear the motor in his brain grinding gears.

Finally, he looked up. "Well, I don't think you have to be a brain surgeon to figure this one out," he said. "I mean, the kid has a highly dysfunctional family. He's obviously acting out. He clearly has an aberrant superego at work. And, of course, there's the pressures of society coming down on him: Be cool, make money, get famous, buy a car, fuck a blonde. I can give you a couple of good quotes along those lines if you want."

"You're saying he's typical?" Sherry asked. It couldn't be!

"Oh, no, don't get me wrong," Klein said, standing up and stretching his back again. "This is a special case. This kid is wacko with a capital W. Most of the kids I see have a relatively good reason to kill—incest a lot of times, or perceived self-defense. We get a couple of real nasty cases, kids who kill during a robbery or something, but usually they're just freaking out and it's a onetime thing. The closest I've ever come to a case of unmitigated evil like this involved a twelve-year-old, actually, a kid up in the Boston burbs who killed his five-year-old neighbor—stabbed him twenty-six times if I recall. A few years later, we found out the kid had been watching his stepfather beat the shit out of his mother for years and years. He killed himself eventually."

"The stepfather?"

"No, the kid," said Klein, "the killer."

"Too bad. For everyone."

"Yeah, it really was. Terrible case."

They sat in silence for a few moments.

"So," Sherry said finally, "can you just talk a few minutes about my case?"

"Well, not specifically, unless I want to get arrested in a few weeks for not traipsing off to the cops with the information you've just given me. I'd get off I'm sure, but it'd be a major hassle."

"How about some general quotes about kids like him?"

Klein nodded happily, and for the next quarter of an hour, he pontificated away as Sherry got as much as she could in longhand.

"Great!" she said when Klein appeared to be done. Jack had been right. This would help the story.

She stood to leave. Maybe Jack could tell her who the butler was.

"You're going?" asked Klein. He sounded genuinely startled.

"Well, I don't want to take up any more of your time." She felt relieved; maybe he would invite her to see the house.

"Sherry, Sherry," Klein said, in an amused and scolding tone, "we haven't discussed the most intriguing thing about this entire case!"

"We haven't?"

Klein motioned her to sit down.

"Sherry," he said excitedly when she had settled back onto the couch, "*lots* of kids kill. But very few go blabbing it to reporters. Didn't that ever occur to you?"

"Of course," Sherry said, her voice intentionally offended. "I've known from the beginning that he's telling me because he wants to start a new life."

"Uh-huh," Klein answered, sounding unconvinced. "And why is it he wants to start a new life?"

"Well, that's obvious," Sherry shot back. "He wants to start a new life because—" She stopped, momentarily confounded. "Because—"

"Because?" Klein prompted her.

"Because . . . well . . . It's sort of hard to explain."

"Hard to explain, hmm?" said Klein. It was the voice of a Boston psychiatrist suddenly.

"Well, everyone I know has a theory or two," Sherry said. "My boyfriend thinks he has a crush on me, and he's coming clean to impress me. My partner, Belinda, thinks he feels guilty. Jack doesn't really have an opinion. Um, let's see, a couple of people in the newsroom think he's actually a genius and has plans to sell his story to Hollywood for a million bucks."

"I see," Klein said, not amused. "But what do you think?"

Sherry closed her eyes for a moment in concentration. She knew *she* understood Manuel completely, but how could she make this shrink feel what she felt in her gut? "Look," she said finally, "maybe it's something you have to live through to understand, but sometimes to start a second life, you have destroy the first one. And that's not something you just decide in your head. You can't say, okay, my old life is dead now. You have to *do* something to make it happen. You have to kill it. You see what I mean? That's what Manuel is doing."

Klein looked at her skeptically. "That's what he's told you?"

"In so many words," Sherry answered quickly. Manuel didn't need to tell her. She knew what the truth was. "Yes, he has."

A few seconds passed, and then Klein shook his head. His expression wasn't angry or adversarial, simply thoughtful and maybe even a little sad.

"Look, I've never seen this kid, or met him, or even heard his voice," Klein said at last, "but I would wager that he has no idea why he's telling you his story. I certainly don't think guilt has anything to do with it. And I doubt he's trying to kill off his old life—that's way too sophisticated a process for a sixteen-year-old with arrested emotional development—"

"So, then what's the real reason?" Sherry interrupted Klein abruptly. All at once, she felt nervous, very nervous. "Why did he spill his guts to me? Why does he want to start over?"

"What do you *really* think?"

"Please!" Sherry jumped from the couch and stood with her back to Klein for a moment. This wasn't what she had come to Boca for. Not at all. She wasn't even sure she wanted to finish this absurd conversation.

She turned to face Klein. "You're not *my* psychiatrist," she said. It was more a plea than a statement. "Just tell me what you think."

Klein sighed heavily, sounding as if he had bad news to deliver. "Well, it certainly has to be a combination of factors, a crush on you being among them, along with his oppressive home life and the years of brutality against his mother," Klein said, "but I'd have to say, Sherry, that the most important motive is something we simply don't know yet. There's a piece of the puzzle missing."

"There is not!" Sherry shot back immediately. This guy was going too far; he hadn't even met Manuel. "Look, Dr. Klein, I've spent one hundred hours with this kid, and I've heard it all. I *understand* him, perhaps on a level no one else can to relate to." She stopped for a moment to let her words sink in, then rushed on. "And let me just add this, Dr. Klein. Your whole argument about him having a crush on me is ludicrous. He has a girlfriend. Her name is Blanca."

Klein shook his head sadly.

"Doesn't matter, Sherry," he said. "Adolescent lust is a powerful thing. I've seen all sorts of murders and suicides and lots of real horrible stuff on account of teenagers in love, or what they consider love."

"I don't believe this," Sherry said, exasperated. She marched purposefully over to Klein's wall of photographs and focused on a picture she hadn't noticed before: the doctor, decked out in an expensive double-breasted suit, posing in front of the New York Stock Exchange with a hundred-dollar bill in his teeth.

"Well, like I said"—Klein was talking again—"his crush on you isn't the most important factor at work, Sherry. He probably didn't start out with a crush on you, but it probably took over his other motives after a while." He paused and waited until she turned to face him again. Then: "But, I mean, isn't the more important question *why* he loves you?"

Sherry thought about it for a second. "He thinks I'm pretty," she said. "And I let him talk about himself."

Klein looked at her dubiously. "No offense, but that's a little simplistic, isn't it?"

"I don't know." Sherry walked back to the couch and sat down again. This was getting exhausting.

"So you're pretty," said Klein. His tone told her he was about to fill in the blanks. "And you're white, and you look rich—sorry, I hope that doesn't upset you—and you represent the *Citizen*, a big, moral, upstanding community institution, and you come into this kid's school, and you say, I'm not here to judge you, I'm here just to listen. I'm here to validate whatever you want to say. I accept you. I love you."

"Oh, come on!" Sherry said. This guy had gone to one too many Grateful Dead concerts.

Klein shrugged. "You asked what I think."

"Well, I have a question for you," Sherry shot back. "Does it really matter why he's telling me?"

Klein smiled. "Not to you, I guess, and that's a choice you'll have to live with," he said, "but to me, it does. Then again, I'm a shrink."

"I don't believe it," Sherry snapped. This guy had a goddamn answer for everything; he was pissing her off.

"You don't believe I'm a shrink?"

"I don't believe that's all you do." She walked over to the window facing Klein's house and jabbed one finger in its direction. "You're telling me Blue Cross built that palace? I don't think so."

"Right," said Klein. He was smiling cheerfully again, un-
daunted and even a bit intrigued by Sherry's sudden explosion of
bitchiness. He liked her a lot. "If I lived off my practice, I'd be
sleeping in a one-room shack under the highway."

"Right," said Sherry. She didn't know if she should feel indignant or embarrassed.

Klein pulled his knees into his chest. "Commodities," he said
simply. "Gotta love 'em."

Then he stood up, walked over to a large armoire next to his
black oak desk, and pulled open the doors dramatically. "Exhibit
A: personal computer," said Klein. "Exhibit B: quote machine."

Sherry walked over to investigate.

"I'm the soybean king," said Klein. "King Klein o' Soybeans." He was watching Sherry's face, waiting for a reaction. He
wanted her to laugh, at least.

"I don't get it," she said quietly.

Klein shrugged. "I trade grain futures, you know, soybeans,
wheat, oats, corn. All that shit," he said. "Started as a hobby.
Now it's an addiction. Thank God I'm good at it. My monthly
Neiman's bill is bigger than the national debt. And then there's
ballet lessons. And vacations to Vail. And Little League uniforms.
And, of course, bread and water. All the essentials."

Sherry was feeling more stupid by the minute. "Is it legal?"
she asked, trying to sound like a reporter.

Klein played along. "One hundred percent," he said,
"though I can see where it doesn't exactly look that way."

"No, not exactly." She dropped onto the couch again, not
sure what to say next but not ready to leave either.

Klein closed the armoire and returned to the chair across from
Sherry. He waited.

"Well, the story is almost over anyway," Sherry muttered
finally. Klein didn't answer. A minute passed. Then: "You know,
I'm really getting sick of everyone asking me all these questions
about it—I mean, Belinda and Brazil and now you. Everyone's
always asking me questions about it, like *I* fucking committed all
the murders or something."

Klein let her talk.

"I'm just doing my job the best I know how, okay? I'm just
being a reporter. Is that really so fucking bad? I want to be a great
reporter. I want people to recognize my byline. I just want to be
myself. You'd think that was a crime or something."

Klein shrugged: I understand.

Sherry slumped down on the couch. She was offhandedly studying her split ends.

"Wait until my parents read it," she said.

Silence.

"My father's going to die. He'll disown me."

Then: "Actually, he'll probably pretend it never happened."

Silence again.

"How do you want him to react?" Klein asked after a minute had passed.

"What? Oh, I don't know," said Sherry. "I don't really care. If I cared, I wouldn't be living in Miami. If I cared, I'd be up in Marblehead, married to Charles, volunteering for the Junior League."

Klein shook his head. "I think you have it exactly backward," he said.

Sherry raised a hand to cut him off. She didn't want to understand what Klein meant; she didn't want to discuss *her* anymore.

"How did you say you knew Jack again?" she asked abruptly enough to let Klein know the subject was changed.

"I didn't," said Klein.

Sherry nodded vaguely. Hadn't he mentioned it when she first walked in? Suddenly, she felt totally confused, as if she had just awakened in a strange hotel room.

"So," she said brightly, trying to sound more connected than she felt, "how *do* you know Jack?"

Klein was watching Sherry closely. She looked as if she might break apart at any moment. He wanted to keep her talking about herself, but it might be too much for her, too dangerous for a onetime encounter.

"I met him at his daughter's murder trial," Klein said matter-of-factly. "I was an expert witness for the prosecution. I testified that the kid who killed her knew exactly what he was doing. The defense was claiming temporary insanity."

"Oh, really?" asked Sherry, trying to look as though she knew Jack's daughter had been murdered. The rumor in the newsroom was that she had died of a drug overdose. She was eager to hear more. "What happened again?" she asked. "The kid got off, right?"

"Nope," said Klein, a little surprised. "We nuked him. Life without parole."

"Why'd he do it, anyway?" Sherry went on in a conversational tone of voice. "Jack never explains that part of it."

"Well, in fact, it was one of those adolescent lust things I was
talking about earlier," said Klein. "He thought she was sleeping
with his best friend. She wasn't, but that didn't really matter. He
thought so, and so he went out and got shit-faced and coked up
to the max, and he found his father's hunting rifle and boom.
That was that."

"Someone told me Emily was a drug addict," Sherry said.

"I wouldn't go that far," said Klein. "Not an *addict*. She was
your typical recreational user. In fact, one big problem the prosecution had was that Emmy was quite coked up when she was
murdered. Had to prove she didn't incite Oliver in some way."

"Oliver?"

Klein smiled. "Yeah, I know," he said. "It doesn't seem like
a killer's name, right? We're used to killers being named Juan or
José or Manuel or something, right?"

"Right," said Sherry. Had Jack told him after all?

Klein stood up and stretched his back again. "Where are my
clogs?" he asked, looking around.

Sherry leaned forward and pulled them out from underneath
his chair, staring at them as if they were two pieces from the
Museum of Modern Art.

"I gotta tell you," she said, "I haven't seen clogs in a long,
long time."

"You're kidding!" said Klein. "You mean all you Miami reporters don't wear them around? I thought wearing clogs was
rule 505-C in the *Citizen* style book."

Sherry finally laughed. "Must of missed that one," she said.

They stood facing each other for a few moments, both of
them looking ready to speak and waiting for the other to go first.

"Well, I guess I better go," Sherry offered at last. It wasn't
what she wanted to say.

"Right," said Klein, looking a little disappointed. This visit
had reminded him of home, not of Marblehead, but of Cambridge
in the early winter, air as brittle as the Cliffies he used to love so
much.

He started to walk toward the door.

"I can find my way out," Sherry said in a voice a bit rougher
than she had intended. She hated saying good-bye to people she
knew she would never see again.

She extended her hand, and Klein shook it warmly. He wanted Sherry to look him in the eyes. He wanted her to know that someone cared, about her and about the kid. But she was looking away, toward the big house and the water beyond.

"By the way," she asked all of a sudden, "what's with your butler?"

"Luke?"

"I didn't get his name."

"Yeah, that's Luke," said Klein haltingly. "We took him in. He lives with us." Sherry held onto Klein's hand. There was more, and she had a feeling what it was.

"He killed his father two years ago," Klein continued. "When he was fourteen. I struck a deal with the prosecutor so he could serve his sentence here, with us. I think he's getting better."

"Was he sick?"

"In a manner of speaking."

Sherry kept her eyes on Klein expectantly. It was his turn to look away, though he kept squeezing her hand tightly.

"Was he sick?" Sherry asked again.

"Yes," Klein said finally. "It's hard—" He met Sherry's eyes. "I guess he had to be, to take the life of another human being."

"Even if the other human being deserved to die?"

Klein dropped Sherry's hand gently and thought for a long minute.

"Even then," he said at last.

It was getting late by the time Sherry hit the highway south, homeward.

The sun was to her right, dissolving pink and orange in the western sky, and the dusk air gusted through her window, filling her head with the scent of papaya and suntan lotion. Even the heat was gone, and in its place, warmth.

The light all around was so soft and radiant Sherry wanted desperately to feel something like peace, but instead her neck and shoulders were riddled with the buckshot of anxiety. She could barely move her body, but her mind was thrashing.

Why, she kept asking herself over and over, why was everyone trying to fuck up her story?

Really, what did Klein know? His patients weren't anything like Manuel. Not at all—even he had admitted that. Manuel was different. Yes, he had been crazy, but now he was breaking free. Klein didn't understand how hard that was. Nobody did.

Christ—soybeans! That's what Klein understood. He was just a looney shrink who played the market to the hilt. He was a businessman.

But then, Sherry wondered, why did she feel as if she were about to break into pieces the minute she left his office? Why did every question he asked her keep playing through her head? He wanted to know if Manuel was telling her the truth. Why he was talking to her. His reason for wanting a new life.

That morning she thought she had the answers. But now, suddenly, she wasn't so sure. And the worst part of it all was the creeping, tingling feeling in her gut that maybe, just maybe, Manuel knew her better than she knew him. Perhaps he had seen right through her, just as Klein had. Could it be?

"Thank you, Dr. Klein," Sherry blurted out loud, and all at once tears began to run down her face. "Thank you, you fucker." The ache of fear and uncertainty was unbearable. "I've been had, fancy that," Sherry mumbled to herself. Then, suddenly. "No I haven't—Jesus Christ! I'm losing my mind!" She wiped the tears off her face with the back of her hand and tried to take a few deep breaths against the tension in her chest. She was a damn good reporter. She had asked all the right questions, gotten good answers. So it was hard to make sense out of Manuel—of course it was! He was nuts. Her story would make that perfectly clear. And it was going to be a great story, she told herself, a story that would prove to anyone with any doubt that she could make it on her own.

Klein had it all wrong, Sherry decided. He didn't understand her. He didn't understand anything.

She knew exactly where Temple Sinai was. And she had *wanted* to go to Marblehead High. And Manuel did feel guilty. He was sorry he had to kill the dog.

The dog—

Sherry was trying to picture it—teeth bared, barking wildly, lunging for the kill—when suddenly she felt gripped by dizziness. Where the hell was she anyway? What was going on? All at once she felt confused again. *Why* was it Manuel wanted a new life? What had she told Klein? She wished the answers would stop flitting around her brain and stay put for longer than a second. And she wished the pain would leave her neck, and the place where it hurt the most, the space between her heart and her gut.

Another few miles slipped by. Then: Exit 24. Hollywood. Sherry felt a brief flash of relief. Wasn't there a nice beach in Hollywood? She'd gone there with Belinda once. That's right, she recalled, last year just before Christmas—and it had been just beautiful. Beautiful like paradise. Paradise found in Florida. Paradise lost.

Milton, right? Sherry had to wonder.

Milton. Wordsworth. Byron. She'd loved them so much in college. Now she couldn't remember who was who. When had she found the time to forget so much?

Exit 24. She pulled off the highway, and at the bottom of the ramp headed east. The sky in front of her was turning from crimson to cobalt blue as the sun slid away in the rearview mirror.

It was just dark when she reached the shore. The beach was empty, and it *was* beautiful, just as she remembered it—expansive like Miami Beach with its glimmer-colored sand, but somehow, strangely, still unspoiled.

Sherry climbed out of her car inch by inch, careful not to move her neck or shoulders. When she was finally done and standing, she kicked off her shoes and left them there, next to the door.

She walked toward the water. The breeze was thick with the dulcet taste of the sea, and she inhaled deep and slow. Long exhale. Her muscles were beginning to unbind.

Sherry dropped her chin forward, and it touched her chest. Some pain was still lodged there, but it was fading. She rolled her head from shoulder to shoulder. Much better, she told herself, just keep breathing.

In front of her, the waves pushed forward again and again against the satiny shore, expiring with the gentleness of a farewell kiss. A memory: winter on Marblehead Neck. The sand is gritty and olive-colored, and the waves assault the shore like sandpaper on bare skin. She used to love the touch of cold salt air on her lips. Would she love it now?

Just so many questions, Sherry thought, one after another. No answers.

Just so many moments that don't make sense.

She shut her eyes to hear the waves better, and all at once Sherry saw her father behind the lids, standing there in the water in his black judge's robes, not seeing her as he extended one hand out to accept a neatly folded roll of bills. "Father—don't!" she shouted out to the sea, and then she laughed ironically at the useless pantomime.

What difference, Sherry asked herself, what difference did it make anyway? She didn't care about him anymore. Klein was wrong. He was wrong. Right?

She opened her eyes to kill the question, but the vision of her father lingered, even though the tears had started falling, accidentally, down her face and onto the sand. Now she could see him sitting in his study late at night, head bowed, as if in prayer, over a foot-thick law book in the light of a green-shaded banker's lamp. She remembered the sonorous sound of his tenor telling her what her last name meant—honesty, integrity, and truth. She remembered the vacant look in his eyes on her last day home and his cursory good-bye at the front door. He didn't even wish her good luck. Had he *ever* loved her?

Sherry was walking at the water's edge now, tears still falling into the current. The undertow would take them away, out to sea, maybe forever.

But somehow the undertow here seemed so benign compared to home.

In the far distance, Sherry could see a couple walking arm in arm, stumbling really, as if the weight of their love might pull them down into the sand. She couldn't tell if they were young or old, but there was something about the way the woman kept touching the top of her hat lightly, as if a coy gust might steal it, that made her think of Alice and her girlish way of moving, like a fairy.

But of course, *Alice*, Sherry thought—shit! What day is it? I've got to get my dress for the wedding, or else she'll kill me.

The wedding—Charles will be there.

Charles.

Suddenly, Sherry found herself remembering their first meeting and smiling to herself, more from bittersweet sadness than joy. He'd been so funny and tender then; they'd both been so innocent and free. It was the first day of classes her freshman year. He'd sat next to her in the back row of a class on epic poetry. Halfway through the lecture, he turned to her and whispered, "You look familiar. Haven't we met before?"

Sherry had burst out laughing. "That has got to be the *oldest, stupidest* line in the book," she said, wagging her head in amazement, oblivious to the glares coming from the more serious students around them. "You have got to be one pathetic loser, buster. I mean it. Why don't you go ahead and ask me my sign now."

"What's your sign?" Charles asked. "Aquarius, right? I knew it."

"Very funny."

"Look, I'm not kidding, you look familiar."

"Oh, were you at Woodstock, too?" Sherry asked.

"Well, as a matter of fact, Muffy, I was. Row 497, seat 702. You were wearing a red bikini and pearl earrings, right?"

Sherry laughed again, but this time with more amusement than disdain. She turned in her seat to get a better look, and surprise, she liked what she saw: a slender, muscular blond, with a shock of hair falling over his forehead in a bohemian preppy sort of way. He was wearing a beautiful beige cashmere sweater—she picked that up almost immediately—and a clunky gold-and-silver Rolex. And he did look familiar. Very familiar.

"Oh, God, maybe we do know each other," she allowed.

"No, no—forget it. Couldn't be." Charles was flirting assiduously now. "It was just a stupid pickup line, and I'm just one pathetic loser. Ignore me, please. *Please.* Don't even look at me. I'm begging you."

"Hey, I'm sorry, okay?" Sherry started to giggle. "Where have I seen you before? Did you go to Saint Mark's?"

"Andover."

"Vacation on Saint Kitts?"

"Nevis."

"Pray at the First?"

"Our Lady of Mercy."

"Never mind," said Sherry. Maybe she was mistaken. Then: "Wait, wait—I've got it—Bluemoor, right?"

Charles broke into a wide I-told-you-so grin, and Sherry couldn't help but notice that his teeth were absolutely perfect. "Bingo! I knew it," he said. "My stepfather is a member. I've been there a hundred times—whenever I visit my mom."

"Who's your stepfather?" Sherry asked.

"Laddie Pasch."

"Doctor Pasch, the heart surgeon, right?—I know him," Sherry said. Of course, she knew him; he lived on the biggest house on the Neck, bigger even than One Hundred Endless Horizon Lane. "He plays golf with my father, Laurence Estabrook."

"The Judge!" said Charles.

And back and forth the conversation went for the rest of the hour and well into lunch, as Sherry and Charles compared acquaintances, exchanged gossip, and started planning their lives together. Even from their first meeting, there seemed no question they would ever be apart again. Everything in their remarkably similar lives had prepared them for each other.

The memory faded, replaced by another: making love with Charles at twilight, the evening before graduation. His face was buried in her neck, and he was murmuring softly as he pushed gently inside. "Can you believe it, Sher?" he asked, "We're just one planet in one huge galaxy, but scientists think there are hundreds, maybe thousands, more galaxies. Can you believe it, Sher? We're just two people in this universe, and here we are together."

She hadn't answered. She was thinking instead of the letter he'd slipped under her door the day before, when she told him she was moving to Miami. *Thank you, Sherry,* he had written, *for everything, good and bad. No one can ever take away the memories.*

So he had won really, Sherry thought. He deserved to.

Suddenly, she stopped walking, all at once too tired to take another step forward down the beach or backward to her car. All she wanted now was to sleep, to black out, to surrender to the undertow.

She lay down in the water.

It felt like heaven.

I could lie here forever, she thought, water washing over me, making me dissolve, making me disappear. In a few days, Brazil will come looking for me. I'll open my eyes, and he'll be there, blocking the sun.

Get up, Sherry, he'll say.

Sherry shut her eyes, and he was gone. But in the darkness she felt someone else nearby, someone achingly familiar but now gone, too, someone like the person she used to be, back before.

"Alice? Is that you?" Sherry asked the question softly; she was lying on her side now, just far enough into the water so that the waves broke across her shoulders and then gently tugged at her arms and hips and legs before slipping back out to sea. "Do you forgive me yet for leaving, Alice? I'll be home soon to see you get married. And then for your baby's christening, and then to attend his first birthday party, and his high school graduation, and on and on for all the babies you have. I'll come back for all the important things. I promise you, Alice."

No more words. Sherry was thinking now, drifting away in her mind, imagining little babies wrapped in blankets, defenseless, eyes shut tight, squeaking like tiny birds. All the mothers in the park that day with Manuel looked so tired. They made me so tired, Sherry thought. They made me so sad. Why do women want babies anyway? Life is already too complicated.

Will Belinda ever have babies? Will I?

They say to give birth is to die a little.

Or is dying a little like being born again?

Manuel, tell me.

You're sorry, aren't you?

Tell me it will all be over soon.

Tell me everyone will forgive me.

Tell me I'm doing the right thing.

Tell me, Manuel.

Tell me.

Belinda had been at work more than an hour when Sherry finally dragged herself in the next morning. She hadn't left the beach in Hollywood until daybreak, though she could hardly remember the hours passing. They had just passed, and then suddenly she opened her eyes and the horizon was shimmering a light and pearly blue, the color inside a mussel shell.

She woke up grieving, feeling incomplete and completely alone.

Even if she had it all wrong, there was nothing she could do to stop the story now. The whole newspaper, from Newman on down, was waiting for it. And, of course, she reminded herself, she didn't have it all wrong. It was a great story, the greatest of her life.

But thank God in heaven it would all be over soon.

And when it was, Sherry decided, she was going back to Klein, and he would have to talk to her some more. Even if he didn't want to.

"Sorry I'm late." Sherry tapped Belinda on the shoulder and tried to camouflage her exhaustion with an unnaturally upbeat voice. "Better late than never, right?"

Belinda spun around in her chair. "Sherry!" she cried loud enough to turn heads around the newsroom. "I'm so glad you're back! I have so much—"

She stopped suddenly and stared at Sherry. She looked terrible, her skin paler and even more transparent than usual and her eyes darker and more intense.

"What is it?" Sherry asked. "I look shitty, right?"

"No, no, you look fine," Belinda said quickly. "I guess I'm not used to you without makeup. You look different."

"I look shitty."

"You look . . . tired."

"I didn't get any sleep."

"But I thought Brazil was out of town," said Belinda. "I mean, Jack just told me that he sent him to Tampa for some trial until the end of the week."

"I wasn't with him. I was alone."

"Oh?" Belinda sounded confused. This wasn't like Sherry at all.

"Don't worry. I'm fine," Sherry said, checking her desk for a message from Brazil. Here it was: *S—Jack is sending me to Siberia, cruel and unusual punishment for "slowing down the progress" (his words) of your little red schoolhouse zombie drug killers from space story. Back Friday night. Kisses, Brazil. P.S. Really in Tampa. Holiday Inn. Call me or no nookie when I get back. Honest.*

"Sherry?" Belinda was watching her, relieved that she was smiling.

"Yeah?"

"Is everything okay, because—"

"Everything is fine."

"Because I have huge news."

"Hold on." Sherry scanned the rest of the messages on her desk. A call from Joe Riccardi. He was a good cop source in Florida City. A message from Manuel. Probably just his daily check-in call. A message from Alice. *Please call ASAP.* Shit—it was that damn dress again! She had to get it tonight after work. She had to.

"Sherry?"

"One second, Belinda." She checked her top drawer to see if Brazil had left her a Twinkie. He hadn't.

"Listen, I have huge news!" Belinda was practically jumping up and down now, and her voice bordered on shrill. "You have to listen to me this instant!"

"Okay, okay." Sherry sat down in her chair and faced Belinda, trying hard to concentrate. "What do you have?"

"This isn't work."

"It's not?"

"Nope!"

"It's Eladio?"

"Yep!"

"I can't stand the suspense," Sherry said dryly. "Go ahead, tell me."

"We're getting married."

Sherry felt a bomb implode in her chest.

Belinda—the most permanently fucked-up, lonely, helpless, rejected, saddest, most accident-prone person on earth—*she* was getting married? To a Miami cop? And living happily ever after?

Sherry stared at Belinda. She could think of a hundred things to say, but none of them would come out.

Belinda stared back, her yellow eyes filled with tears. Sherry had never seen her smile with such joy. She'd never seen anyone.

"We're getting married," Belinda said again slowly, as if she couldn't believe it herself; it was too wonderful.

"But—"

"No buts, Sherry, please."

"I just can't believe it."

"Believe it!" Belinda said. She had pulled her chair close to Sherry and was whispering excitedly. "He asked me yesterday. I'm still shaking, look." She extended her hands for Sherry to see. The fingertips were trembling.

"But—"

"I said no buts, Sherry."

"Just one, please, Belinda."

"Just one."

Sherry scooted her chair closer to Belinda and rested a hand firmly on her knee. "But," she said, "you've only known him fifteen minutes."

"I knew you were going to mention that." Belinda stood up abruptly, disengaging Sherry's hand, and then sat down again, sighing hard.

"Well, it's true," Sherry answered softly. "You barely know the guy."

"Please don't call Eladio *'the guy'* like that."

"You barely know Eladio."

Belinda stood up, circled her desk in a jittery half-step, pushing papers back and forth and biting her lip, and then suddenly sat down again. She didn't look unhappy, Sherry thought, just very, very agitated.

"You know, Sherry," she said finally, "you know, sometimes you don't know anything."

"I know that you barely know Eladio. I hope you're planning on waiting a year."

"No, we're not, and I'll tell you why," Belinda said, her voice so strong Sherry hardly recognized it. "Let me tell you something, okay? One time, Sherry, I was in a van in Niamey, okay? This van took people from the center of town over to the embassies and the banks and the fancy houses on the outskirts of town. Okay, get it? It was a van for foreigners, for people with money, because the poor people who cleaned the floors on the outskirts of town had to walk there, because they couldn't even afford the four pennies it took to board the goddamn bus. You follow me?"

Sherry nodded. What in hell, she wondered, was Belinda talking about?

She went on: "So I was in this van, and of course the windows were open because it was only about a hundred and fourteen degrees outside, okay?"

Sherry nodded again.

"And I'm sitting next to the window, just looking out—actually sort of hanging out—of it, trying to catch a breeze and watching the marketplace, and this woman walks by. Sherry—she was so dirty and poor you could just feel hunger eating away at her insides, and she was pregnant. God—I—"

Belinda stopped for a second to take a deep breath. She didn't want to cry, especially not now.

"You what?" Sherry asked.

"I felt so sorry for her."

"Belinda," Sherry said, trying not to sound irritated, "I'm not sure what this has to do with you getting married to Eladio."

"Well, of course you don't," she shot back, exasperated, "I'm not finished yet."

Sherry shrugged an apology. "Okay, okay," she prompted Belinda, "so, the pregnant woman—"

"Okay. The pregnant woman, she was walking all around the van again and again while it was filling up with French people, and she was holding her hands out like this—begging. She had this weak little voice and she kept saying, '*Cadeau, madame,*' with her head down, ashamed. And, of course, everyone was ignoring her. Everyone always ignores the beggars in Niamey. But then she came around to me, and I was going to ignore her, too, at first, but then something struck me about how terribly cruel life is and how my . . . my *inaction* was only making it worse, and so I told her to wait, and I pulled ten bucks out of my wallet and I handed them to her. I put them right in her hand. It was like putting food in her stomach.

"And, Sherry, she lifted her head and looked at me, right in the eyes. She didn't say a word. She looked at me, and I looked at her, and *something* passed between us. I *knew* her then, and she *knew* me, as if we had known each other for a hundred thousand years. We didn't need to exchange words. Everything was understood.

"And then, of course, the van pulled off, and we never saw each other again."

Belinda sat back in her chair and smiled to herself wistfully.

Sherry wanted to groan. "So you're telling me that you and Eladio have looked each other in the eyes, right?" she asked. "That's really beautiful. Really, Belinda. But divorce in America is a little more complicated than a van pulling off into the sunset."

Belinda leaned forward in her seat and shook her head. "We're not even married yet," she sighed, sounding more amused than angry, "and you're talking about divorce!"

"Please, Belinda, be realistic."

"But there's no reason to be!" she answered happily. "No reason at all! You don't understand, do you, Sherry? *Something* has happened. Just be glad for me! Tell me 'Congratulations' or 'Good luck,' okay? You Americans are so caught up in the temporal world it drives me insane. Forget it—it's meaningless. Let it go."

Sherry started to protest, but she suddenly lost her drive to fight the inevitable. "Okay, I'm forgetting the temporal world," she said wearily. "It *is* meaningless."

Belinda smiled again—Christ, she was practically glowing. Well, Sherry thought, wasn't this just great? Wasn't this just what the Manuel story needed now—a powder puff on the double byline?

"So, Mrs. Almost-Alvarez," she said after a minute of silence had passed between them, "when's the big day?"

"Sunday."

"*Next* Sunday?"

"You heard me, Sherry."

"But what about the story?"

"The story!" Belinda shouted, incredulous. "All you think about is that goddamn story!"

"We have to finish it."

"You finish it, then."

"I'm not doing it without you."

"Why, Sherry?" Belinda asked. "Why can't you do it without me for once?"

"I don't want to," she answered quickly. She needed Belinda now more than ever.

"You just want me to share the blame when it's all over."

"That's completely ridiculous, Belinda. It's unfair. I want you to share the—"

"The glory?"

"I don't know."

"The prize money?"

"I said I don't know."

"What were you going to say?"

"I forget," said Sherry. She had the feeling she was talking to someone else, not Belinda.

"Fine. Selective amnesia. I get it all the time myself," she answered in her new voice. "Well, don't worry, Sherry. Nothing is going to get in the way of the story. Eladio and I aren't going on a honeymoon. We need to save money to buy a house."

"You're not going on a honeymoon?"

"We don't need to," Belinda said. She sounded certain.

"Of course not."

"You're being sarcastic."

"No, I'm not."

"I'm sure when you marry Charles, you'll take a nice three-week honeymoon in Saint Martin. Or maybe that's not chic enough for you. Go to Saint Kitts. Have a blast. Go for it."

Sherry shook her head. "What are you talking about?" she asked. She missed the old Belinda already.

"I don't know." She was mimicking Sherry's voice.

"You don't know?"

"Jesus Christ, Sherry! Have you gone deaf?"

"No." Was she crying again? It was hard to believe she had any tears left, after last night, but she did, and suddenly they were flowing full force.

Then, all at once, Belinda was everywhere, arms around Sherry's neck, face pressed against hers. She could feel her heart beating.

"I'm sorry, Sherry," she said. "I didn't mean to imitate you like that. I'm sorry. Do you forgive me?"

"Forgive you?"

"You're doing it again, repeating everything," Belinda said, but this time the words were tender.

"I think I'm just really tired," Sherry said. She wanted Belinda to stop hugging her; the whole newsroom was probably watching.

"Well, get out of here then," Belinda said. "Go home, take a shower, have a long lunch. When you get back this afternoon, we'll work nonstop to finish the stupid story, and we'll be all done by the time you take off for Boston on Saturday."

"Okay," said Sherry. She felt a little better, but something was still bothering her, gnawing nervously at that place beneath her heart. What was it? She thought for a minute, absentmindedly tucking and untucking the hair behind her ears. What was wrong? Suddenly, it came to her. Of course—she was going to miss Belinda's wedding.

"You're getting married while I'm gone," she blurted out.

Belinda smiled apologetically. "We just want to do it, Sherry," she answered, as if she had anticipated this criticism, too. "It's just going to be me, Eladio, and the justice of the peace. We didn't want a big deal. We just want to be married."

"I could be a witness."

"To tell you the truth, Sherry, I thought you wouldn't want to be there—that's sort of why we went and planned it for next Sunday."

"I want to be there."

"I'm really surprised," said Belinda. She sounded so sincere it made Sherry's heart sting. "But it's too late. Everything is all set. I'm sorry."

Belinda let go of Sherry's hands and then looked down at her own, carefully studying the life lines as if they held some kind of message. Sherry recognized the gesture. It meant Belinda was about to cry.

"I'm going home," she announced quickly, standing up. "I'm just going to return a few calls, and then I'm going to take your advice. I'll be back this afternoon."

Her words seemed to end Belinda's dangerous reverie.

"Great," she said hopefully, looking up. "We'll really start wrapping this story up this afternoon."

Sherry nodded and picked up the phone. Just one call to Manuel, and then she was going home. She needed to put herself back together again. She wanted to look in a mirror. She wanted to sleep without dreaming, if only for an hour.

Sherry hung up after three rings and checked her watch. Of course he wasn't home—it was only eleven. School wouldn't be out for hours. Thank God.

She turned to say good-bye to Belinda, but she was already deep into an animated conversation on the phone, voice peaking and falling in guttural Spanish, hands fluttering left and right like a hummingbird's frantic flight.

She didn't even notice Sherry leave the newsroom.

39 Ever since she'd quit waitressing at the edge of the Everglades and moved into Brazil's little house on Tall Palm Lane, Jeanie's life had taken on a brand-new and completely predictable rhythm. Every single day went exactly the same, from the baby's first diaper just after sunrise to his last bottle halfway through the evening news. In fact, things were so regular that sometimes she would be standing in the supermarket checkout line or pushing John Junior in a swing at the park, and she would stop and ask herself, What day is it anyway? A lot of times, she'd have absolutely no idea, and that thrilled her completely. For the first time in her life, she wasn't waiting for something, or wanting for something. She was just living, simply and finally, without pain.

The baby woke her up about six-fifteen every day, rattling the bars of his crib and calling out "Ma-Ma" in a soft singsong until she appeared at the door to his room. As soon as he saw her, he'd let go a high-pitched squeal of delight, lift his arms to be picked up, and, once Jeanie had him against her chest, he'd hug her so tight it made her eyes water.

After she fed him breakfast, the two of them would take a walk around the neighborhood. It usually took an hour or more because John Junior liked to push his own stroller. She didn't mind. They had nowhere to go.

Then they'd eat lunch together, and she'd put the kid down for his nap. The next three hours were hers alone, which really confused her at the start. She hadn't had free time, all to herself, in the middle of the day, since Lost Corners. But now she'd gotten the hang of it again. She spent the first hour cleaning the house and making dinner, the second taking a nap, and the third watching *Donahue*.

By the time John Junior woke up, it was time for dinner, and sometimes Brazil would be there. Sometimes not. He worked crazy hours, and he spent a lot of time with his girlfriend from the newspaper. Not that he'd tell Jeanie about it directly—he never mentioned Sherry by name. Instead, he'd say, "I've got some stuff to do tonight after work," or "I won't be home until real late, don't wait up." The amazing thing was, Jeanie didn't *care* that Brazil was cheating on her. It didn't even feel like he was cheating, because he wasn't sneaking around and he wasn't lying. They had an *arrangement*—that's how she'd heard a lady refer to it on *Donahue* once. And she liked their arrangement. Brazil gave her a hundred bucks a week just to eat and to spend any which way she wanted, and he gave her a car, and he let her do whatever she wanted with the house. He didn't even complain when she painted the bedroom pink and got a ruffled bedspread to match. He told her it looked pretty.

There wasn't much to their sex life, but she didn't miss it all that much. The way she figured it, she'd had enough screwing in her life to last her until the end of time. Every once in a while, Brazil would roll over in the morning and kiss her neck and rub her boobs with his huge, rough hands, and she knew what he was after. Of course she'd let him have it, but she always wondered a little bit if he was thinking about his girlfriend. He kept his eyes shut.

She asked him about that once. It was just after they got married. "Brazil," she had said, "why don't you look at me when we're doing it?" He had frowned and sighed hard, as if the answer were going to be very unpleasant. But then he had said, "Because I'm thinking about how much I love you and the baby, that's why."

And he did love them, she knew that. Brazil gave her everything a girl like her could expect from life—including respect, which she maybe didn't even deserve—and he asked for nothing in return. And no one could ever doubt how much he loved John Junior. All you had to do was see them together to know that they had a major love affair going. She could hear them Saturday mornings, when Brazil let her sleep late, playing together in the backyard. There were such noisy whoops of joy out there, she wondered if they'd forgotten her entirely and forever. But then at nine, without fail, the two of them would stampede into the bedroom like a herd of deranged buffalo, jump on the bed, and tickle her until she screamed for mercy. At which point they'd start on each other—shrieking and grunting and laughing so loud

Jeanie was sure they'd wake the whole neighborhood. But no one ever complained.

"You know what?" Brazil had asked her recently, one night when they were cleaning up the kitchen after the baby went to sleep. "You know what, Jeanie doll? I love Saturday mornings as much as I love making pictures."

"You're kidding," Jeanie had answered, squinting her gray eyes in disbelief as she wiped a dish dry. "Are you sure about that?"

"I am utterly positive."

A moment passed.

"Well," Jeanie said finally, "that makes me very happy, Brazil. Thank you for saying it."

"I mean it."

"I know you do."

She put down her dishcloth and kissed him, standing on tiptoes to reach his cheek.

"Thank you for everything," she said.

"Thank *you*."

"You got nothing to thank me for," Jeanie said, and she meant it.

"I do, too," Brazil came back quickly. "I thank you for being you." He had stopped bustling around the kitchen and was facing her now. "And for surviving how you did and getting well and for taking such good care of Junior every day. I thank you for all those things. I thank you for understanding."

Jeanie nodded. She didn't want to get into the details of what she understood and why. But she was glad he had come out and said it, and she had thought about the conversation pretty often since then, like every time he didn't come for dinner or called Sherry from the phone in their bedroom while she fed the baby. The memory of his words that night in the kitchen soothed her. How could she ever be angry at Brazil?

The fact was, she could make it through a day pretty much without him if she had to, and that's what she was doing that strange morning when the phone rang at ten.

She knew it wasn't Brazil—he had just left for Tampa to cover a trial. Maybe it was the lady across the street, wanting to borrow more corn syrup. She ran out of the stuff so often, you would think she made a pecan pie every afternoon.

Jeanie caught the phone on the second ring.

"Hello?" she said.

No answer.

"Well, good-bye!" she shouted into the phone, a little pissed off.

Then she heard it: a distant voice, breaking up over the line, but somehow familiar.

"Is this Jeanette Darlene White?" the voice asked.

Jeanette Darlene White? Was there a soul out there who still knew—or cared about—the girl by that name?

"This is Jeanie," she said after a second had passed. She was nervous, but not sure why. "Who is this?"

"Darling, this is your aunt Ardelle calling you from Lost Corners, honey."

Aunt Ardelle? Jeanie vaguely remembered her—a thick-ankled woman who wore mean little glasses and her hair in a bun. That's right—Aunt Ardelle, her father's big sister. She lived on the other side of town in a huge old house with her moneybags husband (he owned the hardware store, Jeanie seemed to recall) and their four snot-nosed kids. She saw them once a year, at Christmas, when they dropped a turkey by the trailer and then took off before things got ugly. Her father always dumped the damn bird in the garbage as soon as they drove off.

So *Ardelle* was calling her. This was bad news.

"Aunt Ardelle—what's wrong with my daddy?"

"Oh, Jeanette, Jeanette—" The woman on the other end of the line was suddenly sobbing. "I have such terrible news, darling—"

Jeanie cut her off. "He's dead, ain't he?" she asked.

"Yes, that's right, honey. He's gone to a better place. I'm so, so sorry," Aunt Ardelle sputtered. "He's left this world, Jeanette. He's at Jesus' side now."

Jeanie smiled tightly. "I doubt that very much, Ardelle," she said. She was tempted to tell her aunt to cut the crap. "I think he's six feet under now and probably dying for a drink."

"Now, Jeanette, this is no time for bitterness. Your father was a good man, a good man gone bad because of liquor," Ardelle said. "But he loved you, darling. He loved you until the end."

"With all respect, ma'am," Jeanie said, "I don't think he knew if I was dead or living."

"That's not true!" Ardelle came back like a boomerang.

"Honey, how do you think I found you? He had a letter from you right by his bed, the one where you told you went and got married and had a baby."

"Oh," said Jeanie. She still wasn't sure why she had written him about that.

"And darling, you were in his last, dying thoughts." Ardelle was still talking. "The fellows down at the Nu-Dy Re-Vu told everyone he said your name when he fell off the barstool. He said it loud and clear: 'Jeanette Darlene.' Just like that."

"He was probably thinking about my mother."

"Oh no, honey," said Ardelle. "I don't think so. I really don't. But, Jeanette, I didn't call to argue with you, honey." Her sad ranting was now replaced by the syrupy-sweet voice of a nurse in a mental hospital. "I called to tell you that the funeral is this Sunday, right here in Lost Corners. Mr. Colefern and I bought your daddy a beautiful final resting place under a big oak tree. He'll be happy there."

Funeral? Someone was going to bury her father in his own grave?

"I can't come all the way to Lost Corners," Jeanie said quickly. "I got a baby to take care of, and I don't exactly have the money right now." The last part was a lie. She had nearly a thousand dollars in a box under the bed, and anyway, Brazil would be happy to pay for something like this, her father's funeral.

"Jeanette, babies can travel!" Ardelle exclaimed. "They do it all the time these days. And don't you worry about the money. Mr. Colefern and I will take care of your expenses. We *understand*."

Jeanie wondered what that meant.

"Look, ma'am," she said, "I really can't travel with the baby."

But then again, maybe she could. Jeanie tried to imagine the trip: It wouldn't be like hitching. They could fly to Chicago, catch another little plane to Rapid City, and then one bus to Casper and another to Lost Corners. It would be a real adventure for John Junior, and it might be sort of interesting to see the old town again, now that it was behind her for good and forever.

"Yes, you can travel, darling," Ardelle said, still yapping away. "And once you get here, we'll all cover the baby with love and kisses. He can play with all my grandchildren! I have six of them now, Jeanette—can you believe that!"

"Great," said Jeanie. She was thinking about the trailer where she grew up. It probably hadn't been cleaned once since she left ten years ago. It probably still smelled like cheap red wine and morning-after puke.

But there were some pictures there, she remembered suddenly, pictures that her father always kept locked in a tin box, to keep her from running away. He always said he'd give them to her when she turned eighteen, but she hadn't lasted that long.

But now, the tin box was hers. She would see her mother at last.

"I'll be there," she told Ardelle.

"Jeanette, I knew you'd do the right thing!" Ardelle practically shouted. "Now, I've already gone and checked out the flights for you and everything. Can you leave tomorrow afternoon? Your flight leaves at one fifty-four."

"I guess so," said Jeanie. Did it have to be so soon? This was happening awfully fast.

"All right, honey." Ardelle was excited now. "You just go to the airport, and you can pick up your tickets there, at the United Airlines terminal. You know where that is?"

"I'll find it," said Jeanie. She'd never been to the airport, but she figured the cabdriver would know where to go.

"You're going to fly into Denver, and then you'll have to wait at the airport a little while," said Ardelle. "Then, you've got to get to the Continental terminal and catch Flight Four-A at four thirty-nine P.M. to Casper." It sounded as though she was reading from a scrap of paper.

"In Casper, your cousin Wallace will be waiting for you. He's got a dark blue Ford Escort with a baby seat in back and a dent on the left side. You can't miss it."

"Oh, Aunt Ardelle," Jeanie protested, "I can take the bus! I don't need nobody driving two hours just to get me."

"Don't worry, Jeanette. It's all decided."

"I can afford the bus."

"I don't want any argument, Jeanette."

"All right, all right," said Jeanie. She really would have preferred it the other way. She was going to need to do some serious thinking before seeing all the old places again. She'd just have to pretend to fall asleep in the car.

"So, we're all set then, aren't we, Jeanette?" her aunt asked.

"Yep," said Jeanie. "We're all set." She was surprised to feel so charged-up. Maybe later she'd cry about her daddy, maybe when it hit her.

She thanked Ardelle and hung up the phone. "John Junior," she said, picking up her son and kissing his face all over, "we're going to Mama's house, but just for a little bit."

The only problem was, how was she going find Brazil?

Jeanie knew she *had* to let him know that she was leaving town for a few days; otherwise he'd get all worried when he called to check in and no one answered the phone.

But where was he?

Jeanie phoned the photo desk at the *Citizen* and asked to speak to Vinnie Baldiso. He was the boss. She'd met him once, at the Bomb Shelter.

"Vinnie," she said when he finally got on the line, "this is Jeanie Brackett calling, Brazil's wife? I'm sorry to disturb you."

"Not at all," Vinnie answered, sounding rushed.

Jeanie spoke quickly. "I need to reach Brazil in Tampa. My daddy died," she said. "Do you know where at he's staying at?"

There was a long pause. Then, slowly: "Gee, Jeanie, I'm terribly sorry to hear about your father."

"Don't worry about it."

"Was it unexpected?" The man sounded so grief-stricken Jeanie felt sorry for *him*.

"Unexpected?" she said. "Well, not really. He was a drunk."

"Oh." Vinnie suddenly sounded less sad and more uncomfortable. "I'm sorry."

"Yeah, so am I, I guess," said Jeanie.

In the silence that followed, she could hear Vinnie's awkward breathing on the line. Was he going to say something else? It sort of seemed that way, but nothing came.

"Vinnie, sir?" she asked finally. "About Brazil?"

"Oh, yes," Vinnie said, startled. "Oh, of course. Jeanie, I'm
sorry, I have no idea where he's staying, but I'm sure someone
else might know. Hold on." He put his hand over the phone, but
Jeanie could still hear him call out, "Does anyone know where
Brackett is parking his ass in Tampa?"

"Ask Sherry Estabrook," came the response. Then laughter
all around.

Vinnie was back on the line. "I'm terribly sorry, Jeanie," he
said, "but no one here seems to know."

Jeanie sighed hard. "Well, can you put Sherry on the phone?"
she asked.

There was a long pause, and Jeanie watched the second hand
tick by on the clock in her kitchen.

"I'll transfer you," Vinnie said after nearly a half minute had
passed, and then the line clicked, went silent, and rang again.

"Sherry Estabrook's desk." It was the voice of a smart person,
Jeanie thought, a person who'd gone to school, cheerful and confident.

"Is this her I'm talking to?" she asked.

"No," the voice came back, still cool and clear as a teacher's.
"This is Belinda McEvoy. Can I help you?"

"I need to talk to Miss Esterbrook," said Jeanie. She had
heard Brazil mention this Belinda McEvoy. He didn't like her.

"Sherry won't be back until later today. She's not feeling well."

"Oh," said Jeanie. She was getting nowhere, and that was
making her begin to panic. Maybe she'd have to call back Aunt
Ardelle and call off the whole thing. She started to say good-
bye, but then stopped. "Hey," she asked Belinda with sudden
urgency, "can you give me her phone number? Can you give me
Sherry's home phone number, please?"

"Who is this?" Belinda asked protectively.

"This is Brazil's wife." Jeanie felt stupid saying it, like an
imposter.

"Jeanie?" Belinda asked, her voice turning almost warm and
familiar. "I've heard a lot about you."

"Oh," Jeanie said flatly. She had no idea how to respond.
"Well, can you give me the number?"

"Um, well . . ." Belinda stalled. She knew Sherry would
kill her.

"I'm sorry, I can't," she said finally. "But I can have her
call you."

"Okay," said Jeanie, feeling more frustrated by the moment. She knew it would never happen—Sherry would never call *her*. She wasn't crazy.

"I'll give her the message," Belinda was saying, but Jeanie had already hung up.

She checked the clock again. A whole hour had somehow slipped by since she'd promised Aunt Ardelle she'd come to the funeral in Lost Corners. Before she knew it, the day would be gone and then the night, and then she'd be on the plane, and Brazil would have no idea where in the world she and the baby had gone. She had to get in touch with him, and she had to do it soon. There was only one thing left to try: She would go to Sherry, find her in person at her house. That way the message was sure to get to Brazil.

Plus, she was curious, just a little curious.

She found Brazil's address book in his underwear drawer and flipped to E.

Sherry was the only entry, listed by her first name. There was a phone number, totally illegible, and underneath he'd scribbled: *43 Lemonlime. The Grove (3rd R off Mango).*

She could find it.

Jeanie wiped the blueberry jam off John Junior's face and tied his shoelaces. Then she buzzed into the bathroom, pulled her hair back with a rubber band, and smoothed a little pink lipstick on her mouth. She looked in the mirror. "Forget it," she said out loud. There was no changing the way she looked now, and it didn't really matter anyway, did it?

A half hour later, she was turning into Sherry's driveway.

Somehow she had expected the house to be much bigger, or at least fancier. Instead, it looked just like a thousand other houses she'd seen in Miami. In fact, it looked a little like the house she shared with Brazil. Real nice, but real ordinary.

Jeanie slowly got out of her car, unhooked John Junior's car seat, and hoisted him onto her hip. All the while, she was trying to figure why in the world she felt so calm and strong doing this crazy thing. Shouldn't she be just a little scared or at least embarrassed? Sure, her heart was banging so hard she could practically hear it, but the truth was, she wanted to meet this girl, at last. She wanted her to see the baby. And she wanted the baby to see her.

Jeanie rang the doorbell, and almost instantly heard the *tck-*

tck-tck of high heels running toward the front of the house. The door flew open.

This had to be Sherry.

She stood there, unbelievably lovely, lips parted in controlled surprise, head tilted like a marionette, wearing a tight blue dress and dozens of tinkling gold bracelets up and down one arm. Her makeup was freshly applied and absolutely perfect.

But she wasn't blond! For some reason, Jeanie had expected that. Instead, here she was with the blackest hair and the bluest eyes and the most glamorous-looking face, almost as if she were from a foreign country. Jeanie never seen anyone like her, except on the cover of a magazine.

"Hi," Jeanie said. She tried to smile.

Sherry nodded. "Hello," she said. Her voice was composed and even a little friendly, as if she had been expecting their visit. "Please come in, Jeanie." She had known who it was the moment she opened the door. The baby had his father's eyes. He had his open-faced Cracker stare.

Sherry stepped back a few feet to let them by and then closed the door quietly.

"Please sit down," she said, ushering Jeanie into the living room. "Can I get you anything to drink? How about the baby? Would he like a little warm water?" The sad exhaustion that had been with her since she left Hollywood Beach was suddenly and completely gone, replaced by a fusillade of adrenaline. She was on automatic.

"No, nothing for neither of us," said Jeanie, still standing, looking around under her brows, trying to see as much as she could before she had to leave. "I'll just take a minute of your time."

"Are you sure you won't have something to drink?" Sherry asked again.

"I'm sure."

"Well, then!" Sherry sat down on the couch and motioned Jeanie to sit in a wide leather chair nearby. She obeyed, reluctantly.

"Well, then!" Sherry said again.

Jeanie was still looking around, more overtly now. She recognized Brazil's photographs here and there, and noticed that the house smelled familiar, like darkroom chemicals. She also noticed that the furniture looked expensive. So much black leather everywhere! And the throw pillows on the couch were covered with the smoothest red silk she'd ever seen.

"I'm sorry to disturb you," Jeanie began, "but I need to get in touch with Brazil right away. I wouldn't have barged in on you if it wasn't an emergency, but I have to leave town for a few days, and I want him to know where I'm going. I know he's in Tampa, but I don't know where he's staying at."

"No problem!" Sherry said. Was that really all she wanted? She smiled brightly. "No problem at all! He's staying at the Holiday—"

"My daddy died," Jeanie cut her off. She had shifted John Junior from her lap to her shoulder and was rocking him gently to sleep.

"Oh, my God!" Sherry gasped. "Jeanie, I'm very, *very* sorry!" She jumped up from the couch and ran to the kitchen. "Here, let me get you a tissue," she said.

"I'm not crying," Jeanie called out to her matter-of-factly.

Sherry walked back into the room and placed the box of tissues between them on the coffee table. "Well," she said, embarrassed and a little confused, "just in case you feel like it." She smiled apologetically.

"But I don't feel like it," Jeanie said. "Isn't that strange? I just found out this morning that my daddy is dead, and I don't feel nothing."

"Maybe you're just in shock," Sherry offered. She was sitting down again, legs tucked under, trying not to stare too hard. She had always imagined Jeanie as ugly, or dumpy at least, but she was actually quite pretty. She had amazing light gray eyes, the color of rain. She wasn't sure she had ever seen that color before.

"Maybe I *am* just in shock," she echoed Sherry. She liked the idea. "Maybe I'll cry at the funeral or something."

"I'm sure you will," said Sherry. It seemed like the right answer. The women looked at each other, and Sherry noticed that Jeanie had settled comfortably into the leather chair, as if she wasn't planning to leave anytime soon. "So," she asked her after a moment had passed, "that's where you're going, then—home?"

"Well, it hasn't been home for a long time, but I guess you could call it that," Jeanie said.

"And where would that be?"

"You ain't never heard of it," Jeanie said. "Lost Corners, Wyoming. Sorta near Casper, but closer really to Blakesfield."

"Blakesfield, of course," Sherry improvised. "That's lovely country, isn't it?"

"Not especially," said Jeanie. "The land is rough. It makes the people that way."

"Well," said Sherry, momentarily stymied, "I suppose they still have some pioneer spirit!"

Jeanie nodded vaguely.

"I mean," Sherry went on, "the land makes them tough."

"I said it makes them *rough*," Jeanie corrected her.

"Right," Sherry said uneasily. Then, suddenly, she stood up again. "Look, Jeanie, I'm getting myself some bourbon," she announced. "Want to keep me company?"

"Why not?" Jeanie answered. "I could use a drink right now."

Sherry was back a minute later with two tall glasses.

"To your father," she said before taking the first sip.

"I guess so," said Jeanie.

They drank in silence for a minute, silence save the baby's muffled snoring and the sound of Jeanie's hand softly rubbing his back up and down.

"Did I tell you Brazil was staying at the Holiday Inn?" Sherry finally asked.

"Yep."

"I can't believe he didn't tell you."

"He never tells me," Jeanie said, her voice a little defensive. "He don't need to. He calls in every few days."

"But look what happened," Sherry said. "Here's an emergency, and you had to come traipsing all the way over here."

"It's all right," Jeanie said. She was almost done with her drink. "I don't mind meeting you."

"Thanks," said Sherry. What was she supposed to say? "I'm glad to meet you, too."

"Oh, sure you are," Jeanie said. She was smiling.

"No, really, I am," said Sherry. "Here we are, sort of sharing the same life, and we don't even know each other."

"I never thought of it that way," Jeanie said, shrugging. "But I gotta tell you, we don't share the same life—we share the same *man*." She patted the arm of the leather chair. "I get the feeling our *lives* have been real different."

The subject made Sherry nervous.

"Is your mother still living?" she asked.

Jeanie shook her head. "She died when I was little. I don't even know if she had blond hair or black."

"I'm sorry," said Sherry.

"Yeah, me, too." Jeanie looked up at the photos on the mantelpiece. She had noticed them when she first walked in.

"Your mama's alive?"

"Yes," said Sherry. "I guess I'm lucky."

"And your daddy?"

"Yes," said Sherry. Then: "But we don't get along very well. We had a falling-out of sorts—a fight, I mean—when I moved to Miami."

Jeanie leaned forward and squinted her eyes. She wanted to hear more. "Why's that?" she asked. "He didn't want you running off to someplace so far?"

"You could say that," said Sherry. "But more that he didn't want me to work at a newspaper. He wanted me to go to law school, I guess."

"On whose dollar?" Jeanie asked, as if money might have been at the root of the problem.

"Oh, on his, on his," Sherry sighed. "That wasn't the issue, really. He wanted me to follow in his footsteps. He's a judge. A big judge. He runs a whole courthouse up in Boston."

Jeanie frowned slightly and took a final sip of her drink. "You're rich then, aren't you?" she asked.

"Yes," said Sherry.

"You don't have to work, but you work anyway?"

"Yes."

"That I don't get at all."

"Well, what do you do all day if you don't work?" Sherry asked.

"You could raise up a baby," Jeanie came back quickly, "or you could go to the beach or go shopping at the mall. Shit, I could think of a lot of things to do."

"But you'd get bored after a while," Sherry said.

"Not after my life, you wouldn't."

Sherry had no idea what Jeanie was talking about. All she knew was that Jeanie had worked at some sleazy truck stop on Alligator Alley.

"I guess waitressing is hard work," she said.

"Shit, no—waitressing is *easy*!" Jeanie laughed. She was sorry to keep cussing, but the bourbon had got to her. "I'm talking about all the other shit, like me giving blow-jobs to strangers just so I could eat, and like me killing my baby by accident on the way back to Boise. I'm talking about *that* shit. That was hard."

Sherry poured herself another tall glass of bourbon, slowly and deliberately, careful not to look at Jeanie. She was afraid the horror would show, silencing her.

"I'm talking about kicking the horse," Jeanie was still talking. "You know what I mean? Horse?"

"Heroin?" Sherry asked. Her voice was just above a whisper, but she was trying hard to sound conversational.

"Heroin, right," said Jeanie. "I'm talking about kicking it cold turkey in the hospital, with no *nothing* to help you. That's hard."

"I'm sure," said Sherry.

"So, you see what I mean? I don't mind *not* working."

"I don't blame you." Sherry was surprised she could speak, her lips were so numb.

"Now tell me we share the same life."

"I see your point," Sherry said. "I had no idea."

"Can I have a refill, please?" Jeanie held out her glass, and Sherry quickly poured bourbon to the rim. "The only thing we've got in common is Brazil and shitty fathers."

Sherry nodded and murmured in agreement.

"I was thinking, though," Jeanie went on, her words beginning to slur a little, "no girl is ever *friends* with her daddy. You can love him or respect him, but have you ever seen a girl who's buddies with her dad? It don't happen. It just don't." She shrugged and absentmindedly kissed the baby's neck. "I mean, we want it to. Shit, I wish I had been friends with my daddy. I wish I loved him. But . . ."

"But?" said Sherry. She wanted to know.

"But he never loved me. It takes two."

"Oh, I'm sure he loved you," Sherry protested. "He just acted like he didn't."

"What good was his love if he never showed it?" Jeanie asked her, eyes moist with a bourbon buzz. "It's not love if it don't get showed."

"Well, maybe I never showed him love either," Sherry suddenly blurted out. She was feeling the bourbon, too. "Maybe *I* didn't show *him*."

"What?" asked Jeanie, but she somehow seemed to know what Sherry was talking about. "Don't blame yourself. Don't do that, honey. Don't make it easy for him. I made excuses for my daddy for a long time. No more. I'm glad he's dead."

"You shouldn't say that."

"It's all right. The baby don't understand," Jeanie said. She seemed changed all of a sudden—her face was lit with energy. "I'm glad he's dead," she said again.

"I don't think I feel that way—no," Sherry said, shaking her head back and forth and talking more to herself than Jeanie. "I think I'll cry. I'll cry for everything that *didn't* happen."

"Yep, probably," said Jeanie. "Sounds right."

"There will be so many people at the funeral," Sherry went on. "They'll be expecting me to cry."

"You do whatever you want," Jeanie said firmly. "They don't own you."

Sherry stared at Jeanie for a long minute. No wonder Brazil loved her.

"What is going to happen to us?" she asked finally.

Jeanie shrugged and took another sip of bourbon.

"I don't know," she said, looking wistful. "And to tell you the truth, I'm not too worried about it. I've already died once. I'm not scared of dying again."

"You've died once?" Sherry asked. Did she hear right?

"When my baby passed on."

Sherry looked at the child sleeping across Jeanie's chest. His tiny hand clutched at her sleeve desperately, even in sleep.

"My first baby," Jeanie said.

"I'm so sorry," said Sherry. She felt as if she might cry, but she was afraid to let go again, after last night at the beach.

"You should have a baby," Jeanie said, her voice suddenly brimming with optimism. "A baby makes you worth something."

Sherry dropped her chin to her chest and let go a sharp sigh. In her mind, she was watching the mothers in the park, eyes elsewhere and glazed with exhaustion, but somehow so full of peace and resolve as they watched their babies run and play and fall, and then get up to run again.

"You don't understand," Sherry told Jeanie when she could finally speak, her voice pitched low with sadness and desire. "I want to be worth something on my own first."

She reached for a tissue and held it against the inside of one eye and then the other.

Jeanie shook her head; she was completely bewildered, and

all at once she felt swamped with pity for this poor girl. Even with her fancy clothes and fancy furniture and her perfect makeup and everything else she owned, she seemed small and lost, like an orphan. No wonder Brazil loved her. "Well," she said, trying to sound kind, "good luck."

"Thank you," said Sherry.

And so the conversation was over; it just felt that way to both of them.

Jeanie pushed a piece of hair off her forehead and then shifted deliberately in the chair, moving John Junior from one shoulder to the other. After a second, she shifted him back again. Sherry knew she was trying to wake him, and a moment later, he did begin to stir, lifting and dropping his head groggily and muttering tired baby noises.

"Guess I better get home and get him a bottle," Jeanie said, standing up. "I didn't expect to stay so long."

Sherry stood, too.

"I'm really glad we met," she said. She wanted very much to embrace Jeanie, but something—maybe it was the waking child between them—stopped her. "I really, really like you."

"Yeah," said Jeanie. "I like you, too. You're different."

Sherry pulled open the front door and let Jeanie and John Junior onto the porch.

"Take care," she said. "Have a good trip home."

Jeanie smiled, moved the baby to her left hip, and then extended her hand for a quick farewell shake. "Thank you for everything," she said. "We'll probably never meet again, so I won't say 'See you later.' "

Sherry nodded.

"I'll just say good-bye," Jeanie said. "Good-bye, okay?" She almost didn't want to leave, Sherry looked so alone and pathetic there on the porch, eyes red-rimmed like a widow. But the baby was starting to fuss, and so finally she turned and walked away.

Over her shoulder, she heard Sherry's thin voice.

"Jeanie," she said, "see you later."

41

For the rest of the week, Sherry and Belinda wrote.

Jack had given them his office, posted a sign on the door that said, DISTURB THEM—YOU DIE, and kept a constant flow of Cuban coffee coming. He even had lunch delivered to them every day. He wanted the story done and out, soon. All the other parts of the package were done, and with the cops climbing all over Belinda, it was too hot a piece to keep quiet much longer.

It was a good thing Estabrook knew how to write fast, good for her sake. She was leaving for that damn society wedding Saturday morning, and if the first draft wasn't done by then, Jack informed the two of them each day, he'd lay his fucking body down in front of the airplane. The first draft would be on his desk Friday night, no excuses.

"Don't worry," Sherry reassured Jack every time he stuck his head in the office and demanded an update. And she meant it. It was coming much more easily than she and Belinda had expected. It was a story dying to be told.

They had decided to go with a short and brutal lead, not very subtle, one that would make the reader put down his blueberry muffin and say, "Holy shit! Mabel—did you read the *Citizen* this morning?" Belinda had resisted at first—she kept asking Sherry if it had to be so darn melodramatic—but pretty soon she couldn't fight the thrill of it. After all, the stuff they had was pretty amazing. Why not tell it that way?

This is a story, the lead went, *about a teenage boy who assassinated seventeen men, one girl, and a dog, for fun, for respect, and for money.*

"Definitely makes you want to read on," Belinda said.

Sherry lit a cigarette. She had started smoking again when they sat down to write. She needed it, especially now. She'd quit later, when it was all over.

"Wait—don't you think we should mention the dog's breed

right up top?" Belinda suggested as Sherry banged down the keys. "It's pretty revealing, I'd say—"

"No, no," Sherry cut her off, "I don't want to bog the lead down with too much detail. Maybe we'll stick it in later."

"Okay," Belinda agreed. Then: "But wait, Sherry, I've got it—I think you should change 'money' to 'glory,' because Manuel was *really* doing it to feel important, right? He wasn't motivated by greed."

Sherry nodded excitedly, tapping the end of an unlit cigarette against her chin. *This* was why she had to work with Belinda. She couldn't do it alone. *This is a story*, she rewrote the lead, *about a teenage boy who assassinated seventeen men, one girl, and a dog, for fun, for respect, and for glory.*

"Love it!" Sherry exclaimed. She typed on:

The boy is 16 years old today. He attends high school in a middle-class Miami suburb. He receives straight B's from his teachers and spends Saturday evenings at the mall with his girlfriend.

In short, he's a typical teenager.

With one exception: The plague of illegal drugs, which has reached so many other levels and corners of Dade County society, has infected his young life.

At age 14, he was recruited by and then joined the Lopez cocaine family, a drug importing and distribution ring that currently operates out of a gracious ranch home in Coral Gables by the Sea. In the two years that followed, he worked as an "enforcer," killing more than a dozen persons, at $2,500 a hit, who stood in the way of Lopez profits.

And, although the boy says he has decided to leave the cocaine business to start a new life free of crime, he has no regrets.

"I made a lot of money. You could say I'm rich now," the boy told the Miami Citizen *in a recent interview, speaking under the condition that his identity would not be revealed. "You could say I'm a classy guy. You can tell by looking at me."*

Belinda was reading over Sherry's shoulder as she wrote.

"Hey, Sherry," she said, "don't you think the second graf gives him away? I mean, Mimi Lopez is going to know instantly who the kid is—"

"She's going to know who it is no matter what we write," Sherry answered quickly. She didn't want to stop for long debates—she was on a roll. "As soon as we state Manuel's age—which we *have* to do—she's going to be able to identify him.

But, look, we've discussed this before. He's going to be okay, remember?''

"Right," said Belinda. She could see Jack pacing back and forth in the newsroom, throwing a nervous glance toward his office every few steps.

Sherry kept writing:

An extensive analysis of police records and an independent lie-detector test, administered by Sherman Otis, Inc., of Miami, confirm that the boy's story is true.

It begins on the football field of his suburban high school, where another player invited the boy, then 14, to a party in one of Miami's glitziest high rises.

Belinda cleared her throat. "Glitziest?" she asked softly. "Is that a word?"

"Let the copy editors worry about it," said Sherry.

For the next hour, she typed nonstop, seamlessly churning out everything she knew about Manuel's induction, apprenticeship, and career. Every few paragraphs she would ask Belinda to find the right quote from the pile of transcripts she held on her lap—"Get me the one on how good he thinks he is," she would say, or, "Read me the stuff he said about killing Eddie." And Belinda would oblige.

By Thursday night at seven, they were almost there.

The story was long, but it was an easy read. Jack would be pleased.

"We just need to stick in the stuff Adam Klein gave me," Sherry said.

"Oh, yeah—the shrink," said Belinda, unenthused. "Was he any good?"

"Believe it or not, he helped a lot," Sherry answered.

She scanned the copy for the right spot and found it not far beneath the lead.

Adam Klein, a Boca Raton psychiatrist who specializes in youths who kill, said that many young murderers commit their crimes because they feel pressured by society to achieve fame, fortune, and greatness, Sherry wrote. *Klein, who spoke in general terms and is not familiar with this case specifically, added that some teenage murderers are "acting out" hatred for family members who have hurt them or someone they love.*

She looked at Belinda. "Do you think the reader will put this together with what happened to Manuel's mother?" she asked. "Or should I spell it out?"

Belinda scrunched up her face in thought. "No, I think it's clear," she answered after a moment. "I mean, even if you didn't have Klein saying it, any dingdong would realize that Manuel had to be affected by his mother getting beat up all the time and then killing herself. You don't want to sound like you're making excuses for the kid."

"You're right," said Sherry. "You're always right about these things."

"Oh, please, Sherry," Belinda sighed, "you're sitting there writing the whole thing, and all I'm doing is answering dumb little questions."

"You're writing, too," Sherry said. "You're my muse."

"That's wonderful." Belinda rolled her eyes. "Can we get on with the story, please?" She wasn't angry, but she was meeting Eladio for dinner at nine. They were eating Chinese at her place.

"Right," said Sherry. She inhaled sharply. Her lungs hurt from cigarettes, but she didn't mind. "Do you think I've got enough from Klein?"

Belinda read over Sherry's shoulder. "I guess so," she said. "Since he couldn't talk about Manuel directly, he doesn't really add that much. She groaned and went on: "I hate psychiatrists," she said. "So many questions, so few answers. What good are they?"

Sherry paused for a long minute to stub out her cigarette and light another. Suddenly, she was dying to tell Belinda about Klein's doubts—in her head, she could hear his flat Boston voice saying Manuel's motives were darker than she knew—but telling Belinda now would only slow down a process she, and everyone else, wanted done and over.

"I guess," Sherry answered at last, "I guess psychiatrists are good for people who don't even know what the questions are."

Belinda shrugged and scanned the copy on the screen again. "I think you've got enough Klein," she said. "Did he say anything about rehabilitation?"

"We didn't talk about it."

"Okay." Belinda reached over Sherry's shoulder and hit the Scroll key. She was reading quickly, correcting typos and spelling mistakes every few lines. Sherry was a terrible speller. Very irritating.

After a few minutes, she stopped. Something was wrong with the description of the Lulu LaTerche hit. She read it over again twice.

The boy's next job, his thirteenth, took place in Homestead, a small town in southern Dade County. He was assigned to silence a young prostitute suspected of informing a rival cocaine ring of Lopez family drop-off locations.

The victim, identified as Lulu LaTerche, 15 years old, was shot in the face as she smoked crack cocaine in an abandoned shack in the town's poverty-stricken Belleville section.

Belinda shook her head. She was beginning to feel tired and frustrated with this whole project again.

"You've got this Lulu part all wrong," she said, standing up and walking over to the window. Her back was to Sherry.

"Okay. *No problema, señorita.*" Sherry swiveled around to the computer and held her fingers over the keyboard, ready to type. "Go ahead, hit me with the right stuff."

Belinda said nothing.

"Hello," Sherry called out in a singsong. "I'm waiting."

Belinda turned around. "Well, *señorita,*" she began coolly, in that new voice Sherry recognized from the other day, "you got the facts right, you just happened to miss the truth on this one."

It was Sherry's turn to groan. They had got this far without one of Belinda's self-righteous outbursts; why couldn't they go the distance?

"What's the truth?" she asked. "Tell me."

"The truth is this: Manuel murdered a little girl—my God, Sherry, she was fifteen years old!—and he did it in cold blood for absolutely no reason on earth," Belinda said, the words rushing out indignantly. She was thinking about the big cop's watery blue eyes. "Manuel blew her head off. He stuck the gun up her nose, for God's sake! And he says he was just following orders—he had no idea what she had done wrong, and he didn't care."

"He didn't stick the gun up her nose, Belinda! Jesus Christ," Sherry said, exasperated, rolling her eyes, "don't be ridiculous."

"The cop said he stuck the gun *in her nose,*" Belinda answered quickly, but even in the saying of it, realized the assertion sounded preposterous. "I'm telling you, that's what he said. . . ." Her voice trailed off.

"I think he was employing what is commonly referred to as *hyperbole,*" Sherry pretended to tease Belinda good-naturedly, but

they both knew how irritated she was feeling with the delay.
"You know, Belinda, cops are always exaggerating. And this cop
sounds like he had a rather *preternatural* interest in the victim, if
you get my meaning. If you'd given him the chance, he'd probably
have told you Manuel raped and scalped her while he was at it."

"I guess so." Belinda dropped her head dejectedly. "But the
other stuff I said is true," she muttered. "I mean, Sherry, let's not
lose touch with the fact that Manuel murdered a little girl just
because someone told him to. He didn't even ask why."

Sherry reread the copy.

"The story says her age," she said. "Look, Belinda, it's up to
the reader to realize the murder was in cold blood and that he
was just following orders. All Manuel's murders were that way,
if you want to get technical about it."

"This one was worse," Belinda answered softly.

"It was worse because the victim was a female," Sherry said.
She could feel Belinda retreating and wanted to give her a way
out. "It feels closer to home."

"Maybe," Belinda said wearily. She walked back to Sherry
and sat in the chair behind her right shoulder. "And he didn't
have to kill the dog . . ." she suggested meekly. It was her last
shot.

"No, he didn't," Sherry said, the irritation no longer hidden.
"But he thought it was going to bite his leg off—"

"What? A little tiny Pekingese? Sherry, come on!" Belinda
scolded her with a renewed burst of energy. "It would have felt
like a mosquito stung him—"

"*Pekingese?*" For a moment Sherry wasn't sure she had heard
right, but then, all at once, she knew that she had. She stood up
abruptly and walked to the corner of the office, resting her body
against the wall so that she could gaze out the window at the bay
and still keep her back to Belinda and the computer where the
Manuel story was nearly complete, save for their double byline.
But the view, usually so soothing, did nothing for Sherry now.
Her stomach churned with queasiness, and again her skin began
to tingle with the painful onset of prickly heat. "Pekingese?" she
repeated finally. "Manuel said it was a Doberman pinscher."

Belinda let out an ironic laugh. "Is that what he told you,
Sherry?" she said. She wagged her head incredulously. "What a
fake little macho man he is! The cop report says he blew away a
Pekingese—says it clear as day."

Sherry said nothing, but inside, her head was clamoring with voices of fear and doubt, voices now familiar to her, voices she was getting very good at silencing. Perhaps, she thought, perhaps this is exactly what Sherman Otis meant when he said Manuel's story was only true "by and large." Or perhaps she had heard Manuel wrong that day in the car as he described the D'Escara hit. Or perhaps he mixed up the names of the breeds in his own head.

Or perhaps Belinda had it bang-on. Perhaps Manuel was a strutting, preening little fake, in love with his myth as much as he was in love with himself.

But the fact remained: He had killed eighteen people for the Lopez family cocaine ring, and he had told her all about it. For so, so many reasons, Sherry reminded herself, the story had to run.

She turned back to face Belinda. "Fine, a *Pekingese*," she said, her voice resolute. Her skin still hurt, like a lingering case of sunburn, but the nausea had vanished. Nothing had changed, she decided—the detail actually helped the story. It showed the depth of Manuel's savagery; it made the story that much more shocking. "Let's stick it in the lead," she said.

For the first time in hours, Belinda smiled, a smile of triumph and relief. "Thanks, Sherry," she said. "We've got to show him for what he really is."

But Sherry was too busy fixing the copy to hear her.

When she was done, she motioned Belinda over to her side. "Sit down," she said, "and let's give this one last look-see." And for fifteen more minutes, they read together in silence, occasionally squeezing hands, until they reached the end. And even then, they sat side by side, wordlessly, for another fifteen, letting the story roam in their heads. There was so much to say, neither of them could speak.

It was dark outside by the time they were done, but the bay still sparkled, lit by the big houses of the causeway islands.

"I guess that's it," Sherry said finally. "We can just spend tomorrow really fine-tuning the writing. Maybe we'll even get out of here early."

"That sounds wonderful," said Belinda. She checked her watch. Eladio would have to let himself into her apartment. "You want to go out and celebrate tomorrow?" she asked, standing up and pulling on her jacket.

"God, I'd love to," Sherry said. "But I promised Manuel I'd see him for dinner. He *insisted*. He wants me to let him read the story."

"You're not going—"

Sherry cut her off. "Of course not," she said. "I'm going to give him an idea of what it contains, but he can read it with the rest of Miami."

"Read it and weep," said Belinda. Her mind was already someplace else. "Okay, so we'll go out and celebrate when you get back from Boston."

Sherry nodded. When she got back, Belinda would be married. Would Eladio come along?

"Great," Sherry said. "We'll celebrate when I get home."

She checked her watch. It was Thursday—department stores were open late—so there was still time to get to Fort Lauderdale to buy the dress for Alice's big day. At least she'd be ready for one wedding.

Manuel told her he'd pick her up at eight, at her place.

Sherry wasn't thrilled about the plan, but at least this visit would be short. She was determined. There would be no lingering over photographs, no tears in the kitchen. The story was done, on Jack's desk and out of her hands forever. This was going to be good-bye, finally and thankfully, whether Manuel liked it or not.

And the fact was, she had a great excuse for an early evening. Her plane to Boston would leave at 7:42 A.M., and she wasn't even packed. Manuel would *have* to understand: Dinner would take an hour, maximum. She had to be home by nine, in time to catch Brazil's call, throw together a suitcase, watch the news, and get some decent sleep. Perfect.

So perfect that Sherry felt nearly ecstatic as she hurtled around the house waiting for Manuel, emptying ashtrays and stacking old magazines and newspapers that were thrown every-where. Manuel was just *hours* from being out of her life! Sure, she might have to see him again—in court or at the D.A.'s Office or maybe at a police-orchestrated press conference if he ended up turning state's evidence—but she would never, ever, have to be alone with him again, never hear him talk about murder with his mouth full, never have to wonder if she had lost her mind to feel sympathy for someone so capable of evil, never have to scour his words for the mystery of his soul, and best of all, never have to fight with Belinda about it all. After one last dinner, she would only have to deal with Manuel in black-and-white, in the comfort and safety of the newsroom. Every other story in the "Baby Lips package," as Jack called it, was written and edited. All the art was shot—Brazil had got a terrific telephoto color picture of Mimi Lopez herself watering the flower boxes in front of the Gables house—and the big map of Manuel's hits had been drawn. The plan now was for Jack to spend the next week editing Sherry and Belinda's piece with a bunch of his favorite sons: Joe Mooney, the hard-ass who ran the city desk, Gene Beloit, who won a Pulitzer in '78 for getting an innocent guy off Death Row in Tallahassee, and Radewski, that mole with the beady eyes. As much as every-one hated him, the guy knew how to write.

Jack told Sherry that he expected to be done by the following Friday. He wanted the package to run, and run big, in Sunday's paper.

Sherry was thinking about just how big when she heard Man-uel honk his horn outside. She slipped on her shoes and ran to the front door. If she moved fast enough, he wouldn't even have to come inside.

But by the time she reached the front porch, she could see Manuel was out of his car and walking up the driveway, smiling broadly.

He was carrying a large box with a handle. Sherry groaned. What in the world could this be about? How long would it take?

"Hi!" she called out, trying not to sound too irritated.

Manuel continued to walk toward her, and his smile seemed to intensify with every stride. It made Sherry nervous. She stepped outside and pulled the door closed behind her.

"Why don't we just go?" she said, pretending not to see the box and feeling ridiculous. "Unfortunately, I'm really crushed for time tonight."

Manuel kept smiling. He walked past Sherry and into the house.

She followed him; what choice was there? He had placed the box on the coffee table in the living room and settled into the couch, arms folded smugly. For the first time, Sherry noticed that Manuel smiled without showing his teeth. Just as she had thought the first time she saw him—he *was* repulsive.

"I've got bad news," Sherry started right away. She wanted to sound breathless and panicked. "Manuel, my plane leaves first thing tomorrow morning, and I'm not even packed, so we really can't spend too much time together tonight." She was still ignoring the box—but did she just hear something inside it rattle? She went on: "I figured we'd just catch a fast bite. Like I said, I am really, really short on time tonight. So why don't we head out now? We can take my car."

Manuel continued to smile at her. Then he tilted his head toward the box in that exaggerated Latin way that drove Sherry crazy.

"I've got something for you," he said. The voice was seductive, ingratiating.

"This?" Sherry tried to sound surprised. "This is for me?"

Manuel nodded. "For you," he said. "Open it."

Sherry took a step backward. She didn't want to open it. She was through playing by his rules. The game was over.

"I'll open it later," she said, "tonight, when I'm done packing."

"Open it now," Manuel said. The voice was still smooth, cajoling.

"No," said Sherry. "We don't have time."

"I said you should open it." A little harsher.

"I'll do it later."

"You'll do it now." This time, a command.

Manuel kept his eyes focused on Sherry. He wasn't going to surrender.

"You'll do it now," he repeated.

Sherry couldn't bring herself to look at Manuel, so she turned her eyes to the box, staring so intently she thought she saw it move. Maybe she was making too much of this. Maybe she should just play along a little longer, until the end of dinner, until they finally parted ways.

"Okay, okay," she said. She smiled and then let out a coquettish giggle. She figured Manuel would never know she was faking it, and she was right. His sickening smile was back. He looked like a snake with hair.

Sherry sat down on the couch, as far from Manuel as she could without making a point of it, and then leaned toward the box on the coffee table. The top flaps weren't sealed, she noticed. How odd.

How terribly odd.

Sherry looked around the room, suddenly feeling a little frantic and searching for a diversion. She was just about to get up to grab a half-empty can of Coke on the mantelpiece when Manuel touched the curve of her back with his two fingers.

"Go ahead," he said. "Open it."

"This really wasn't necessary."

"Yes, it was."

"No, it—" Sherry stopped cold. The box *was* moving, and something inside *was* making a noise, a strange scratching noise.

She looked at Manuel. He raised his eyebrows and nodded slowly, looking unbearably smitten with himself.

"Go ahead," he said.

Sherry stood up and pulled open the lid of the box, ready to jump back fast if she had to. But nothing leapt out at her. Nothing except a tiny, scared *meow*.

Sherry's heart surged with hope. Could it be?

She stared into the box, and yes! it was—there in the corner: a kitten, curled into a frightened ball but utterly and completely beautiful, a sweet little short-haired gray with crooked white paws and bewildered orange eyes. It looked just like Pansy.

How absolutely wonderful, Sherry thought, and how absolutely horrible. How could Manuel do something like this to her? Especially now, when she was so ready to hate him?

She picked up the kitten and held it to her face. After a second, it began to purr, softly at first, and then with increasing conviction. It even sounded like Pansy.

How could Manuel do this?

How could he make her so happy?

Sherry sat down again and laid the kitten on her lap. She stroked Pansy's favorite spot, top of the head, between the ears— and the kitten lifted its little head in approval.

"You're crying," said Manuel.

"Yeah, I know," said Sherry. She couldn't help it.

"I wanted to get you one just like your old cat," Manuel went on. He was watching Sherry closely, loving every detail of her reaction. His plan was working to perfection.

"But—"

"I know, I never saw your cat, right?"

"Right," said Sherry. She was sitting on the floor now, watching the kitten explore a few square inches before darting back to her side.

"But I did see your cat"—he stood up—"right here." He triumphantly pointed to a photograph on the mantelpiece. It showed a young Pansy, eyes half-mast and front paws tucked under, relaxing the day away on a big brocade couch in the Marblehead house.

"So, how did I do?" he asked. "Great, right?

Sherry nodded.

"I want you to know I thought of everything." Manuel was still talking. He reached into the cardboard box and pulled out two cans of cat food. "Just in case you threw everything out after your old cat got wasted."

"Thanks," said Sherry. She couldn't take her eyes off the kitten. It kept tripping over its tail—too adorable!

"Now," Manuel continued, standing above Sherry, gloating over her drippy tears, "I'm sure you're wondering what to do with the kitten when you go away tomorrow."

The thought hadn't even occurred to Sherry. "Oh, yeah," she said. She'd have to ask Brazil to come feed it. He wouldn't be overjoyed, but he'd do it.

"Well, don't worry about it for a second," Manuel said. "I'll keep the thing until you get back. We can get together Monday, and I'll give it to you again."

Sherry scooped up the kitten and jumped to her feet.

"Absolutely not!" she said, meaning to sound friendly but unyielding. "You've really done enough, Manuel. And I thank you. I really do. I love the kitten, but don't worry about it anymore. I'll get my boyfriend to stop by while I'm gone. He'll feed it and play with it, and you won't have to bother."

Manuel's narrow face contracted into an aggravated grimace.

"You're still going to go out with that guy?"

"Yes, I still go out with him," she answered vaguely, knowing she was missing something.

"You're still going to go out with him after this?" Manuel pointed at the kitten.

"I don't follow you," Sherry said, but suddenly she did, and it made her stomach turn with loathing.

Manuel stared at Sherry. He was angry.

"You'll follow me," he said.

"What?" said Sherry.

"Just give me time, twelve hours, you'll follow me then."

"What?"

Manuel smiled, lips sealed together, eyes potent with spite.

"You'll see," he said.

"I'll see?" said Sherry. The kitten was purring again.

Manuel nodded briskly.

What in the hell was happening here? Whatever it was, it gave her the creeps.

Sherry checked her watch; it was quarter to nine. She wanted Manuel out, but not this way. She wanted to part with all loose ends tied neatly. She wanted to part as friends.

"Did you say if the kitten was a boy or a girl?" she asked after a minute had passed, her voice artificially bright.

"Boy," Manuel said glumly.

"Great!" said Sherry.

He shrugged.

"No, I mean it! Boy cats are so much better than girl cats. Pansy was a boy cat," Sherry lied. "Boy cats are great! I can't thank you enough, Manuel. You really, really made my day."

"Your day?" He was displeased.

"I mean my week—my month! I mean, God, you made my *year*! I love this kitten!" She hugged the animal to her chest.

Manuel studied Sherry's face. She seemed to be telling the truth.

"So, he looks like your dead cat, right?" he said, his voice warming up again.

"Exactly," said Sherry. She smiled cheerfully and then checked her watch, this time pulling back her sleeve in an exaggerated motion. "Wow!" she cried. "It's really getting late."

Manuel didn't answer, and Sherry could feel the prickle of cold sweat on the back of her neck.

"It's really getting late," she repeated. "Manuel?"

He looked up from the couch, expressionless.

"We're going to have to say good-bye now."

The grimace returned, just briefly, and then a hard grin, lips pressed shut as usual. He stood.

"I'm glad you like the cat," he said.

"I *love* him," said Sherry.

Manuel started for the door.

"I'm sorry we didn't get to go out for a farewell dinner," said Sherry, following him.

He didn't turn around. "We'll see each other when you get back," he said.

"I'm sure . . ."

But she didn't want to lie.

"Listen, Manuel," she corrected herself, "the story is finished."

He faced her now.

"I know," he said.

Sherry was confused; she had expected him to sound sad or disappointed. He sounded just fine.

"That means we don't need to have any more interviews." She spoke slowly, using the same voice she put on when she first addressed his high school rap room. She wanted to be trusted, liked—understood.

"Good," said Manuel. "No more interviews. They were getting boring."

His response made Sherry very nervous. Maybe he didn't get it—their relationship was over.

"It was very nice working with you," she said. Could she be any more clear? "I really learned a lot, and I appreciate all the time you spent with me. I wish you a lot of luck in the future."

Wait—was he smirking? What was this?

"You're very smart, Manuel, and I know everything will work out for you," Sherry filled the silence, hoping he would interrupt soon. "I hope you like the story. It will probably run next Sunday—that is, a week from this Sunday, okay?"

He *was* smirking.

Then: "You're talking like we're never going to see each other again," he said.

"We may not," said Sherry.

"No, we will," Manuel answered. There was no doubt in his voice.

Sherry looked at him, incredulous. What could she possibly say to make him understand?

She opened her mouth to try again, but then stopped. There was nothing to say, and she knew it. Nothing that would convince him of something he didn't want to believe. He'd just have to learn the hard way: From now on, she wouldn't return his calls, meet him for dinner, or answer any letters. She was grateful for the kitten, she really was, but if he came to her house again, she'd call the police. Trespasser on the premises.

Sherry smiled at Manuel and extended her hand.

He shook it, a little too hard, and then left without saying good-bye.

Nothing had changed in Lost Corners, except the name of the bank and the priest at Fourteen Holy Helpers Church and Parish House.

Back when Jeanie was still living in the trailer, the old priest, Father Vernon, used to stop by about three times a year to gently remind her to come to mass soon, as if church had just happened to skip her mind for the past twelve or fifteen years. The funny thing was, she wanted to give it a try, but somehow she always seem to spend Sunday mornings cleaning up Saturday night benders. So she never ended up getting to church in her life, and that's why she never ended up believing in God.

Anyway, she wasn't in Lost Corners five minutes when Aunt Ardelle told her that Father Vernon had been reassigned down the road to Deluxeville, and now Fourteen Holy Helpers had a new and young and handsome priest named Father Ray, who had doubled attendance Sundays and instituted a Christmas play, in which her grandson, Lloyd III, had played Jesus Christ Himself this very past year.

Wasn't that wonderful?

Jeanie agreed: just wonderful.

But she was actually a little sorry Father Vernon wasn't going to be the one to bury her daddy. Would she know a soul there besides her relatives? They were all being nice enough to the baby, but then . . .

But then, they all seemed to feel so very terribly sorry for her or something, as if she were *still* living in that stinking trailer with the town drunk, as if she *still* had a reputation at school, as if she were *still* the same Jeanette who was seen one Christmas morning eating a burger in Poison Ridge at the White Castle, with its little blinking tree in the window. So it was true. All those things happened in her past, but nobody seemed to realize she was a different person now. She lived in Miami, Florida, with her husband, who was a famous photographer, and her baby, who had everything a baby could ever want, and they owned a nice house that was just a few blocks from the ocean—for crying out loud, she could go swimming every single day if she felt like it! Nobody seemed to realize that *she* had made it out of Lost Corners, and they were all still stuck there. She felt sorry for *them.*

She missed Brazil already.

She loved him more than ever now that she had met that poor girlfriend of his. He was always trying to help everybody, even those completely beyond repair. And he had been such an angel when she finally reached him at the Holiday Inn, offering to fly to Lost Corners from Tampa that very same day. Why had she told him no?

Maybe because she was just so used to making life uncomplicated for him. And maybe because she knew the searing pain of coming home to a place like Lost Corners was something he just wouldn't understand.

And so here she was, alone except for her only son, in the neat little guest room of her aunt Ardelle's house.

Jeanie quickly unpacked her suitcase—she didn't want her funeral dress getting wrinkled—and then pulled back the sheets on the double bed to warm them up for the baby.

"John Junior," she asked after she was done, "you want a bath, sweetness?"

"Da-da," the baby babbled back.

"You want your daddy? Me, too, honey."

He was asleep before Jeanie could even kiss his forehead.

Jeanie checked her watch; it was just past seven, their time.

She was beginning to feel tired, but it was still early enough to get done what she came for. She headed downstairs to see if Ardelle was still around.

And she was, bustling from one corner of the kitchen to the other, apron over her old-fashioned print dress and glasses low on her nose, consulting a worn-out cookbook and then throwing this and that into a gigantic black pot.

"Aunt Ardelle?" She said it softly.

"Jeanette!" The old woman spun around, surprised and little confused. She was used to being alone. "Why aren't you resting? You've had a long trip today, honey."

"I'm not tired."

"You've got a big weekend ahead of you. You need your sleep."

"I'll be fine, like I said."

"But you don't want to weaken your fragile constitution at a time like this," Ardelle insisted.

Jeanie wasn't interested in fighting about it. There were more important things to discuss. She cleared her throat purposefully and stepped closer to her aunt.

"Ardelle," she said firmly, "when can I go to the trailer?"

Her aunt dropped her jaw. "You don't want to go there, Jeanette," she answered hurriedly. "I've been there. It's not very nice."

"I *know* what it's like," Jeanie said. She didn't want to sound angry, but for God's sake, she didn't *need* anyone's permission to go to her own house. She just needed a ride.

The two women faced each other for a long minute. Finally, Ardelle spoke. "Jeanette, I can't let you go there *alone*," she said. "It's not cleaned up yet. You can't see it by yourself. It will be . . ."—she was struggling uneasily for the correct words—"it will be too much for your heart, honey."

Jeanie thought about it for a second. She'd rather go there by herself, of course, but was it worth one of those stupid back-and-forth arguments with Ardelle? No way.

"All right," she said. "You want to come with me?"

"Heavens no!" Ardelle shot back before she knew what she was saying. "I mean, Jeanette, I've been there once. That's enough. I'll send you with Father Ray."

And so her aunt picked up the phone, and a few minutes

later Father Ray was at the door. He was young, but he sure wasn't handsome. Ardelle had lousy taste in men. He was too thin, for one thing. After living with Brazil, Jeanie had come to like the feeling of a big man. And this Ray was too pale and weak-looking. He reminded her of a kid they used to taunt back in elementary school; they called him Wimpy Wales, but his first name was really Pierre. One time all the eighth-grade boys chased him down in the playground and stripped him naked for the world to see. He never came back to school.

The priest shook Jeanie's hand, laying both of his over hers. His palms were damp. She hated that.

"I am so pleased to meet you, Jeanette," he said, all the while looking at Aunt Ardelle with dreamy eyes. "I am very glad to be of service to any member of the Colefern family."

She was going to tell him she was a White, but the fact was, she didn't want to get into any big conversations with the man. He probably already knew too much about her. "Thank you," she said instead. "Why don't we get going?"

They didn't talk much in the car ride over; Jeanie was grateful for that. But she noticed that every time Father Ray opened his mouth, he had to say something complimentary about her aunt Ardelle or her uncle Lloyd. He just loved them to death, and it was beginning to get irritating.

"What the hell, did they give you a lot of cash or something?" she finally asked.

Father Ray gulped so hard, he looked like a cartoon character with an Adam's apple as big and bouncy as a beach ball. Jeanie noticed his lips were moving slightly; he seemed to be thinking very hard, practicing what he might answer. A half-minute later, he shifted in his seat, side to side, and the car swerved with him. He was a terrible driver; Jeanie thanked her lucky stars there was no one else on the road.

"The Coleferns have been extremely generous to Fourteen Holy Helpers," he said at last. He laid into the words "extremely generous."

"Well, I guess they're just made of money, then," Jeanie said. She'd been meeting up with rich people left and right lately. First Sherry, who looked as if she were about to fall into a million pieces if you touched her, and then Ardelle and her family, who all seemed very, very nervous for some reason. If they all had so much money, why couldn't they be happy?

"I guess they don't know how lucky they are," she said out loud.

The priest nodded and murmured in agreement, but when Jeanie glanced over at him, he looked completely perplexed, Adam's apple still bobbing up and down.

She laughed to herself and looked out the window. They were on her side of town now—no more houses, just narrow tin-sided trailers stuck here and there on the sandy ground, and lots of mangy barking dogs running in a pack, searching for supper in every other rotting garbage heap. It wasn't like a regular neighborhood. Far from it. The trailers were arranged at skewed angles, as if they fell from space, and separated from each other by unfriendly acres of rough grass and haphazard hills and old cars on cinder blocks, their engines scattered around them, like gifts under a Christmas tree. Jeanie noticed the moon was out, showering down a surreal and lovely ivory glow, but in the end everything in Lost Corners looked just as hard-edged and ugly as when she left. There was no place on earth more different from Miami.

"Here we are," Father Ray said in a high, thin voice meant to sound cheerful. He pulled the car right up to the front door of the trailer where Jeanie once lived.

It looked sort of spooky without the lights on.

Maybe this was a stupid idea, Jeanie thought. Why go in now? Wasn't it enough just to be here for the funeral?

But, of course, she had to go in. The past was sitting right in front of her, waiting to be finished.

"I'll be back in a minute," Jeanie said. She'd go in, she figured, get the box from under her daddy's bed, stick it in her bag, and then get out of there. The end.

But Father Ray was already out of the car and headed up the three steps to the trailer's door. "Your aunt Ardelle asked me to go inside with you," he said. He sounded sorry.

"You don't have to," said Jeanie, "I won't tell her."

"It's all right," the priest answered in a sad-voiced way that almost made her like him. "I'd better do what she asked."

Jeanie shrugged. "Go on in, then," she said. "The switch is on the right."

The priest reached inside the trailer and tripped the light, a single uncovered bulb hanging in the middle of the main room, where every day Jeanie used to cook three cheap meals, watch nine hours of black-and-white TV, sleep on a sagging old couch, and clean up puke on her hands and knees with Spic & Span. The priest stepped inside, and Jeanie followed.

The place was a shit hole. It even smelled like one.

Father Ray ducked his head in embarrassment. But Jeanie wasn't ashamed. She suddenly felt prouder than ever, proud she had escaped, free and clear.

"You should see where I live now," she told Father Ray. "It's a friggin' palace compared to this—"

Jeanie looked around: The kitchen sink was overflowing with dirty dishes, encrusted with egg yolks and hash—obviously her daddy never lost his taste for junk from a can—the floor was covered with shirts turned inside out and Mabel Black Label empties and girlie magazines with centerfolds open wide. The little Formica table where Jeanie had tried to do her homework after school was piled high with tabloid clippings about UFO sightings in Canada and alien attacks on midwestern farmers. Jeanie walked over to the table. The last clipping was dated November 12, two days before the old man died. She held it up for Father Ray to see: ALIENS MAKE DAKOTA BABY'S HEAD EXPLODE. HYSTERICAL MOTHER CRIES, "I BEGGED THEM TO KILL ME INSTEAD!"

"As you can see," Jeanie said, "my daddy believed in little evil creatures from outer space."

"I see."

"I guess he was a real fruitcake, when you get down to it."

"I wouldn't say that, Jeanette," Father Ray said, suddenly animated. "He was a sinner. But God loves those who sin."

"How about those who get all broken and used up by those who sin—does God love them?"

"God loves them, too."

"Well, that's real nice of Him," Jeanie said. It sounded like a bunch of bullshit to her.

"You should forgive your father, Jeanette," Father Ray said. His thin little voice was insistent.

"What for?"

"The Bible says—"

"With all due respect, sir, I don't care what a *book* says," Jeanie interrupted him, "I want to know the *real* reason."

"All the real reasons are in the Bible."

"I guess I got to read it someday, in that case." Jeanie didn't care if she sounded bitchy. Father Ray was turning out to be a complete wimp. First he had been bought by Aunt Ardelle and Uncle Lloyd, and now he was telling her to forgive her father. He didn't even *know* her father.

"Yes." Father Ray seemed oblivious to Jeanie's sarcasm. "You must meet the Lord."

"Fine," she shot back, "is He staying around here?"

"He is everywhere."

"How convenient."

"Yes," said the priest, "isn't it?"

Jeanie nodded vaguely. Had everyone in this town had their brains baked?

She dropped the clipping back on the table and maneuvered around the priest to get to the tiny cubicle that her father used as a bedroom. It looked just the same: naked mattress on the floor, soiled clothes hanging out of drawers and over the garbage pail, cigarette butts everywhere.

Jeanie noticed some of the butts were smudged with red lipstick, and suddenly the thought of her father screwing some girl made her sick to her stomach. How could anyone touch him on purpose?

"Jeanette, are you feeling all right?" The priest, still standing out in the main room, had noticed Jeanie's breathing had turned rough.

"I'm fine, I'm fine," Jeanie answered quickly, but the fact was, she was feeling so terrible she thought she might pass out. "Be right there," she told the priest.

Jeanie dropped to her hands and knees and peered under her father's bed.

No box.

Fucker!

She stood up and dusted the ashes and grit off her hands. Where else could it be?

Jeanie began to search through her father's dresser drawers, reluctantly at first, and then frantic all at once, pulling out clothes with both hands and flinging them to the floor like a crazy woman. She hadn't come all this way to let the bastard rob her again.

Jeanie looked left and right. Where the hell was the tin box? Had he tossed it when she left? That wasn't like him; he kept everything, even the little umbrellas they stuck in fancy drinks. He had a whole collection of those.

Then it occurred to her—of course!—she knew where he'd put it. She pulled two flannel shirts and a pair of boxer shorts off the garbage pail and stared inside. There it was.

She could tell right away the top wasn't locked. This was her lucky day.

But then it wasn't at all. The box was empty.

"That no-good son of a bitch from hell!" The words flew from Jeanie's lips like spit onto hot coals. "That no-good fucking bastard went and killed my mother! That low-lying pool of pond scum! Now I'm not ever gonna see her." Her voice was loud now, more a wail than a shout, made heavy and hoarse with the kind of anger and heart-crushing regret that can make a person crippled. "Now I'm not ever gonna see her."

"Jeanette?"

Father Ray was standing above her in the bedroom, hands clasped together on his breastbone. "Let me help you," he said, but he didn't move.

"I'm fine, I'm fine," Jeanie muttered to herself. She stared into the empty box. "Now I'm never gonna see her," she said again.

"See her?"

"My mother." Jeanie was sitting on her knees, chin on her chest, eyes closed. She was hugging herself as tight as she could, imagining it was Brazil there with her.

"You were expecting what? Photographs?"

"Right."

"Maybe they're elsewhere in the trailer," Father Ray offered in that same fake-cheerful voice he'd been using since they arrived. He couldn't have Jeanie returning to Ardelle red-eyed and surly.

"They're not anywhere in this trailer," Jeanie snapped. "There probably never were any pictures. He just lied and lied and lied and lied. That's all he ever did. Get drunk and lie. I'm glad he finally croaked. I hate his dead stinking guts."

This was too much! Father Ray suddenly crouched down by Jeanie's side, unwrapped her arms, and took her hands in his. "Look at me," he insisted.

Jeanie opened her eyes. The priest's face was barely a half-foot away.

"Hate is evil!" he exclaimed. "Pray with me, Jeanette! Pray

with me that you'll be released from the Devil! Seek forgiveness
for what you have just said!"

Jeanie tried to pry her hands away, but Father Ray was holding on too tight.

"Father, forgive Jeanette, for she has sinned!"

The priest was looking skyward now, and his eyes were suddenly so glassy Jeanie could barely see the pupils. He looked
stoned.

"I haven't sinned," she corrected him, and all at once, she
felt completely clearheaded and even a little bit giddy. Everything
was finally done and in its place. No more dangling questions, no
more dangling lives. Her father was dead, and so, at last, was her
mother. The truth was, really and completely, that she had *one*
family: Brazil and the baby, both living. They loved her, and she
loved them. The past was over. She was ready to bury it all.

"Father Ray," Jeanie said, trying to see into his eyes, "if you
don't drop my hands this instant and stop asking God to forgive
me, I can assure you that from this point forward my aunt Ardelle
and uncle Lloyd will have nothing further to do with your friggin'
Fourteen Holy Helpers, if you follow my drift."

He followed it. A moment later, he was standing near the
door of the trailer, smoothing his hair with one hand and fumbling
for the car keys with the other.

"Are we done here?" he asked.

"I'm finished, yes," Jeanie said. She stepped by him and
into the cold mountain night. A second later, he was beside her,
walking in short, fast steps toward the car.

But suddenly Jeanie stopped and spun herself around and
around in a circle, arms flung glad and wide like a child getting
ready to make an angel in the snow.

"I'm looking all around, and I'm hugging it all up inside,"
she pronounced loudly, knowing Father Ray wouldn't understand her, but feeling good just to get it out. "I'm looking all
around because I'll never see this place again."

The priest nodded, and Jeanie spun around one last time.

"This is how I want to remember it," she said, "all blurred."
She laughed because it was true, she had made the world around
her look as fuzzy as an old photograph. "I don't want to remember
any of the real stuff," she said.

"I see," said Father Ray, stooping into the front seat and

turning over the engine. A second later, Jeanie plopped into the car next to him and, without really noticing it, started to whistle happily, which apparently bugged the hell out of Father Ray.

"Jeanette," he said, "would you like me to turn on the radio?"

"No thanks," she said. She had switched to humming now, and the priest was rubbing his neck as if a fly were crawling on it.

He cleared his throat loudly. "How long will you be staying?" he asked.

"Just until Sunday." She picked up the tune where she left off.

"How nice," said Ray, now trying harder than ever to keep the conversation going. "And then, will you be taking the bus or flying?"

"We're taking a plane."

"And will your husband be meeting you at the airport?"

The mention of Brazil stopped Jeanie cold. Nobody had said a word about him since she arrived, as if they didn't believe he existed or something.

"Yeah, he'll be there," she answered, suddenly pushed back against the car seat by an almost physical pang of longing. "He promised to be waiting for me and the baby."

"How nice," said Ray. "And what does he do for a living?"

"He's a photographer at the *Miami Citizen*. That's a big newspaper down there."

"How nice," said the priest.

"He's really good," said Jeanie.

"I'm sure," said Father Ray.

They had just crossed the railroad tracks and were back in Ardelle's neck of Lost Corners. But Jeanie wasn't watching the scenery anymore. She was thinking about her husband, about his beautiful face, with not a line of meanness in it, and about the way his big arms felt when he held her in bed at night, safe and warm like a cloak of love. Had she ever told him how very, very much she loved him? Had she ever thanked him for loving her the way he did, after she was all used-up and useless? Maybe he didn't even know how she really felt about him and their baby and their marriage. She let him have his girlfriend, right? That was her way of showing him that she appreciated him, that she respected who he was, that she understood the limits of their relationship. But maybe that was all wrong. In fact, suddenly she was *sure* it was all wrong. All she had on this earth was Brazil and their baby, and she was being insane to share her family with someone else. It was *her* family. Her *only* one. And it was too precious to just give it away to some girl who didn't even need one. Hadn't Sherry said her mother and father were still living? So she didn't get along too well with her father—but it didn't sound like she couldn't ever, with a little effort. The fact was, Jeanie suddenly realized, Sherry had her own family. She couldn't have Jeanie's anymore.

"What time is it?" Jeanie's urgency caught the young priest off guard. He'd been enjoying the silence.

"Just past nine."

"Making it what in Miami?"

Father Ray thought for a moment. "I guess that would make it just past eleven."

"Great," said Jeanie. There was still time to call Brazil. She had to talk to him tonight, to tell him that everything had changed. "Honey," she was going to say, "you can't see that girlfriend of yours anymore because—"

Because . . .

How was she going to put it?

Because . . .

Because you just can't.

Because we can't go sharing our family all around with everyone.

Because I love you too much.

Because you're all I've got.

She could hear the silence already. Brazil wouldn't say anything mean. He wouldn't disagree. He wouldn't argue. He just wouldn't answer.

All right then. Maybe it would be better not to come on too strong, announcing that from now on everything was going to be totally different, sounding like a dictator on the TV news or something. Okay, that was the wrong approach for Brazil, now that she thought about it for a minute. It would be better to bring it up gently, in bed one morning, or in the kitchen after dinner one night. "Honey," she might begin, "our little family is really special to me. Since I been to Lost Corners, I realize you and the baby are the only two people I got in this world. And I'm wondering if it might be better for all of us if we keep a little bit more to ourselves." Something along those lines might work. Maybe. She would have to try.

"Well, we're back!" It was Father Ray talking again in that

now familiar high-pitched voice that was supposed to sound cheerful. He pulled into the driveway, and Jeanie quickly saw Ardelle's bulky silhouette in the living-room window. A few seconds later, the front door opened, and her aunt peered out, looking worried and sad.

"Well?" she said, her voice matching her face.

"Mission accomplished!" Father Ray announced.

Ardelle looked into Jeanie's eyes for the real story, but she couldn't read them. She'd never been able to read her brother's either.

"Everything's fine," Jeanie said quickly, when she noticed her aunt's desperate stare. "I got what I wanted. More, even."

"More?"

"Right," said Jeanie, in a way that made it clear she wasn't going to explain. "How was the baby?"

"Not a peep," said Aunt Ardelle.

"Thank you for watching him."

"He's an angel."

"I know," said Jeanie.

She turned to the priest. "Good-bye, Father," she said. "See you at the funeral."

Ardelle and Jeanie stood in silence watching him go. Ardelle was smiling. Jeanie was not.

"God bless the good father," her aunt said as Ray pulled open the car door and twisted his skinny body inside. Then, suddenly and almost too eagerly, she lifted her little pinched chin and waved her hand in small circles like a queen. "God bless you very much!" she called after the priest.

In the distance, they could see the glint of Father Ray's teeth through the windshield. Obviously, he had heard.

The whole scene made Jeanie sick.

"Oh, please, Aunt Ardelle," she said. "How come you're asking God to bless him when he needs it least of everyone?"

"Jeanette?"

"I mean, there are people out there who really need God's help, if there is a God, I mean. And Father Ray isn't one of them. He's all taken care of. I'm telling you."

She expected Ardelle to disagree quickly, but there was silence for a moment instead, and then she answered, speaking in a soft murmur of a voice, a voice filled with thinking.

"It's true," she said, "a lot of people need God's love more than Father Ray." She paused and wet her lips before going on.

"I suppose you're thinking of yourself, Jeanette," she said at last. "And I'm sure—"

"Not at all!" Jeanie came back right away. "I'm not thinking of me at all!"

"You don't mean you?" Ardelle sounded doubtful.

"No," Jeanie said firmly. "I'm thinking of someone else. Someone who really could use some love right now. I mean, she'll be okay in time. I'm sure she will. But her life is about to change, and she's not the strongest person in the world. But she's probably a lot stronger than she realizes, and maybe someone like God could help her realize that."

"You don't mean you?"

"No, Aunt Ardelle," said Jeanie, "I'm thinking of someone else entirely."

"Well, I'm sure God blesses *her*," she said, turning to go inside the house for the night. It was getting cold standing out in the driveway. "I am sure God blesses her."

Jeanie hoped Aunt Ardelle was right, not just saying it this time, for Sherry's sake.

 It was past midnight when Sherry finally finished packing for her trip to Boston. It shouldn't have taken so long, but she couldn't decide what to wear to the rehearsal dinner. She knew she'd be sitting next to Charles. She didn't want to send him the wrong message, of course, but she wanted him to remember, the way she would be remembering.

So finally she settled on a black Chanel she'd only worn once in Miami, on a date with the Colombian doctor, months ago. It was too sophisticated for Brazil. He liked more skin.

And then, after that was decided, she realized she had never asked Alice what shoes to wear, so she stayed up another hour trying on the bridesmaid dress with every pair of black heels in her closet. None of them looked right.

Finally, she picked two pairs to take with her, and then she needed to wash some stockings, and do her nails, and shave her legs. . . .

The fact was, she was too pumped-up to go to bed so early.

She was going back; for the first time in the longest time, she was going home.

People she had known forever would be there, watching her, waiting. Would she remember everyone's name? Would she still smoke her unfiltereds and swear in front of the grown-ups and laugh that bitchy laugh? Would she dance the slow dances with Charles? Would the Judge pretend to kiss her hello? Would he ask about her work? Would he even look her in the eye?

The phone rang. Brazil, late.

"I knew you'd still be up," he said as hello, voice made smaller by the connection from Tampa.

"What if I wasn't?"

"Not a question. I knew you would be. You're all bent out of shape about this wedding," Brazil said matter-of-factly. "It's that faggot. Seeing him again has you hot as a pig on a spit."

"Please."

"Admit it, you can't wait to jump into bed with him."

"You know, Brazil," Sherry said, "you really can be a jerk sometimes." She laughed.

"You didn't say you wouldn't."

"Wouldn't what?"

"Fuck him."

"This is stupid," Sherry said. She knew better than to promise fidelity to Brazil. No matter what he said, he liked it better uncertain.

"Are you saying I'm stupid?"

"Forget it," Sherry said. "Why are you calling so late?"

"Emergency at home."

"Is everything okay?" Sherry asked quickly. The image of Jeanie, sleeping baby on her hip, flashed through her head, making her heart ache a little with affection.

"Everything's fine. Jeanie's father kicked. She had to go all the way back to—"

"Lost Corners. That's right. I know."

Silence on the line.

Then: "You *know*?" It didn't even sound like Brazil.

"Yeah, I know," Sherry said. "Jeanie came over here yesterday. She needed to find out where you were staying in Tampa."

"Oh."

"Uh-huh," Sherry said. She couldn't help smiling, thinking of Brazil sitting alone in his hotel room, freaking out.

"She went over to your house, huh?"

"That's what I said."

"And you gave her my phone number?"

"Yep."

"And then?"

"And then—what?"

"Fuck it, Sherry, you just want to make me squirm, right?"

"Yep."

"Well, fuck you." He slammed down the phone.

Sherry checked her watch. She'd give him five minutes.

The phone rang in four.

"Hello, dearest," Sherry said, picking up.

"Let me guess—you two bitches sat around all afternoon complaining about me, right?" Brazil sounded as if he had just taken a flight of stairs.

"Something like that."

"Well, the both of you obviously don't know how good you've got it with me."

"Damn straight!" Sherry giggled. She couldn't help herself.

"Fuck you!" Brazil slammed down the phone again.

"Very mature," Sherry said. She checked her watch. She'd give him three minutes this time, then she'd call Tampa and apologize.

He called in one.

First words: "You're loving this, aren't you?"

"No, no, no!" Sherry was beginning to feel sorry for him. "Brazil, sweetheart," she said, "I don't think we even talked about you."

"You didn't?" Obvious displeasure.

"We talked about Jeanie's father and my father and going home and babies and life in general. I think your name was mentioned once. Once."

"Once?"

"Just once, sweetheart, okay?"

"Okay." Brazil cleared his throat, still uneasy. He tried to picture the two of them, facing each other in Sherry's black leather and rosewood living room, chatting away the afternoon.

"Did you like her?" he asked at last.

"Well," Sherry said slowly; she hadn't expected this from Brazil, "I thought she was great, actually. She's really survived a lot."

"Yeah."

Neither of them knew what to say for a minute. Finally, Sherry spoke. "Your kid's real cute," she said. She was surprised the words hurt so much coming out.

"He's a good little guy."

"Yeah," Sherry said. "So, how's Tampa?"

"Okay. Just your typical, run-of-the-mill triple murder trial." Brazil was trying hard to be his old self again, with some success. "You know—virgin sacrifices, corrupt cops, missing corpses. All in a day's work."

"Right," said Sherry. She was rummaging through her suitcase now, making sure she hadn't forgotten anything. "Well, at least it doesn't sound boring."

"It's okay." Pause. "But I miss you."

He missed her? Suddenly, the words sounded strange and misplaced.

"Do you miss Jeanie, too?" Sherry asked. She wasn't angry, just curious.

"Oh come on, Sherry," said Brazil in his best good-ol'-boy voice, "give me a break."

"Do you?"

He waited a few moments before answering, but he knew he had no choice but to tell the truth. Sherry already knew the answer. "As a matter of fact," he said, "I do."

"That's nice."

She said it without emotion because she had no idea how to feel. On one hand, she was relieved to know that Brazil had enough goodness in him to care about Jeanie, because she deserved that from him, but at the same time, she was struck by the realization that he had been loving Jeanie and missing her and caring about her all along—*all this time*. It had never been just the two of them, Sherry and Brazil. In fact, it had always been the three of them, always. And she was the interloper, not Jeanie.

"Sherry?"

"Yep."

"You know I love you, darlin'."

"I know it."

And the truth was, she did know. He did love her.

"But you love her, too," she said. "Right?"

"Right." He sounded sad.

Sherry sighed.

"Are you crying?" Brazil asked.

"No. You want me to or something?"

"I want you to say something at least."

"There's nothing to say."

Sherry lay down on the bed and closed her eyes. A minute passed with dead air between them.

"Sherry?"

"Yes."

"You're never coming back to Miami, are you?"

Sherry opened her eyes in surprise, both at the idea, which had never crossed her mind, and at the unmistakable sound of fear in Brazil's voice. So exposed. So unlike him.

She sighed again. "I'll be back," she said. There was really no choice.

"But then you'll leave and go back to him."

She thought of Charles for a second, his voice of tears, his slender shoulders, and his murky green eyes.

"I doubt it," she said.

"You doubt it?"

"Brazil!" Sherry sat up on her bed and dropped her legs over the side, "this conversation is absurd."

"You're mad as hell at me, aren't you?" he answered.

"Not mad, just—"

"Just?"

"Just—I don't know."

"Christ! I've never heard you say 'I don't know' so many times in my life," Brazil shouted.

"Sorry."

"Sorry!"

More dead air. It was almost one. Sherry knew if she didn't sleep now, she'd sleepwalk through the wedding. And there was nothing left to say. There was nothing to say, period.

"I've got to go," Sherry said. "My plane leaves really early."

"Wait." Brazil was still using his loud voice. "We can't hang up until we're back to normal here. Let's talk some more. We can work everything out. I know we can."

"Look," Sherry said, "nothing has changed, okay?"

"You mean it?"

She hated to lie, but—"I mean it," she said.

"All right," said Brazil. He was onto her, but he knew he couldn't push it. "All right," he said again. Then: "Did you wrap everything up with that sicko Manuel?"

"Oh, shit!" She had completely forgotten.

"What?"

"God, I'm really glad you asked," Sherry said. "You've got to do me a big favor."

"Anything."

"You've got to come over here and feed my new kitten this weekend."

"Wow, Sherry darlin', that's wonderful," Brazil said, suddenly sounding a little perplexed. Maybe she would stay in Miami after all. "I didn't know you were going to replace Pansy."

"Well, I did." She couldn't tell him, not now anyway. She was too tired. And it was all too complicated.

"Pansy Junior is in good hands."

"I know," Sherry said. "Thanks."

"Thank you!"

He began to hum to fill the silence.

"Brazil, I've got to get some rest," Sherry said. She felt so exhausted that she could barely whisper the words.

"Okay . . ." He wanted to keep talking. As long as he could hear her voice, she was still his.

"I'm going to hang up."

"Wait—"

"No, really, I'm hanging up now."

"Just another minute."

"No," said Sherry, and then, without pause, she clicked the receiver down to cut their connection. " 'Bye," she said into the silence of her room, but in the stillness, she was sure she could hear Brazil weeping.

Because he was.

**45** She had set the alarm for 6:00 A.M., but the doorbell woke her up first, stabbing the dawn hard and loud in the middle of a dream about babies and blood.

Sherry jackknifed up in bed and grabbed her clock.

Five forty-seven A.M.

What the hell?

The doorbell rang again, seeming louder and angrier than ever in the grainy azure quiet of first light.

It rang again, insistent, three times.

Sherry sat paralyzed in bed, scared to move, scared to find out who could be outside wanting some part of her now, some explanation or apology or answer.

Was it Belinda—distracted and confused and needing to talk the darkness away? Something was wrong with the story, right? She was having second thoughts again. She wanted her byline off it. She wanted to go to the cops. She wanted Sherry to tell her one more time how Manuel would survive.

Or maybe it was Brazil at her door—breathless and hokey-faced and bursting with guilty love. He had driven the night through from Tampa, right?—rehearsing some story about his everlasting devotion, omitting Jeanie as usual, hoping Sherry would tell him that she loved him just the same as before, no hard feelings.

Or could it be Manuel? He was angry and vengeful and feeling betrayed at last, there to claim his property, demanding she tell him the truth, but then somehow not caring as he stepped closer and touched her—

No!

No, it couldn't be. He wouldn't bother with the bell; he'd simply slip the lock and come inside.

So then, who?

Sherry listened for the sound of the buzzer again, but in the silence she suddenly heard something else, something terribly familiar: the noisy crackling of a dozen cranked-up police radios, crashing against each other in the thin dawn air like an orchestra of bad news.

Cops? On Lemonlime Road? There had to be some car wreck or fire going down, or maybe there was another riot in the Black Grove. Or maybe the wife across the street had finally figured out the maid wasn't just cleaning her husband's socks.

The terror dropped off Sherry like dead skin. She pulled on a robe, ran to the front of the house, and pulled open the door.

A smiling almost-bald man in a wrinkled plaid jacket stood on the porch. Behind him, the street was filled with a squadron of police cars, sirens silent but flashing blue-and-white, two ambulances, and the boxy brown van of the Medical Examiner's Office. Cops were everywhere.

"Well, well! If it isn't Sherry Estabrook, *Miami Citizen* staff reporter—I didn't know you lived here!" The man on the porch was talking to her in a friendly voice, as if they were old pals. Sherry stared at him for thirty seconds before she realized it was Teddy Wasynczuk, from Miami Homicide.

"Sergeant Wasynczuk?" She rubbed her eyes and looked over his shoulder for the story. All she saw was chaos, more chaos than normal for a crime scene, cops running and shouting in every direction, neighbors holding hands and crying, police dogs on long chains howling like wolves at a fading moon, and overhead the dull *thud-thud-thud* of low-flying helicopters. *She'd been dreaming of babies and blood.* Maybe this wasn't happening.

But it was. It was. She could smell the pungent aroma of Cuban coffee wafting over from a group of detectives, huddled in a tight circle, talking excitedly on the street in front of her house. She knew most of them, but not well enough to dream them up on a night when she needed sleep so desperately.

"Look, it is five forty-seven in the morning," she told the cop, hoping not to sound too bitchy but feeling that way. She wanted an explanation, fast.

The cop checked his watch. "It's early, I know," he answered apologetically, sounding weary himself. He stepped inside and motioned Sherry to sit down on the foyer couch. "But, Sherry Estabrook, my dear *Miami Citizen* staff reporter, we happen to have a double next door, and I need to ask you some questions. Soon as I'm done, you can go right back to bed. I promise."

A double?

The cop moved to close the door, but Sherry pushed by him and took a dozen fast strides across her front lawn. Just beyond the driveway, she could see two investigators she recognized from the D.A.'s Office taping a yellow crime-scene ribbon over the Beauregards' garage door. One of them was still wearing his slippers.

Sherry turned frantically to find Wasynczuk—there had to be some mistake—but he was still inside. She ran back to the house.

"A double *homicide*?" she asked him, a little surprised she was able to speak. Her whole body was suddenly rigid with horror, rigid except her heart, which jumped wildly in her chest with the power of canon fire. She could barely feel the tiny kitten rubbing her legs, waiting to be fed.

The cop nodded and held up two fingers. "Homicide times *dos*," he said. "An old couple. Husband and wife. Execution style—doesn't even look like a robbery." He shook his head sadly. "Good Lord," he went on, sounding resigned, "what is Miami coming to?"

Sherry dropped to the couch in one stiff, trancelike move. Her mind, too, had stopped functioning. She couldn't think of anything to say. She couldn't think of anything to think.

Wasynczuk sat beside her and pulled out a small pad.

"Were you home last night?" he asked, rolling his eyes familiarly. He recalled chatting it up with Sherry just a few weeks earlier, at the scene of some routine cocaine hit near the dumpster at the Seven Stars restaurant. She'd been her usual self that day— funny and hard-assed and ambitious as all get-out. She obviously took mornings hard. Especially mornings when her neighbors got wasted. "Sherry," he asked again, "were you home last night? Just bear with me, okay?"

"Okay," Sherry managed to answer numbly. "Yeah, I was here." She couldn't even feel her lips moving.

"What time?"

"All night."

"Help me out, Sherry," the cop said, still sounding friendly. "Starting at?"

"Um, I don't know," she said slowly. "I guess I got home around six or seven."

"Hear anything? See anything? Anything unusual?"

"Am I a suspect?" Sherry blurted out. She meant it seriously, but the cop took it as a joke and laughed politely. "You reporters!" he said. "Always looking for the angle."

Sherry didn't understand. Was he kidding? She stared at him for a minute, waiting for more. He stared back.

"You're tired, huh, Sherry Estabrook?" he said finally. He sounded terribly sweet. She remembered suddenly; Wasynczuk was a good guy. He liked the *Citizen*. Loved to see his name in print. He wasn't angry at her. He wasn't even going to yell at her. He had no clue.

"Yeah, I'm beat," she said. She instinctively reached down and petted the kitten still brushing her ankles plaintively.

"Let's just get this over with, okay?"

"Okay." She nodded once.

"So, did you hear or see anything suspicious last night?"

"Nothing."

"Have you seen anyone unusual coming or leaving your neighbors' house in recent days or weeks?"

"No." She shook her head for emphasis. It was the truth.

"Did you know them?"

"Not really."

"Just hello and good-bye? Those kind of people?"

"Not even," said Sherry. She wondered if she should tell him about Pansy.

No, of course not. Was she out of her mind? If she mentioned Pansy, she would sound insane. And it was such a long story. And he might not understand. And he might wonder what Pansy had to do with anything. And she might have to answer more questions, and by accident she might end up telling him about . . .

No—

Not yet, anyway. She couldn't.

It was too awful to believe. So awful it couldn't be. Right?

Sherry looked at the cop. He was checking his watch.

It occurred to her that even if she wanted to tell him everything, he was done with her already, standing up, tucking his pen and pad away into an inside coat pocket.

When he noticed Sherry looking at him, he smiled wanly and then shrugged.

"Who knows," he said, "maybe we'll find ten tons of coke in the garage."

"Maybe," said Sherry.

"My opinion? This was way too brutal to be random," he

added, as if he were answering a question. "I mean, it's not like he got 'em while they were sleeping or anything."

Sherry wasn't sure she wanted to hear more. She already knew the ending.

"Terrible," she said.

"Nope"—Wasynczuk was rolling now—"whoever it was woke them up, gagged them good, made them strip naked, and then tied them into their lawn chairs in the living room!"

Sherry nodded and inhaled deeply. Her stomach was upside down, but she had to hold on. She had to—to survive, to escape, and then to come back and make everything right again.

"Lawn chairs," she said, trying to sound like a reporter.

"He even made them face each other so they could see what was going to happen next," the cop continued, scratching his chin, "but we don't know who he wasted first. We'll have to wait for the autopsy, I guess." He grimaced.

Sherry inhaled again, and all at once she knew she needed to get outside. She bolted for the door. The cop followed her.

He caught up with her at the edge of the driveway. "You look shook up," he said, laying a hand on her shoulder.

"You just never think," Sherry inhaled deeply again and then exhaled a long sigh, "you just never think it will happen in your neighborhood."

Wasynczuk bobbed his head knowingly. "I've heard that a hundred times," he said. So had Sherry.

A uniformed officer stepped out of the Beauregards' front door, scanned the scene, and then, spotting Wasynczuk, frantically waved him inside.

"Oh, well, duty calls," he told Sherry. He nodded politely and then started to walk off, but Sherry stopped him, catching him by the back of the coat a few yards from the spot where Alvin had killed her cat a month before.

"Teddy!" she frantically called out. "Teddy!"

The cop twisted around, a bit taken aback, and looked at Sherry. She was a wreck, eyes just beginning to bleed tears, face all splotchy with fear and confusion. Poor kid.

He held her by both shoulders. "Now, Sherry," he said, "pull yourself together. I'm telling you, we'll get the killer who did this. You will be safe. I promise you."

She shook her head. That's not what she wanted, not at all. She wanted something else: to be absolutely sure.

"I just have to know," she asked, gasping lightly between the words, "please tell me—where were they shot?"

Now, Wasynczuk thought, this was like the old Sherry Estabrook, always digging for the grisly details. He obliged her. "Well, he cut 'em up pretty good first, but as far as we can tell, he got 'em right here." Wasynczuk folded his right hand into the shape of a gun and laid his index finger against his neck. "Right here," he repeated, "both of them."

"Both of them," Sherry repeated mechanically. She stared into the blur of space beyond Wasynczuk and waited to feel something, like outrage or shock or fear. But nothing came.

The neck. Of course. She knew that.

Manuel.

The cop was watching her, she could sense it. He was confused by her reaction—so dazed! Especially for a reporter. Maybe, Sherry thought, maybe I should act surprised. But she couldn't muster the energy to pretend. She could barely muster the energy to stay standing. She leaned slightly toward the cop, looking woozy enough to faint.

Wasynczuk caught her by the elbow, steadied her, and then squeezed her shoulders familiarly. "Do you have a friend you can call?" he asked. "Someone to keep you company?"

Sherry shook her head vaguely. "I'm going home for a wedding in an hour actually," she answered, all emotion drained from her voice. "I'm leaving Miami."

"Great!" said Wasynczuk, and he seemed to mean it. "By the time you get back, this will all be solved. Don't think about it for a minute."

"I won't," said Sherry. Then she smiled as best she could and walked away.

 She was the last one on the plane, and the only passenger in first class. The stewardess greeted her by name a few seconds before the engines turned over.

Sherry nodded brusquely and looked away. She didn't want to connect with anybody for the next three hours. She needed to be alone, to think, to prepare, to remember, to listen for answers in the silence above the clouds.

"Coffee, Miss Estabrook?" The stewardess was suddenly leaning close beside her, floppy red bow at her neck, plastic grin in place, talking in a loud, deliberate Carolina drawl. "We have French Roast, Colombian, good old Sanka, decaf, and something called Mocha Java, which I hear is just wonderful though I must admit I've never tasted it myself, which, of course, isn't to say that y'all might not be brave enough to give it a go and—"

Something stopped her cold. It was Sherry. She had removed her sunglasses and launched an atomic acid-rimmed glare through eyes turned almost ruby from crying.

"Now listen," she said, speaking in a low voice intended to sound scary and tragic, "I cannot be disturbed. That's the rule for today. All I want is a Coke with lemon every half hour. That is it. Don't ask me any questions about my work. Don't make small talk about my family. Don't tell me about the weather in Boston. Just leave me alone. That's what I'm paying for."

The stewardess smiled tightly and then turned and took off down the aisle at a clip, cheap stockings scratching beneath snug polyester. A moment later, Sherry twisted around in her seat to see her whispering with the other red-bowed stewardesses, pointing toward first class. They were all shaking their heads and frowning.

"Oh, excuse me," Sherry said sarcastically, but not loud enough for anyone to hear. She twisted back and looked out the window.

It was beginning to rain.

Would it be snowing in Boston? It was unlikely so early in the season, but hoped so. The thought of snow, so peaceful, falling to earth with the gentle soundlessness of death, made her want to sleep, if only for a few minutes.

She shut her eyes and let dark exhaustion swallow her. It felt like drowning, but that was okay, drowning was release. . . .

"I'm sorry, Miss Estabrook, I hate to bother you, but could you please fasten your safety belt?" A different stewardess this time, same sixty-decibel accent. She stood by uneasily until Sherry was done and then scurried away.

A moment later, the plane began to back out of its berth. Sherry shut her eyes again and waited. When she opened them later—she wasn't sure how much time had passed—the plane was airborne but still flying low enough to see the massive hotels and apartment buildings cluttering the shoreline from Miami up to Boca.

A dip, then a lift, and they were above the clouds at last.

This is what she had been waiting for, hanging suspended between two places, out of reach of everyone except herself, with time enough to breathe and dream awake and decide. There were so many decisions to make.

The first one was this: Should she tell the cops who killed the Beauregards? The crime was so grotesque—why did he have to make them *strip*, for Christ's sake?—that she knew the *right* answer immediately. The answer was yes.

But then—

Sherry squeezed her eyes shut tight and clamped her hands over her ears, trying desperately to stop the next thought from being born in her mind. It came anyway, and it came fast.

If she turned Manuel into the cops, she knew, the story would die. Her story would die.

She could say good-bye forever to the huge front-page package featuring one very quotable sixteen-year-old cocaine assassin played prominently beneath her byline in 18-point type. She could forget the awards, the dinner with Newman and the publisher, the thoughtful interviews on TV about crime reporting and journalism ethics. Instead, the Manuel piece would become humiliating fodder for supermarket tabloids: teenage hit man, infatuated with pretty reporter, kills neighbors in cat-murder revenge plot.

Sherry dropped her head into her hands and began to cry.

Her sadness was so overwhelming, she was surprised the tears came so quietly, without sobs. Still, her entire body was shivering, as if she had suddenly been caught in a freak spring snowstorm. She pulled her jacket tighter to her body and pulled up the collar to cover her neck; as she did, she suddenly had a flash of the Beauregards bound and gagged, heads slammed back by the force of gunshot, blood spurting from their eyes and mouths.

"Oh, God, no!" she said out loud, but in her horror, the words came out as a whisper. "What have I done?"

All at once, Sherry was struck with a crushing hammer blow of grief, and she didn't have to think long to remember why it felt so terribly familiar—she had felt it exactly three times before. First when she saw her father, standing in the center of his grand law library and smiling obsequiously, pocket a neatly folded roll of bills. Second, when he told her that a young girl had, in truth, been raped, and raped brutally, at One Hundred Endless Horizon Lane. And finally, a moment later, when he sanctimoniously informed her that she would never have gotten into a respectable college at all if it hadn't been for his deceit.

Now, she thought, wouldn't the Judge just *love* the irony of her horrible predicament? What had he called her that day in his library? Spoiled and naive, Sherry remembered, and the pain of the epithets bruised her still. He had claimed she would never find success on her terms, and now—

And now, Sherry knew, she was about to prove him right.

No!

Suddenly Sherry knew what she had to do—she would not let the story die. Not like this. Someday soon, very soon, she would tell the cops who killed the Beauregards. But first the Manuel story would run as it should. Everyone wanted the story to run—Jack and Newman, and even Belinda to a degree. Christ, even Manuel wanted the story to run. He was dying for his story to appear in black-and-white so that he could get on with his new life, just as she planned to get on with hers. So he was a sick kid, very, very sick, Sherry thought, and another grotesque image of the Beauregards bound and gagged flashed through her mind. All at once she knew Manuel Velo, age sixteen, would probably never stop killing. He'd never escape his past. But once his story ran on the front page of the *Miami Citizen*, at least he'd be killing far away from her and everyone she loved, in Mexico, if that's where he really planned to run.

The tears stopped, and Sherry sat up in her seat, letting go a long, relieved sigh.

The plan wasn't so bad, she told herself—it wasn't bad at all. After all, if the Baby Lips package ran, Manuel would leave Miami forever, and a whole cocaine ring would be closed down. Countless murders would be *prevented*. She was doing the right thing, and not just for herself. What difference did it make *why* he was telling her, if the outcome was so damn respectable? She'd have to take a drive up to Boca to ask that exact question of Dr. Klein once this whole story was done and buried.

Sherry sighed again and waited for the tension twisting up her shoulders to dissipate, and it did, but not completely.

I guess, Sherry said to herself, I guess I am waiting to feel ashamed. Another flash of the Beauregards—this time a close-up of Laura, desperately begging for mercy. Sherry looked out the window, anticipating more tears, but none fell. Instead, slowly but surely, all she felt was the creeping prickly heat of fear— fear that someone would figure it all out too soon—someone like Belinda or Brazil or Eladio.

"I'm so fucking alone," Sherry blurted out, her voice so desperate she barely recognized it. "And I'm so fucking scared."

Sherry felt someone standing above her. Yet another stewardess.

"Did you want something, Miss Estabrook?" she asked, tilting her head to one side, smiling bravely.

"No." Sherry said it firmly, but not harshly. The poor woman was just another human being; who knows what troubles she had.

She turned back to the window.

Pretty soon, the plane would dip again, this time beneath the clouds, and Boston would open up before her like a mirage. Before she knew it, she would be face-to-face with her past: her parents, Charles, Alice. . . .

Damn it all, Sherry thought, why did Alice have to get married now?

Why indeed? She broke into a short, unhappy laugh. "You're just jealous," she scolded herself, this time so softly no one could hear her. But the thought stuck in her mind anyway, the way the truth always does. She imagined Alice walking down the aisle of the First, her lovely hazel eyes glistening with tears of joy. In a year or two, there would be a cute baby and a nice house and then every other accoutrement of domesticity: a Volvo in the garage, piano lessons at the local music school, PTA meetings on Tuesday nights. It's as inevitable as slush in March, Sherry thought. Poor Alice.

Another ironic laugh. Poor *me*, Sherry thought, poor me.

She closed her eyes and all at once heard Jeanie's wide-open, honest twang filling her living room on Lemonlime Road, talking about her life and her baby and *her* husband. Of course she sounded honest, Sherry thought, she had nothing to hide. She was the one wearing the wedding band. In the end, she was the one Brazil went home to.

I am the one, Sherry thought, who wakes up alone.

A small fluttering to her right. A stewardess, of course.

"Are you done with these?" she asked, gesturing toward the tray table of the next chair. Sherry looked over to see three plastic cups of Coke with lemon, bubbles gone flat, ice melted.

"Holy shit, I'm sorry!" she said quickly. She hadn't even heard them arrive. Just as she had ordered.

The stewardess raised her eyebrows into a dainty arc. "So are you through here?" she said with just enough sweetness and sarcasm in her voice to make Sherry feel terrible. "I can get you a fresh cup if you want."

"Listen, I'm sorry—"

"It's perfectly all right."

"I was so busy thinking that I didn't even remember I'd asked for them—"

"That's just fine," said the stewardess. She had finished gathering up the glasses on a tray and was about to take them away when suddenly she turned back to Sherry and smiled. "It's clear and cool in Boston," she said. "But they say it might snow this weekend."

Sherry smiled back. "Thank you," she said, and she meant it.

A minute later, the plane began its slow plunge toward Boston, finally piercing the broken clouds above the choppy brown waters of the harbor.

In the distance, Sherry could see the city, its serious black and gray towers lit dimly by the midmorning winter sun. She picked out the voluptuous golden dome of the State House and then the clumsy silhouette of the Pru Tower. Finally, almost unintentionally, she spotted the austere gray courthouse, built square in the heart of the city, where her father passed judgment day in and day out.

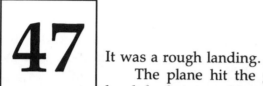 It was a rough landing.

The plane hit the ground too fast and too hard, brakes crunching too loud, before it finally and abruptly hurtled to a stop just short of the end of the runway.

After a moment of silence, the pilot's voice came over the loudspeaker. "Sorry about that," he said in a good-ol'-boy drawl that automatically made Sherry think of Brazil. But just for a second. She had to put Miami out of her mind, completely, for the next two days. She had to, to stay sane.

"Miss Estabrook?"

It was the first stewardess, handing Sherry her carry-on suitcase from the overhead compartment.

Sherry took the bag and then headed for the exit.

"Miss Estabrook?"

Sherry turned back to the stewardess, half expecting a few final words of reproach.

But instead, the woman was smiling warmly at her. "Don't forget your coat, Miss Estabrook," she said in an accent somehow less irritating than before, "it's brutal out there."

A coat? Sherry groaned out loud. In her rush out of Miami, she'd left it hanging in the front hall closet.

"Miss Estabrook?" The stewardess was considering Sherry closely, looking concerned."Is everything all right?"

"Fine," said Sherry. "It's nothing. I just forgot my coat at home."

"Oh, dear! That's just dreadful!"

"No problem," Sherry came back fast, but frustration and dread were already taking hold. "I'll survive," she said.

"Well, I'm sure you will!" The stewardess laughed lightly, faked an exaggerated shiver, and then stood back to let Sherry off the plane. "But you be careful," she said sweetly in parting, "you be careful out there, or you just might end up with ice in your veins instead of blood."

Her father's driver, Lewis, was waiting for her at the main terminal. As usual.

And as usual, he escorted Sherry to the car without a word. A few minutes later, they were zooming up Route 1A toward Marblehead.

It was a familiar ride—in the old days she used to count the seconds between potholes and bumps—but this time Sherry couldn't help leaning forward in her seat, as excited as a tourist, to stare out the window and watch the city turn into suburb and finally into the narrow, peaceful roads of home. But then . . .

But then, something stopped her cold. She had to look away. It was too much to see it all at once—the leafless trees covered with new snow, skeletons against the white sky, the careful clapboard mansions of the Neck, windows framed by rigid gowns of flowered chintz, the stiff-backed runners defying the cold to race along the shore, exhaling tiny puffs of frozen air and Yankee anxiety. It was too much all at once, like seeing a photograph of someone recently dead, someone once beloved.

She lay down on the seat and closed her eyes to shut out every particle of light, only opening them again when she felt Lewis take the turn to the house.

The car stopped, and a second later the back door swung open.

"Is something wrong, miss?" Lewis asked, peering inside at Sherry lying curled on her side, one arm flung over her face.

"No," she replied quietly. "Just remembering . . ." She shook her head to shake away the thoughts tangled inside.

Then she pulled herself up, got out of the car, and slowly walked toward the house where she grew up.

48

She arrived at the wedding rehearsal with five minutes to spare, but already the block was parked up on both sides. After circling twice, Sherry ended up wedging her mother's too-wide, too-long Mercedes onto a shoulder of dirt down a hill near the end of the street, against a hedge at the edge of someone's tennis court. The spot was illegal, but cops didn't visit this neighborhood too often. It was one of Marblehead's oldest and the second-most exclusive, after the Neck, of course. The houses were rambling, dramatic Victorians mainly, with a few stately brick Georgians thrown in, all of them set far back from the road on an acre or more of formally groomed lawn. The cars parked outside were Jaguars and Cadillacs in somber shades of gray and blue. And except for the warm yellow lights glowing from within each house, there was not a sign of life anywhere.

Sherry pulled up the emergency brake and headed for the First, built on the corner of two of the neighborhood's most lovely streets, surrounded by arching maples and sycamores. She could see the church from a hundred yards; it was all lit up like a stained-glass candle, beckoning with its sedate and gracious beauty.

How many Sundays, she wondered, had she trudged up this road, five steps behind Mother and Father, to hear Reverend Foster intellectualize God, make brief mention of Jesus, compliment the junior choir, wax poetic about the upcoming bake sale, and finally conclude with a few words about the cost of the church's upkeep?

Hundreds, probably . . .

She hadn't been back for years, since she'd left for Miami, actually. But still, she knew the place by heart. Just reaching for the front door brought back memories, how crazy. . . .

Sherry stepped inside.

That smell! Linseed oil and Norell perfume—

She took one stride forward, but then . . .

312

But then, how was she going to do this—this entrance part? She hadn't planned it at all; she needed to get her bearings first. Without thinking, she dodged left, into a corner of shadow near the last pew.

Okay, where was Charles?

Nearly a dozen people were gathered at the front of the church, laughing in that loud and artificial way she recognized too well, shaking hands, chattering away, heads aslant. But not him.

Near the altar, she could see Alice and Jamie holding hands as if for life, conferring seriously with Reverend Foster, who looked so much older than before but still wore his stature in the community like a crown. He had the carriage of nobility, shoulders thrown back, chin always tilted slightly skyward, lips pursed in an expectant, slightly bemused expression. He wore his pure white hair in an old-fashioned crew cut, and underneath his robes on Sunday, Sherry remembered, he wore Topsiders. His sailboat was named *Saving Grace*.

Alice smiled suddenly, a huge smile, putting practically every perfect tooth on display. She rose to her tiptoes, kissed Jamie, then turned back to the minister and asked an earnest question, and the three moved closer together.

A group of guys—they all looked like Jamie, same preppie haircut, same skinny loafers, same former-jock gait—were hanging together, joking and milling around the first pew. Sherry recognized most of them from school or the Bluemoor. The blond in the red sweater was named Tyler or Taylor or something like that, and he was supposed to be a fantastic water-polo player in college. She recognized the guy in the beige cardigan as Robbie Hazard. He went to Darmouth, then worked as an analyst on Wall Street, making eighty grand the first year out. For some reason, everyone knew about it.

And there was Paul, Alice's older brother, looking sweet and befuddled as usual, smoking a pipe, off by himself in a corner. He was a huge disappointment to them all, but naturally no one ever mentioned that. He'd dropped out of Williams after freshman year and then hitchhiked to Oregon in search of the meaning of life, only to return three years later with the notion he was a poet. And in fact, he eventually did get a book published—it was called *I've Seen the Sandinista Sunrise*—and his father threw a huge party at the Copley to celebrate, only Paul didn't show up.

Where was Charles?

Sherry stepped out of the shadow and took a few steps toward the front of the church. She couldn't see him anywhere.

But she could see Alice's mother, whispering in an agitated manner with Charlotte, Alice's little sister, who wasn't so little anymore. They were huddled together in the second pew, looking furtively at the man and woman sitting stiffly across the way—Jamie's parents, no doubt. Then came Alice's father out of nowhere, grinning wide, standing over them in his bright green sweater, talking in his chummy way, thumping his chest and then clasping his hands together in delight, and suddenly everyone was smiling and chatting as if they were the oldest friends on earth.

Sherry took a few steps closer, moving into the light.

And that's when Alice saw her.

"Oh, my God, you made it!" she cried out in a delicate voice, wriggling out of Jamie's hand and running toward Sherry. "I can't believe you're actually here."

The two friends embraced, just for a moment, and then Alice pulled away and took a long look at Sherry.

"I just want to make sure you're real," she said.

Sherry smiled awkwardly and shrugged. Why did she feel so embarrassed? "Hi, darlin'," she said finally, to break Alice's stare. "I'm real, okay?"

"You called me *'darling'*? I love it!"

"Oh, sorry," Sherry quickly backpedaled."That's just a habit I picked up in Miami. Everyone calls everyone darling."

"I *love* it!" Alice said again. She grabbed Sherry's hand. "Come say hello to Jamie. He's dying to meet you again. I'm always talking about us."

Sherry felt herself smiling, but she wasn't sure why. "Great," she answered and followed Alice down the aisle.

Jamie bounded forward to greet them.

"The famous Sherry Estabrook!" he said as soon as they were face-to-face. He took Sherry's hand in both of his and squeezed. "I know we met a long time ago at a party, but that was before I knew you were my future wife's best friend!"

"That was before you knew your future wife!" Alice chimed in. She sounded fine, but suddenly Sherry noticed that she was thinner than ever, and up close, her hazel eyes, usually so mesmerizing and bright, were shell-shocked. Even her lipstick wasn't on quite right; she'd missed the edges.

Sherry extricated her hand from Jamie's vigorous grasp and moved closer to Alice. "Are you all right?" she whispered, hoping Jamie would take the hint and get lost. "You look exhausted."

Alice smiled weakly, chin up, eyes scanning right and left to locate her mother. Jamie didn't move. He was waiting for the answer.

"I'm wonderful, Sherry," Alice said after an uncomfortable half minute had passed. "It's just that planning a wedding has been the hardest thing I've ever done in my life."

Jamie sighed loudly. "Tell her the truth, for God's sake, Alice," he snarled, "I thought you told her everything."

Alice dropped her chin to her chest and exhaled a little humming sound. It was a mannerism Sherry had almost forgotten. She said nothing.

"Well, fine!" Jamie said a few seconds later, and then turned and marched off to join his buddies near the first pew.

Sherry watched Alice, waiting. She exhaled, humming, once more, and then looked up and started to talk, in a frail, frantic voice Sherry did not recognize at all.

"Our parents aren't speaking," she said at last. "It's been hell, Sherry, they *hate* each other. We've almost had to cancel the wedding twice. They keep threatening not to come." She cast her eyes toward the second pew, where Jamie's parents were now in what seemed to be a pleasant conversation with Reverend Foster. "I can't take the pressure another minute. I just want it to be over. I don't even care about the wedding anymore."

Sherry pinched Alice's arm above the elbow. "Don't say that," she said. She didn't come all this way to see Alice and her marriage fall apart. She didn't come all this way for nothing.

"No, I mean it," Alice answered sadly. "Jamie and I have had some terrible fights. I'm not even sure I know him, really, I'm not sure I—"

"I said, don't say it!" insisted Sherry.

Alice shrugged. "Okay," she answered vaguely.

Sherry looked around the church again for Charles. No sign of him.

"Hey, tell me," she began, meaning to ask where he was, but then noticing Alice was struggling not to cry, "tell me what the problem is with Jamie's parents."

"It's *too* ridiculous."

"These things always are." Sherry's voice was soothing, full of old affection. "Tell me."

A pause. "It's money," Alice said finally, "if you can believe it."

Sherry couldn't. Between the two families, there was probably enough cash to buy and sell Mimi Lopez.

"Money?" Sherry asked.

"Money," said Alice, still sounding as if she might shatter. "Jamie's parents wouldn't pay for the honeymoon unless we went to Caneel Bay, where they went on their honeymoon a hundred zillion years ago, and we know it's very nice, but we really really wanted to go to this new resort in the Seychelles which is supposed to be fabulous, so my parents ended up paying, which isn't fair—"

"No—" said Sherry, shaking her head earnestly. She had already stopped listening—this *was* ridiculous—and was searching again for Charles.

Just then, Reverend Foster's voice filled the church, calling them all to the altar. "Let's get started," he was saying in that crotchety Brahmin accent Sherry had imitated for Brazil a dozen times, "We've got to make sure these two lovebirds get married without any mishaps or missteps or misbehaving."

Everyone laughed.

Except Charles, who was slowly emerging from his own black pillar of shadow near the side of the church. He had been there an hour, waiting. His eyes were fixed on Sherry.

They exchanged one glance, and then Sherry tried not to look back again. Oh, my God, she thought, completely stunned by the ache and power of what had just passed between them, this is going to hurt like hell.

She looked back at him, just for a second. But it was too late, already.

Charles was still standing at the edge of the crowd, half in darkness, eyes focused on Sherry. She took one look at the tender pull on his lips, and she knew what he wanted. *We never finished what we started*—he'd said that to her a million times since she moved away. It was killing her. *He* was killing her. She wanted him, too. How could this be?

She glanced over at him again. He was waiting. Their eyes locked for ten seconds, and then she broke away.

She had forgotten how beautiful he was, how fragile and

seductive, his olive eyes, his shoulders, his long and bony hands. Suddenly, she wanted to hear his sad voice against her neck again. Would Brazil ever love her the way Charles did? Could he, even? She had forgotten what it felt like to be loved that way. It was so wonderful, overwhelming, so complete. She had forgotten.

Sherry took a few steps closer to the altar, a few steps closer to Charles. How could this be, she wondered, this explosion of regret, so fast? Then she remembered—Brazil had loved Jeanie all along. She knew that now. And *here* was Charles calling her with his eyes, and she wanted to run to him and hold him and let him rest his head on her lap to cry. She wanted to cry with him, for everything.

But they stood apart and waited.

Reverend Foster was talking: "Now, this is a very straightforward affair," he said. "Should be very familiar to one and all. The groom and his best man—that would be Taylor, correct?—come out that door, the music starts, the ushers seat the mothers, the wedding party descends, we see the maid of honor come down by herself, that's lovely Charlotte, and then at last we have the immense pleasure of seeing Mr. Wheelwright escort dearest Alice down the aisle to her destiny.

"Shall we practice?"

Everyone nodded. Sherry and Charles exchanged another glance. He was smiling at her now, a smile filled with heartbreak. She recognized it from their last night together.

"Okay, let's move to the back of the church!" Alice was trying to sound cheerful, but her voice came out distant and strained. "I'll tell you the order of the wedding party." She started to prattle off names. Sherry and Charles were almost the last ones to march.

They walked toward each other.

"Hello, Sherry," Charles said, so softly she could barely hear him. "Welcome home."

"Thanks."

They stood in awkward silence for a moment, but then, suddenly, Charles took Sherry's left hand and lifted it into the light, inspecting her fingers closely. After another moment, he let it go and exhaled a long sigh of something that sounded like relief.

"Just checking," he said gently, looking away, embarrassed.

Sherry shook her head. Was he was looking for a ring? How insane—

"You were checking for what?" she asked.

Charles didn't answer, instead tilting his head toward Reverend Foster, who was in front of them all, waving his arms for quiet and shouting at the same time.

"Ladies and gentlemen," he said, "please pay attention! We are at that critical juncture where the music begins." He hummed a few bars of the wedding march and cued two ushers to seat the mothers. He hummed a minute longer and then started to wave the couples down the aisle.

It was their turn.

"Sherry and Charles!" announced the minister. Then, as they walked by: "Isn't it wonderful to see you two again!"

Charles smiled at Reverend Foster and then looked meaningfully at Sherry. She automatically smiled back, but inside she felt almost too weak to keep moving. All at once, she felt a relapse of unbearable fatigue—had everything really happened this morning? The Beauregards, the cops, the horror, the escape? It seemed so long ago, so far away from this church and these people. So far away from Charles.

He was watching her.

"I can tell something huge is bothering you," he said out of the side of his mouth as they continued slowly down the aisle. His tone was so intimate it made Sherry's heart contract in pain.

"I'm fine," she said.

"Sherry, you're talking to *Charles*," he chided her gently. "I know when something is bothering you from a hundred paces. I know when something is bothering you when you're in the next room."

Sherry inhaled sharply. "You *used* to know," she said. It was a weak defense.

"I still know you, Sherry," he said. "We had a lot of days and nights between us." His voice brimmed with sadness and regret.

She had no time to answer. They were near the end of the aisle, and Alice's mother directed them to opposite ends of the altar.

Reverend Foster's humming was suddenly louder, and Sherry looked up to see Alice walking down the aisle, reluctantly, on her father's arm. She stopped dead at the first pew.

"Few more steps!" urged Reverend Foster, "all the way up to the groom, please!"

Alice's father was beaming, oblivious. He strode forward,

pulling Alice along. A second later, Jamie stepped up and took command.

"Get it together, dear," he ordered Alice loudly enough for everyone to hear. "Come stand next to me."

Alice obeyed.

"Good girl," he said.

Everyone looked away and waited.

Finally, Reverend Foster came through. "Perfect performance," he pronounced. "I certainly don't think we need to do it again!"

Nods and murmurs of agreement all around.

"Basically, after everyone is all arranged just so, I say this and that and tie the knot, and then Alice and Jamie march off to blissful matrimony, and everyone follows. Very straightforward. Couldn't be more straightforward. Marvelous."

Sherry looked over at Alice. She was still facing the altar where Jamie had positioned her, standing motionless.

But Jamie was in action. He clapped his hands to get everyone's attention and then opened his arms wide as if he wanted to embrace them all with one grand gesture.

"Friends," he began, "friends and family members—all of you are especially important to me, to me and my lovely bride-to-be. We adore you all!" He didn't bother to look at Alice. "Please go home, get an hour or two of rest, and we'll see you all at eight at the rehearsal dinner at the club!" He started to give directions, but Sherry had already turned him off. If she moved fast, she could get out of the church before Charles forced her to tell him why she looked upset, she could escape before he forced her to surrender—

But, of course, he was already at her side, hand resting lightly on her lower back, whispering as he guided her away, down the aisle.

"I *hate* Jamie," he was saying. "He treats Alice like she's invisible. She deserves better."

"Yes!" Sherry said, suddenly energized. This was completely unexpected—Charles had never liked Alice in the old days. He thought she "encouraged" Sherry too much. But now—

"What really gets me is the way he orders her around, like she's a bimbo or something." Charles was still whispering urgently, holding Sherry's arm conspiratorially. "I don't understand why she takes it."

"She's numb," said Sherry.

"Numb?"

"You know, she's freaking out. She's getting married tomorrow, that's a gigantic thing, and they've been having some problems," Sherry went on, drawn in almost against her will.
"Weddings are always full of little miseries. Remember when
Nina and John got married? Nina's mother almost smacked John's
mother with her purse during the reception—"

They both laughed.

"But then everything was kissy-kissy a year later when Nina
had the baby."

"Oh, yeah," Charles remembered.

"So everything will be kissy-kissy with Alice and Jamie, I'm
sure—"

Charles shook his head. "This is *much* worse, Sherry," he
said, pulling his eyebrows together in that wonderful, serious
way that she hadn't seen in so long. "I'm not even sure Alice and
Jamie *like* each other."

"Well, I've got to admit, it sort of looks like that," Sherry
found herself agreeing.

"It's not too late for her to call it off." Charles was still excited.
"Sherry, what do you think? Maybe you should talk to her tonight."

They were huddled close, standing just outside a side door
of the church. Charles had led her there; it was behind a tall
hedge, out of sight of everyone.

"Tell her to call it off? Are you kidding?" Sherry said. She
couldn't believe Charles cared so much.

"What are friends for?" he asked.

"Look, they're just having a fight about their honeymoon,"
Sherry came back quickly. Things were bad, but she definitely
was not going to tell Alice to cancel the wedding. "Everything
will be fine once the wedding is over and they're lying on the
beach in the sunshine. I'm telling you, Charles, heat has a way of
healing—"

He cut her off, his face suddenly clouded by sadness again.
"Like it healed you in Miami?" he asked.

"I'm not healed," Sherry answered without thinking.

"Neither am I," said Charles. He stepped closer to Sherry;
she could feel him breathing. They were almost touching.

And then they were. Charles wrapped his arms around

Sherry and pulled her into him, burying her with his chest and shoulders and mouth. He held her face in his hands, forcing her to stay close, until she had no more desire to fight it.

She could hear him say her name over and over again, lips against her neck and chest and forehead—he sounded as if he was crying—and then he drew her down to the ground with him, onto him, still holding her as he had to, to stay alive.

She pulled away.

"What is happening?" she asked. She was breathless and freezing and swamped with hope.

"Don't ask," said Charles, "just feel." His eyes were closed.

"I feel snow in my shoes," Sherry said. "Can't we go somewhere?"

Charles shook his head and pulled Sherry close to him for another rough kiss. "Let me have you here," he said. He reached for Sherry's belt.

"*Here?*"

"Sherry—please—" She'd never heard him so full of longing.

"Charles, I'm cold."

He pulled her close again and covered her face with his lips. It was too much . . . Yes, she wanted him inside her, she did, right now, but not here. Definitely not here in the shadow of the First.

"Let's go to my car," she said. "It's right down the road. Please."

"How far?"

"Less than a block. Near that tennis court."

"All right."

He stood up, and not looking at Sherry, starting walking fast down the hill. She followed, finally catching up with him a few feet from the Mercedes.

"Backseat," he said.

Sherry nodded. She unlocked the car, and they climbed in, Charles first.

And a second later, he was all over her again, calling her name desperately, running his hands across her breasts, up her thighs, down her back. He remembered everything.

"Sherry," he moaned, pulling off her stockings, "you still want me, don't you?"

"Yeah . . ." She didn't want to talk, but he seemed to need it.

"You want me as much as before, right?" He was insistent.

"Yeah, Charles, yeah."

"Do you want me more? More than before?"

"Yeah . . ."

He pushed forward, inside her.

"Say my name," he moaned.

"Charles, Charles . . ."

"You never used to say my name."

"I'm sorry."

"You were afraid you'd say someone else's name by mistake." He was fucking her hard, and it hurt.

"That's not true," Sherry said. "Please, Charles, slow down."

"You were afraid."

"I was not—"

"Say my name now—"

Sherry said it again and again, but her passion was gone, replaced by guilt and grief and fear, fear that she could never make everything up to him, not in a million years of trying. She waited for the end to come.

It did a minute later, silently.

Charles rolled off her and zipped his pants, looking out the window.

"Christ . . ." he sighed heavily.

Sherry waited, half expecting him to start talking about the stars and planets. This time, she wouldn't tease him.

"Christ," Charles said again. Then: "I'm sorry, Sherry. I don't know what came over me. I don't know."

"What do you mean?" she asked. Why was he apologizing? Was he sorry he came so fast? That was okay. They were out of practice; they'd get better again.

"I don't know," Charles went on muttering, still staring out the window. "I just lost it when I saw you in the church. It just brought back so many memories." He laughed ironically. "I guess I got horny or something. You look really terrific, Sher. Really skinny."

"Thanks," she said. Horny?

"I'm really sorry I did this to you."

"Did what?"

"You're still on the pill, aren't you?"

"Yeah—"

"Thank God." He shuddered.

"Charles, what's happening?" Sherry asked. Her hands were

beginning to tremble, and she clasped them together to make them stop.

"Oh, Christ . . ."

"Charles?"

No answer. He looked down at his knees, and then at Sherry, briefly.

"Tell me what's wrong," she pleaded when their eyes met. "I won't be mad." But already, she was slamming closed the doors to her heart. Something terrible was coming, but she wasn't going to feel it. At least, not now. Not in front of him.

"All right," Charles said finally, sighing again. "I can't believe this happened, Sherry, because I have a girlfriend. Alice fixed us up a few months ago. I'm sorry. I have a *fabulous* girlfriend, and I'm in love with her and everything—"

Sherry stopped him with an airy wave.

"It's okay. Don't worry about it," she said, voice remote. "I have a boyfriend. No problem."

Charles broke into a wide, relieved grin. "Whew!" he said, jokingly dragging one hand across his brow. "Well, that makes me feel a lot better!"

"Don't worry about it," Sherry said. "These things happen."

"I guess we just got carried away." Charles shrugged. "Nostalgia, maybe."

"Maybe," Sherry said. Maybe not. All at once, she couldn't remember why she had loved him once. Had she ever known the reason?

She turned to Charles but looked past him, into the darkness.

"Can you get out that door?" she asked.

"I think so," he replied cheerily, leaning across her legs to straighten his tie in the rearview mirror.

"Sherry," he said when he was done, "let's just keep this between us, okay?"

She nodded. "No problem."

Charles put on his coat. "The funny thing is, I think you're really going to like Jessica."

"Jessica?"

"My girlfriend. She'll be there tonight, of course."

"Oh," said Sherry, trying to sound interested. Then: "That's too bad."

"What's too bad?" said Charles. He was suddenly concerned.

"Um, it's too bad I won't get to meet her," Sherry answered

matter-of-factly. "I can't make it tonight. I'm having dinner with my parents."

Charles frowned. "Oh," he said, "well, then maybe you'll meet her at the wedding."

"Maybe," said Sherry. She picked the car keys off the floor and climbed into the front seat, making sure Charles couldn't see up her skirt.

She turned over the engine. "This is where you get off," she told Charles.

"Okay," he said. "See you."

And one heartbeat later, he was gone, bounding up the hill, away from her, for the last time.

 Sherry drove home slowly, taking every back road she remembered, taking the long way back to Endless Horizon Lane.

She wanted to stop shaking before she walked through the front door to face Eleanor and Laurence. She wanted to look happy for them.

And a half hour later, she was fine; she made herself fine. There was no choice. First, she forced Charles out of her mind with the speed and determination of an autumn hurricane, wiping out memories one after another until none remained. By the time she'd circled Old Town twice, he had vanished for good. Soon, Alice was gone, too, probably forever. After that, Manuel, the Beauregards, Brazil and his uneven love—all purged, sent away. And when her head was clear, at last, she filled it anew with thoughts of Belinda and Eladio, of their simple joy and golden future, of how the three of them would all be together again soon, free and clear in the healing heat of Miamiville.

Sherry cut back onto Pleasant Street, past the red brick high school where Adam Klein went, picked up Harbor Avenue, and headed home, the short way.

Her parents were eating supper when she walked in the door,

of course. It was seven o'clock. She could hear the clinking of silverware against china and the soft melody of her mother's voice, filling the silence.

Sherry walked into the dining room, her footsteps muffled by two thick Oriental rugs. They didn't hear her coming, and for a minute, she stood in the door and watched them.

Eleanor was in her usual seat, catercorner to Laurence, her elbows resting in front of her, beautifully manicured hands cradling a glass of dark red wine. The cavernous room was lit by candles, and in the dim yellow glow her mother looked somehow soft and vulnerable and young. She looked happy.

Her father, too. He had taken off his tie and jacket—they were thrown haphazardly on the marble-topped credenza near the door—and unbuttoned the top of his stiff white work shirt, revealing a V of wiry silver chest hair. He looked just like a regular man. Sherry noticed he was done with his meal and was leaning toward Eleanor, listening to whatever she was saying, listening closely. Every few seconds, he smiled and rubbed the back of his wife's right hand with his. Nothing had changed at One Hundred Endless Horizon Lane.

Sherry took a long step into the room. "Guess who," she said quietly.

Her parents both jumped up from the table.

"Oh, my word!" her father exclaimed. "Sherry—we weren't expecting to see you tonight at all!" He fumbled to close the top button of his shirt.

Eleanor looked shocked, too. She took a quick sidestep next to her husband, and then they both stood, maybe ten yards away from Sherry, unable to move closer.

But Sherry was on automatic. She pushed herself toward them, reaching her father first and placing a quick, dry kiss on his cheek. Then she hugged her mother briefly and pursed her lips in the air just below her left ear.

"I should have rung the doorbell," she said. "I'm sorry for surprising you."

Both her parents started chattering at once.

"You don't need to ring the doorbell to your own house," the Judge said. "Don't be ridiculous, Sherry!"

Eleanor echoed his words exactly, but then went on. "It's just we were so sure you weren't coming home until after the rehearsal dinner."

Sherry shook her head. "I decided not to go," she said.

Eleanor Estabrook raised her eyebrows. "To *Alice's* rehearsal dinner?" she asked.

"That's right," said Sherry. "I decided not to go."

Her father shook his head, looking worried and frankly perplexed. "Is something wrong?" he asked, and Sherry was startled at the unfamiliar kindness in his voice. What was the Judge up to this time?

"No, nothing's wrong," she answered flatly. "I'm just very tired, and I need some sleep." She paused for a moment, deciding if she should say the words banging to get out of her throat. She looked directly at the Judge, and he returned her glance, his expression unexpectedly receptive. Sherry took a deep breath and continued, purposefully keeping her voice low and controlled. "I happen to be very tired," she said, "because I happen to work very hard at the *Citizen*. As a matter of fact, I've just wrapped up a major piece about a young man who—"

She stopped abruptly. The last thing she wanted to do was get in a debate with her father about the legality of keeping Manuel's crimes from the police.

"A young man who *what*, Sherry?" It was the Judge, still speaking in the strangely kind and welcoming voice. He had settled back into his chair and was motioning Sherry and his wife to do the same.

Sherry reluctantly followed his lead, but she was not going to divulge any more details about Manuel. The story was precarious enough already.

"He's a young man who has had a long association with a major crime family in Miami," she said. "His information is really going to have a major impact on the city."

She paused momentarily, anticipating a litany of skeptical questions. Instead, there was a brief silence, then:

"Wow, Sherry, that is fantastic, I mean, really *super!*" It was the Judge again, his voice so enthusiastic Sherry searched his face for signs of sarcasm or ridicule. "I'd love to hear more about this!"

"Right, you would," Sherry replied dryly. Her father certainly looked sincere, but she had no other reason to trust him. No reason in the world.

"I mean it, Sherry," he said.

Eleanor Estabrook nodded vigorously by his side. "We have

so much catching up to do," she said. "Sherry, we've lost touch with you, darling. We both feel that way—"

"Lost touch with me?" Sherry shot back incredulously. The last thing she needed now was to let her parents engage her in some kind of crazy mind game. She was barely holding it all together as it was. She jumped out of her chair and started backing out of the room. "You two were never *in* touch with me. I can't believe my ears. I mean, you started sending me to summer camp as soon as I could dress myself, and you never ate one goddamn fucking dinner with me, and—"

"Sherry, Sherry, let's not argue." Laurence Estabrook held up both hands to stop his daughter. He was standing now, too. "We obviously have a lot of talking to do. Your mother and I have been counting the days for you to get home, we really have, dear. It's just as I told you on the phone last month, Sherry—your mother and I have done some serious thinking since you left home the way you did, and—"

"Uh-huh," Sherry cut him off laconically. She remembered the call. For some reason, both of them had been on the extension at once, and her mother had kept piping up in an ingratiating voice about a series of visits with a "Dr. Cunningham," as if Sherry had known or cared who he was. She hadn't given it a second thought, until now, when suddenly she realized Eleanor must have been referring to Miles Cunningham, an old golfing buddy of the Judge. Had her parents been seeing a *shrink*? The idea was too outrageous to believe. Then again, she recalled, her parents' stilted letters had been arriving at Lemonlime Road more frequently lately, each one with a new and oddly gushy sign-off paragraph. She'd chalked it up to that ancient rule of WASP etiquette that says parents and children should at least pretend to love one another. What else could explain it? "Look," Sherry blurted out cursorily, "I've got to go. I need to sleep. I can't deal with this . . . this *insanity* tonight."

"But we have so much we want to tell you!" Her father was practically pleading now. "Sherry, darling, your mother and I, we're at the age—" He paused for a moment to pull his wits together, taking a deep breath and running a hand through his close-cropped silver hair. "It's as I said, Sherry. We've spent many, many hours trying to make sense of what happened—"

"*Many* hours," Eleanor Estabrook interjected, and Sherry recognized the hopefulness of her tone from the phone call about Dr. Cunningham.

"And, Sherry darling," the Judge went on, "we both think that there are some apologies that should be said all around—"

"Apologies *all around*, huh?" Sherry was nearly shouting. This was too much! Too much posturing to bear at one time! "You expect me to apologize to you? I haven't done anything wrong! I'm not the one who took a bribe! I'm not the one who paid off the family of a poor girl who got raped."

"Please—" Eleanor Estabrook had lowered her face into her hands and was weeping delicately. "Please, Sherry, don't open old wounds."

"Okay, fine, I won't," Sherry said. And for a moment she stood, silent and paralyzed by confusion, near the door to the dining room. Her head was telling her to bolt—to run upstairs and away from her parents' unexpected peace overtures, but her heart was begging her to stay, to hear them out, to make amends.

In the end, it was her father who made the decision for her.

"I know you want to leave, Sherry," he said sadly. He took a short sip of water and cleared his throat before going on. "I guess I don't blame you. We're not going to agree. I know that, and you know that. It's just that your mother and I thought we should try to work things out a little bit."

"A truce," Eleanor Estabrook suggested meekly.

Sherry shook her head. She wasn't disagreeing. She was just too overloaded with emotion—first the Beauregards, then the decisions of the plane ride home, then Charles, and now *this*—to know what to think about anything in her life.

"All right then, go," Laurence Estabrook said. There wasn't the slightest hint of judgment in his voice, only regret. He sat down again and tilted his chin to his chest, as if he were carefully studying the pattern of the tablecloth. After a moment, his wife leaned over and kissed him softly on the cheek.

And before they looked up again, Sherry was gone.

50

Even in the dead of winter, the moonlight filled Sherry's Marblehead bedroom with the unearthly glow of a kerosene lamp. That was always the most wonderful thing about being on the third floor. She felt close to heaven.

She lay down on her bed and prayed sleep would come quickly. It did not, of course. An hour passed, and she struggled not to remember, everyone and everything. She tried to concentrate on Belinda and Eladio. What colors would they wear tomorrow? What promises would they exchange? What kind of love would they make?

She should call them . . .

Sherry reached for the phone on her night table and dialed Belinda's number in the dark. Ten rings. No answer.

She tried to sleep again, and for a moment she seemed to drift, but then . . .

She should call Brazil. The thought occurred to her like a revelation. They had left it so terribly, so indefinite and discordant. He could be thinking anything. He could be thinking everything was the same.

She lifted the receiver and dialed.

But he didn't answer at all. His wife did.

"Brackett residence," Jeanie said over the line. In the background, Sherry could hear a baby's delighted laughter mingled with Brazil's noisy guffaw.

Sherry couldn't speak.

"Hello—Brackett residence," Jeanie repeated after a second had gone by, louder this time. "Hey, you two, quiet down over there!" More laughter and noises.

Sherry found her voice. "I'm sorry. I must have the wrong number," she said. "Please forgive me."

She hung up and pushed the phone away. A minute later, she was asleep.

And until morning came, she dreamed of babies and blood, both her own.

51 They planned the wedding for sunrise, on the beach where they first made love.

Eladio had to pay the justice of the peace fifty extra bucks to wake up at six in the morning and traipse all the way out to Key Biscayne, but it meant so much to Belinda, he would have paid a thousand. Whatever it took to make her happy.

And so, just after the sun cut through the horizon and lifted above the glimmering bay, they stood at the edge of the water and were married.

The ceremony was just a few lines. Belinda had written it.

"If loves beckons you, dare not say no," it began. She remembered the line from a well-worn book of Farsi poems she found in her father's desk drawer after he died. "If love beckons you, say yes, for there is no other answer to life."

The justice paused, reading ahead, and then continued.

"Belinda, do you say yes to Eladio, to love, to life?"

"I do," she answered.

He turned to Eladio.

"Do you, Eladio, say yes to Belinda, to love, and to life?"

"I do," he answered.

The justice looked back and forth between them, waiting for a cue to continue, but Eladio and Belinda were too busy looking at each other to notice. They faced each other, crying from wonder and joy and hope, holding hands, letting the surf break over their ankles for ten minutes or more. It was an amazing sight, the justice would tell his wife later. In all his years at this game, he had never seen two people more consumed by love. They looked as though they were about to faint dead away.

Finally, when he figured he'd better get on with things or risk bumping into the first sunbathers, the justice cleared his throat, pushed his glasses up on his nose, and read the legally required words binding Eladio and Belinda, forever and ever, in the eyes of God, Amen. Eladio had asked him to mention God, at least once.

"Now, with the power vested in me by the state of Florida, I pronounce you husband and wife," the justice concluded. Usually, he went on to tell the couple to kiss, but Eladio and Belinda were already in each other's arms, down in the water, and not just kissing, but laughing and hugging and rolling in the sand and generally making quite a scene. Truly, he'd never seen anything like it. These two people seemed so happy and young and free, he had to wonder why no one was there to watch them get married.

No one, that is, except for him, and his secretary and her sister, whom Eladio had paid ten bucks apiece at the last minute to serve as witnesses. They had spent the wedding in the car, dozing.

There were supposed to be other witnesses, of course, Eladio's brother and his wife, but the day before the wedding, they backed out. It wasn't their fault, Eladio told Belinda. His mother objected—too fast, no church, no priest. To her mind, it wasn't right. But she would get used to it, Eladio promised Belinda. Someday.

But Belinda didn't care. She wasn't planning on telling her mother for another month at least, or maybe she'd wait even longer. She didn't want the perfection of it all cracked by Katherine McEvoy's objections, her scolding, her jealousy, her remorse. She'd tell her eventually. Someday.

And so Eladio and Belinda were married at sunrise, alone, on the beach where they first made love.

52

The next night, Brazil waited for Sherry at her house on Lemonlime Road, asleep on the living-room couch, an empty pizza box on the coffee table in front of him. Her plane was due in at eight; it was already close to midnight.

Still, despite all the delays—the plane had circled over Atlanta for two hours—Sherry wasn't really surprised to find him there, and maybe even a little relieved. Brazil was her best friend, perhaps her only friend, Sherry thought, even knowing what she did about poor, sweet Jeanie.

She dropped her suitcase in the bedroom, brushed her hair in the bathroom, and then wandered back to the front of the house to kiss him awake.

"Hi, darlin'," she whispered as she leaned down to touch his cheek.

Brazil nearly jumped out of his skin.

"Whoa!" he cried, bursting out of slumber and lunging off the couch as if he'd just seen a rattlesnake. "Whoa, darlin'!—you can't creep up on a man like that! You nearly gave me a heart attack."

Sherry took two steps back and took a long look at Brazil. He *was* really scared—white-faced, trembling, and lips turned skinny and silver.

It didn't take him long to recover, though. A minute or two later, his color was back, and he sank into the couch again, propping his feet on the coffee table.

"Darlin', come sit down by me," he said sweetly, once he got settled. "We gotta talk."

Sherry groaned. She'd just lived through the worst weekend of her life, she'd been traveling for hours, and he still wanted to hash out that stupid phone call about Jeanie. There was nothing to talk about, really, or at least nothing that would make everything all right again.

But then, why not hear him out? He probably hadn't stopped thinking about their argument since Friday night. That's the way he was—once he latched on to something, he wouldn't let it go. He was trying so damn hard to save them, it almost hurt to watch. She sat down.

Brazil took both her hands in his and squeezed them gently. "Sherry," he began in the sugar-coated version of his best Cracker voice, "I've been waiting for you 'cause I've got some bad news about something that happened here on Lemonlime Road, sweetness, and I didn't want you to be all alone when you found out."

On Lemonlime Road? Oh, Christ no, Sherry thought, this isn't about the phone call at all. It's about Alvin and Laura. Just as she had feared—

"Now, Sherry"—Brazil was still talking away in a syrupy voice meant to sound soothing—"the morning you left for Boston, somebody went and killed your neighbors over there, the Beauregards." He pointed toward Alvin and Laura's house and then held up his hands in a calming gesture. "Now don't you panic, darlin'. The cops are pretty certain it was a drug hit. They found a bunch of cash in the house, so they don't think there's a lunatic running around your neighborhood randomly killing innocent folks. Okay?"

Sherry stared at Brazil, waiting. Was he going to wink at her now, or make a face, to let her know that he knew the score? Why wasn't he just being straight about the whole thing? When would the yelling and recriminations and I-told-you-sos begin?

She waited some more.

Finally, Brazil spoke again. "I guess you must be in shock, darlin'," he said, putting his arms around her. "But I want you to let your feelings out, okay? If you're scared, you can tell me. If you want to cry, just go on ahead and cry. That's what I'm here for."

Sherry didn't know what do—could it possibly be that Brazil was sincere? Or was he testing her? He had to be.

She leaned forward and looked in his eyes. "The cops think it's a drug hit," she said, trying to keep her voice expressionless, "but what do you think? Really now—what do you think?"

Brazil shrugged noncommittally. "Well, I can't say I disagree with them, darlin'," he said. "I mean, there was a bunch of cash in the house. Now that could mean the old geezers were too senile to trust the local bank, but it is usually a sign something a little bit illegal is going on."

Brazil paused and checked to see if there was anything left in the pizza box. "Jeez, Louise!" he said, "I can't believe I downed that whole mother!"

Sherry watched him still, mute with confusion.

He kept talking. "To tell you the truth, Sherry," he said, "I'm surprised you're not more flipped out, and I'm proud of you, darlin'. I thought you'd want to move into the Intercontinental tonight, or put bars on your windows, or buy a gun or something."

Sherry shook her head in wonder. "I guess I've just seen so many cocaine murders they don't even register anymore," she said. It was the best she could come up with.

"And I guess the Beauregards weren't exactly your favorite people," Brazil added. He kissed Sherry's cheek and smiled sympathetically.

"Not exactly," she said.

They looked at each other in silence for a few seconds, and then Brazil nodded once, firmly, as if he could officially mark the end of the conversation that way. But, of course, he couldn't help making a few final remarks. "Well," he said, "I just want to say I'm real glad to see you're not taking this hard, Sherry." He slapped his knees twice for emphasis. "You've really toughened up since we got you out of that city of wimps and sissies up in the north woods there."

Sherry smiled weakly. What the hell was going on?

Brazil stood up and wandered toward the kitchen in search of more to eat. "True, true," Sherry heard him mutter as he walked away. "You seen one, you seen 'em all." A second later, she could hear the cabinets opening and slamming. Then: "Dang it! You ain't got an egg to suck on in here! No, wait, maybe I'll drink this year-old carton of buttermilk. Oh, yeah!"

Words weren't important anymore. Sherry was listening to the tone of Brazil's voice. He sounded so real. . . . Could it be he didn't make the Manuel connection?

Then, suddenly, it occurred to her. Of course he didn't— there was so much he didn't know. He didn't know that she had told Manuel of Pansy's murder in detail, and that she had wept at the telling. He didn't know who gave her the new cat as a valentine to the future. He didn't know about Manuel's creepy promise the day she left for home: *You'll follow me.*

Of course he didn't know. Yes! A bolt of relief, but then

suddenly Sherry felt a shard of fear scrape down her spine. Would the obvious escape Belinda, too? Could she be that lucky?

She headed for the kitchen and found Brazil leaning against the counter eating peanut butter from the jar with a knife. "Tell me," she said to him, "was this thing with the Beauregards all over the paper? Did Jack give it huge play?"

"Pretty big, but not gigantic," he answered matter-of-factly. "Metro front." He dug in for another knifeful. "I think if it had been random, Jack would have plastered it all over page one, but it was like you said, you know, just another two cocaine casualties." Brazil let out a short, ironic laugh. "I just remembered that Jack was moaning and groaning all over the newsroom that he was dying to call these two geezers 'elderly grandparents' in the lead—for that extra added dramatic effect, you know?—but the cops said they couldn't find any living relatives. Poor little Jackie! I hate that asshole."

Sherry forced a smile. Brazil caught it instantly.

"Now that wasn't very convincing," he said. "Maybe you're more freaked-out about this than you're willing to let on."

She nodded and lowered her head. She didn't want him to look at her too closely tonight. Who knows what else he'd figure out with a few clues.

Brazil put down the peanut butter and opened his arms wide. "Come here and give me a hug," he said. She obeyed.

He pulled her close, kissed the top of her head, and then held her that way for a long time. It felt so wonderful and terrible she wanted to cry, but no tears came.

"Thanks for being here," she said finally.

"Well, well . . ." he murmured back. "Well, I knew you'd read the Sunday paper before you went to bed and . . ."

"And what?" she prompted him.

"And nothing," he said, hugging her tighter.

"Come on—"

Brazil sighed. "And I had to make sure you didn't go and get dirty with that Charles faggot," he said. "But I guess you look clean enough." He pushed her away a few inches and surveyed her up and down, self-satisfied smile breaking across his face. "You pass."

"Thanks," Sherry said.

He gave her another quick hug. "Okay," he said, "I gotta split now."

"Leave?" Sherry was at his heels all at once, following him to the door. "You can't leave now—I can't be alone tonight." The image of Manuel breaking through her bedroom window flashed through her head, and she saw blood dripping from his lips the way slobber drips from the jaws of a Doberman pinscher. "I mean, what if the killer comes back to get me?"

"You been selling cocaine?"

"Come on," Sherry pleaded. "This is a special circumstance. I'm telling you, Jeanie will understand."

But Brazil was already on the porch. He turned to face Sherry to say good-bye, and that was when she noticed his eyes; they'd clouded over. He suddenly looked so defeated, she barely recognized him from a minute before.

"I don't think so," he said. His voice had changed, too—it was more serious and plain than she had heard it in a long time.

"What?" Sherry asked.

"I don't think Jeanie will understand."

He was being ridiculous and melodramatic, as usual. Just forty-eight hours earlier, Sherry reminded herself, Jeanie had sat in her living room, matter-of-factly admitting that they shared the same man. Sherry laughed at Brazil affectionately. "Darlin'," she said, "I'm sure she will—"

"No." The word came out like a bullet. "She won't." Brazil paused and let out a long stream of breath between tightened lips. He hadn't intended to talk about this tonight. But now there was no getting out of it.

"Look," he said, voice taut, "I don't know what happened in Lost Corners, but something did, and Jeanie came back different. She's got all sorts of different ideas about how things have to be. I don't know why. . . ."

Sherry said nothing. There was nothing to say. This time, there was no easy escape, no "Don't worry, I have a boyfriend" to throw out fast, no trapdoor to another place conveniently far away. She had no choice but to keep listening.

"So now, for some reason, Jeanie is all uptight now about our family. She's been saying 'our family this' and 'our family that' ever since she got off the plane," Brazil went on. "I don't know what came over her, but I'm getting a feeling she wants things to be different with, you know, with, uh—"

"With us?" Sherry helped him out.

Brazil raised his palms skyward and wagged his head, as if he didn't know the answer. But they both knew he did.

"Like, she doesn't want you to see me anymore?" Sherry asked.

"Well, she hasn't said that."

Sherry felt a quick burst of relief, but then, just as fast, she wasn't so sure.

"She hasn't said that?" she echoed Brazil. "What has she said?"

He scrunched up his face as if he'd just bitten into something bitter. "She keeps saying we gotta talk."

"Talk?"

"About 'our family.' " He leaned into the last two words and braced them with quotation marks in the air.

"Your family," Sherry said, "and what do you think she *really* means?"

There was a long minute of silence before Brazil answered. "I think she means something about me and her and our baby and what we're all about, like, what we want to be. Something like that."

"Your baby, right." Sherry closed her eyes and took a few steps backward to lean against the open doorframe. She'd been so wrong about Jeanie it was staggering.

She had been wrong about everyone lately.

"Are you okay, darlin'?" She could hear Brazil talking to her, but she knew he hadn't moved any closer. Of course he hadn't.

She nodded. "Just tired," she said. "Let's talk about this later, okay?" She opened her eyes just in time to see him bobbing his head eagerly in agreement.

"That's a fine idea," he said, trying to sound cheerful again and half succeeding. "Now—I want you go to bed this instant, and don't you worry one second about anybody coming to hurt you in the night. I promise you, you're perfectly safe here."

"Thanks," Sherry said, backing into the house and closing the door.

She didn't want to say good night to him. She didn't want him to kiss her this time, the last time, whether he knew it or not.

53

Belinda was in the newsroom at eight—she couldn't wait to see Sherry, to hug and kiss her hello, to welcome her back, to tell her how wonderful it felt to be married. She wanted her to know that it had been the right decision after all, to do it so fast and to do it alone. She hoped Sherry wasn't angry anymore. She couldn't wait to see her.

But at quarter to nine, Sherry still hadn't shown up, and Belinda began to panic. There was a story conference on the Manuel piece in fifteen minutes, and Jack was already watching the clock, pacing anxiously around his office with the jerky movements of a man who'd survived on coffee and unfiltereds for two straight days, which he had. He and his squad of hit men had spent every minute of the weekend fighting over every word in the story, stopping only to pee or run down the hall to buy a couple more packs. One of the overnight guys had told Belinda that they'd finished at four Monday morning, and Jack sent everyone home. He was staying just until nine to tell Sherry and Belinda what was left of their masterpiece, and then he was going home himself, to crash.

Belinda's phone rang. It was Jack. "Where the fuck—" he shouted.

But Belinda wouldn't let him go on. "She'll be here any minute now," she said reassuringly, as if she knew for a fact that Sherry was parking in the garage five flights below. "Don't worry, Jack—"

He slammed down the phone, and across the newsroom Belinda could see him check his wall clock and then his watch. It was three of nine.

Maybe, Belinda thought, maybe Sherry had missed her plane, or maybe she was stuck in traffic on 95, or maybe she was just too exhausted from Alice's wedding to get out of bed this morning. That had to be it.

At 9:10 the elevator door opened, and Sherry stepped into the newsroom. Belinda expected her to look tired and harried, yes, but not like this. At a distance, Sherry looked as worn-out and fragile as an old wedding gown. Up close, she looked as wasted as a new widow. Something very bad must have happened in Boston, something with her parents, maybe—

Belinda ran up to Sherry and grabbed her hand. There was no time to talk. Jack was getting more pissed-off by the second. "Sherry," she whispered frantically, "we've got the Manuel story conference with Jack right now, this minute—okay? Just follow me." She looked into Sherry's eyes and saw nothing. "Just follow me," she repeated.

Sherry nodded vaguely and obeyed Belinda's orders. A second later, she looked up to see Jack sitting behind his desk, head in hands, watching the ashes from his cigarette float around a half-full coffee cup in front of him. He didn't look mad, she thought, just burned-out, and didn't she know how that felt—

"Close the fucking door and sit down," he ended Sherry's musing. "I'm just assuming Estabrook has a good excuse for being late. I'm just assuming. I don't want to hear about it."

"Actually—" Sherry began. She was going to tell him that her life was such a disaster—such a *fucking* disaster—that she hadn't managed to fall asleep until dawn, but he jerked his hand across his throat. "I don't want to hear about it," he said. "Got it?"

"Yes," Belinda answered brightly. "Sure do."

Sherry looked over at her, and Belinda smiled warmly. "Sure do," she said a second time, and then turned her attention back to Jack. The sooner this ended, the better. She had to take care of Sherry.

But suddenly Jack was in no hurry. He straightened up in his seat and took a fresh unfiltered from the pack on his desk. "I trust you had a nice time in Boston?" he asked Sherry.

"Very nice," she answered, though Belinda wasn't sure she moved her lips.

"And I understand you had a busy weekend, Miss McEvoy," he said to Belinda.

Belinda giggled. "That's Mrs. Alvarez," she said, holding up her left hand to display a narrow gold band. "You understand right. I got married."

"Very nice," Jack said laconically.

"Very nice," Sherry echoed him.

Jack lit the cigarette, then stood up and walked slowly to the window. For a full minute or more, he watched the bay.

Finally, he turned around, exhaling a column of smoke toward the ceiling.

"Me and my guys," he began, "we were very busy this weekend, too."

He took a few steps closer to Belinda and Sherry and leaned against his desk. "We spent the weekend reading all about your friend Manuel. Nice kid, this Manuel. Very nice."

"Very nice," Sherry said. She was looking away from Jack, into the newsroom, though from where Belinda sat, her eyes didn't seem focused.

Jack went on. "We read your piece about a hundred fucking times," he said. "We analyzed every fucking word and every fucking sentence. We busted it apart, and then we stuck it back together"—he paused to take a drag—"and the amazing thing is, girls, it doesn't look too different from what you handed us to begin with."

Jack smiled. "You done good."

He returned to his chair and waited for the reaction—he didn't compliment reporters very often—but oddly, there was none. Of course McEvoy was smiling, but she was a fucking bride, for Christ's sake. Estabrook—well, she looked like she was in a goddamn trance.

Finally, Belinda spoke. "We thank you—*both* of us!" she said, looking toward Sherry for agreement. Sherry nodded her head. This was good news. She should say something—

"I'm so happy, Jack," she blurted out.

Belinda wondered if she was trying to sound sarcastic, because she did.

But Jack didn't seem to notice. He was standing again, and he'd pulled a printout of the story from his top desk drawer. He waved it triumphantly.

"This is it," he said. "I want you both to read it over. There are some changes. Not major ones. We spend more time describing Manuel—you gotta paint a better picture of this kid, what he looks like, what he wears, what kind of car he drives. That kind of thing, that's all."

Belinda waited for Sherry to object, but she was listening calmly, expressionless.

"We fixed up some of the language, made it a bit more explicit." Jack laughed. "I mean, you kids write about Manuel's hits like you're describing a fucking polo match. This was murder. *Murder*. So we made that a little clearer."

"Yuck," said Belinda.

Jack rolled his eyes.

"So, just read it over. If you have problems, I'll listen to them, but I'll tell you now, I don't think much is going to change," Jack said. "The lawyers are looking at it today. I told them we have to have it back by Thursday. It's running Sunday."

He dropped his cigarette into the coffee cup and reached for another.

"Okay, you can get lost," he said, without looking up. "Take it easy this week. I'll tell the desk you're not free agents yet. So go home early. Come in late. Relax a little."

He took a quick peek to gauge the reaction to this news. Again, McEvoy was smiling like a clown, and Estabrook looked— what was with her, anyway?—she looked as though she couldn't care less.

"So, get lost!" Jack said again. Belinda quickly stood up, and Sherry followed. He knew he shouldn't, but one last time before they were out the door, he spoke.

"You done good," he told them. This time he didn't wait for a response. He was already on the phone with Garrett Newman, telling him to clear a spot on his desk for all the prizes Baby Lips was bringing home for them real soon.

 They were back at their desks, well out of Jack's line of vision, before Belinda tried to rattle Sherry back to reality.

"Hey, you," she said, scooting her chair over to Sherry's desk, where she was absentmindedly looking through old phone messages. "How are you?"

Sherry didn't look up, although she wanted to. She was afraid if she looked up, she'd see Brazil. He'd come into the newsroom while they were meeting with Jack, and he seemed just fine, thank you. He'd probably slept like a baby.

"Oh, Belinda," Sherry sighed. "It's like the song says: Life sucks and then you die."

"That's not true!" Belinda looked aghast.

Sherry shook her head. "Of course you think it's not true," she said. "You're in love. You just got married. You're going to live happily ever after." She was surprised it felt okay to talk about it. "On the other hand, both of my boyfriends just dumped me. Charles screwed me in the back of a car and then informed me he's in love with someone else. Brazil says his wife wants to circle the wagons. And, oh yes, my parents suddenly want to kiss and make up, just like that. Not to mention the fact my neighbors were murdered—"

"They were?" Belinda was completely caught off guard. She hadn't read a newspaper since Friday. She and Eladio hadn't even turned on the TV.

"Yeah," Sherry said. Belinda's surprise was a huge relief. "Good old Alvin and Laura Beauregard. Someone killed them."

Belinda gasped, and Sherry took the opportunity to read her gold-flecked eyes with all the energy she had left. Belinda definitely looked upset, yes, but she wasn't horrified. The Manuel connection did not compute, at least not yet.

"The cops think it was a drug hit," Sherry went on quickly. "It was execution style."

Belinda leaned back in her chair and clucked her tongue like an old lady. "Everyone involved in drugs!" she exclaimed. "This whole city is infected—it's like the plague!"

Sherry nodded. As long as Belinda didn't know the details, the secret was safe.

She changed the subject fast, before Belinda started asking questions. "Alice's wedding was a bomb," she said. "I just sat in the corner drinking Stoli, and if you can believe it, Charles kept asking me to dance, 'for old times' sake.' Then I was forced to sit next to his girlfriend, little Miss Jessica, at the luncheon, and she kept calling me *Cheryl*. Not Sherry, but Cheryl. I guess I can safely conclude Charles doesn't talk about me too much, wouldn't you agree? So much for four fucking years of my life."

Belinda seemed distracted, but she followed Sherry's lead. "What a jerk," she said.

"Then I get home, and I find out Jeanie has decided Brazil

can't see me anymore. She's decided to reclaim her family, which means bye-bye to you-know-who. Got to *love* her timing."

"Well," Belinda said, perking up—this was a subject that interested her much more that Sherry's plush and sordid past—"maybe it's for the best that you get out of that relationship anyway. Brazil is married, I mean. It's not healthy."

"I know," said Sherry. She knew.

"And what happened with your parents?" Belinda asked. It was best to get everything out on the table right away. Then they could start to think of solutions.

"Oh, nothing, nothing," Sherry said. "I don't want to go into it. Just very, very strange and extremely suspicious behavior." She knew Belinda hated to hear her talk against her family. It was that whole thing with her father's suicide.

And anyway, Sherry figured, there was no reason to keep talking about her trip home. It was too depressing, and as far as she could tell, Belinda had already forgotten about the Beauregards. Maybe they should take the rest of the day off and go to El Roda for plantains and beer, and maybe she would smoke a cigarette or two. What did she have to lose?

"Look," Sherry said, "Let's stop talking about me. My life is a total disaster."

Belinda shook her head no—she wanted to help Sherry feel better—but already Sherry had grabbed her left hand and was examining her wedding band.

"You are a wife!" she gushed, hoping to pull Belinda into a better mood with her. "I can't believe it!"

"I can't either."

"So, how was it?" Sherry asked, though she wasn't sure she could bear to hear the play-by-play. "Tell me all about the wedding."

Belinda glowed, and Sherry suddenly realized she looked more lovely and peaceful than ever. "Well, it was beautiful," she began, "we did it at sunrise, out on Cape Florida—"

She stopped. Sherry's phone was ringing.

"Hold on," she said, motioning Belinda not to move.

She picked up the phone and put on her work voice. "Sherry Estabrook," she said. *"Miami Citizen."*

Long pause.

"You're back."

Manuel.

"Yes," said Sherry. She grimaced, and Belinda immediately understood. She rolled her chair back to her desk and started wading through the Spanish-language Miami dailies that had been piling up in her In-box since last week.

"Did you have a nice trip?" Manuel asked.

"Very nice," Sherry answered coolly. She could tell by the edge to his voice he was anxious to talk about the Beauregards, to boast about what a great job he had done. But she wasn't going to let him.

"Manuel," she said, "I can't talk to you." No excuses.

"Is someone listening?" he asked again.

"No."

"Is your boyfriend there?" He suddenly sounded frantic and paranoid, so out of control Sherry barely recognized his voice.

"No."

"Then what's the matter?" he barked. He was surly.

Sherry lowered her voice to a whisper. "Look, Manuel, I don't like what you did," she said. "I don't want to talk to you again. What you did was wrong."

There was a moment of silence, and then Sherry thought she heard Manuel snicker.

"Yeah, that was a mistake," he said.

What was this? "Pardon me?" Sherry said.

"I said it was a mistake," Manuel answered snidely; he was obviously leading to some kind of punch line, and Sherry could picture his face, twisted into an evil smile. "I shouldn't have iced them in the neck."

"That's right," she said hopefully.

"I should have nuked the old guy in the balls, and that bitch, I should have blown her face off."

Sherry felt her stomach turn over, and all at once she was swept with a full-blown case of rocking nausea, so severe she thought she might faint or vomit, or both. She inhaled deeply over and over again and quickly wiped her forehead, now covered with a patina of sticky sweat, with the heel of one hand. Not only was Manuel a perpetual killing machine, as she had finally and horribly realized during her plane ride back to Marblehead, but he was getting crazier by the minute. She barely recognized the boy on the other end of the phone—his cool, self-restrained swagger was gone, replaced by a lunatic edge. And knowing that she had played into it, that she had stupidly told him about Pansy's murder and set the Beauregards' gruesome killings in motion, made her want to scream with shame. Sherry reached over to a nearby desk and finished the contents of an old can of Coke—it tasted repulsively sweet, but her throat had gone so painfully dry she didn't care. A moment later, she felt the seasickness in her gut fade slightly. Thank God, she thought, thank God in heaven this whole terrible mess is almost over. As soon as the story runs, she decided, I'm going to take a long vacation someplace very far away, and when I get back, I'm going to tell Jack he's got to take me off the news for a while, put me on features, let me write puff pieces for the Living section. After the story runs, Sherry thought, he won't be able to say no. No one in the newsroom will be able to say no to Sherry Estabrook.

Sherry shook her head twice to bring herself back to the present, and she realized Manuel was still ranting at her through the phone. "I should have stuck my gun up that bitch's nose, baby, because everyone knows that the neck is Manuel's *firma.*" He let out a snicker. "It's my signature."

"Yes?" Sherry asked wearily. What was he getting at?

"So, it was a mistake."

"Why, Manuel?" She hadn't wanted to volley, but he made it impossible not to play, as usual.

Another long pause. Then: "Because Mimi Lopez is all over my case, man, she wants to know why I did it."

Of course, Sherry thought, of course she knew about the murders! Jack had given them enough play to catch anyone's attention. Manuel was going to have to cut out for Mexico faster than he thought.

"I keep swearing to her that it wasn't me." Manuel was talking again, voice popping with anxiety. "And I think I may have convinced her last night. I just kept saying, 'I only pull the trigger when I get paid, Señora Lopez.' She didn't say anything, but I think she finally bought it."

"Good," said Sherry. She looked up to see Belinda scrutinizing her. She covered the phone. "What is it?" she whispered.

"Sherry, I don't think you should talk to him anymore." She sounded concerned.

Sherry nodded. "I'm getting off," she said. "One minute."

"Is someone else there?" Manuel asked.

"No."

"Your boyfriend is there."

"No, he's not." The words came out slowly, as if she were talking to a mental patient.

Manuel let out a long cackle. "I can't believe you're still going out with him after what I did for you," he said. He was expecting her to correct him.

Sherry didn't answer.

"I ended it with Blanca this weekend," he said.

"I'm sorry," said Sherry.

"It was getting too complicated."

"Uh-huh," Sherry said laconically. Now she was really through listening to him forever.

"So I told her it was over."

"That's too bad. Look, Manuel, I have to go—"

"When can I see you today?" he cut her off.

"You can't," Sherry answered, raising her voice loud enough for Belinda to hear. "I told you, Manuel, we aren't going to see each other again. The interviews are over. The story is over—"

"Don't bullshit me!" he barked. "You'll see me whenever I tell you to."

"No, I won't see you whenever you tell me to," Sherry said, knowing Belinda was watching and listening. "This is the end, Manuel. Good-bye."

She started to put down the receiver, but Manuel was still yelling. She held the phone up for a second longer.

"You can't do this to me," were the last words she heard. "I know where you live."

And so Sherry spent the next few nights at Belinda and Eladio's apartment.

Her bed was a scratchy old couch under the window in the living room, but it wasn't as if she actually spent many hours asleep. Instead, she stayed awake past three, waiting for the door to come crashing down and for Manuel to come rushing at her, pants undone, ready to penetrate her at last.

Usually, she would fall asleep just as it was getting light, only to be awakened an hour later by the muffled sounds of Belinda and Eladio making love in the next room. She didn't mind; it was a wonderful noise, so full of truth. They always laughed afterward.

Of course, it stung a bit to hear their happiness, too, sometimes terribly, and from the very first day away, she longed to be back at her own house, sleeping in her own bed, waking up to silence. It killed her to run away, but then, she had no choice.

Brazil wouldn't help her this time.

"I can't stay over at your place anymore, darlin'—it's Jeanie, like I said," he told Sherry that morning of Manuel's phone call, sounding pained and apologetic but looking neither. "She's gotten all bent out of shape about our family. She says we can't go sharing our family with strangers if we're gonna stay together."

They were standing a foot apart in one of the *Citizen's* tiny darkrooms, where Brazil was printing pictures of fluffy cakes for a Food section feature on birthday parties.

Sherry was crying, and in the red glow of the enlarger, her tears looked like drops of blood. Brazil felt sorry for her, sure, but somehow Jeanie's tears were harder to take, and there had been plenty of them lately.

"Please, Brazil, please, this is the last time," Sherry pleaded with him, "tell Jeanie this is an emergency, or just lie for Christ's sake—tell her you're shooting art for some overnight police stakeout or something."

Brazil shook his head. He couldn't, unless he wanted Jeanie to leave town, taking his best buddy, John Junior, with her. Who knows where they'd go, or if they'd ever come back. She had never stayed in one place very long. Of course, he hoped, he truly did, that someday Jeanie would get back to being her old self, but right now it was too risky to push her. He couldn't let Sherry screw things up.

But damn, she was trying. "I promise I'll never ask again," she was saying, voice propelled by a frantic second wind. "We don't even have to stay in the same bed. Tell her that—tell her you're sleeping on the couch. She can come check for herself. Tell her she can stay over, too. Tell her to bring the baby—"

This was getting crazy. "Sherry!" Brazil snapped, grabbing

her by the shoulders and squeezing tight. "Everything is going to be okay."

He transferred the last photo from the developer to the stop bath and flipped on the light.

"Now, just listen to me," he said firmly. "I want you to tell Jack you need to stay at a hotel—"

"But I don't want to stay at a hotel—"

Brazil rolled his eyes. "Fine," he said, "stay with Jack or Radewski. Go stay with Newman, all right? Just don't stay at your house. Tell Jack you don't feel safe. He'll love it. He'll make sure you've got a place to stay and—"

"But I have to stay at my house to feed my cat," Sherry protested.

Brazil rolled his eyes again and checked his watch. He had to be across town in fifteen minutes to take a head shot of the Dade County Boy Scout Troop Leader of the Year. He had to end this quick and clean. "Look, Sherry," he said, "I'll feed your goddamn cat, okay? I'll take it to my house and keep it until this whole thing blows over."

He reached behind her and pushed open the door to the darkroom.

"Out we go," he said. "I gotta be on an important assignment in about two seconds."

Sherry sighed and stepped outside. A second later, Brazil was past her, at his locker, strapping on cameras and stuffing his pockets with film. And then, without a word, he was out the door of the photo lab, practically sprinting to the elevator.

She ran after him, catching up just as the doors opened and he stepped inside.

"I'm sorry I even asked you," was all she could think of saying as good-bye.

She couldn't tell if he answered.

And so, she ended up with Belinda. Jack had wanted her with him—he said his house was a "fucking A-1 fortress"—but Belinda had insisted. They could go swimming together every morning at Cape Florida, and then stop by work for their messages, and then spend the afternoon shopping, every day a different mall. Except for Wednesday. Wednesday they would go to the zoo.

And that's exactly what they did.

At first, it felt too quiet, like too easy an escape, and Sherry saw Manuel everywhere—behind every car, behind every clothes rack, behind every window. She even saw him at the snake exhibit at the zoo. But in truth he was nowhere. He didn't even call the *Citizen*. And pretty soon, Sherry was feeling better, as if all her fear had been some overblown, paranoid daydream.

Maybe, she told Belinda, just maybe he's beginning to forget me. And on Friday night, she went home again.

 Later, Sherry would remember that she had killed the engine the instant she turned onto Lemonlime Road that night, gliding down the block in neutral, swinging into her driveway with only the muted sound of crunching gravel. She remembered that she waited a few careful minutes, if not more, behind the wheel of her car before getting out, looking left and right for nothing and everything in particular, finding only the remote stillness of a picture postcard beneath the fuzzy glow of streetlights. She remembered feeling such relief that she began to whistle, and she even remembered the song, a plush Top-40 ballad from Spanish radio that Belinda liked, "*Soy Tuyo Para Siempre*," Forever I'm Yours.

And later, when she remembered that night, Sherry would wonder why, in the slow-motion hush of her dark return, she hadn't seen the moonlit glint of steel on her porch or heard the scrape of leather soles against cement. But the truth was, she had noticed nothing, except how good it felt, all through her heart and head and limbs, to be home again.

Manuel felt her happiness, too—he saw it in the way she walked up the path in a fast-giddy lope—and it almost made him laugh. She was too easy.

He had been waiting for her, of course, as he had every night since their last conversation, leaning against the frame of her front door in a narrow wedge of charcoal shadow, waiting and thinking of her see-through eyes and the way she moved her lips, waiting and knowing that eventually she would come back. It was just a matter of time.

Manuel checked his watch. In fact, it had just been 103 hours, 14 minutes, and 56 seconds. Now she was his.

He stepped into the light at the moment Sherry slipped her key into the lock, took a quick step behind her, and pressed a gun into the soft flesh of her waist.

"Don't bother screaming," he whispered behind her right ear. "Something tells me your neighbors won't hear you."

He had been waiting for her. Of course.

Sherry stood paralyzed, face two inches from the door, an arm's reach from the refuge inside, her heart ramming against her breastbone like manic hammer-fist punches. She couldn't have screamed if she wanted. She could barely move her lips. "What do you want?" she tried to say, but she knew Manuel couldn't hear the airtight voice creeping out of her throat. And so she squeezed her eyes tight and waited for the tiny click of Manuel's safety, and then the sound of her own body hitting the ground.

But silence.

Then a sharp jab of the gun, pressed so hard into her side that it ached.

"After you, *señorita*," Manuel said. His voice was suddenly businesslike, not completely unfriendly, and Sherry wished she could see his face. But that was impossible. He had lifted the gun inside her shirt, grazing the muzzle along her spine, and was guiding her to his car, parked in the long shadow of the Beauregards' garage.

Then: "Get in."

Sherry stared at the glossy black Camaro, unable to move. With its shiny mirrored glass and sleek devil's-tail wing, it looked more like a Miami coffin than a car. She glanced at the door and expected to see her own initials embossed by the handle, but instead saw neon-yellow racing stripes, curled around each other in an elaborate, flowery design.

"Get in," Manuel repeated. "Now."

"But—" Again, Sherry's voice stuck in her throat. "Please—"

"I can't hear you," Manuel replied after a moment had passed, his voice changed into something low and surly, as if he couldn't care less what she wanted to say. He readjusted the muzzle of his gun so it fit more snugly in the curve of her waist.

Sherry took a deep breath, exhaled, and this time pushed the words out. "Please don't hurt me," she said. It sounded weak and pathetic, and Manuel laughed bitterly, a laugh that seemed to last for a long time. Afterward, he raised one slender finger and slowly traced a line from the crown of Sherry's forehead to the base of her throat, like a surgeon plotting the path of an incision. His eyes were focused beyond her, far off. He was frowning.

"Get in," he said, and this time Sherry obeyed. A moment later, he was next to her, behind the wheel. He locked her door from a control panel at his left elbow and then turned on the air-conditioning full blast.

"I like it cold," he said.

Sherry nodded.

"It's good for you." He circled the gun in the air above his head for emphasis.

Sherry nodded again. She wondered when Manuel was going to put the car in gear and take off, but suddenly he seemed utterly uninterested in her. Instead, he was angrily fiddling with a loose thread hanging from the crinkly golden robe of his dashboard Jesus.

"I thought I fixed this yesterday," he complained loudly, wagging his head. Another voice now: choppy, shrill. "That's what you get for paying too much—junk." He tugged on the thread a few more times, and in an instant, the bottom hem came completely undone.

"*Junk!*" Manuel exploded. Sherry turned just in time to see him crack the figure over the head with his revolver. It fell to the floor in three pieces.

"Pisses me off!" Manuel was still shouting. "I bought that piece of shit two days ago."

"I'm sorry," Sherry said.

"Yeah, you should be."

"I am," Sherry repeated with more feeling, trying to reach the Manuel who had brought her pink roses, however deep he was buried now. "I really, really am."

Manuel turned abruptly to face her, and for a second Sherry thought that maybe the softness in her voice had worked, jostling some memory of their intimate hours together, but then she saw his dark lips, twisted into the same tight, ironic grin that should have chilled her blood that first day in the park.

"Fuck you," he said. The words came at her like two daggers. The smile lingered.

Sherry felt her heart stop cold, and then suddenly start again, banging harder than ever, shoving the blood of fear through her veins so hard and fast it hurt. What was going on? Manuel had to know he couldn't get away with killing her—too many people at the *Citizen* knew too much about him, too many neighbors had the chance to see him casing her house. It wasn't like him to be so sloppy, Sherry told herself, so unprofessional. But then, she thought, but then, it wasn't like the Manuel she had *wanted* him to be when this whole thing began—a misguided boy who killed other men because he wanted to avenge his angelic mother's death in a city where cocaine was a business. But maybe it was just like the Manuel beside her now, the *real* Manuel, whose disjointed voice changed with every thought, who waved his gun in the air like a maestro gone berserk—a boy she barely knew, a liar and a killer on a mission she did not begin to comprehend.

All at once, Sherry knew this Manuel didn't want a clean ending, one bullet to the neck, no fingerprints, no witnesses.

He wanted a new ending, his own. She had to make him understand that couldn't be.

"Manuel," Sherry began, voice small and desperate, "I can explain—"

"Fuck you," he fired back. "You can't explain nothing. You lied."

She opened her mouth to protest, but Manuel swiftly raised his gun and laid it against her chin.

"Shut up," he said.

Sherry pressed her lips together.

Manuel smiled, then waited a few seconds. "Okay, talk now," he said, taking the gun away, and Sherry opened her lips to speak. But before she had a chance to begin, the gun was on her face again, and Manuel was grinning. "I change my mind," he said. "Shut up."

Sherry nodded.

And then once more Manuel pulled the gun away.

"Go ahead, talk," he said.

"Manuel, please—"

"I change my mind." Gun pressed to forehead. "Shut up."

Ten seconds of silence, and then the same routine, this time with the gun pressed to her cheek. Then again, with the gun pressed to her lips, and again . . .

On the fifth round, Sherry didn't even try to speak. She closed her eyes and let out a painful, furtive sigh of despair. He had been waiting for her, of course, long before tonight. How could she have missed the signs? She suddenly thought of Sherman Otis, of his cranky voice over the phone line after the lie-detector test in his office a hundred million years ago, telling her Manuel could not be trusted, and how she had hated him for saying something so prissy and naive. She thought of Adam Klein and his words of warning—the kid isn't telling you something important, he said, be very careful. And she thought of Belinda calling Manuel crazy, too, for killing husbands and sons and brothers, and she thought of her own answer that day, and the answer was cocaine. As if that explained everything.

"Now you're angry with me, right? Well, fuck you." Manuel was talking again, and Sherry knew she was hearing his real voice for the first time, the voice of a madman. In her frantic, tunnel-vision rush for the story—her gut-propelled pursuit of all those shocking quotes and sordid details that would make the story front-page news and her along with it—she hadn't been listening before.

She dropped her chin to her chest and covered her face with her hands.

"I'm not mad at you," she whispered. "I'm mad at me." It was the truth.

The comment caught Manuel by surprise, and he shifted back in his seat for a moment. But a split second later, he lunged forward again. "You should be," he blurted out. "Fuck you."

"Okay," Sherry said, and suddenly she felt some fear draining away, replaced by a sadness so overwhelming and harsh she could hardly breathe. She knew there was nothing she could do or say to make him understand who she was or why everything had happened as it had. The game was over. She'd lost. She stared at the revolver in Manuel's right hand. It was compact and silver, polished to a reflective shine. She knew if she asked, he would gladly tell her the price. "I'm sorry, Manuel. I'm sorry for everything," Sherry said. "Just tell me what you want." She uncovered her face and looked him in the eyes. "What do you want?"

"I want you to stop using that tone," he answered.

"I'm sorry."

"Fuck you."

"I'm sorry," Sherry said again. It was the wrong answer, she knew that, but she doubted a right one existed. And if it did, she was too numb to know it.

Manuel said nothing. Suddenly, he was busy again with the air-conditioning, pushing the dashboard vents around in a panic, sliding the temperature knob left and right for what seemed like five minutes. Then, just as abruptly, he turned his focus back to Sherry with the force of a stun gun. Her attitude was pissing him off! She was just sitting there as if she were bored, eyes unblinking and blank, lips open just wide enough to breathe in and out with the steady rhythm of a sleeping baby. Manuel let out an angry grunt. So she still thought she could blow him off, he raged inside, even now!

He could fix that.

He grabbed Sherry roughly by the chin, then raised his gun slowly and pressed it against the triangle of flesh between her eyebrows. Almost instantly, two tears fell from her eyes.

Much better.

"Please don't," she whispered.

Manuel didn't move.

"You lied to me," he said.

Sherry blinked, and two more tears fell into her lap.

"You used me."

"I didn't mean to."

"Yeah, you did," Manuel cut her off. He took a deep breath and exhaled slowly. Sherry could tell he was ready to explode again; his jugular stood out from his neck like a rigid rubber tube, bulging with mercury instead of blood. He clenched the steering wheel with both hands and then swiveled to face Sherry with a condemning glare.

"And the worst thing is, you said you loved me, and you don't. You *promised* me you loved me. You promised."

Love?

The word slapped Sherry across the face. Manuel thought she loved him? He was a thousand times sicker than she had ever imagined—even in these terrifying last few minutes. And she was in his abyss of insanity far too deep to fight back and live. He thought she loved him? Christ—she hadn't promised love to anyone for as long as she could remember, and maybe she never had. And maybe that had been her most terrible mistake. So many people would never know—

Except Manuel. He would go to his grave believing she loved him once. And she had no choice now but to tell him he was right.

For the next minute, Sherry heard nothing. She saw nothing. She could only feel, and what she felt was darkest grief, lying heavy on her body, embracing her with the sadistic passion of a rapist.

Then: Manuel's voice again, devoid of anger, full of pleading. "You don't love me, do you?" he said. "You promised you would." He sounded like a little boy, and Sherry suddenly realized he wasn't talking to her at all, but to someone totally imagined. He was talking to a dream of Sherry Estabrook, to the woman she had pretended to be, all those hours and days when she had listened to his stories with the kind of unconditional mercy offered only by a mother. Or a lover.

"I'm sorry you don't think I love you," Sherry said at last, feeling as if her heart were being slowly crushed by an iron glove. "I do love you, Manuel. I really do."

Manuel leaned back in his chair, smiling triumphantly.

"I knew you did," he said, "so you better start acting that way."

"It's just—" Sherry started to answer. She was sobbing softly now. "It's just hard to show it when I feel like you're about to kill me."

Manuel lowered his gun, and for the first time, let it rest in his lap.

"But I'm not going to kill you," he said quietly, in a sweet, surprised voice that filled Sherry with relief and terror at the same time. She would live, but—

"Then what are you going to do to me?" she asked, trying to stop the tears. She was looking at him now, trying to read his expression in the dim light of the car but finding nothing there.

A minute passed, and in the silence Manuel fiddled with the remote-control door locks, popping and closing Sherry's at least ten times.

"What are you going to do to me?" Sherry finally asked again.

"You can't leave me," Manuel answered. The little boy had vanished, and he sounded like his old self suddenly—polite and controlled—but Sherry was too raw to believe it, too smart now to disagree.

She nodded.

"I want you to be with me forever."

"Okay." She would agree to anything—all she needed was a chance to get out of the Camaro. A chance to scream, make a run for it, a chance to hurl herself off a balcony or between two cars. "Fine, Manuel," she said.

More silence.

Then: "We're doing a hit together."

He said it calmly, as if he'd been planning it a long time.

"What?"

"We're doing a hit together tonight, you and me." The calmness was gone now, replaced with edgy insistence.

"Manuel," she said lovingly, like a sister or a friend, "I don't know if that's a good idea—"

His laughter stopped her. "Shut up!" he ordered. "Fuck you."

"I'm sorry," Sherry said, but it was too late. His rage had returned, double force. How dare she tell him what was a good idea? All of a sudden she knew everything! All of a sudden she could tell him what to do! Well, the story was over—she'd said so herself—now it was time for him to claim what was his. She had promised.

A second later, Manuel jammed the Camaro into Reverse and backed out of the Beauregards' driveway at a rip. On Lemonlime Road, he turned left and sped north, through Coconut Grove, onto South Dixie Highway, and then east over the first broad white causeway to Miami Beach, moving so fast that oncoming traffic looked like one unbroken blur of phosphorus light. They were gunning along the shore, weaving recklessly between traffic, before he spoke again.

"We're doing a hit together, right now, you and me," he said.

He turned to her, nodding his head vigorously, his opaque eyes glistening with excitement. He wanted a response, Sherry could tell, and she struggled to find one that wouldn't spark another brutal outburst.

"Who?" she finally asked.

Manuel smirked, self-satisfied. "You'll see," he said. "Somebody famous." A pause. "I wanted to make sure we did one we would always remember, you know?" Sherry noticed that his hands were trembling and that his voice was rising and rolling dreamily the way it did when he described his meeting with Mimi Lopez.

"You're going to love it," he told Sherry, voice at full boil now. "You'll finally understand, you'll understand everything about me." He licked his lips like a wolf. "You're going to know what it feels like to be me, to be Manuel—fantastic! You're going to be me!"

Suddenly, Sherry felt overwhelmed by nausea, and she covered her mouth with both hands to hold back a surge of vomit. She was gagging, forcing herself to swallow, but Manuel seemed oblivious. He was still talking fast and loud, staring straight ahead, eyes in an unhooded-serpentlike trance.

"We're never going to be apart now, you know what I mean?" he said, words slurred in the rush. "Once you've killed someone together, that's it—you're married by blood. Everyone knows that."

Sherry inhaled through her nose, still fighting the pressure of vomit in her throat. She felt certain she couldn't go on, the pain everywhere was too much: needles of regret in her heart, thumping terror in her gut, and now the stinging force of her insides fighting to get out. She leaned forward and put her head between her knees, waiting for blackness, but none came.

Instead, Manuel roughly pulled her back by the hair. "Sit up!" he ordered. "Don't be nervous, you'll fuck everything up."

"I'm sorry," she said. "Manuel, I love you, but I can't do this—"

"Shut up! You'll do what I say."

"I can't—"

"I told you to shut up!" He slammed the dashboard with his gun on each word. Then, more gently: "The first time is always hard. It gets easier. Trust me. It's like a drug, you know? You do it once, and then you got to do it again and again. It's like"—he stopped for a second and then bit into the next three words—"you get addicted."

Sherry shut her eyes, begging for an escape, searching for one in the blackness. But all she found were a hundred blurry images dashing behind the lids, and in each one, she was young and home again, watching snow drift down from heaven, covering the earth with the crispest layer of white, the texture of an angel's wing. In her mind, she heard a sea gull's plaintive winter call and then the crackling sound of ice breaking up on Marblehead Harbor with the spring thaw.

"I'm sorry," she whispered. She was thinking of her father, and how he clenched his broad Yankee jaw when he was too angry to speak.

"I told you, there's nothing to be sorry about," Manuel answered. "This is the best thing that ever happened to you." An instant later, he swerved the car through a hard left, onto Ninety-sixth Street, and then slowed down. He was looking for street signs. A few blocks later, he turned left again into a high-priced neighborhood Sherry vaguely recognized from an assignment two years before. A lot of rich Latins lived here, barricaded into their designer-done split-level homes, high-intensity burglar beams crisscrossing every mauve and marble room. The ornamental front doors, carved of the finest endangered redwood, welcomed no one.

"Look for number fifty-six," Manuel instructed Sherry.

She glanced out her window, pretending to obey.

"See it?"

"No."

He slowed down again. They were creeping down the street now, the houses getting bigger and more ostentatious as they drove closer to the canal. In one driveway alone, Sherry spotted two tangerine Rolls-Royces. The license plates read HIS and HERS.

"Aha—wait, this is it," Manuel said a moment later. He stopped the car and rolled down his window to double-check the number. "Yeah, we're here." He pulled the Camaro into the semicircular drive and killed the lights.

"Nice place, right?" he asked Sherry conspiratorially.

"Very nice," she answered. She was on automatic now. All she had to do was close her eyes when the moment came. She could be there for the hit, but she didn't have to watch.

"You know who lives here?"

"No."

"Someone super-famous." Manuel said, stretching out the last word like a gushing TV emcee.

"Okay." Sherry glanced at the house. Like all the others in the neighborhood, it betrayed no hints about the people who dwelled inside, except that they had too much cash. The shrubbery was clipped to symmetrical precision, the lawn watered to an unnatural shade of green, the garage built big enough to hold four limousines. Every light was on, but the place was sealed up in a silence so dense, even the palmetto bugs didn't dare to scratch through it.

Manuel leaned over Sherry and reached into the glove compartment. A moment later, he pulled out a shiny silver tube—it looked like a short piccolo—and started to screw it onto the muzzle of his gun. "Silence is golden," he whispered just loud enough for Sherry to hear. His breathing was heavy now—she could hear each sharp inhale and labored exhale—and he twisted in his seat uncomfortably. He checked his watch.

"So this is it," Manuel said finally. "Don't try anything stupid. If you do, I'll have to hurt you. I don't want to, but I'll have to. Don't make me. Just follow me."

Sherry nodded. *Follow me*—he'd told her that before, weeks ago. She hadn't understood.

Before she knew it, Manuel was standing outside her car door, waving for her to get out. The gun was hidden in the palm of his right hand, and Sherry knew only a neighbor with binoculars would be able to see it.

Manuel laid the gun sideways against her back and guided her down a winding flagstone path to the front door. He rang the buzzer, and Sherry could hear the faint clanging of chimes inside. Then: footsteps and the sound of someone looking through the tiny peephole. Manuel smiled as if he were posing for a yearbook photograph.

The door slowly swung open.

"Manny—hey! This is a surprise, man. Long time, no see!"

"Yeah, right, *amigo*!" Manuel responded in voice oozing with friendliness. "I was just in the neighborhood, so I thought I'd drop by."

"All right! Great . . ." The man, Sherry noticed, didn't look especially pleased, but he waved them inside anyway, faking a polite smile.

Manuel pretended not to see the invitation. "Hey, man, I brought along a friend of mine," he said instead, tilting his head toward Sherry. "Hope you don't mind."

"No problem." The man motioned them inside again, and again Manuel ignored him.

"You alone?" Manuel asked.

"Yeah, yeah," said the man, and it seemed to Sherry that the admission came reluctantly. "Yeah, uh, Andrea's in transit."

Manuel laughed knowingly and then pushed Sherry forward. "Go on in," he insisted, as if she had been holding up the works. "Go on in and tell Pepe how much you love him. She couldn't stop talking about you in the car."

Pepe? Of course! Pepe Reboredo—that was it! Sherry knew she recognized him, but she wasn't sure how. And no wonder! He was so ordinary-looking close up—with an outdated John Travolta hairdo, thick center paunch, and droopy black eyes. He looked like a thousand other Cuban men in Miami fighting middle age with too much hair spray, too much gold chains, and too few shirt buttons fastened.

"Pleased to meet you," Sherry said, extending her hand, which Pepe lifted to his lips and kissed dramatically. Sherry lowered her eyes and noticed he was wearing turquoise alligator cowboy boots. No scuff marks.

"*Muy, muy bonita,*" he answered, addressing Manuel. His tone was friendly, but Sherry couldn't lose the sense that he was very uneasy with their visit. He stood firmly in the foyer, legs spread like a cop guarding a bank vault. The message was clear: You're not going any farther than this.

Manuel grinned smugly at Pepe's compliment. But then, almost instantly, he lost the smile and put on an aggressive grimace. "Hey, man," he said, taking a few steps toward Pepe, "we got business—"

"What a wonderful house you have!" Sherry suddenly cut Manuel off in an exaggerated burst of enthusiasm. "What a wonderful house! How long have you lived here?"

Pepe shrugged. "Two, three years—"

"How wonderful!" Sherry exclaimed. "It's just so—big!"

She didn't know what to say next, but she knew she wanted to keep talking. It was a long shot, she told herself, but maybe if Manuel had a little more time to think about it, he would realize it was insane to kill *this* man. Insane! Pepe Reboredo—for Christ's sake!—lead singer of Bernie Badillo and the Havana Boys! The guy was a fucking Miami icon—king of the cha-cha dance-hall set, the Cuban Frank Sinatra and, of course, a Bay of Pigs hero with scars to prove it! He ate dinner twice a month at the mayor's house. He had an extremely popular call-in talk show on an extremely popular Spanish radio station. Thousands of Cuban women kept a photo him in their wallets, his velvet-painting eyes looking longingly into the distance. There was even a street downtown named after his sappy band.

"Thank you for your lovely compliments," Pepe answered, seeming relieved at the distraction and a little amused at Sherry's sputtering. "Everything you see is all thanks to the beautiful people of Miami."

"And aren't the people of Miami just beautiful!" Sherry agreed heartily. From the corner of her eye, she could see Manuel was getting fidgety, but she went on. "It's amazing how well known you are, Pepe—how well loved by everyone, including the mayor, and the police and everyone. I mean, the *police* love you. Everyone—"

"That's enough!" Manuel had stepped between Sherry and Pepe now, and was frowning angrily. "Pepe knows who loves him."

"It's just that everyone *knows* him, Manuel," Sherry gushed, but she knew already that her plan had failed. Manuel's face was screwed into a frown rigid with hatred, his eyes popping like a freak-show corpse and his lips covered with frothing yellow bubbles of spit. "Back off," he shouted at Sherry, and a heartbeat later, she saw the flash of his revolver, and heard the thick thud of two gunshots, the sound of lead plugs dropping through water.

"*Jesucristo! María!*"

Pepe Reboredo fell to the floor in a pile, groaning hoarsely, clutching at his meaty left thigh with both hands.

"What the hell—" he grunted at Manuel. He stopped to gasp for air, his eyes scrunched shut in pain. "What you do this for, man? You're fucking crazy, just like everyone said—"

Manuel cackled with laughter. "*You're* crazy," he fired back. "You owe Mrs. Lopez a hundred grand, and that makes her very unhappy."

Pepe was writhing on the blood-covered marble floor of the foyer, twisting and turning as bolts of agony shot up and down his leg.

"Mimi didn't send you," he managed to say between clenched teeth. "You don't work for her anymore—everyone knows that, man. Slicing up faces, blowing away that little girl for nothing, for nothing . . . *Jesucristo*, Manuel, you *are* out of control—"

"*Jesucristo*, Manuel, you are out of control," Manuel mimicked Pepe in a whiny, high-pitched voice, and he turned to Sherry for a reaction. She stood motionless, back flat against a far wall, so paralyzed by terror she wasn't sure if she was still breathing. "Hey," he demanded. "They said I was bringing too much *attention* to the family. They didn't like my style. Ha! *You* tell me, who's crazy—me or them?"

"Them," Sherry whispered. "They are, Manuel."

Manuel snickered triumphantly and turned back to Pepe. "This is Sherry Estabrook," he told him. "She's a reporter with the *Miami Citizen*. She's my girlfriend. We're getting married soon."

Pepe groaned. The puddle of crimson blood underneath him was growing wider by the second. "Please help me, Manuel," he pleaded weakly. "Help me and I tell Mimi to take you back. I'll tell her you're not crazy, I swear. I swear to you on my mother's grave."

Manuel shrugged. "I'm not scared of Mimi," he answered. "Mimi said I was fucking up her business. Well, Mimi's gonna get hers soon, and everybody's gonna thank me." He turned to Sherry for acknowledgment, and in her shock and final, terrifying comprehension, she nodded obediently. "I'm gonna be a superstar." He turned back to Pepe Reboredo. "More famous than you, you little prickface."

Pepe tried to lift himself up on his elbows, but Sherry could tell he was losing consciousness. His eyes were covered with a slimy gray glaze, and his lips were almost purple.

"Hey, Pepe, wake up!" Manuel said, laughing bitterly. "Hey, Pepe, wake up and say good-bye!" He looked again at Sherry and wondered why she wasn't laughing, too.

He walked to her side and squeezed her arm just above the elbow, as if he were about to lead her onto the dance floor. "Okay, it's your turn," he said. Then, swiftly, he stooped down and pulled a small black pistol from his ankle holster.

He handed it to her.

"Finish the job," he said.

Finish the job?

Manuel wanted *her* to shoot Pepe Reboredo? Sherry began to shake all over, uncontrollably, as if a frigid wind were suddenly wrapped tight around her, turning sweat into ice. Manuel could force her to watch, yes, but he could not force her to kill a man. Never—

She let the gun drop to the floor.

"Pick it up," Manuel commanded.

"Manuel, I can't do this—"

"I said, pick it up!" His voice was low and urgent, followed quickly by the clicking sound of a safety being released. Manuel raised his gun and pointed it at Sherry's face.

"Do it," he said.

Sherry obeyed, moving in slow motion, feeling as if she might faint, wishing she would.

"Now, listen to me," she heard Manuel say, "you're going to finish the job, understand?" Without waiting for an answer, he moved his gun closer to her face—she could almost feel the silencer's muzzle touching her cheek—and with his left hand, he dragged her over to Pepe's limp body. They were standing right above him, and Sherry could feel his warm blood seeping through the toes of her sandals.

"He passed out," Manuel said, sounding a little disappointed. A shrug. "So," he said, "it couldn't be easier. You're lucky, I guess." He popped the safety on Sherry's pistol for her and then pressed it more firmly into her hand.

"Okay," he said flatly, "go ahead." His gun was planted now against Sherry's left temple. "You'll thank me when it's over. I'm doing this for us."

"Please—" Sherry protested, but she knew there was no point. Manuel's gun was pressed hard into her skull, making her jaw ache and her eyes water. "I can't," she whispered through tears. "I can't."

"You can," Manuel answered. "You will."

 In the car ride back to Coconut Grove, Manuel couldn't stop chattering, voice zooming up and down two octaves, fingers twitching on the wheel, eyes jumping around like two black beetles on a camphor lantern.

"I can't believe you got him right in the brains!" he kept telling Sherry. "What a mess, man! No open casket for Pepe!" He laughed raucously.

Sherry sat silently beside him, watching the road spin by, counting up to ten and then back to zero again over and over. She was trying to block out Manuel's words with her own mind's static, but it was impossible. The ranting was too loud and horrifying to ignore.

"You did great, baby," he said repeatedly. "I knew you were a professional. I knew you had it in you. You did great."

Then, sympathetically: "Like, maybe you want to work on your aim a little bit in the future or something, but I don't mean to criticize you, baby, you did great."

Sherry nodded. The truth was, she didn't aim at all. She had lifted her right arm up from her side with the little strength she had remaining, and then squeezed the trigger. When she opened her eyes, Pepe's face was gone, and Manuel was dragging her out the door. She hadn't even heard the blast.

"Do you think he died right away?" she asked Manuel as they turned onto the causeway and sped back toward the mainland. "I mean, did he move or anything after the bullet went in?"

"He wiggled for a second," Manuel answered matter-of-factly. "But I think he was dead already. You know what I mean? Like snakes. You cut up their bodies, and they keep wiggling all around for a few minutes."

"Uh-huh," Sherry said.

Manuel snickered. "Shit! You got him right in the fucking forehead."

"Oh."

"You did great, baby," he went on. "And now tell me, you're a little freaked-out, right? But it feels great, doesn't it? It feels awesome, right?"

"Right," said Sherry. She felt dead. All her nerve endings had gone cold, and her limbs were stiff, as if blood had stopped circulating through her veins. A dewy patina of cold perspiration coated her skin like a funeral shroud of damp silk.

"You can't wait to do it again, can you?"

"No," said Sherry.

Manuel nodded gleefully. "We can do another tomorrow night or something. No—shit—it's my father's birthday. I've got to make him dinner. Maybe next week—yeah!" he suggested. "I got to think of someone to kill first. Maybe that asshole who kicked me off the football team for fighting too rough. He said I had to go see the school counselor if I wanted to keep playing. He said I had a 'problem with authority,' just like that!" Manuel laughed raucously. "What a fucking idiot! Let's get him."

"Okay."

He reached over and squeezed her thigh. Sherry could tell he was looking at her meaningfully, and she struggled to turn her head slightly in his direction.

"You feel it, too?" he asked softly. It was more a statement than a question.

"What?" Sherry said. She didn't want to spark his anger, but in her heart she knew there was nothing left he could do that night to crush her soul any smaller. Manuel hadn't hurt her body, and maybe, she told herself, she should be thankful for that. But he had raped her life raw, and the pain of it was going to go on forever.

"You feel it, too?" he said again. "The thing between us now?" He was still squeezing her thigh, and the sensation of his skin against hers made her muscles clamp tight to the bone.

"Uh-huh," she answered.

"It's like"—he smiled shyly—"it's like we had sex, or something."

"Sort of," said Sherry.

Manuel was steering the car through the center of Coconut Grove now, driving more slowly, taking in the spandex-and-linen night-life scene spilling out of the bars and onto the streets, smirking as if he owned it all.

"Want to get something to eat?" Manuel asked her.

"No, no thank you," Sherry answered quickly. "I'm really tired. But thank you."

Manuel nodded knowingly. "Like I said, you're sort of freaked-out now," he said, "but believe me, you'll feel great in the morning."

Sherry murmured in agreement. She had barely heard his words, she was thinking instead about what Pepe Reboredo had said in his dying moments and Manuel's horrible answers—horrible because they were the truth, at last.

"Manuel," Sherry said quietly, "Mimi fired you, right? That's the real story, isn't it?"

"She's a cunt!" Manuel shot back. He jerked forward in his

seat and shoved the air-conditioning up a notch. A full minute of intense, angry fidgeting with the controls passed before he went on, and when he did, his words came like an explosion. "She calls me into her house after I killed Eddie and she tells me I'm too *violent* for her—hah!" He slammed the dashboard with the heel of his hand and then punched the roof with the same hand, fist clenched. "What a joke—too violent for Mimi Lopez!" he shouted. "She tells me I gotta stop cutting people, and she was all pissed-off that I shot that little whore down in Homestead and I shot that guy's dog a few times—she said the police were noticing *her* because of *me*." He shifted uncomfortably, pulling the steering wheel with him, and the car swerved into the oncoming lane and out of it in a wild seesaw ride. "So, I told her that I knew what I was doing—I know how to make people respect me. It's like I told you that day, I'm *advanced*. I told her that, you know, and she and her fucking sons stood there and laughed at me like I was a fucking joke. Well, fuck them."

He looked at Sherry for her approval, and she forced a meek smile.

"She said I should be *happy* she was letting me live," Manuel surged on. "She said she felt *sorry* for me! She tried to kiss me good-bye. Hah! I didn't let her touch me."

"Of course not," Sherry muttered, surprised any words even came out. The numbness had given way to a stabbing pain in her chest, and she curled into herself as much as she could without drawing Manuel's attention. But one quick sideways glance told her Manuel was oblivious to her anguish. He was staring out the window with a wicked grin, steering the Camaro along the center line, forcing oncoming traffic to swerve onto the shoulder or stop dead to avoid a collision. For a moment, it seemed to Sherry that he had forgotten his tirade against Mimi completely, but then just as suddenly, he flared up again like a cheap firecracker.

"My story's gonna get them," he announced. "They'll be sorry they fucked with Manuel Velo."

"They're going to jail?" Sherry sighed, sickened by the perfect logic of his plan. "That's what you think, right?"

"Right!" Manuel said cheerfully.

"And you're going to Mexico?" Sherry asked, but she knew she was hoping against hope.

Manuel burst into laughter. "I don't have to run, baby!" he said, smirking knowingly. "I'm gonna go pay a visit to the chief of police Sunday just about ten o'clock after everybody over there at headquarters has had a nice chance to read the newspaper, and I don't have to tell you, baby, the cops are gonna *love* me. You said so yourself, remember, that day in the park? I'm gonna be famous!" he exclaimed, stretching out the last word as if each syllable thrilled him endlessly. "I got us all set up for life," he told Sherry. "You and me, baby. They could even make, like, a TV show about us or something."

"Sounds great," Sherry said. Tears started dripping down her face again, but she quickly looked out the window and wiped them away. "Really, Manuel," she repeated, "a TV show. Fancy that." She paused for a moment to catch her breath because there was one last question she needed to ask, a question she should have asked at their first meeting in the park that day, under the lush, protective canopy of the spreading banyan tree.

"Tell me, Manuel," Sherry said, "tell me something, would you, okay?" She inhaled sharply to fight back the sudden, forceful urge to hang her head and weep. "Why did you tell *me* your story? I mean, if what you wanted was revenge, why didn't you just go to the cops right at the start?"

Manuel flashed an insinuating smile and then shrugged as if the answer were obvious. "Because I loved you," he said blithely, still staring out the window, "from the moment I saw you."

Then, turning to face Sherry, he finished his answer. "But you knew that," he said matter-of-factly, "didn't you?"

Sherry felt her heart contract once, a spasm of pain so profound she imagined a poison arrow piercing it at the core. "Yes, Manuel," she said finally, "I guess I did."

They drove in silence for a minute or two longer, and then Manuel turned onto Lemonlime Road and into Sherry's driveway. He cut the engine.

A minute of silence.

Then: "You want me to come inside?" he asked, sounding a little embarrassed. He was staring at his lap, where his gun had rested, snug between his thighs, since they left Pépé Reboredo's house. "Or you want to wait?"

"Let's wait," Sherry answered. This was not the good-bye she expected at all. She had tried to block it out of her mind until now, but in truth she had expected something far worse—his bony, grotesque body penetrating hers in a dry and painful imitation of passion, the final humiliation in a night of indelible horrors.

"Okay, let's wait," Manuel agreed, sounding a little relieved, and suddenly it occurred to Sherry that he had never once mentioned sex to her in all of his boastings. Yes, he had complimented her lips and talked ravenously about the women at Mimi Lopez's parties, but he had never mentioned having sex, not with Blanca, not with her, not with anyone.

And, of course, Sherry realized, it made perfect sense. Manuel was a virgin. He had never made love, and probably never would.

He didn't need to.

She turned to face him now, her dread redoubled. Manuel didn't want her body, she knew all at once. He wanted her mind, her heart, her soul—and he wanted them in the permanent, obsessive way no physical act could satisfy.

She bowed her head in resignation and waited for Manuel's words of parting.

Finally, they came, and she took them in without surprise: "We've got all the time in the world," he said, "because you know, from now on, we're never going to be apart."

Then he kissed her tenderly on the cheek and unlocked the door.

Sherry stepped inside her house and quickly snapped the lock behind her. Then, in the pitch-darkness and without thinking, she shoved the large black oak credenza in her foyer across the doorway—it was heavier than hell—and scrambled into the dining room to grab a chair to stack on top. And then another chair, and then two more.

When she was done, Sherry ran to the kitchen. There, in the yellow-blue light of the gas stove, she pulled a tray from the cupboard and methodically started covering it with her crystal—the fluted champagne goblets from her grandmother, the Baccarat wineglasses from Mother, the matching cognac snifters from Charles. Sherry stared at each piece regretfully, momentarily sorry to see them go, but she knew—she absolutely *knew*—that something had to be done. She had to protect herself. She needed time to think, to recover, to plan.

For the next five minutes, Sherry frantically carried the tray from room to room, slamming every window shut and carefully placing two or three glasses on each sill. Manuel was bound to smash one breaking in, if not tonight, then tomorrow night, when he came for her again. The noise would wake her. And then she would—

She would what?

The question stopped Sherry cold, and she slumped backward onto her living room couch, two of the glasses falling to the soft cushions beside her, the rest hitting the floor and delicately shattering into glittery shards.

She would what?

Sherry stared into the blackness of the room, knowing the answer but hating it with the kind of sorrow and desperation she had not felt until that night.

She would call the police.

And then what?

She would tell them there was a man forcing his way into her house.

And then?

And then, the police would come and arrest Manuel for trespassing.

But it wouldn't end there. Not at all. It would be the beginning of something worse, Sherry felt in her gut, something much worse.

Manuel wouldn't be in handcuffs before he started a campaign of revenge he would gladly die to win. Sherry had lied to him again, hadn't she? She had attempted to get free. But they were tied together forever—*we're married by blood*, he had said a dozen times in the car ride back from Miami Beach that night—and nothing was going to change that now.

He would start by telling the cops who exactly killed Pépé Reboredo. And maybe that wasn't so terrible, Sherry told herself. There would be an avalanche of gory publicity at first, of course, her face plastered on every news show and across every front page for a few days. The headlines were predictable: WEALTHY REPORTER FORCED TO SLAY MIAMI SUPERSTAR, JOURNALIST WEPT AS SHE PULLED TRIGGER, ATTORNEY CLAIMS. And then, after a few weeks, GRAND JURY CLEARS MIAMI REPORTER OF MURDER CHARGES; SAYS HOMICIDE WAS "AGAINST HER WILL." She would probably lose her job in one of those please-quit-or-be-fired deals, and she would go home to a graciously lukewarm welcome—how terribly embarrassing this would be for her parents—and she would start looking for another life, someplace else, far away, where no one would know her name or recognize her face.

So maybe that was the price she would have to pay for killing a man, Sherry told herself, sitting in the darkness of the living room, surrounded by broken glass. And maybe that wasn't so terrible given what she had done.

But she didn't want to call the police, not now, not ever.

Because they would set Manuel free, just as he intended.

It would take a while, of course, for *the People* v. *Mimi Lopez et al.* to work its way through the justice system—Manuel had so many stories to tell and so many people to send down—but eventually his testimony would win him a new name and a new place to live.

He would walk out of court unshackled, Sherry knew for certain, and he would come looking for her.

She shut her eyes and let the tears fall.

Manuel *had* won—they were never going to be apart again.

Her mind traveled in fast-forward. Suddenly, it was Christmas, and she was at her grandmother's house on Beacon Hill, looking down at Joy Street from the bowfront parlor, hoping to catch a glimpse of the carolers who paraded at dusk in their red wool mufflers, but seeing instead Manuel, all alone, looking up at her, smiling bitterly. And then suddenly she was someplace hot and dusty and unbearably poor—it had to be one of the African cities Belinda was always talking about—and she was waiting at a bus stop to get to the other side of town, where she taught in a school made of straw and mud. She turns around to ask someone the time, and out of the corner of her eye sees Manuel walking toward her in a lazy gait, hand outstretched, as if they are old friends. She turns to run, but an instant later she feels his hand on her shoulder and his breath on her neck—

Sherry cried out in the silence, a cry from so deep inside it didn't sound human.

There was only one solution, she knew all at once. Manuel had to die.

He had to die, or she would.

Sherry took a deep breath and stood up. "I want to live," she said out loud, and she was surprised how much it sounded like an apology. "Please let me live."

She wandered to her bedroom and lay on the floor, her mind hurtling all over with ideas, each one more horrible than the last. She could try to kill Manuel herself, she thought, but then she remembered the sickening last moment before she shot Pepe Reboredo, and she knew she didn't have the guts to pull a trigger again, ever. Or maybe she could hire someone to do the job, but then she ran the chance of getting blackmailed forever, trading in one psychological prison cell for another.

Or, Sherry thought, or maybe this isn't a problem at all. Maybe the story will kill him. The story will kill him, she told herself, if I let it. Its publication has to catch Manuel so off guard he doesn't have time to get to the cops. It has to catch him so off guard Mimi Lopez will find him first.

Impulsively, she rolled onto her stomach and crawled over to the phone, dialing Jack's number in the darkness.

His wife picked up. "Yes?" she said, obviously irritated. It was after eleven.

"Mrs. Dougherty, I'm sorry, but I need to talk to Jack."

"Who is this?"

"Sherry Estabrook. I'm a reporter—"

"Oh, yes."

A muffled sound and then Jack's groggy voice: "Jesus fucking Christ, Estabrook, this better be front-page news." He had been sleeping.

"Jack, hey, look, how you doing? Jack, I've been thinking," Sherry began, but he cut her off.

"Why the fuck are you whispering?" he demanded.

"Gee, I'm sorry. I didn't realize," Sherry answered, trying to speak up. "Is this better?"

A moment of silence.

"What the fuck is going on?"

"Jack, I've been thinking, um, pretty seriously here tonight, and I just had to talk to you," Sherry said. "I mean, I couldn't sleep until I talked to you about this—"

"Spit it out already!"

Sherry cleared her throat. "Jack," she said, "I think we need to run the Baby Lips package sooner than we've planned—like I think we should run it tomorrow," she said. "I think maybe we're giving the cops a chance to break the story before we do—"

"Wait a minute, Estabrook," Jack cut her off. "You called me at home at eleven twenty-seven on a Friday night because you had a hunch that *maybe* I hadn't already given the scheduling of your fucking story enough thought?" In the background, Sherry could hear Jack's wife muttering something unpleasant.

He went on: "I mean, Sherry, if it was something important, I wouldn't mind. You know that. But this is fucking ridiculous. It's my job to think about this kind of thing."

"I'm sorry, Jack," she said. "It just sort of seemed like a big risk to me."

"Let me assure you it's not," Jack answered. "I had Belinda check it out today. The cops haven't got a clue about this kid. And believe me, she asked a lot of leading questions. The story stands. For Christ's sake, Sherry, we want this piece to run on a Sunday so it gets all the attention it deserves. You're going to be famous."

"Great," Sherry said immediately.

"So forget about it."

"But, Jack—" Sherry knew her voice was too shrill, and she didn't care.

"I said forget about it!"

And then the line went dead.

Less than a minute later, Sherry was dialing Belinda, her last hope.

"Alvarez residence." Belinda's voice was chirpy, and in the background Sherry could hear Eladio warbling along with a scratchy mambo record.

"Hi, it's me."

"Sherry! I've been trying to reach you." Belinda sounded anxious. "Where have you been all night? Did you get home okay?"

"Yeah—"

"Did you go out to eat or something?" She didn't sound convinced.

"I just drove around thinking," Sherry answered after a moment had passed. She hated to lie to Belinda, but if she told her the truth, she knew her plan to get Manuel killed would be destroyed by noble intentions. Belinda believed in the system, especially now that she was married to it.

"Well, sometimes just being alone is the best thing," she said sympathetically. Then: "I guess I was sort of worried." The truth was, she had been so nervous she had been pacing the apartment since seven, calling Sherry's house every five minutes. Eladio had been furious the whole time, damning Sherry in Spanish and English for making his wife act so *loco*.

"I'm fine," Sherry assured her. "I'm sorry I didn't call sooner."

"No, no. It's okay. I'm sorry." Belinda collapsed into Eladio's easy chair and covered the mouthpiece of the phone while she let out a long, noisy sigh of relief.

"Don't be sorry, Belinda."

"No, I am."

"Oh, Christ!" Sherry exploded. Why was Belinda always apologizing? She had nothing to be sorry for. Absolutely nothing.

"Sherry?" The voice was tiny, tentative, and suddenly Sherry felt a surge of love for Belinda, and guilt for never having told her.

"Yes, Mrs. Alvarez?" she answered.

"Did you get a decent dinner?"

"Yeah."

"So, everything's okay, right?" Belinda looked up to see Eladio waving for her hang up. Time to go to bed. "Everything's okay?"

"Right."

"So, maybe I'll see you at work—"

Sherry stood up abruptly, pulling the phone off her night table with a loud clatter. She couldn't let Belinda off the line without getting her to agree to talk to Jack about changing the story's run date.

"Wait, don't hang up yet!" she pleaded. "I have to tell you something."

"What? What is it?" Belinda's voice was instantly attentive and soothing. "Is it Brazil? I saw you talking to him the other day near the elevator. It didn't look too great."

"No, no, it's not that," Sherry came right back. "It's not him at all. It's the story."

"The story?" Belinda sounded incredulous. "Sherry, the story is done. Let it go."

"I know it's done," Sherry tried to sound sincere, "but I was thinking that maybe we need to get the story out sooner, like tomorrow. I mean, I don't know what in the world we're waiting for—"

"Sherry?" Belinda said. "The story is over. We can't change it now. It's too late."

"It's not over until it runs off the presses," Sherry insisted. "So much has changed—"

"It's over for me," Belinda cut her off quietly, and Sherry noticed Eladio's singing and the mambo record had gone silent. "I can't talk about Manuel or Mimi Lopez or cocaine murders anymore. I just can't. Eladio could lose his job, Sherry. He really could, knowing what he does and not telling anyone."

"Well, don't tell him anything!" Sherry shot back as if the answer were obvious. "Just don't tell him!"

A half minute of silence passed before Belinda finally spoke again.

"But, Sherry," she said, "he's my husband."

Sherry felt her heart drop. She was alone.

All she could do now was pray that Mimi Lopez moved faster than Manuel as he strutted into police headquarters.

"I understand," she told Belinda. "He's your husband."

"I'm sorry."

Sherry lay down on her bed and inhaled deeply, trying to sound like herself but not really knowing how.

"Don't be," she told Belinda, and she meant it with all her heart. "So long."

A moment later, she closed her eyes, and overcome by suffocating fatigue, she fell into a sleep so close to death it felt divine.

Sherry thrashed awake four hours later, tangled in sweat-drenched sheets, thrown from bed by the force of her dream and the perfect, terrifying solution it contained. If Jack and Belinda would not save her, she would save herself, and now, all at once, she knew how. But she had to wait until Sunday, Sunday morning to be exact, just after two, when the piercing all-clear bell sounded in the cavernous pressroom of the *Citizen* and the machines started to rumble and then churn, spitting out newspapers faster and faster and faster until another bell clamored and the machines roared into a deafening silence.

She would be there, she knew, to catch the first copy off the press, its paper still hot and its ink still damp. Being there was her only hope.

And so, Saturday night, Sherry did not go to sleep. Instead, she waited for the hours to pass into Sunday in her living room, sitting motionlessly on the floor, slowly smoking one cigarette after another in the pitch-blackness, listening to nothing, not even the ragged sound of her own breathing, and thinking of nothing, except what she had to do to survive.

At one precisely, Sherry stubbed out her last butt, crawled on her belly to the kitchen to make sure she cast no shadows behind drawn curtains, and slipped out her back door, immediately scrambling into a triangle of darkness near the steps, her face tucked to her chest and her body pulled into a tight crouch. Then, for ten long minutes after the lock clicked shut, she waited just as she had planned—waited for the sound of a twig snapping underfoot or a branch being pushed aside. She waited for the sound of Manuel's sickly-sweet greeting—"*Well, what have we here?*"—or the touch of his rawboned fingers on her neck. But nothing. Nothing but silence. And so, slowly, she stood, and after one final excruciatingly careful look left and right and left again, she began to run and run fast, past the avocado tree in her yard, over the fence to Christmas Day Park, through the swing set, under the slide, and across the playing field, until finally, wet with perspiration and gasping for breath, she came to Persimmon Lane, a narrow, unlit dead end, where only two houses stood, and they were hidden behind high white stucco walls. The road itself was unpaved and overgrown with leafy vines, muffling the sound of her footsteps as she approached her car. She had hidden it there just after dark, and in the sliver of moonlight above, it was barely visible, just as she had hoped.

Sherry climbed into the front seat and immediately locked the door. Again she waited, twelve minutes this time, banking on her gut's guess that if Manuel was watching, he wouldn't have the patience to hold back that long. With the windows jammed tight against the humid night, the car was sweltering and airless, and Sherry's black sweatsuit stuck to her skin like a damp wash-cloth. Even her scalp was soaking wet, with ripe rivulets of sweat dripping down her face and off her chin. Still, she forced herself to remain curled in a ball on the front seat, counting off the seconds to dull her sharp-edged anxiety, until at last she knew it was time to drive, via a twisted and irrational route she devised herself, to the *Citizen* building on Biscayne Bay.

The ride took a half hour, twice as long as usual, exactly as planned, and as soon as she arrived, Sherry headed for the far corner of the guest parking lot—a place no one would look for her conspicuous red BMW with its conspicuous Massachusetts plates. Again, she parked, curled into a ball, and waited in total darkness. Three minutes passed, then five more. She checked her watch—it was nearly two. She had just a few moments to spare.

Then, suddenly: footsteps, heavy footsteps, scraping the pavement and stomping toward her in an angry, purposeful clip.

Sherry felt her heart dive-bomb into her gut painfully—how could she have missed Manuel behind her? What a fool she was! She had checked the rearview mirror as often as she stared straight ahead, she had U-turned three times, backtracked twice, stopped at yellow lights, and run red ones—and still he had caught her—

Sherry instinctively pushed herself forward, off the seat and into the tiny well of space near the accelerator, pulling her body into an even tighter fetal hug, eye sockets pressed hard into knees and arms wrapped tight around her shins. And then, her voice squeezed to a strident whisper, she prayed to God for mercy as she never had before. "Oh, Father," she began, "forgive me for all of my sins—"

More footsteps, closer and closer, seeming to take forever to reach her, then—*crack crack crack*—three harsh, insistent raps on her window, the unmistakable sound of a steel muzzle on glass. Instantly, Sherry felt her bladder go, warm piss running down her thighs in gushes and filling the car with the fetid stench of failure and terror. Still she prayed, eyes jammed shut in concentration: "Father in heaven," she chanted fervently, "I promise, oh God, I promise to be good from now on—"

"Open it up, lady!"

Sherry screamed.

It was a short, breathless, high-pitched scream of sheer relief, but enough of a scream to send the security guard outside her window backward a few steps in shock. He recovered quickly and

approached again, holding a black nightstick out in front of him
in a feeble attempt to look menacing.

"Okay, get out with your hands up," he ordered, voice no-
ticeably quavering.

Sherry quickly uncurled her body, scooted back into her seat,
and stuck her palms in the air, trying hard not to laugh, not just
at the nervous security guard, but at herself, her sudden attack
of religion and her puddle of stinking pee. She used her foot to
snap open the door handle and then stood up beside her car.

"I can explain everything," she said, as cheerfully as she
could muster. She was still trembling all over, trying to shake free
of terrifying *what-ifs* racing through her head. "I work here," she
said. "I'm a reporter on the city desk."

"Let's see some identification."

Sherry shook her head. She was traveling light on purpose.
"Look, I don't have any on me," she said, smiling reassuringly.
"But I can promise you I'm Sherry Estabrook, employee number
2430, extension 3004, Social Security number 118—"

"That's enough," the guard cut her off, and not in an unfriendly way. Apparently, the intentionally self-confident and bemused tone of Sherry's voice had done the trick. That, and the
fact that he wasn't standing close enough to her to pick up the
smell of urine. He lowered his nightstick and relaxed his hunched-
up shoulders, and Sherry noticed he was probably about her age,
pudgy with baby blubber, with lovely light blue eyes and the
sallow skin of a man who sleeps all day. Every few seconds, he
rubbed the side of his nose with his forefinger, as if to shoo away
an invisible fly, and then tugged on a curly clump of red hair near
his left sideburn. She wondered if the twitches were simply that,
or if he was still petrified from their encounter, the way she was.

"Oh, well," Sherry sighed, to break the tension. "Nice night,
wouldn't you say? No moon to speak of, but still quite nice."
Overhead she heard two sea gulls cawing back and forth on their
way toward the water.

The guard nodded agreeably, and, smiling awkwardly, motioned for Sherry to drop her hands. "You know," he said, all at
once sounding quite brotherly, "you shouldn't park all the way
out here, Miss Estabrook, it's not safe."

"Really? Well, I'll say! I do it for exercise," Sherry improvised.
"You know, you can burn a lot of calories just walking longer
distances, or ironing standing up, or washing the dishes by hand

instead of using the machine. I read that someplace. So, anyway, that's why I like to park out here."

The guard nodded again, this time with even more vigor. "There's supposed to be a new pill coming out that just dissolves fat," he volunteered.

Sherry smiled. "That so?" She turned her back and opened her car door again, pretending to search for something under the front seat. But the guard didn't get the hint to leave. He hovered closer now, watching her with interest.

"Well, you going in?" he asked at last.

"Yep," Sherry agreed. "Just got to find something here." She motioned him to go ahead without her. The last thing she wanted was to draw attention to herself.

"I'll wait," the guard offered. "The night shift's gotta stick together."

"Oh, I'm not night shift," Sherry answered, quickly turning to face him. The guy was obviously going to be persistent. "I couldn't sleep, so I thought I'd drive over to pick up a copy of Sunday's paper. The presses rolling yet?"

"Just started."

"Great," Sherry said. "Gotta go." And before he could answer, she waved and started to jog toward the building. Over her shoulder, she could hear him shout good-bye, and then, faintly, wish her good luck.

But by that time, Sherry was almost at her destination. She could hear the low rolling thunder of the presses, and a few yards off, she could see dozens of truck drivers, pacing back and forth on the sidewalk behind the building, gabbing and drinking coffee, gearing up for a long night of deliveries. A few steps closer and she saw the massive conveyer belt into the loading dock start to jerk forward, and on it, the day's first editions. Down below, ready with wrapping wire and metal dollies, was a horde of bleary-eyed men in dreadlocks, the army of Haitian refugees who ferried the paper from inside the building to outside, where the trucks waited with motors running.

All the noise and confusion—the people shouting and milling around in anticipation, the buzz of boom boxes blasting reggae, the din of the presses, and the stink of truck diesel—was just what Sherry was counting on. Head ducked, she deftly elbowed her way through the crowd and grabbed a copy of the paper off the conveyor belt before anyone even noticed she was there, and she was gone just as fast, back into the darkness of the parking lot.

A minute later, she was in her car, doors locked again, windows shut. And there, in the dim light of the overhead bulb, she saw the story, stripped across the top of the front page, under a stacked headline:

YOUTH, 16, ADMITS CAREER AS COCAINE HIT MAN;
DESCRIBES LIFE INSIDE MIAMI'S DEADLIEST BUSINESS

The double byline read, *Sherry Estabrook and Belinda Alvarez*, Miami Citizen *Staff Reporters*.

Sherry tucked the newspaper into her lap and turned over the engine. She had one more stop before she was through.

Her route this time was more direct: south on 95, left on Red Road, and then four twisting single-lane miles more. At last, just before three, the moon now totally hidden by silver clouds, Sherry saw the sign for Gables by the Sea. She pulled a hard left, and then, in her head, listened as Manuel directed her again—take this left, he had said, now right, okay left again. Finally: "This is it. This is where she lives. Mimi Lopez."

Sherry killed the lights, shifted into neutral, and glided into the driveway. The house, just as it had been on that sunny afternoon with Manuel, was as closed-up as a coffin. The curtains were drawn, and on the first floor even the shutters were shut, as if a hurricane were expected soon. Still, Sherry couldn't help but admire the restrained elegance of the place, with its gracious, arching front door and low, sloping tile roof. It quietly announced wealth and all its accoutrements, but unlike Pépé Reboredo's glitzy stucco palace, it also said this: Stay away, no visitors, we're serious people inside.

Sherry ignored the message.

Just as planned, she pulled open her glove compartment, pulled out a comb, mascara, and red lipstick, and quickly pulled her face together. She had anticipated the sweat wrecking her looks, but she hadn't planned on pissing in her pants. She just had to hope that the stench had faded—she had driven down 95 with every window hanging open—and that she wasn't there long enough for anyone to notice the look of damp discomfort and disgust she couldn't manage to completely camouflage with her new, completely fake blank expression.

Inside, she was dying with fear.

Sherry got out of the car, newspaper under her arm, and swiftly walked toward the front door, amazed that her legs were even working. Her mouth was filled with charcoal cinders, and she wondered how she was going to get out the six short words she planned to say—*Give this to Mimi right away*. If worse came to worst, all she had to do was shove the paper at whatever burly bodyguard answered the door, jab one finger at the front-page headline, and then turn and run. She'd left the car door open and the key plugged in.

With three paces to go, Sherry dropped her chin to her chest and quietly tried out her voice. "Please," she murmured, surprised it sounded so calm, "give this to Mimi." She cleared her throat and started again. "Please give—"

"Yes?"

Sherry looked up to see the door in front of her wide open, and leaning to one side, the silhouette of a tiny birdlike woman, legs crossed at the ankles, hair pulled back against her skull, one frail arm supporting the other, holding a cigarette to her lips. "Who are you, please? Yes?" she said again in an aristocratic Spanish accent, the kind used by people who learned English in school instead of the streets. "Who are you looking for?" The tone was not unfriendly and certainly not scared, Sherry noticed at once, just mildly curious.

"I'm looking for you," Sherry said simply. She took a few steps closer, close enough for her face to show in the light of the foyer chandelier. Close enough for her smile to be seen, a smile that begged, trust me, if just for a moment.

Mimi Lopez tilted her head to one side and frowned slightly. She was studying Sherry intently, cigarette poised against her lower lip, eyes wide open and critical. Instantly and unexpectedly, Sherry was struck by the undertow of her flawless beauty—Manuel had told her of it, of course, but she had chalked it up to teenage adoration or mother worship, she forgot which now. All she knew was that Mimi Lopez had to be fifty at least, but still she had the humble, enchanting face of a virgin, full of light and promise. She wore her hair long, pulled off her forehead and over her shoulder in a loose French braid with an organza bow at the end. She didn't wear a trace of makeup or a piece of jewelry, and she was dressed plainly, in blue jeans and a tucked-in white T-shirt. She was barefoot.

It was only after a full minute had passed that Sherry saw a hint of the Mimi Lopez she had expected, and she saw it in her eyes. Just for a brief flash—it must have lasted less than a second—her eyes turned opaque, pupils absorbing the light and spinning into vacant black pools. Then, just as suddenly, the light came back into them, and she smiled one of the sweetest, most forgiving smiles Sherry had ever seen.

"You're not *policía*," she said at last, sounding absolute certain. "You must be one of Roberto's girls—poor thing." She uttered the last two words deep from her heart, mouth turned into a compassionate frown, right hand outstretched in an invitation inside. "He's not here, *mi bebé*, but let me fix you something to eat."

Sherry shook her head. She knew from the reporter on the Lopez family sidebar that Roberto was one of Mimi Lopez's eight sons, the eldest and reportedly the most brutal. He was said to be a flagrant and abusive womanizer, a speed addict, and his mother's successor, a very anxious successor.

"No, I'm not one of Roberto's girls," Sherry said, and she couldn't help but sound slightly apologetic. Mimi Lopez had looked so hopeful, perhaps even desperate for company. "Who I am is not important. I'm just here to give you something I think you should read right now." She handed Mimi Lopez the newspaper, front page unfolded.

For the next five minutes, both women stood motionless, Mimi Lopez reading and Sherry watching her. She had intended to leave—she was already off schedule by ten minutes or more if she was to get home and still get three hours of sleep—but the expression on Mimi Lopez's smooth face compelled her to stay. She looked deeply, affectingly sad.

"Oh, little Manuel," she sighed when she was done scanning the copy inside and out. "I warned him, you know, he's so young. . . ."

For a moment, she scrutinized the grainy picture of herself on the front page and shrugged. "Could be anyone," she said. Then, carefully, she looked up and directly into Sherry's eyes.

"Thank you," she said, and suddenly Sherry heard the arch businesswoman in her voice, a shrewd *don't-fuck-with-me* undercurrent. "If you tell me who you are," she said, "you will be rewarded."

"I don't want anything," Sherry shot back automatically,

knowing the lie was obvious. "I just wanted you to see this before it was too late."

"Too late?" Mimi Lopez asked. She took a deep inhale on her cigarette and then threw it to the marble floor. "Are you telling me—"

"Yes," Sherry cut her off abruptly. "Yes, I'm telling you Manuel plans to go to the police this morning. He's going to testify against all of you if—"

Sherry stopped cold. She'd already said more than she intended, but then again, she had never expected to be face-to-face with Mimi Lopez. Perhaps she should take advantage of the opportunity, say *exactly* what had to be said—

"If what?" Mimi Lopez demanded.

Sherry took a few steps backward, ready to flee. "If you don't stop him first." She turned and started to sprint back to the car, but something stopped her just as fast—the clear, tinkling, carefree sound of Mimi Lopez's laughter behind her.

"Come back here," she called to Sherry, her voice now warm and bemused, like a mother talking to a silly two-year-old. "Come back here for a minute, then you can run away forever."

Sherry obeyed.

"Now, you, whoever you are," Mimi Lopez began when Sherry was standing in front of her in the doorway, "I guess you want Manuel dead, huh? And you're afraid he's going to get to the police before I get to him, right?" She laughed again. "Don't you worry, *señorita*, because I know exactly what I have to do to make sure this article"—she slapped the paper dismissively with the back of her hand—"means absolutely *nada* to anyone trying to hurt me or my boys."

Sherry bowed her head, all at once exhilarated by her success and profoundly ashamed by her complicity. She had won, yes! But she was a hypocrite and a liar now more than ever. Suddenly, she felt a bolt of tenderness for her father, so strong and unexpected it made her heart ache with regret. She thought of him standing in the dining room, face ashen with sadness, asking for her forgiveness, and she thought of her own horrible refusal, as if she had the right to judge him still.

"Thank you, Mrs. Lopez," Sherry murmured.

"Thank *you*!" Another sweet smile. Then: "You're Eddie's wife, aren't you?" she asked softly. "Your brother works over at the paper, no? He runs the big press machine?"

Sherry nodded meekly. It was just one more lie.

"That's a good brother," Mimi Lopez said, "to call you so early in the morning."

"Uh-huh," Sherry agreed vaguely.

"And you," Mimi Lopez said, leaning close to Sherry, "are a good friend to me." And with that, she stood on her tiptoes and delicately kissed Sherry on the cheek. "God bless you," she whispered. "Now, I have work to do. Good-bye."

60

The next morning, Sherry was at work by 6:00 A.M.—those were Jack's orders. She hadn't slept anyway when she got home—she was shaking too violently, replaying her meeting with Mimi Lopez over and over again in graphic slow motion. She couldn't even force herself to lie down. Instead, she'd paced the house until daybreak, darting from window to window, checking for Manuel in every shadow, imagining the sound of his seething, sickly-sweet voice demanding entry. Just before dawn, when the cerulean light of morning began to creep into the sky and birds began to call to one another in the avocado tree out back, Sherry finally collapsed onto the living-room couch and began to doze restlessly. But then, not ten minutes later, she awoke abruptly in a freezing sweat. She'd dreamed Manuel was alive—that somehow, *somehow*, he had escaped Mimi Lopez's wrath and was on his way to get her before running to the cops. She would never be free! Sherry let out a frenetic scream and leapt to her feet—she had to get out of the house before it was too late; she had to get to the *Citizen*. She checked her watch. It was almost time for Jack's meeting anyway; no one would wonder why she was there early. She hurtled toward her bedroom, bumping into furniture and pushing herself off the walls in panic, and dressed in two minutes flat, pulling the first thing in her closet off the hook: a short floral skirt she'd bought for a party the summer before and a bright red University of Georgia T-shirt Belinda had given her for her birthday. Then she grabbed her bag and ran for the door. She was almost there when she tripped over a pile of newspapers in the hallway and went sprawling, facedown, to the floor. But she didn't even feel the impact of her fall, and it wasn't until she was in the car, racing downtown at eighty miles an hour, that she realized her elbows and knees were dripping blood all over the car. Instantly, she grabbed a tissue from her purse and started mopping it up, then stopped just as fast. There were more important things to worry about than a few stupid bloodstains, she told herself as she pushed the accelerator to the floor, much more important things.

She made it to the *Citizen* building in record time, careered her car into the No Parking zone at the front door, and sprinted inside. All she had to do was make it to the elevator, she thought, then she would be safe, *then* she would stop trembling. And that's what happened. The moment the elevator doors closed in front of her, guaranteeing safe passage to the protective sanctum of the *Citizen* newsroom, Sherry felt her muscles unclamp from the bone. She took a long, slow inhale of breath and let it out twice as slowly. By the time she reached the fifth floor, her terror was ebbing away, replaced by fatigue, complete and total fatigue, marrow-deep. She could barely lift her feet to drag herself to her desk, and when she finally made it, she slumped into her chair and rested her head on her arms in front of her. All around her, the newsroom was rumbling into motion. The overnight shift was lazily packing up to go; the day crew was reading the wires and tanking up on coffee. Small clutches of reporters were chatting here and there, most of them—voices hushed with undisguised envy—about the huge front-page spread starring an eminently quotable teenage assassin named Manuel. But Sherry was oblivious. She was swamped with dizziness, so swamped that she didn't notice a few minutes later when Belinda bounded up to her, chirping away cheerfully.

"Well, you've got to admit we did it! We really did it, Sherry!" she exclaimed. "And I've got to say, it looks pretty darn awesome, Miss Estabrook!" She waited a moment for a response, got none, forged on. "*Yoo-hoo*, sleepyhead, wake up and celebrate!" She tousled Sherry's hair familiarly.

The touch jerked Sherry out of her daze, and she lifted her head to see Belinda sitting on her desk, decked out in a cheery yellow pantsuit covered with orange polka dots. As usual, or at least since she'd met Eladio, Belinda was also wearing turquoise eye shadow and pearly lipstick. She was smiling broadly, still babbling away, but Sherry couldn't make out the words. She stopped her with a tense wave of the hand.

"Hey, *amiga*, slow down, I'm begging you," she whispered hoarsely. "Let's just take it easy here. I'm not feeling too hot."

Immediately, Belinda opened her eyes wide in concern. Sherry did look terrible—her face a lurid white, her eyes, ordinarily such a vibrant shade of blue, were cloudy and bloodshot. Her whole body sagged. "Maybe you're getting the flu," she suggested solemnly. "And, oh, boy, what a great time to get sick!" She reached out and squeezed Sherry's shoulder comfortingly. "You need a break, Sherry, you really do."

"Yeah, I do," Sherry answered right away. The idea of a vacation was enough to lift her spirits, if only slightly. As soon as she was out of this mess, that's exactly what she would do—take some time alone, sort out what went wrong, decide how to make everything right again. "I think I really do need a vacation," she told Belinda. "A long one, a few weeks or something. I think I've got to get out of town for a while, maybe go to Japan, or Australia, even, I've never been there. Or maybe Africa, right? You can tell me—"

Her rambling was cut off by a sharp bark of commands from Jack Dougherty, who'd just marched into the newsroom surrounded by the other "Baby Lips package" writers, Radewski, three general-assignment reporters from Metro, two attorneys from Babcock, Bauer & Wold, and two translators. "Everyone in my office, now!" he hollered, and everyone obeyed. Sherry was the last one to make it, but she did, with Belinda supporting her lightly at the elbow.

Jack leaned back on his desk and lit a butt. "Okay, listen up," he began curtly; he was in high gear, just as he always was after a blockbuster ran on the front page. "I figure the phones are gonna start ringing by seven, and by late afternoon we ought to have enough calls for one of you to throw together a solid reaction piece for Monday's front page, got it?" Everyone in the room nodded. In his head, Jack was already fiddling with the headline—COMMUNITY SUPPORTS *CITIZEN* STORY 2-TO-1. SOME SAY PAPER SHOULD HAVE GONE TO POLICE, or MIAMI RESIDENTS SPLIT ON HIT-MAN STORY: CRITICS SAY YOUNG KILLER GLORIFIED. Something like that. The story, he told himself, would write itself.

And it did, but not exactly as he'd planned. Quite the opposite. By noon, more than five hundred people had called, most of them *enraged* that the *Citizen* hadn't turned Manuel over to the cops, some of them worried that the *Citizen* had jeopardized his life, a couple of them ranting and raving about the story's impact on Miami tourism. "I hope you all go to hell," one woman screamed at Radewski, "for what you're doing to this city. No one is ever going to visit here again. The *Citizen* killed Miami."

By three o'clock, more than a thousand readers had called—every able body in the building was answering the phones—and most of them were furious, canceling subscriptions, screaming for the publisher's resignation. They wanted to know Manuel's name. They wanted to know where the *Citizen* was hiding him, and what the hell for. And they wanted to know when the police were going to arrest him on TV.

But by that time, Jack wasn't counting callers anymore. He was in another office, two doors down from his, huddled with the lawyers and Garrett Newman. From her desk, Sherry could make out that Jack didn't look pleased. In fact, he looked *extremely* pissed, his face set in a dark growl, his hands jabbing the air like a boxer gone ballistic. She wondered what in the world was going on, but overcome by exhaustion and anxiety, she didn't have the energy to stand up and find out. Instead, she lowered her head to her desk again, just in time to miss seeing Jack open his mouth to start shouting.

The fact was, Jack was getting killed. Not by the outpouring of anger about the story—he was used to that kind of garbage—but by Newman's unexpected about-face. Suddenly, the *Citizen* had to "realign" its policy toward Manuel, he announced, straightening the hanky in his suit pocket. He had assiduously avoided eye contact with Jack since their meeting alone began. Dozens of readers and many *major* city leaders had been in contact with him, he said, and more than a few advertisers as well. He saw now the story had been a mistake. The bottom line was that the *Citizen* simply couldn't be in the business of *protecting* a self-avowed assassin; it didn't look right. It wasn't good for Miami, he said, it wasn't good for anyone.

Not only that, Newman informed Jack officiously, but the publisher himself had just received a call from the D.A., and he had two subpoenas ready to go, one marked "Estabrook" and the other marked "Alvarez."

"But it's not going to come to that, you understand," Newman stated dryly, sounding as if he were reading from a prepared statement, and in truth, most of what he was saying had been dictated to him earlier in the day by his bosses on the eighth floor. "Due to the heinousness of the crimes involved, management has decided that the *Citizen* should work with the authorities at this point." He paused to fidget with his hanky again, then proceeded in a stilted voice. "Now, I know, Jack," he said, "that this plan isn't going to sit well with you—"

"You bet your *fucking* ass it's not going to sit well with me!" Jack bellowed back. He pulled his fly-fishing cap off, rubbed his forehead angrily, then pushed it back on his head again with a snarly grunt. "Since when do we turn our fucking sources over to the cops? Jesus Christ, Newman! What's going on here? This is a fucking *newspaper!*"

"We have a responsibility to our readers—" Newman shot back. He was getting drawn into the argument against his will. He had his orders, and that was that. "The *Citizen* exists for its—"

"We got a responsibility to our fucking *profession!*" Jack wouldn't let him go on. "Reporters aren't cops, man! Come on, you know that." He shook his head disbelievingly at what was happening. He might have expected the publisher and his bean-counting cronies to wimp out, but not Newman. He'd been a newsman once, and he'd stood by him on lots of tough stories in the past couple of years. "Fuck it, Garrett," Jack blurted out, "I thought you were one of *us.*"

That was all Newman would hear.

"Cool down, Dougherty," he snapped. "The decision has been made." He stood and walked toward the window, back to Jack. "Get the girls in here," he said quietly. "We need Manuel's location, and we need it now."

Again, Jack shook his head. "You oughta be ashamed," he muttered, lighting another cigarette. He inhaled a long drag, then exhaled it toward the ceiling, thoughtfully watching the smoke billow out above him like a dusky gray cloud. Maybe it was finally time for him to get out of newspapers, he told himself, spend some time in the Everglades, casting for tarpon in the glorious solitude of daybreak. Maybe the news business was just getting to be too damn much of a *business* business for him to stick around. He lowered his gaze to the newsroom and spotted Sherry with her head on her desk and Belinda beside her reading a magazine.

Alvarez looked fine, he decided, but Estabrook looked totally wiped-out. Poor kid, he thought, she didn't know what was about to hit her. She was like him when it came to the cardinal rules of journalism—a good old-fashioned hard-ass. He'd always admired that about her. Turning Manuel in was going to break her heart. If they both were lucky, Jack sighed to himself, Manuel had already cut out of town.

He picked up his phone and banged in Belinda's extension. "You and your pal there," he said, "come on over to my house for a spot of tea." He threw Newman a sardonic glare and got one in return. "And I mean pronto."

A half minute later, Sherry and Belinda appeared, and Newman stood up to greet them with a gruff nod. Immediately, Sherry sensed something was wrong, terribly wrong. For one thing, Newman looked as stiff and uncomfortable as a marionette, decked out in a sharp-pressed gray suit and a red power tie. No one dressed up like that at the *Citizen* on a Sunday, no one from the newsroom at least. For another, the man was wearing a severe frown. For three years running, Sherry had known him only as a jocular, good-ol'-boy comrade—but right now, the corners of his mouth were pushed far down into his jowls. Sherry cast her attention to Jack. He was frowning, too, but from the opposite corner of the room. Instinctively, Sherry took a quick read of his mood. He was pissed-off all right, but not at them.

"Sit down," he ordered, then let out a long, resigned sigh. He dropped his head for a moment, as if in prayer. When he raised it again, his eyes were in the distance, considering the buzzing activity of the newsroom.

"Okay, girls," he said finally, "tell me: Where the fuck is Manuel?"

Sherry nearly jumped backward at the shock of what she had just heard, and suddenly—painfully—she was wide awake. Her fatigue had vanished, replaced with a thumping, raging attack of fear. What was this? What in the world? She couldn't believe it— was Jack, of all people, going to lasso Manuel for the cops before Mimi Lopez could find him?

"Where's Manuel? That's what you're asking?" she practically sputtered. "Why, I-I-I don't know. I haven't the slightest idea." It was the truth, thank God.

"You don't know?" It was Newman speaking, and the tone of his voice redoubled Sherry's fear. It matched his expression to a

T—strident and indignant. He wasn't playing around. He wanted Manuel, and he wanted him right away.

"No, I don't know where he is," she snapped, surprised by how self-confident and self-righteous she sounded. She was neither. "And, as you are well aware, I guaranteed him confidentiality—"

But Newman cut her off. "Belinda," he asked, "do you know where Manuel is?"

Belinda shook her head. Poor Sherry—she knew something like this was going to happen to her. "I never even met him," she offered.

Newman looked startled.

"But, Sherry, you have, correct?"

"Correct," she answered.

"And now you're saying you have no idea where he is at this moment, correct?"

"Correct," she said again, this time more firmly. She knew how to play this game.

"Do you know where he lives?" Newman asked.

Sherry wanted to slug him. Of course she knew where he lived. Hadn't he read the story? *The teenager lives in a modest three-bedroom home in one of Miami's well-kept middle-class suburbs. There are two cars in the driveway—his, a fancy sports coupe, and his father's, an aging American sedan.*

"Yes, I know where he lives," she answered coolly.

"Can you call him there?" Newman asked.

Sherry closed her eyes for a second to gather her thoughts. She could, yes, she knew that. But she wouldn't, no. She *couldn't* be a part of his rescue. As long as Manuel was alive, she was his prey. She knew that as sure as she knew her name was Sherry DuFraine Estabrook. Even if Manuel went to jail—and that was unlikely given the bounty the D.A. was sure to pay for his testimony—someday he would get out. And even if the government set him up with a new name and a new house in the boondocks, he could still roam free. *And he would find her.* In a flash, Sherry imagined waking up one sunny morning to discover him standing over her bed, leering triumphantly, her room torn apart around them. She pictured him bursting into her house in the dead of night, gun in hand, trigger cocked, lips frothing with blood like a wolf after a kill. He lunges toward her and—

Sherry opened her eyes in terror and looked forcefully at

Newman. "No, I cannot call him," she said, "because, as I've just explained, we had an agreement—"

Suddenly, unexpectedly, Sherry noticed that Jack had backed up to the window, out of everyone's view, and he was sending her an urgent message in pantomime, shaking his head *no*, just slightly, but enough for her to see it. Don't tell Newman anything, he was saying, keep it to yourself.

"Now, um, wait a moment here," Sherry improvised quickly, forcing a tight smile. She licked her lips and cleared her throat, buying time to let the meaning of Jack's gesture sink in. He was with her—*yes!*

She cleared her throat again. "You know, uh, I can't call him," she said, backpedaling furiously and trying to sound contrite. "It's just that, um, yeah, part of our agreement was that I would never call him at home. I don't even have his number. And it's unlisted. His dad, you know . . ." She shrugged apologetically.

Newman visibly clenched his jaw, bulging out the muscles in his neck. His face, so clean-shaven and golden tan, was beginning to flush pink.

"I see," he said.

All at once, Jack was back at the table in the middle of the room, looking smug, or close to it. "Okay, that settles it," he said, waving his cigarette in the air, "even if we wanted to turn this kid over to the cops, we couldn't. The girls have no idea where he is. End of story. Tell the D.A. he can subpoena them if he wants. We got lawyers galore who can fight jail for a week at least." He shot Newman a sanctimonious smile. "And so, folks," he said, "it looks like we've done our job here. Now let the cops do theirs."

Sherry was swamped with relief. She started to back out of the room, pulling Belinda with her, but Newman wasn't buying Jack's pitch so fast. He swiveled around to face Sherry.

"What are the odds of this young man calling you?" he asked angrily.

Sherry shook her head noncommittally. He had called her the morning before and left a gushy message on her machine, but she hadn't heard from him since. He'd mentioned something about his father's birthday, but he was so wired and crazy, he was also probably lying very, very low, because of the uproar over Pepe Reboredo. Two dozen police detectives were assigned to the case around-the-clock, and the whole city was screaming for a public lynching. "I don't know," she said. "He hasn't called me for a week."

Newman looked around the room in frustration. "I want Jack to know the *minute* he calls you," he said, standing up. "I'll call the D.A. now and push him off for forty-eight hours. I'll tell him we're trying very hard to find the boy. I'll tell him we're cooperating fully."

He nodded brusquely and then left. Sherry and Belinda stood, too, but remained.

"Sit down," Jack told them when they were alone. His voice was quiet, measured. He sounded weary, so weary they could barely hear him speak.

For a minute or more, he stood with his back to them both, staring out at the bay. The evening sky was turning charcoal gray, he noticed, there was a storm rolling in. It would probably hit by nightfall. He dropped his head to his chest and exhaled a harsh, melancholy breath.

When he finally turned around again, Jack walked slowly over to the table where Belinda and Sherry sat, side by side. He lowered himself into a chair across from them. Slowly, an ironic smile uncurled on his lips, and he leveled his eyes at Sherry with a careful stare.

At last he spoke.

"I don't want to know if Manuel calls," he said simply. "Don't tell me. I'm not cooperating with the police. I'm not a judge, I'm a goddamn journalist."

Belinda was stock-still, but Sherry nodded, saying a silent prayer of thanks. Thank God for Jack's diehard ethics, she told herself, they're going to save my life.

"So"—Jack was still talking—"you do what you want. You do what you have to do." He let out a small cough, and Sherry noticed that he wasn't smoking. "But for the sake of reporters all around the world, for reporters and editors everywhere, don't turn the kid over to the cops."

He stood up and returned to the window overlooking the bay. His back was to them again. There was silence for a moment, and then, finally, he broke it.

"Don't turn him in," he said softly. "Don't do that."

61

Belinda was starving. More hungry, she told Sherry, than ever in her entire life.

"We've got to go out to eat," she said as they were getting ready to leave the newsroom after their meeting with Newman and Jack. "There's not enough food in our apartment to feed all of us." Sherry had arranged to move back in with Belinda that morning; she said someone kept calling her house and hanging up.

"Let's go out someplace and celebrate!" Belinda was insistent. "Let's go hog-wild!"

Sherry shrugged distractedly. She hadn't had an appetite for days.

"I could really go for a huge pile of black beans, lots of rice, a big palomilla steak, the works," Belinda chattered gleefully. "And I have such an urge for flan, I can't tell you."

"Okay, okay," said Sherry, stuffing a blank notebook into her bag, just in case Manuel's body turned up in the Miami River overnight and Nerve Central gave her a call. After all, the whole day had gone by without him showing up at police headquarters, as he'd so carefully plotted; perhaps he'd been dead for hours. She nodded at Belinda vaguely. "Fine, fine, let's go out," she mumbled. "I don't care."

Belinda clapped in delight. "Let me call Eladio," she said, "he'll meet us at—"

She stopped and frowned. Sherry's phone was ringing. "Make it short!" she ordered, only half-joking. "I've got to eat something soon or I'm going to die." She sat down at her desk and picked up a battered copy of *People* magazine she'd found in the ladies' room.

"Sherry Estabrook, *Miami Citizen.*"

"Hello, Sherry."

It was him.

He was still alive—*damn it!* Sherry felt her heart explode like a

Roman candle. How could Mimi Lopez have screwed up? Manuel must have gone into hiding, someplace so obscure even her henchmen couldn't track him. *Damn it all!* she screamed inside, her gut twisting into a knot of dread so tight she could barely draw a breath. Just hearing his voice again redoubled what she already knew. Her career, her life, her *freedom*—everything she'd worked so hard to earn for herself in Miami—were slipping away from her with every second Manuel was alive. She couldn't let it happen. She couldn't let them go without a fight.

She waved frantically at Belinda to leave for dinner without her, but she was still buried in the magazine. She didn't even look up.

"How are you?" Sherry asked. Instantly, she knew that she needed to engage Manuel in conversation, draw him out, find out where he was, maybe even convince him to meet her some-where—somewhere Mimi Lopez was sure to see him.

"I'm fine," Manuel answered tonelessly.

"Did you see the article?"

"Uh-huh."

"What did you think?" she asked, forcing herself to sound friendly, interested—sincerely concerned.

"It was okay."

Sherry thought she heard another voice in the background, but no—Manuel always called alone.

"How are you?" she asked again. She was afraid her loathing was seeping through, and she softened her voice. "Where are you? Are you okay?"

No answer.

"Manuel?" Sherry ventured gently. "Manuel?"

The answer came in a burst: "What?" he snarled. Then, abruptly: "I need to see you."

"Oh, really?" Sherry felt a bolt of relief ricochet through her body. This was *just* the break she needed. "You want to see me? All right, fine, Manuel," she said. "Let's meet somewhere." All at once, her mind started whirling with plans. They could rendez-vous in the parking lot of Lincoln High—Mimi Lopez was certain to be staking out the place—or perhaps somewhere near his house. The park with those giant banyan trees—

But Manuel spoke before she could suggest either.

"I'm leaving town," he said sullenly. "I want to say good-bye. I want to say good-bye to you tonight. Okay?"

"Okay, sure," Sherry said automatically, but suddenly she began to tremble, her legs shaking so hard she could no longer stand. She fell into her seat and quickly swiveled away from Belinda. She didn't want her to catch the hysteria playing on her face; she could feel it there, screwing her mouth into an ugly grimace, filling her eyes with scalding tears. Manuel was leaving town *tonight*? That was barely enough time to do what had to be done. All at once, Sherry knew she needed to keep Manuel in Miami longer, long enough, at least, to let Mimi Lopez exact justice.

"Manuel," she said, struggling to keep her heart from catching in her throat, "I've got a great idea, why don't we meet over by the high school—"

"I *know* where we're meeting," he cut her off with a growl. "Devotion City." Sherry recognized his tone of voice instantly. He wanted her obedience, just to have it. "I want you to meet me at that trailer I showed you. Meet me there tonight, at midnight. You remember where?"

She did. It was the scene of Manuel's fourth or fifth hit. Some coke runner who was skimming.

"Yeah, right, that place," she said agreeably, but feeling more panicked than ever. Mimi Lopez would *never* spot them out there; the place was a fucking swamp. "Hey, Manuel," she rushed on, "can't you walk to a gas station or something? Devotion City is sort of out of the way." It wasn't a lie. The place was stuck ten miles out of town in the shadow of the airport, surrounded by chain-link fence, inhabited by freaks and losers and prison escapees who only came out at night. A couple of years ago, some developer was supposed to turn the place into a little oasis of sun and fun, but the deal went bust, and the land had been unattended ever since, growing mangy. A couple of squatters had put up tents, but every time the county tried to install electricity and running water, the lines were sabotaged. The people who lived there wanted it dark.

"I don't want to meet at a gas station," Manuel shot back.

"How about that restaurant near the Perimeter Road?"

"No!" Sherry could feel Manuel's fury start to ignite. "I can't go nowhere," he barked. "I don't want to be seen. Got it? I just want to say good-bye to you, that's all. Then I'm getting out of here. So it's gotta be Devotion City. It's safe there."

"Oh, I see." Sherry played for time. She was searching her

mind for a way out—she knew she *had* to see Manuel to convince him to stay in Miami, but she desperately did not want to see him in Devotion City. She was terrified to her core of being alone with him, of being forced to renew their blood-soaked wedding vows. He might touch her, claim her as his own, kidnap her.

Or kill her.

She knew that. But still—

Sherry felt the seconds ticking by as she wrangled with every crazy, convoluted idea that whizzed through her mind. Logic slipped in and out of her thoughts like gusts of fog over water. Maybe now was the time to call the police and confess everything, she thought, or to find Jack and explain what had gone wrong. Maybe her only choice was to run away herself, to a place so far away and so obscure no one would ever find her. She could start all over again. In turn, every possibility thrilled and mortified her. Every choice seemed to be wrong, every choice seemed to be right. The dizziness and fatigue of the morning returned to her in full force, and she had to fight the overpowering urge just to let the phone fall to the ground, and her body after it. Every path open to her led to *certain* disaster and disgrace, every path but one, and it was the most dangerous of all. But it was the only one with redemption at the end of it. All at once, Sherry knew that she had to play out what she had started in Miami. She would go to Devotion City.

Manuel had to die. He had to, or else she would.

Sherry eyed Belinda. She was done with the magazine and was now straightening up her desk busily, happily dumping the notes from the Manuel story in the trash. After a moment, she felt Sherry's glance, looked up, and smiled.

"I'm hungry!" she mouthed. "Let's go!"

Sherry nodded numbly. She cleared her throat again to let Manuel know she was about to speak. "See you soon," she said flatly, and without watching, cut the connection with her thumb. At the sound of the dial tone, her mind went blank; there was nothing left to decide.

A few feet away, Belinda tilted her head and frowned. "Sherry," she said leadingly, "who was that?"

"Um, oh, no one," Sherry mumbled.

Belinda considered her skeptically. "You can tell me, Sherry," she said. "Are you back with Brazil? Was that him, because—"

"It was my hairdresser," Sherry cut her off. "He loved the story."

"Oh!" Belinda came back brightly, clearly relieved. "Well, that makes one person." She smiled and picked up her phone to call Eladio, and a minute later they were out the door, on the way to a tiny Cuban place off Calle Ocho. Belinda swore it had the best margaritas in town.

When Manuel hung up, Roberto Lopez took the gun off his face.

There was a minute of silence, and then Mimi Lopez ordered her son to back off, leaving Manuel standing alone in the middle of the room.

They were in her office, the thirty-eighth floor of a skyscraper on Brickell Avenue, not far from the *Citizen*, but with much more expensive views. Everyone was there, everyone whom Mimi Lopez trusted, fifteen men in all, eight of them lining the walls of the room, the others standing behind Mimi Lopez at her desk, a massive Louis XVI period piece she'd picked up at an auction in Paris.

Mimi Lopez took off her glasses—she only needed them for reading small print, and she had been doing plenty of that since the paper had been hand-delivered to her early that morning— and threw Manuel an incredulous look.

"So your reporter friend, she said yes?" she asked. "She bought the crap about you wanting to say good-bye?"

Manuel nodded.

"¡Estúpida!" Mimi Lopez exclaimed, laughing and throwing up her hands in amazement.

"¡Estúpida! Estúpida!" Now it was a chorus in the room.

After a moment, Mimi Lopez raised one slender hand for silence.

"So, Manuel," she began again, standing behind her desk, "she'll meet you at midnight?"

"Yes, *señora*."

Mimi Lopez sighed and walked over to one of the picture windows facing the bay. The view was so glorious in spanking shades of blue and green, it was hard to believe what a dirty mess reality had suddenly become. She should have known better than to let Manuel live. But she had chalked his excesses up to youth. She had imagined she was his mother. She had set him free. What a mistake that had been. And if it hadn't been for Eddie's pretty wife, she thought, she and her sons would have paid a terrible price for it.

Now, of course, the police were going to be working like madmen to find Manuel. That jackass D.A. was probably delirious, dreaming of turning him into the state's star witness before remaking his face and sending him to live in a trailer in Wyoming.

But he would never get the chance.

Mimi Lopez turned and took another step toward Manuel.

"Did anybody but this Sherry Estabrook interview you?" she asked. Her precise mind was considering the power and beauty of a simple warning, executed swiftly. "This Sherry Estabrook woman, she was the only one, right?"

"Yes, *señora*."

Mimi Lopez shook her head.

"I know this is *los Estados Unidos*, but we can't let journalists run around thinking they can write this way about our private *business*," she said with obvious distaste. Then: "She has to die, Manuel," she stated flatly. "But I know you won't mind proving your loyalty by doing the job."

She waited ten seconds for an answer.

"I don't mind, *señora*," Manuel said. He was looking past her, out the window of her office.

Suddenly, his inattentiveness struck Mimi Lopez as insulting. She lunged toward him, grabbed his chin, and pulled his face up to hers. "How could you be such an idiot?" she snarled.

There were murmurs of agreement from around the room.

"One thing holds the family together," she was shouting now, still one inch from Manuel. "One thing—loyalty. I thought you knew that!"

Manuel swallowed hard. "I'm sorry, *señora*," he said, "I really am. I'll prove it to you."

"I know you will."

Mimi Lopez shoved Manuel away in disgust and then turned

her back to the room. She spit out a few words, and though no one could make them out, the meaning was unmistakable. A moment later, she returned to her desk, lowered herself slowly and straight-backed into her chair, and coolly considered the front page of the newspaper again.

"And who is this Belinda Alvarez?" she asked, squinting at the double byline.

Manuel shook his head. "I don't know," he said. "I never met her, ever."

Mimi Lopez paused for a moment and then shrugged. He was telling the truth.

"She can live," she said simply.

Joey Lopez stepped forward to object, but his mother stopped him with one look.

"Let her live," she said. "If we can't make an example of her corpse, she's more trouble for us dead. The impact of our message may be . . . diluted."

Joey Lopez nodded reluctantly and stepped back to his post near the door.

Twenty minutes passed. Mimi Lopez had returned to her desk; she was rereading the story from beginning to end.

"You really said this?" she asked Manuel when she was done.

He nodded.

How sad, Mimi Lopez thought, and how terribly pathetic. She admired the boy for being honest at a time like this, but pitied him for thinking it would help.

"Manuel," she said, this time softly, "Sammy and Mike are going to take you to Enrique's house now. You're going to stay there until eleven-thirty, understand? Have a nice big dinner and something to drink. Relax, okay? And then Joey and Roberto are going to come get you for the trip to Devotion City. They're going to keep you company tonight."

Manuel nodded again, lips sealed into a colorless grimace, but for the first time since he'd been hauled before Mimi Lopez at 4:00 A.M. that morning, he felt like talking. He wanted to beg to see Sherry alone. He *had* to see her alone, to tell her to get out of Miami, to go hide in Canada or someplace until he could come and join her forever. But now . . .

But now, there was no way out. He should have known Mimi Lopez would send her dogs along to stand guard. The fact was, if he wanted to live, he'd have to waste Sherry Estabrook.

She had to die, or else he would.

A second later, Mimi Lopez was talking again. "Take him away," she said, waving one hand in the air carelessly. Sammy and Mike jumped forward and wedged Manuel between them, hustling him out the door and into the elevator before he could bow a deep and grateful good-bye to the *Señora*.

After they were gone, Mimi Lopez dismissed her other lieutenants, one by one, leaving Joey and Roberto for last. She waved the two men close and then kissed each on the lips, a thank you in advance, one they would not forget.

"When he's done tonight," she said afterward, wiping her mouth with two delicate fingers, "kill him."

 Just after eleven, Sherry pulled back the blanket covering her on the couch and slipped on her shoes. She hadn't bothered to get undressed when they got back from dinner. She hadn't even tried to sleep.

In the next room, she could hear Eladio snoring so loudly it almost made her laugh, but her chest and neck and shoulders were frozen stiff in fear. She massaged one shoulder and then the next. They were so tight, she wondered if she would even be able to drive.

She had to leave right away.

Sherry stood and started peeking around the living room for her purse. She didn't want to turn on the light and wake Belinda or Eladio and then have to make up some ridiculous excuse, but where the hell was it?

After five minutes of searching, Sherry finally spotted the bag on top of the TV and reached forward to grab it, accidentally hitting the spindly antenna contraption that Eladio had just rigged up and sending it hurtling to the linoleum floor. The clatter lasted a half minute.

But when the silence finally returned, Eladio was still snoring. Sherry opened her purse and pulled out her keys. She had her wallet. Did she need her address book? No—she pulled it out of her purse and stuck it on her pillow. And she didn't need this lipstick either. . . .

"Sherry?"

Shit! It was Belinda, standing at the door to the living room, wrapped in a fuzzy yellow robe, rubbing her eyes like a sleepy child.

"Go back to bed," Sherry ordered. "Everything is okay."

But Belinda was awake now, and she could tell by Sherry's bitchy voice that everything was not okay. She closed the bedroom door and flipped on the light.

"You're totally dressed," she said, startled, stepping closer to Sherry. Then: "Are you going to meet Brazil?"

Sherry started to say yes, but the disappointed look in Belinda's eyes stopped her.

"No," Sherry said.

Belinda rubbed her eyes again. Sherry was acting so skittish it really worried her. "Can you tell me where you're going?" she asked gently.

Sherry shrugged. "Nowhere," she said.

The answer made Belinda want to cry; she imagined Sherry driving around Miami aimlessly, probably smoking cigarettes nonstop, feeling lost and ashamed and mourning the man she loved as if he were dead. Her life *was* a disaster.

"You're just going out?" she asked. "Just going to drive around and think?"

"Yeah."

"Well, then," Belinda asked, "can I come with you?"

"No!" Sherry jumped back a step. "No, absolutely not."

Belinda shook her head in amazement. She had it all wrong. Sherry wasn't just acting strange, she was hiding something. But what? If it wasn't Brazil, could it be—

"Sherry," she said firmly, "are you meeting Manuel?"

No answer.

Belinda moved close enough to Sherry to grab her wrist and stop her from sidestepping out the door. "You *are* meeting him!" she said. "I can't believe it! You have got to be out of your—"

Sherry cut her off. "Look, Belinda," she said, "you never understood what was going on with us, and I don't expect you to start now, okay? It's just—" She wished she could tell her the truth, but she knew it was too late for that. "It's just incredibly complicated."

Belinda squeezed her wrist tighter. "The story is over, Sherry," she said. "It's over. Let it go."

"It's not over," Sherry shot back, keeping her voice low not to wake Eladio. "He called me today and said he's ready to go to the cops. It was *his* decision. I didn't tell him a thing about Newman. So, look, we're meeting at Devotion City to talk about it." She paused for a second to let the lie sink in. "I have to see him," she said, "that's all."

Belinda was stunned. Manuel was going to turn himself in? Why didn't Sherry mention this at dinner? Was it because Eladio was there? It had to be.

She took a deep breath, still holding tight to Sherry. "Manuel wants to bury Mimi Lopez?" she asked.

"Right," Sherry answered. "I guess he figured out it was the only way he was going to stay alive."

Yes! Belinda repeated the word, clapping her hands in delight and relief. "This is great!" she said.

She wanted to hug Sherry, to celebrate somehow, but Sherry was acting too darn agitated to let her get close.

"Belinda," she was saying, tapping her watch frantically, "I've got to go now. It's already twenty past, and we're meeting at midnight."

"Okay," Belinda answered quickly, "give me one second to pull on a pair of pants," and before Sherry could stop her, she was gone, slipping into the bedroom as quietly as she could.

But it was too late. The click of the door had awakened Eladio, not a lot, but enough for him to know his wife was missing from the bed beside him.

"Angel?" he asked drowsily, lifting his head an inch above the pillow.

Belinda leaned over and kissed his brow. "Go to sleep," she said softly. She pulled open a bureau drawer and took out a pair of pants and a white sweatshirt.

"Why are you getting dressed?" Eladio asked. Now he was really up.

Belinda climbed next to him and gave him a hug. "I have to go on assignment with Sherry to Devotion City. I'll be home in an hour, maybe even less."

Eladio sat up in bed and stretched. "What time is it?" he asked.

"It's still late," Belinda answered. "Go back to sleep."

Eladio turned to check the clock.

It was almost midnight. What in the world. . . ?

He leaned over to the night table to turn on the light, but Belinda blocked his reach.

"Don't wake yourself up, sweetheart," she whispered.

"I'm awake."

"Well, don't get more awake."

Eladio sighed and dropped back to the pillow. He was going to need all the strength he could muster for work tomorrow, with everyone screaming and yelling about his wife's screwed-up secret source and his screwed-up loyalty to the force and the country's screwed-up First Amendment. He'd spent the whole day practicing answers.

Belinda was ready to go. She bent over once more and kissed Eladio, this time on the lips. He was so perfect, it took everything she had not to lie back down by his side.

"See you soon, honey," she said.

But Eladio was already half-asleep. He murmured good-bye.

Then, just as Belinda reached the door, he floated awake long enough to ask one last question.

"Where did you say you were going?" he said, just loud enough for his wife to hear.

"Devotion City," Belinda whispered back. "Manuel."

And then she was gone.

 It took five minutes for Belinda's words to cut through Eladio's swirling dreams and into the tiny part of his mind that was still, barely, on alert. But when they did, he sat up in bed as if lightning had struck his heart.

They were meeting Manuel? At midnight? In Devotion City?

Eladio jumped out of bed and wrapped himself in Belinda's yellow robe. He ran into the living room, turned on the radio to the all-news station, and flipped on every light. And then he simply stood there, wondering what in the world to do next.

If he followed them to Devotion City, Manuel would think he was being set up, not to mention what Belinda might think. She would say he was being overprotective. He didn't trust her. He didn't like Sherry.

She would be furious.

But then . . .

But then, the whole idea of a midnight rendezvous out in that weird swamp made him very nervous. Jesus Christ—he was shaking from head to toe!

He should get in his cruiser and just get out there—

His cruiser . . .

He couldn't be seen out there in a cop car, not by Manuel, or Belinda, or maybe even worse, by other cops. It could mean his badge.

Eladio lifted the phone to call his brother. He had to borrow the Regal, it was an emergency, please don't ask questions.

But Tommy would ask questions. He always did.

So who else was there?

Eladio sat down and stood up and then sat down again, getting more panicked as each second ticked by on the noisy kitchen wall clock. He could call Tim Cooper, he was a buddy, but he was also a cop. Everyone he knew was a cop.

But didn't Sherry have a boyfriend? She did—that's right— a photographer at the paper named Brazil something, what was it? Brazil, Brazil . . .

Brazil Brackett. That was his name. Brazil Brackett.

Eladio ran to the phone and started to dial the *Citizen* news-room, and that's when he saw Sherry's address book, resting on her pillow like a gift dropped from heaven. He flipped to the *B*s and there it was, first entry: *BB—beeper 320-1922/car 267-1651/ darkroom X2121/desk X2157/with parents in Chiefland (904)786-0984/ home 678-8903*.

He banged the last number into the phone. A pause, a click, and then ringing.

Across Miami, on Tall Palm Lane, Brazil reached over his sleeping wife to grab the receiver. It had to be the office.

"This better be good," he said as hello.

There was a heartbeat of silence, then a Latin voice he didn't recognize. "Brazil Brackett?" it asked.

"Yeah?" Who the hell was giving out his home number?

"Mr. Brackett, you don't know me, but this is Eladio Alvarez. I am the husband of Belinda McEvoy, the partner of your girl-friend, Sherry Estabrook." It was more a question than a statement.

"Yeah?" Brazil looked over to see if Jeanie was awake, but she looked pretty dead. She'd had a long day; the baby was cutting a molar and had cried from noon to dinner.

"Mr. Brackett, I'm calling because I'm very concerned about the assignment that Belinda and Sherry are on right now," Eladio went on, his voice barely under control.

"What assignment?" Brazil rolled over, back to Jeanie.

"You know, the meeting with Manuel in Devotion City to-night, at midnight," Eladio said. "That assignment."

"And?" Brazil didn't know what the hell this guy was getting at.

"And I'm very concerned." Eladio waited for a reaction, but there was none. "I'm very concerned for their safety."

Brazil groaned. That's right—it was beginning to make sense. This moron had just married McEvoy. He was a friggin' newly-wed, all bent out of shape about his bride's health and welfare. If he weren't so tired, it would sort of be cute.

"Look, *amigo*," Brazil said, trying hard not to sound like an asshole, "you're wasting your time, okay? The girls are going to be just fine. I don't know about Belinda, but Sherry's a tough broad. Nothing hurts her. She'll make sure your wife gets home safe and sound. I guarantee it. Okay?"

There was a long pause, and Brazil could hear Eladio's ner-vous breathing at the other end of the line. He didn't sound convinced.

"It's just that Devotion City is a, you know, a strange place to meet, wouldn't you say?" Eladio asked after a half minute of silence had passed.

Brazil yawned. "Well, it sure as hell will be quiet out there," he said. "I mean, I guess the kid doesn't want anyone to know he's meeting with them. He's probably more scared than a pig in a slaughterhouse if you ask me."

"Well . . ."

"*Amigo*, listen," Brazil went on, "you just married Belinda, right? This isn't the last time she's going to get up and disappear in the middle of the night on some assignment. Get used to it."

Eladio sighed uneasily. "So, you're not worried?" he asked.

"No, I'm not worried," Brazil said in an authoritative voice he hoped would do the trick. "So they're meeting Manuel. Fine— he's their big source, right? So they're meeting him at midnight. Name a better time if you want to be invisible, right? And so they're holding their little hoedown in Devotion City. I can think of worse places." He laughed, thinking of all the truly terrifying holes he'd seen in Miami. Hell—Devotion City was Disney World! "Let me say it again," Brazil told Eladio, "go back to bed."

Eladio checked the clock. It was 11:35. If they weren't home by one, he was calling this man again.

"All right," he said. "I hope you're right."

"I'm telling you, *amigo*," Brazil said, "trust me."

65

In the silence of the bedroom, Jeanie swore she could hear her heart beating. It was the only way she knew she was alive, because she was sure she'd stopped breathing. And she didn't think she could feel her fingers and her toes anymore. Or her eyes blinking, even.

All she felt was her heart, slamming away, hurting like a hammer on flesh.

She should have known.

Everything had been going so good with her and Brazil and the baby, it couldn't last. They were a family now, really a family, and it hadn't even been that hard. She should have known it would all come crashing in.

Jeanie suddenly felt tears running down her face and dripping onto her neck. So she was still alive. But maybe that wasn't so good.

God, she hated Sherry!

She hated her because Brazil was never going to stop loving her, ever. She hated Sherry because she didn't want to go home where she belonged, away from Miami, away from them both. She hated her because she'd been so nice. But she didn't hate her enough to let her die.

She couldn't do that and go on living with herself. She was a mother, for crying out loud; you can't go and raise a baby up when your soul is no good. Jeanie rolled toward Brazil and tried to take a deep breath. It came out like a gasp, and it cut into her chest like the thrust of a knife.

The sound startled Brazil. He was still awake from that stupid call, but he was sure Jeanie was out cold. "Honey?" he asked. "You okay?"

Jeanie tried to breathe again, and this time it didn't hurt as much. She inched closer to Brazil, pushing her whole body against his, her lips at his cheek. Finally, she pushed the words out, and tears fell into her mouth as she spoke.

"Brazil," she whispered, "he's gonna kill her."

Brazil twisted toward his wife. "What are you saying here?" he asked. "Who's gonna kill who?"

"Brazil," Jeanie was pleading now, "don't be blind, honey. That kid Manuel is gonna kill Sherry tonight. That's why he's meeting her. You read that story in the newspaper that she wrote. You think his boss didn't read it, too? They're gonna force Manuel to kill Sherry, and then they're gonna kill him, too."

Brazil burst into a harsh fusillade of laughter. "Holy shit, Jeanie!" he said. "You've been watching too many of them damn soap operas!"

Jeanie had her full voice back now. She sat up in bed and leaned over Brazil, talking right at his face. "I have not!" she shouted. "Don't be an idiot, Brazil. He's gonna kill her, I'm telling you that. Why else would he be meeting her out in the middle of nowhere, in a place where they won't find her body for a week if the wolves and rats don't get it first? You've got to get out there and save her."

Brazil could feel Jeanie's tears splattering onto his chin and neck. He didn't want to believe her, but maybe she had a point there, about meeting in Devotion City. Because if Manuel was really scared of getting nuked by Mimi Lopez, wouldn't he want to meet Sherry at the friggin' police station or something?

He pushed Jeanie to one side and hurtled out of bed, pulling on a pair of pants and a T-shirt in one move. Then he reached for the phone and dialed the *Citizen*. One of the overnight geezers on the city desk picked up, but Brazil didn't even give him a chance to say his name.

"This is Brazil Brackett, goddamn it," he was shouting into the phone like a madman, "get me McEvoy's home number this fucking second. This is a fucking emergency."

The geezer started to protest. They didn't give out reporters' home numbers—

Brazil cut him off. "This is Brackett, asshole," he shouted, "and I'm telling you you're fucking fired if you don't give me McEvoy's new home number now."

There was a pause and the sound of shuffling papers. A minute later, the geezer cleared his throat and quickly read off seven digits. Brazil dialed them just as fast. Eladio picked up on the first ring.

"Hey, man, we've got to get out to Devotion City right now," Brazil was still shouting. "Meet me there as fast as you can get there. You were right, man, okay? Just meet me right at the entrance there, near the big sign that says No Trespassing, okay?"

"Right," Eladio said. He slammed down the phone, reached for his gun, and ran out the door. He was already dressed, waiting.

 Sherry found the trailer at three minutes to midnight. It had taken five wrong turns and ten minutes of frantic circling. Even in the light of the full moon, Devotion City was shrouded by a mist so murky that every bough-heavy tree and every abandoned tar-paper shack and every burned-out car seemed to emerge from a dark nowhere, like ghosts slipping in and out of the night. More than once, she was sure she had seen Manuel dart out from a blind spot beside the dirt road, his body lit up like a skeleton in the piercing glow of her high beams. Each time, she swerved the car into a hard left or right, only to realize a moment later that all she had seen was a flickering shadow, of what she could not tell, just that it was

not him. Finally, more by luck than intention, she came upon the muddy, darkly canopied clearing where she and Manuel had sat in her car, windows down and rock and roll humming in the background, only three weeks before. They had come to take a look at the rusty bullet-shaped trailer where Manuel had executed a half-blind, smiley Mariel refugee called "Padre Pablo" who, according to someone—Manuel didn't know or care who—had kept a little cocaine for himself before distributing it to his *socios* around town. As usual, Manuel had described the hit to Sherry in officious detail, but now, as she stared at the trailer again, all she could remember was the fact that Padre Pablo, knowing he was a dead man and weeping like a baby, had begged Manuel not to kill his pet dog, too. At the time, in the rush of recording so many other details about gun angles and bullet trajectories, Sherry hadn't bothered to ask Manuel if he had honored the plea. She knew the answer now, of course, and she wondered if anyone would ever find both corpses inside the trailer before they'd turned to a muck so vile that even Devotion City's rapacious black flies would stay away.

Sherry inhaled deeply, hoping against hope that one strong pull of oxygen might soothe the acid bath of anxiety pulsing through her veins. It didn't—it only made her feel more alert, and so, more edgy. What if Manuel wanted her to stay with him tonight, she asked herself, to talk or plan or reminisce? What if he demanded another vow of love? What if he tried to kiss her? Sherry's body jerked painfully at the thought—she could still feel the twitching, intrusive weight of his hand on her inner thigh after Pepe Reboredo's murder—but then she remembered that Belinda was beside her now; an accidental bodyguard, but a body-guard nevertheless. She wouldn't get in the way of Sherry's plan as long as she stayed in the car, out of earshot of Sherry's conversation with Manuel. Sherry threw her a grateful sideways glance and, in the veiled moonlight of the swamp, caught a brief glimmer of her fragile beauty, made even more ephemeral by the shadows playing across her face. For the first time in as long as Sherry could remember, Belinda's long, wavy red hair was hanging loose over her shoulders like a silky shawl. But even as Sherry watched, she pulled it back off her forehead with a sweep, tying it into a loose knot at the base of her neck. The gesture allowed Sherry to get a clear view of Belinda's golden eyes, open wide and fluttering as they took in the murky surroundings with childlike curiosity.

She looks utterly at peace, Sherry thought enviously—calm, bright, and even a bit amused by sitting in the heart of a forsaken swamp called Devotion City in the dead of a balmy Miami night. Maybe, she told herself, maybe it *is* for the best that we're together in this.

She pushed the shift into neutral, then turned off the engine. Another deep breath, and this one worked better. Her fear was still there, but hope was creeping in. Belinda was her excuse; she would spend just as long as it took to persuade Manuel to stay in Miami, and not a heartbeat more. She checked her watch.

"Well, how'd you like that?" she said to break the silence. A little conversation wouldn't hurt. "He's late."

Belinda looked at the dashboard clock. "Nope," she answered, "he's got a few."

"Well, because he's usually so early, I would consider this late."

Belinda shrugged agreeably. "Okay," she said. She was relieved that Sherry was talking again; she hadn't said a word since they left the apartment, and her face had been set in such a forbidding scowl that chitchat was obviously out of the question. Now, however, Belinda noticed that Sherry had eased up a little; her shoulders had dropped down from near her ears, her lips had relaxed into a faintly expectant expression. Belinda shifted in her seat to face her. "You know, it's sort of creepy out here," she said, and she hoped her voice sounded lighthearted enough to let Sherry know she was only half-serious. "I sure hope Manuel isn't up to something naughty."

Sherry immediately and vigorously shook her head no. "He loves me too much to hurt me, if that's what you're getting at," she said, trying to mimic Belinda's tone. "You wouldn't believe how much he loves me." She struggled to press an image of Pepe's faceless corpse out of her mind. "It's practically *sick* how much he loves me."

"I believe you," said Belinda. She touched Sherry lightly on the knee as a show of sympathy, but pulled back quickly when she felt Sherry shudder beneath her touch. "Hey, is something wrong?" she asked gently. "You scared or something, *amiga*?"

"No!" Sherry shot back, and then she forced an incredulous-sounding laugh. "Of course not! I told you, Belinda, he's out here all by himself. He needs to talk to me about going to the cops. He's not going to hurt me, for crying out loud!" She abruptly leaned forward and clicked on the radio, listened to a short burst of cheery Cuban dance music, and snapped it off again. Did she hear something? Something like footsteps?

"What was that?" she whispered urgently, instinctively crouching down in her seat. "What was that noise?"

Belinda seemed oblivious to Sherry's cowering. She stuck her head out the window and cupped one ear purposefully. A moment later, she pulled it back in and threw up her hands, as if she was simply stumped by a silly question. "I don't hear anything, Sherry," she said perkily. Then, with a giggle: "But *of course*," she said in a delighted, mock-peeved voice, "I'm probably going deaf from listening to Eladio singing all the time to his *six hundred* Pepe Reboredo records played at *one thousand* decibels. Day in and day out! In the morning, in the evening! During breakfast, during dinner! I mean, he can't stop playing them, especially since—"

"Shut up about Pepe Reboredo!" Sherry snapped angrily, but she felt terrible the second the words came out. Instantly, she covered her face with her hands and sucked another deep swallow of air into her lungs. It was a full minute before she felt controlled enough to speak, and then her voice barely eked out of her throat. There was so much she wished she could say to Belinda, but couldn't. At least not yet.

"Hey, Señora Alvarez," she finally said, and this time the words were a docile peace offering, "just forget that I said that, okay? I think I might be losing my mind a little bit, but you just have to bear with me for a little while. You've got to do that for me, okay? It's just that—" Sherry took another deep breath to plan her next lie and then let it go in a slow exhale—"it's just that I'm getting pretty bored of everyone talking about what happened to Pepe Reboredo, okay? Just forgive me for that, okay?"

From the corner of her eye, Sherry could see Belinda smile tenderly and reach toward her for a hug; then, at the last moment, pull back. She clasped her hands in her lap awkwardly. "No problem, Sherry. No problem at all," she said, and although she sounded sincere, the hurt was still there. "I'm tired of hearing all about him, too. I mean, *really*, the cops are saying now he was all involved in drugs, just like everyone else. I mean, what's the big deal—"

"Wait, what's that?" This time Sherry silenced Belinda as gently as she could. "I think I hear something." As if on cue, a swamp owl screeched in the distance—a sound, Sherry thought, that came eerily close to the voice of a little girl screaming in fright, over and over and over again.

"That's spooky!" Belinda giggled.

"You're telling me," Sherry answered, forcing a small laugh in return. She checked her watch. "Now he's really late," she told Belinda, grateful for a change of subject.

"Yeah, well maybe he's having second—"

Again, Sherry cut her off. Against her will, she was getting too nervous to talk. "Let's just be quiet for a few minutes, okay?" she asked, and without even looking, she knew Belinda was nodding.

Ten minutes passed in silence, except for the occasional jolting cry of the owl on the other side of the swamp and the rustle of ferrets and snakes in the thorny underbrush all around them.

"Now he's *really* late," Sherry finally said.

"Yes, now he is," Belinda agreed. "Maybe he changed his mind."

"No, I don't think so," Sherry sighed, a ragged and frustrated sigh. The hope she had felt just a few minutes earlier was fading with every moment that Manuel kept her dangling. Suddenly, she was overwhelmed with the urge to start the car, jam it into gear, and speed out of Devotion City, foot to floor. But then, just as fast, she stuck her hands beneath her legs on the seat. She had to stay, she reminded herself, letting the reasons spin in her head like a silkworm's web, she *had* to.

"It's crazy," she told Belinda, to make her decision real. "I don't know where he could be. He sounded so determined to see me. I just don't get it."

"Me neither."

"Me neither," Sherry echoed her. She peered out her window into the gray haze of the swamp and saw nothing, absolutely nothing. The wind—it had been little more than a breeze to begin with—had dropped off, and the air seemed to thicken with its absence into alternating layers of gauze and burlap. The light of the full moon still flickered through the lush treetops overhead, but its glow seemed duller now, Sherry thought; she could barely see the trailer where Padre Pablo and his dog lay dead inside, or the rough dirt road where she planned to escape, and escape fast, the moment her work with Manuel was done. And she heard nothing, too. Even the swamp owl had turned mute in the sky, and the creatures on earth had fallen silent for the night. It was as if she and Belinda were the only living souls left in Devotion City. Maybe, she thought suddenly, maybe Belinda *was* right. Maybe Manuel had changed his mind. Maybe he went to the cops on his own. Or took refuge with his father. Or waltzed into a TV station for his premiere moment of public glory.

Or maybe, she thought, maybe he couldn't wait—an assassin's bullet had grazed his cheek, perhaps, and he had decided to make a run for the border without saying farewell. The possibility terrified her to the core. She imagined him in Mexico, biding time by a shimmering turquoise pool, planning his return. She heard his laughter, all these miles and miles away, and the cruel sound of it made her body go numb and her blood flow backward, just as it had during their final night together. She opened her eyes again, stared desperately into the darkness, and prayed that Manuel hadn't got free before she had.

He hadn't.

The truth was that Manuel was terribly close by and had been for a half hour, zigzagging through the potholed dirt roads of Devotion City, pretending to be lost, hoping enough time would pass so that Sherry would give up and leave. The plan had occurred to him at dinner. It was his last hope to salvage their life together.

But Joey Lopez was getting tired of it. He was sitting in the backseat of the car, but leaning far forward into the front, his hands nervously banging out a salsa rhythm on the armrest beside Manuel. Every few seconds, he checked his watch with a flourish and then turned to Roberto beside him and pointed at the dial with an exaggerated roll of the eyes and a loud groan. He'd had enough; it was time to get back to Miami, report his success to the Señora, and accept the inevitable accolades. He pulled a gun from inside his leather jacket and rested the muzzle against the back of Manuel's head.

"Let's find the trailer," he said edgily, *"comprendes?"*

"Yes," Manuel agreed instantly. *"Sí, sí, hermano."* Out of the corner of his eye, he tried to check his own watch, but couldn't without being obvious. He just had to hope he was late enough.

He turned right, then left, traveled another half-mile, and finally turned off the road into the clearing. Across the way, he could see the outline of the trailer, but did he see. . . ?

Yes, dammit, Sherry was there, he snarled to himself, waiting in her car like a chicken in a coop. *¡Estúpida!*

"That's her," Manuel said, struggling to sound nonchalant. In the fog, all he could see was the glinting metallic trim of the BMW, and he slowly pulled closer to it, until his car faced Sherry's at a distance of twenty yards.

"Beautiful," said Joey Lopez. "Very easy."

"*Very*," snickered Roberto. He popped a piece of chewing gum into his mouth and leaned back for a lazy stretch. This was going to be fun to watch.

"Okay, Manny." It was Joey Lopez talking again, his voice smooth and cajoling. "I just want you to put on your low beams and get out of the car. Right, *hermano*? Walk toward her until you're close enough to get a clean shot, then waste her, and we're out of here. Right? You follow?"

"I follow," Manuel said tensely. "I follow you all the way." He swallowed hard against the painful lump in his throat, and then, instinctively, tucked his chin into his bony chest and squeezed his shoulders together across it. All at once, he knew the fear and dread and hopelessness his mother must have felt as his father stood above her, hand poised to deliver another ruthless blow. Now he was the one who was trapped. He was going to have to kill the only person in the world that he loved, the only person who had loved him since—

Suddenly, Manuel was blinded by a vision of his mother, hovering as if on air, in the center of the clearing. He hadn't allowed himself to think of her like this—to think of her *alive*—since the day he'd found her in his bedroom with her opaque eyes open in terror and mouth gushing torrents of crimson blood. But now, he could not stop himself. She was standing not far from Sherry's car, and although her face was eclipsed by darkness, Manuel was sure he could see her smiling with the sad tenderness she had shared with him alone. The sight of her was stunning. Her serene face was lit from within, her body fluid with grace, her long black hair flowing. She lifted her hand and waved at him, beckoning. "My baby," Manuel heard his mother call, but then, just as suddenly, she vanished into the night. Before he could catch his breath, Manuel felt tears burning the corners of his eyes. Tears! At once, he was crushed by horror—this was something Joey Lopez could not see! Not now, at his final trial! He jammed his teeth together and squinted tight to stop the flow. It worked almost instantly. He was dreaming, he scolded himself angrily, and this was no time to dream. This was the time to act like a man, and he was a man, if nothing else. He checked the clearing for his mother's image again, and it was gone, as he knew it would be. He tilted his chin up, pushed down his hunched shoulders, licked his lips, placed a blank expression on his face. He forced himself to think of the target: Sherry's neck, of the tender, graceful spot just beneath her chin that he had so often admired in their hours together as the perfect place for a kiss. He would never have the chance.

Then, just as he did before every hit, Manuel shut his eyes as if in prayer, and emptied his mind of all but one stark image: himself as a boy, crouched in a pitch-black closet, sobbing silently as he listened to the crack of his father's fist on soft skin and his mother's anguished cries. Slowly, methodically, he let himself be overcome by the feeling of powerlessness that had engulfed him then, and then just as slowly, let it build and build and build in his gut until it had turned into a rage so potent it could only be extinguished one way.

He was ready for business.

Manuel jumped out of the car, straightened his back, tightened his buttocks, and started walking briskly toward Sherry with new confidence, and even a sense of release. He was about to prove just who he was, to start over once again. Mimi Lopez would be proud, he told himself with every step, she would forgive. Instinctively, he kissed the gun in his right hand and then quickly tucked it behind his back, trigger cocked, ready to make its final judgment call.

Manuel was suddenly walking faster, taking one eager stride and then another and another. In seconds, he was just feet from Sherry; his whole body twitching with anticipation, and now—all at once—with frustration. Why didn't she get out of her damn car, he wanted to know. What was she waiting for? Was she playing games? He repressed a shout of seething impatience and forced a rigid smile on his face. "Hey, Sherry, it's me, Manuel," he called out in a strained voice. "Come on out. I need you."

Silence.

Then, just a moment later, he heard a door open, and the sound of Sherry's pretty voice tinkling, "Hi." It was more a question than a statement, and he could tell immediately she was scared. So scared she could barely move. Her head was down, eyes averted, her body pressed against her car. There was nowhere for her to run, except closer to him. Yes, yes, *very* easy! he told himself gleefully, and best of all, she was standing far enough away and her head was hanging so low that in the fog he couldn't make out the expression on her face. From where he stood, all she looked like was another mistake that had to be corrected. His last mistake. Manuel carefully brought the gun around, raised his taut arm shoulder level, and—

Wait! What was this? Manuel suddenly heard another car door creak open.

Holy Mother of Jesus, he swore—Sherry wasn't alone! She'd brought along some *girl*! This fucked up everything!

Manuel frantically spun around to search for Joey and Roberto hiding in the darkness behind him. Did they know what was happening? Or were they too far off to see it?

And that's when he spotted the headlights—a cop car zooming at him at eighty miles an hour, high beams flashing, siren shrieking, horn blaring hard.

"Lying bitch—you set me up!" The scream came from so deep in Manuel's gut it barely sounded human, and he spun back toward Sherry, gun leveled and ready to explode. Like a cresting wave of a violent ocean storm, his anger redoubled and then peaked as all at once he knew Sherry for who she was: a killer. *His* killer. Every word from her mouth had been a lie—she had never loved him! She had used him to find fame and fortune and respect—to find freedom. And now, just before it was too late, she was going to destroy his. From every direction, cop cars were screeching into Devotion City, and over the earsplitting cacophony of their horns and sirens, Manuel could hear voices booming from rooftop megaphones, ordering him to freeze, to drop his gun, to surrender. *Never.* He had to kill Sherry first. He was dying to.

Manuel pointed his gun straight at his victim, and—just for a heartbeat, no longer—he paused to smile, a victorious smile so powerful that it sliced his narrow face in half and drained the luminous white light from the moon. It was a smile so huge and gleaming with hatred that, five feet away, standing by Sherry's side and peering at Manuel through the mist for the first time in her life, Belinda could see it, and she knew instantly what it meant. It meant death.

"Sherry, watch out, look up, look up—look at him!" she cried, but her voice was hardly louder than a whisper, because every ounce of strength she'd ever had was surging to her hands as she desper-

ately shoved Sherry to the ground and, in the same frantic move, leapt toward Manuel to grab the gun from his grasp. She was halfway there, practically flying through the gauzy air like a swamp angel, when the first bullet caught her in the chest and brought her down to earth. "Oh, Sherry," she called out, and this time her voice was stronger, so strong that Manuel knew she was alive, and so he lunged forward, stood over her crumpled body and fired again, this time directly to the neck. The last sound Belinda heard was his laughter.

Sherry heard it, too, but not for longer than a second, because the next sound she heard was Eladio shouting, "FREEZE, PO-LICE!" and then the fast, thick thud of his bullets, five of them in an uninterrupted row, puncturing flesh. The next sensation she felt was Manuel falling hard against her body as he slowly collapsed to the ground, leaving a ragged trail of his warm blood from her chin to her feet before he landed, facedown, in the mud. In his descent, he had reached for Sherry, clutching at her shoulders for help, but she had let him go. She was staring at Belinda's lifeless form an arm's reach away, her golden eyes still open in wonder, her lovely hair splayed across her back, her lips closed lightly, as if in peaceful sleep, but her body gushing blood into the damp earth.

Belinda was dead. Dead for her. Dead because of her.

The next thing Sherry knew, she was running madly, running away, she didn't know where or why, only that she had to run as far as she could, and that she had to keep running forever. All around her, the swamp rose up, as if to consume her, but she forced her way through its bristling thicket and sticky mud, pushing branches aside frantically, crawling between prickly bushes and tripping over piles of stinking garbage, until suddenly she slammed, and slammed hard, into a wall of steel—the trailer. The impact nearly knocked her out, but instantly she was on her feet again, ready to run, but then, all at once, knowing that she was running in circles. She was exactly where she had started from. She threw back her head and let out a howl of grief so wild, the release of it tore her insides out. Across the clearing, Brazil heard it, and in the darkness he called her name desperately, but Sherry didn't hear him. She didn't hear anything.

She had dropped to the ground—her running, she knew, was over forever. She'd run too far already. Now, she needed to get back, to find Belinda in the clearing and close her eyes, and then to find Manuel and open his.

Sherry started to crawl, hesitantly at first as she felt her way through the mud, then faster and faster, until her whole body was coated with gluey dirt, slimy swamp bugs, and hot vomit—her own. Once, and then again, she tried to stand, but her legs were trembling too violently to support her. Still, she could not stop. She pushed her way back toward the center of the clearing with her elbows and knees, and soon they were dripping with blood. Underneath her, she was sure, the ground slithered with snakes, and the sky above was suddenly blacker than ever. She could barely see her way. In the distance, she could hear the clamoring of police radios and see the sharp-edged beam of powerful searchlights scanning the swamp. She lifted herself to her elbows and stared frantically through the fog—and yes—a few feet away lay Belinda and Manuel, their bodies covered by white sheets. Cops were everywhere, taking notes, picking through the ground for bullet casings, dusting her car for prints—but it didn't take Sherry long to pick out Eladio. He was standing above his wife, absolutely motionless, head bowed. Brazil was by his side, holding him standing.

Sherry inched closer, and then suddenly was there, still lying on her belly and covered with blood, but where she needed to be. Brazil saw her first.

"Darlin'!" he shouted, and Sherry could tell right away he was weeping. "Oh, darlin', you're alive!"

Sherry hardly heard him. She pulled herself over to Belinda's body and dropped her head so that her forehead was touching her friend's. Then, instinctively, she threw herself forward, hugging the body through the sheet. Even in death, it was warm and yielding. "No," she answered Brazil at last, although she was speaking more to herself. "I'm not alive."

Then, with all the love she could muster, Sherry carefully peeled back the sheet, and gently pushed closed Belinda's eyes.

"Darlin'!" Brazil shouted again, this time reaching down to pull Sherry up by his side. But she pushed him away and scrambled the inches over to Manuel's body. This time she pulled back the sheet more roughly, and in her haste—Brazil was grappling for her now—she shoved open Manuel's lids with her thumbs and threw herself on top of him, laying her chest against his

blood-soaked one and bringing her face so close to his that their lips were almost touching. Then she looked into his eyes for the answer, and what she saw there would stay with her forever.

She saw herself.

"I killed Belinda," Sherry cried, but her voice was so twisted with anguish that Brazil couldn't make out the words. Instead, he lifted her body up like a baby against his and cradled her there as he carried her toward the waiting ambulance.

"Sherry, now listen to me, darlin'," he whispered tenderly in her ear. "We're gonna get you out of here, okay? They're gonna take you to the hospital now, fix you all up like brand-new, okay?"

He hugged her tight for a brief moment and let loose a hoarse sob into her hair. "Sherry, darlin'," he cried, struggling to regain his voice, but failing. "How'd you let this happen? Why'd you go and get into this mess?"

There was no answer.

Because Sherry was counting her heartbeats, waiting to die, hoping it was soon.

Two days later, Sherry opened her own eyes. She'd kept them fastened shut since she arrived in the hospital emergency room, squeezing them tight against the fluorescent light while some doctor with a thick Spanish accent and delicate fingers washed her torn skin and probed her from top to bottom for broken bones and bleeding organs. There were neither. But when Sherry wouldn't answer the doctor's questions—over and over, he kept asking her how she felt—someone called the psychiatric resident on duty, and suddenly she was gingerly being lowered into a wheelchair and carted away to another floor. Sometime later—Sherry had no idea how much time had passed, and she didn't care—she felt the sting of a needle in her arm, and then slowly, the bittersweet blackness of dreamless sleep.

When she finally awoke, it was morning, or at least it looked that way. The room around her was suffused with sunshine—sunshine so lucent it nearly blinded her. Instantly, she jammed her lids closed again, but it was too late. Someone was calling her name, insistently. Her instinct was to pull the sheet over her head and scream to be left alone, but the voice was too familiar to ignore. Cautiously, she opened her eyes again and saw a blurry group of people standing by her bed. It took two minutes for her to focus—her pupils were dilating mercilessly in her head, spinning open and shut from the cocktail of sedatives pumping through her veins—but at last she did. And the first person she saw was the Grim Reaper—or at least that's what she used to call him. Everyone in the newsroom called him that; it was a joke. He was the Miami coroner; she'd interviewed him at dozens of homicide scenes. He was a huge block of a man, with a beefy square face and linebacker shoulders. He always wore a misshapen black suit and a limp black fedora. His expression was cynical, weary, and sad all at once.

"Hello, Miss Estabrook," he said in a pallid voice when Sherry met his gaze. "I believe we've met before. I'm—"

Sherry cut him off with a sudden shake of the head. "I know who you are," she muttered. The words ached coming out—her throat was rough as sandpaper and her lips dry and cracked. "I know what you're here for." Inadvertently, tears started dripping from her eyes, and she let them fall unabated. "You've got the autopsy, right?"

The coroner nodded solemnly, then tilted his head toward a uniformed cop next to him. "And we need you to sign a witness affidavit," he said. He paused for Sherry's response, got a slight nod, and went on. "Officer Malina here just needs to go over the facts of the double shooting in Devotion City with you."

"Right," Sherry repeated to him numbly. "Facts . . ." Desperately, she tried to focus on the cluster of people by the coroner's side, searching for the person who had called her name. She knew now who it had been—Jeanie. She said the name out loud.

"Yeah, Sherry, I'm here," came the reply. She stepped closer to the bed, John Junior hoisted on her hip, fast asleep. "Brazil and I are here for you," she said, reaching out with her free hand and smoothing it through Sherry's tangled hair. "We're gonna stay till it's over, okay?"

"Uh-huh." Sherry pushed out the sound. For an instant, she lifted her eyes to find Brazil's face, but could not. He was by the door, leaning against it awkwardly, his eyes averted, his fingers fiddling anxiously with a set of car keys. She only had to watch him for a moment to know he would not look back.

Sherry let her eyes drop and rolled slowly toward the coroner; her whole body was sore, as if she'd just run a marathon in the cold rain. "All right, let's get it over with," she whispered to the cop. "You want me to sign a witness affidavit, right?"

"Yes, I'll just run it by you, and that will be all, Miss Estabrook, just that," he said, and Sherry had to wonder why he was being so damn nice to her. She expected nothing, deserved less.

"Go on," she said.

The cop nodded began to read in the inflected language of law and order that Sherry recognized too well: "Witness, Sherry DuFraine Estabrook, twenty-five years old, Forty-three Lemonlime Road, Miami, Florida, states that at midnight of above date, she and victim, Belinda McEvoy Alvarez, drove to Devotion City to meet with Manuel—" Here the cop stopped.

"We need to fill in the boy's last name," he said.

Sherry let go a long sigh. "Velo," she said simply. It was just one word, she thought, one word she should have never kept inside.

"Um, uh, to meet with Manuel Velo," the cop continued, "who was acting as a source for an article published in the *Miami Citizen*."

A pause. "Is it correct so far, Miss Estabrook?"

Sherry nodded, closed her eyes, saw black. A minute passed, maybe more, before she realized the cop was waiting for her to open them again, and so she did, letting the light assault her from every angle.

The cop cleared his throat and went on.

"Witness states that shortly after she and victim got out of her car, late-model red BMW with Florida plates S-duF-E, Manuel, um, Manuel Velo started to discharge gun, silver Ruger .357 magnum reported stolen eight-eighteen-eighty-four Metro case number B78-521A, at her and victim, Belinda McEvoy Alvarez.

"The physical evidence indicates that victim pushed witness Estabrook to the ground and ran toward assailant to grab weapon but was struck twice in the process."

Sherry held up her hand for Officer Malina to stop, and he did. In the silence, she felt herself slipping away again, but not for long.

"Miss Estabrook?" the cop prodded her gently. "Can we finish, please?"

"Yes . . ."

"Autopsy shows that victim was shot in the chest and neck and died of massive trauma to the left carotid artery. Blood tests indicate victim was four to six weeks pregnant."

Silence.

Then: "A baby, oh, God, no—a baby . . ."

The words came out in a hoarse singsong, unstuck from a place between Sherry's heart and her gut, sounding as agonizingly mortal as a death rattle, but without the same grateful release of pain. The pain was still inside, worse now than before, and Sherry tried to kill it by squeezing her eyes shut again. But the blackness beneath her lids had abandoned her, replaced by the sulfur light of the park where she had first met Manuel and by dizzy Day-Glo images of the smiling, tired mothers there, arms folded across their chests, watching their children run and fall and run again.

Sherry opened her eyes and twisted her neck to look at Jeanie, but she couldn't find Jeanie's eyes. Her head was bowed. She was weeping.

"I'm so sorry, darlin'," Jeanie said when she looked up at last. She hugged John Junior against her breast. "You had no way of knowing. You made a mistake, Sherry, it was a mistake, that was all," she said, her voice filled with kindness. "You're just human like the rest of us, darlin'. How could you have—"

Sherry stopped her. She shook her head and held one finger to her lips. "Not a mistake," she said, "a judgment call."

Jeanie said nothing.

Instead, she turned to the cop, nodding at him to continue.

"I think we're almost done," he said uneasily. He was anxious to let these people alone, but had a few more quick questions. He already knew the answers, just like every cop on the case, but he had to ask anyway.

"Miss Estabrook," he said, "did Manuel indicate to you that he was involved in the murders of Alvin and Laura Beauregard of Forty-five Lemonlime Road?"

Sherry nodded yes.

"And Señor Pepe Reboredo of Fifty-six Gladterrace Lane?"

"Yes," Sherry said, trying to sit up. Suddenly, a bolt of urgency riveted through her body. "I was there for that one," she said, frantic to tell the truth at last. "He kidnapped me. I was afraid he would kill me if I told—"

The cop cut her off as if he already knew somehow. "Yes, Miss Estabrook," he said. "We matched the fingerprints last night."

Sherry looked down at her hands and noticed they were black with ink. "I'm so, so, so sorry." She wouldn't let the policeman stop her now. "I didn't want to kill anyone. There was a gun to my face. I had to make a choice." Again, she started to weep, but then forced herself to stop so she could go on. "Maybe I should have let him kill me," she said, more to herself than anyone else in the room. "But I wanted to live. I don't know why, but I wanted to keep trying."

The cop nodded sympathetically, but he wondered why Sherry was even bothering to explain, and explain with such agony that it was tearing her face apart. Everyone already knew the D.A. wasn't pressing any charges against her. The big chest-thumpers at the courthouse had struck a deal with the big chest-thumpers at the *Citizen* that morning. The reporter walked in return for all her notes on Manuel and Mimi Lopez. The cops in Homicide expected to close a slew of unsolved cases with the dirt, not to mention the off-chance they might send someone to jail. So Sherry Estabrook didn't need to shed another tear. She was home free.

"Well, I think we've got everything," the cop said. He handed Sherry the affidavit and a pen and then waited, shifting from one foot to the other, as Sherry struggled to sign her name. Her hands were shaking so badly it took three tries, and then all she managed to put on paper were her initials in small, wobbly script.

A moment later, the cop was gone, and with him the coroner, backing out of the room in complicit silence.

Brazil turned to leave, too, but Jeanie blocked his path. She stepped closer to Sherry's bed and pulled him with her. "We'll stay with you, darlin'," she said, again smoothing the hair off Sherry's forehead. "We won't leave you alone."

Sherry sighed hard. The truth was, she wanted to be by herself. She needed to be.

"No," she said, "please don't stay. I just want to sleep." The drugs were pulling her away, unrelentingly, like the undertow along Marblehead Neck, but there was one last detail she had to take care of. "Do me a favor," she said, reaching for Jeanie's hand

and squeezing it with all the love she had left. "Call my parents, okay? I don't want them reading about this in the paper. Call them, okay?"

"You bet we will, darlin'," Jeanie assured her. "We'll call them as soon as we say good night to you."

"Thanks."

Jeanie didn't move.

Five minutes passed. She was waiting for Sherry to fall asleep, and it looked as though she was going down, but then suddenly Sherry whispered something so softly Jeanie had to lean down to hear it.

"How's Eladio?" she asked.

It was Brazil who answered. "He's holding up," he said. "He's home with his family. They're taking good care of him, Sherry. Don't you worry."

"Okay."

She was ready to drift now, ready, except . . .

Sherry opened her eyes and found Brazil again. "And Jack?" she asked.

Brazil looked away.

"Where is he?"

Brazil looked at the floor. "He's with Belinda," he said. "He won't leave her body alone down there." He pointed toward the hospital basement, the morgue. "So they're just letting him, you know, stay with her, until he can deal. So he's just sitting there. I saw him. He's holding her hand."

Sherry shut her eyes again.

"Okay," she said. Her mind was so fuzzy she couldn't even picture it. "I'm leaving now," she went on, voice failing. "I'm gone."

68

Two days later, Sherry went to the funeral alone, swathed in layers of anonymous black despite the suffocating heat, wearing impenetrable sunglasses and a veil to hide her face and the ravages of exquisite grief.

But her attempt at camouflage backfired. The moment she arrived at the tiny Catholic church in Little Havana where Eladio's family had gathered to bury Belinda, dozens of unfamiliar reporters descended upon her shouting questions, yelling her name over the snap and pop of camera shutters and klieg lights. Even in her benumbed, listless stupor, their presence shocked Sherry—hadn't the *Citizen* just issued a press release that answered everything? Manuel's story, it said, was—by and large—the truth. The only missing detail was one the paper could never have confirmed—and that was the fact that Manuel Velo, sixteen, had apparently been fired by the Lopez family for excessive use of force. The *Citizen*'s management deeply regretted that the boy was killed after making his story public, and it considered Belinda McEvoy Alvarez's death a tragic accident in the line of duty. The *Miami Citizen* planned to establish a journalism award in her name. Sherry Estabrook, the press release concluded, has been relieved of her duties as a staff reporter at the *Miami Citizen*. However, the district attorney has decided not to bring charges against her in the shooting of Pepe Reboredo because of the forced circumstances of her involvement and her agreement to turn her notes over to prosecuting authorities. All questions should be directed to Garrett Newman, Publisher's Office, *Miami Citizen*.

But all questions were suddenly hurtling toward Sherry as she tried to make her way up the narrow steps into the church.

"Miss Estabrook, is it true you were having an affair with Manuel Velo?"

"Sherry, did Pepe beg for mercy?"

"Sherry, did you know Mimi Lopez planned to leave the country?"

"Sherry, how do you feel about Roberto Lopez's arrest?"

"Miss Estabrook, in your own words, why didn't you turn the kid in to the cops?"

Sherry held up her palms in submission. "No answers," she managed to say in a voice creaky from weeping, but the crowd of journalists surged closer to her, and she felt herself stumbling, as if she might collapse completely, knees to pavement. Then, suddenly, there was a firm hand on her arm, pulling her toward the door of the church where a police officer was stationed to keep out the press. Sherry looked up and saw Adam Klein. "Let me help you," he said softly. He put his arm around Sherry and forced a path through the crowd.

A moment later, they were inside, squeezed together in the last pew, and Adam Klein was gently hugging Sherry, holding her head to his chest and rocking her. "I'm sorry, kiddo," he murmured. "I don't know what else to tell you."

Sherry shook her head. His attempt to comfort her only intensified her anguish. "You already told me everything," she said. "I should have listened to you, but I was only listening to myself. I had this plan—" She stopped to wipe a fresh explosion of tears off her face. "I was going to show my father—" Again she stopped, choking on the words, and she dropped her head to her chest as if she might never lift it again. "I can't blame anyone but myself," she wept.

Adam Klein pushed Sherry back slightly, holding her by the shoulders so he could look into her face, and the vulnerability and sorrow he saw there almost broke his heart. "We can talk about it some more," Adam Klein suggested in a low, comforting murmur. "We can get through this thing—"

"There's nothing left to say," Sherry whispered back. "I killed Belinda, and I killed her baby. It should have been me." She shut her eyes for a moment and once again imagined Belinda's lifeless body in the muck of Devotion City, her head turned to one side, a faint smile on her lips but her neck spilling blood. "Oh, God," she said, "it should have been me."

At the front of the church, the priest began to pray. He was a young, fresh-faced man, wearing a simple white robe and a large, unadorned wooden cross around his neck. He swung a ball of incense over Belinda's closed white casket. "We gather here today in the name of Jesus Christ," he intoned, "to send our sister Belinda to the home of the Lord." Over his voice, Sherry could hear the hoarse sobs of many women and a lone man—Eladio. He had been sobbing when he visited her in the hospital to ask her if she remembered Belinda's dying words. Sherry had started to tell him no, but then changed her mind. "She called your name," she told him. "She said she loved you."

It was, she promised herself, her final lie.

"Look, Sherry." Adam Klein was talking again, now caressing her hand warmly, "if you want, you can come to my office tomorrow—"

"No," Sherry cut him off. "I'm going home tomorrow."

"Home?" Klein sounded startled. "You're going back to Marblehead? After everything you did to get free of the place—"

"Yes, *because* of everything I did to get free of the place," Sherry sighed, "I have to go back." The decision had come to her the night before as she lay in the utter darkness of her bedroom, trying to make sense of her life, and all its horrible errors of judgment, from beginning to end. Time and again, she was so paralyzed by a memory that all she could do was moan out loud in anger and self-loathing. Perhaps it was just as Jack had told her before he left for Detroit: She and Manuel were just two very sad, very love-starved, very ambitious people on a fatal collision course. But Sherry knew there was more to it than that—more because the collision could have been prevented if she'd had the moral strength she demanded of everyone else. There had been so many clues—so many messages—all the way, telling her to stop. She heard Manuel's seductive voice under the banyan tree saying he'd been waiting for her; she remembered Sherman Otis's ominous warning, she thought of the little yapping Pekingese, with its mosquito-sting bite. And she saw Laura and Alvin Beauregard, naked as newborn babies, tied in their plastic lawn chairs, dripping in blood.

But it was the memory of her own grotesque reflection in Manuel's dead eyes that made her realize she had to go home. In truth, she knew, she'd never left. Home, with all its lies and deceits and missed connections of love, was as much a part of her as her soul. She'd been running away all these years just to run back again.

"I wanted to start over," Sherry told Adam Klein. At the front of the church, the priest touched Belinda's casket with holy water. "I wanted to be someone else, and now I am." She tried to laugh ironically, but only a tight gasp of pain came out. "There's no place else for me to go but back where I belong."

Klein nodded and gave Sherry one last hug. Then they both turned to watch as six pallbearers, led by Eladio and Brazil, carried Belinda's coffin down the aisle and out of the church.

The next morning just after daybreak, Sherry left 43 Lem-onlime Road forever. There was nothing to bring with her except one suitcase of clothes; she sold everything in the place for two hundred dollars to the new tenants, an elderly couple from New Jersey, renting for a while to make sure they liked Miami before settling in for good. Sherry wished them well and assured them they would. There was so much to love about Miami, she said, it was a city of glimmer-colored sand, cerulean skies, of tender sea breezes and unending hope. It was city of crazy, impossible dreams where everyone was free to make mistakes. The trick, she told them as they stared at her, smiling but completely perplexed, was never to make the same one twice.

The morning after the nightmares stopped, Sherry came out of her room. It was March. Three months had passed since she had returned to One Hun-dred Endless Horizon Lane and her parents' tenderness, three months of remembering and asking why, and now, it seemed, perhaps three months of healing.

From her bedroom window, Sherry could see testament of the previous night's heavenly midnight snowfall, and just as she had guessed from her rooftop perch, Marblehead Neck was covered with a thin, crisp layer of white, as if everything were brand-new. She had never seen such a breathtaking view in her life. She opened the door to her room, and on legs weak from days and nights curled in a tight fetal hug, she walked downstairs to look for her father.

She found him in the kitchen, alone, drinking black coffee from a china teacup and reading the newspaper through tortoise-shell bifocals. For a moment, she stood in the door to watch him in wonder—how he had changed, Sherry thought sadly. Gone was the sturdy Yankee expression, the ramrod back, the critical blue eyes. Since she'd come home, he'd let his hair grow longer— it hung over his ears messily now—and his eyes had aged and lost their exacting glance. His lips sagged slightly into a melancholy frown, and his whole body had slouched earthward, as if it was an effort to stay erect. Even his way of dressing had changed, from his proper dark suits to a pair of old work pants and a wrinkled blue denim shirt with a sloppily knotted red bow tie. It looked like he'd been up all night or slept in his clothes, Sherry couldn't tell which.

"Hi, Dad," she said softly.

Laurence Estabrook jerked up his head in shock, dropping his newspaper to the table and pulling off his glasses. "Sherry!" he said. "You're here—I mean, you're out of your room—I think that's just grand—"

"Thanks," Sherry said. She sat down at the table beside him and folded her hands in her lap to keep them still from trembling. "Where's Mom?"

Laurence Estabrook checked his watch, and Sherry couldn't help but notice his hands were trembling, too. "Well, let's see, it's just after nine, dear, so I'd say she's probably at the homeless shelter." He smiled tentatively, and Sherry realized his voice had lost its bold patrician tenor. "You know," he said, "she still feels quite an attachment to the place, and I think it's a wonderful service, too, I really do—"

He stopped suddenly and jumped up from his seat. "But let me fix you some breakfast!" he said, clapping his big hands together as if he liked nothing better than to cook. "Let's see, I can just mix up a few eggs—"

Sherry motioned him to sit down. "Dad," she reminded him gently, "one of the housekeepers already brought me something."

"Oh, yes, of course," he said, falling back into his seat. "Yes, yes, why, of course." Since her return from Miami, Sherry had taken three meals a day in her room. They always arrived at the same time, arranged on the finest Limoges, delivered by a maid and left outside the door with a soft knock. At first, Laurence and

Eleanor Estabrook had put small notes on every tray—*We love you, Sherry,* or *Please let us know what you need,* or once, in her mother's hand, *Dear, was the pot roast too dry? I'm so sorry.* But Sherry hadn't answered, except once, to write, *I'll come out when I can.* She had run out of things to say after her first night home, when she sat her parents down in the living room and talked to them, her head bowed or her eyes averted out the windows toward the sea, for five hours straight. She told them the whole story of her failed escape to Miami, from the moment she talked her way into a job in Jack Dougherty's office to the moment she saw herself reflected in Manuel's eyes. She told them about the day she dumped her trash on the Beauregards' front lawn, about the raucous sound of Brazil's laugh, about Jeanie's rain-colored eyes and her baby's innocent Cracker stare. She told them about getting screwed by Charles in the backseat of the car before Alice's wedding, about her dead-of-night meeting with Mimi Lopez, about the lovely look on Belinda's face as she lay dying. Every word she spoke was the truth, at last. When she was done, she looked up to see her parents still sitting side by side, holding hands in the faithful way she knew so well, looking exactly as they had when she began, except that their faces had gone ashen with shock and their clothes were drenched with tears. The only times she had seen them since then were from her third-floor window—her mother frantically forcing dormant rosebushes in the frozen ground of February, her father walking on the seawall in his shirtsleeves late at night, both of them looking lost and half-mad. She barely recognized them. And now, in the kitchen, she knew why. They had changed as much as she had.

"Dad," Sherry said abruptly, "I want to tell you that I'm really sorry—"

But Laurence Estabrook wouldn't let her go on. "Don't apologize to me, Sherry," he said quickly, as if he'd been waiting to say the words for a long time. He leaned back in his chair and placed his arms across his chest awkwardly. "It's my fault, everything is. Your mother and I have discussed it—and it's really my fault, Sherry. It was the way I handled that thing"—his face closed down in a pained grimace—"that incident in my study. Terrible. Just terrible, Sherry. I shouldn't have told you those things." His voice trailed off.

But Sherry wanted him to go on. "Told me what?" she asked

him urgently. "That I caused a rape? That you got me into college? Those things?" Her voice came out a little gruffer than she intended. She was surprised how much it still hurt to talk about it. "No, Dad," she said. "You did the right thing—"

Laurence Estabrook let out an ironic laugh. "Was the little payoff you witnessed the *right thing*, too? Sherry, don't tell me you believe that now, after all this."

Sherry said nothing for a full minute. She didn't know what she believed anymore, except that she would never be able to judge anyone again—anyone except herself.

"I don't know, Dad," she finally answered, her voice drained of every emotion but mournful affection. "I guess I wish it had never happened, but I feel that way about almost everything these days."

"Me, too," her father said, and they laughed sadly together for a moment.

Another minute of silence. Sherry stood, walked to the window, and faced the water.

"Looks pretty rough out there," she said at last. In the distance, she could see the Marblehead fleet heading into port, white flags flying in surrender to the violence of the waves. "Maybe a storm is coming. I saw it snow last night."

"Yes, I see, I see," her father agreed quickly. "It certainly did snow. Not too bad, though. Not too bad. I think I'll still be able to drive into town."

"Work?" Sherry asked.

"Yes," he said reluctantly. "Work." The word came out as an apology.

"So, how's it going, anyway?" Sherry tried to sound interested, casual.

"Fine, fine, just fine." Laurence Estabrook copied Sherry's tone, but then looked into his empty cup and sighed wearily. "I retire next year, you know. It's coming up faster than I ever thought. Next June, in fact. After that, your mother and I think we might travel a bit. We've always wanted to take a long cruise, maybe to Alaska—"

Sherry nodded vaguely. "How about Florida?" she asked without thinking. "The three of us—"

She stopped and dropped her head to her chest, shaking it back in forth in wonder. "Forget it. Crazy idea," she murmured, scolding herself. "It's just that I want you to meet my friend

Jeanie, and to see the city, to see how beautiful it is, how it makes you feel free. Maybe then you'll understand a little better . . . I don't know. It's a crazy idea. Forget it."

But Laurence Estabrook had already agreed to the plan with his whole heart. He was standing up now, striding toward Sherry, arms outstretched, and when she looked up at last, he was reaching toward her, welcoming her into their first forgiving embrace.